KU-513-143

A NURSE AND A PUP TO HEAL HIM

KATE HARDY

A NURSE TO TAME THE ER DOC

JANICE LYNN

MILLS & BOON

First Published in Great Britain 2019
by Mills & Boon, an imprint of HarperCollins*Publishers*
1 London Bridge Street, London, SE1 9GF

A Nurse and a Pup to Heal Him © 2019 by Pamela Brooks

A Nurse to Tame the ER Doc © 2019 by Janice Lynn

ISBN: 978-0-263-26982-6

MIX
Paper from
responsible sources
FSC™ C007454

This book is produced from independently certified FSC™ paper
to ensure responsible forest management.
For more information visit www.harpercollins.co.uk/green.

Printed and bound in Spain
by CPI, Barcelona

A NURSE AND A PUP TO HEAL HIM

KATE HARDY

MILLS & BOON

For Archie—
whose love for the beach inspired this book.

CHAPTER ONE

GREAT CROWMELL SURGERY. More than a hundred miles away from his old life in London. Right on the Norfolk coast, a place of wide sands and big skies. Peace. Quiet. No complications. *No lies.* Just him and his new job.

A fresh start.

Ben Mitchell took a deep breath, then pushed the door open.

The receptionist looked up. 'Good morning, Dr Mitchell.'

'Ben, please,' he said with a smile.

'Ben. Welcome to the surgery. The kettle's hot and I made choc-chip cookies yesterday. They're in the staff kitchen. Do help yourself.'

'Thank you, Mrs Hartley.'

'Do call me Moira.' She smiled at him. 'You look like a schoolboy on your first day. Just remember, Ranjit gave you the job because he thought you were the right one for it. You'll be fine.'

Did his nerves really show that much? 'Thank you.' It was ridiculous to feel this nervous. For pity's sake, he'd worked as a GP trainer in London. He was thirty-five. Experienced. He'd done this job for years and years and he knew he was good with patients.

But the first day in a new place would make adrenalin

pump through everyone's veins. Having to fit in with an established team; getting to know new people and learn their quirks, their strengths and their weaknesses. Getting to know your patients and working out what they weren't telling you during the consultation so you could help them with their real problem.

Of course he'd be fine. He'd do the job he'd trained to do. The job he loved. Only this time he'd be coming home to a house with no memories and no misery, which made everything a lot easier.

He opened the door with his name on it—*Dr B Mitchell*, in neat capitals—dropped his bag next to his desk and went in search of the staff kitchen to grab a cup of tea and maybe one of Moira's cookies.

But as he turned round the corner he stumbled over a brown and white dog, who yelped and looked sorrowfully up at him with huge amber eyes calculated to extract as much guilt as possible.

'Archie?' The kitchen door opened abruptly. From the dark blue uniform she wore, Ben realised that this must be one of the practice nurses, probably the one the senior partner had mentioned being on leave when Ben had come for his interview and met the rest of the team. What was her name? Terry?

She frowned at him and bent down to stroke the dog, who whined softly. 'What happened?'

'I didn't see the dog and I tripped over it.'

'Him,' she corrected, her eyes narrowing. Beautiful grey eyes, like the sky in November. It shocked him that he'd actually noticed.

'I'm sorry,' he said, knowing that he was in the wrong for hurting the dog, albeit completely unintentionally. But at the same time nobody would expect to find a dog in the corridor in a family doctor's surgery. 'I didn't mean to hurt the dog. But it shouldn't be here. What if it bit a patient?'

'*He*,' she corrected again, 'barely even nipped when he was a puppy. He's incredibly gentle.'

'There's always a first time,' he said crisply, 'and our patients' health and safety have to come first.'

The look she gave him said very clearly, *You're throwing your weight around this much on your first day here?* 'It does indeed,' she said, surprising him, as he'd expected her to make some kind of protest.

She wasn't smiling when she added, 'Though our patients happen to like having Archie around on Mondays. As do the rest of the staff. And there's an infection control policy in the surgery.'

On Mondays? Why was the dog specifically here on Mondays? But, before he could ask her, she clicked her fingers and the dog got up and trotted behind her to the door next to his, which she closed a little too loudly behind them.

Nurse Practitioner Toni Butler.

Toni. He'd remembered a masculine-sounding name. Short for Antonia? Not that it mattered.

He'd just got off to a really bad start with one of his new colleagues.

But he stood by his view that a dog had no place in a family doctor's surgery, regardless of an infection control policy being in place. Some patients were frightened of dogs; others were allergic and the dander from the dog's fur could trigger an asthma attack in a vulnerable patient.

Nobody said a word about the little spat when he walked into the kitchen, but he was pretty sure from the awkwardness in everyone's faces that they'd all overheard the conversation. He felt embarrassed enough to do nothing more than mumble a brief hello and go straight into his consulting room without bothering to make himself a mug of tea.

At least his patients all seemed pleased to see him during the morning's surgery, welcoming him to the village. He settled into the routine of talking to his patients and suggesting self-help measures as well as medication.

At lunchtime, Toni and the dog were nowhere to be seen.

'How was your first morning?' Moira asked.

Apart from having a fight with the nurse practitioner over her dog? 'Fine, thanks,' he said.

'Good. If you haven't brought anything with you for lunch, there are a few cafés plus the deli and the fish and chip shop along the harbour front—and of course Scott's do the best ice cream in the area. Abby Scott— well, Powell, since she got remarried to Brad—has even developed a special ice cream for dogs. Toni's one of her most loyal customers.'

'Ice cream for dogs?' He'd never heard of such a thing.

'Archie loves it.' Moira smiled. 'Everyone loves Archie.'

Pretty much what Toni had said to him. In his view, the dog still had no place in a doctor's surgery; though Ben rather thought he'd be on a losing wicket if he protested any further.

'Hello, Ginny.' Toni kissed the elderly woman's papery cheek and sat down next to her. 'How are you today?'

Ginny didn't answer. She hadn't said a word in three months, now. Given that her dementia was advanced, she'd either forgotten what to say or she couldn't quite piece together what Toni was saying enough to answer her. But she smiled, and her smile brightened even more when she saw Archie.

This was exactly why Toni had trained her spaniel as a therapy dog. A dog could sometimes get through to someone when a human couldn't, and could bring a spot of brightness into a sick person's day. Residents at a nursing home had often had to leave a much-loved pet behind, and the chance to relive happy memories was so good for them. When Toni's grandmother had been in the nursing home, a visitor with a dog had really helped brighten her mood. Toni desperately wanted to give something back—to help someone the way her grandmother had been helped. And Ginny had been one of her grandmother's best friends and who'd been like a second grandmother to Toni and Stacey when they'd been growing up; Toni desperately wanted to make a difference to Ginny's last days.

Archie, once his fluorescent coat was on, went into work mode, being gentle and sweet and sitting perfectly still to let an elderly patient or a young child pet him, suppressing his natural instinct to bounce everywhere. At the nursing home, Toni came to the lounge so all the residents could spend a few minutes with the dog in turn, and it also meant that one of the staff would be present at all times, in accordance with therapy dog visiting rules.

'Hey, Toni. Hello, Archie, you gorgeous boy.' Julia, the nursing home manager, came over to them and scratched behind the dog's ears. 'Look, Ginny, it's your favourite visitor.'

Ginny didn't reply, but she smiled.

'Catch me in my office on the way out, Toni?' Julia asked quietly.

'Sure.' Toni knew it was Julia's way of saying that she wanted to talk to her privately about a couple of potential health complications among the residents.

'Thanks.' Julia patted her shoulder.

Toni spent a few more minutes with Ginny, letting her stroke the dog and hopefully latch on to happy memories of dogs in her past, then said gently, 'Ginny, Archie needs to go and visit Ella now. We'll come back and see you next week. Say "bye", Arch.'

The dog gave a quiet 'woof'.

Toni did her usual round in the lounge, chatting with the residents in turn and letting them make a fuss of the dog. At the end of her allotted two hours—the maximum length of time for a therapy dog session—she made a fuss of Archie, said goodbye to the residents and headed for Julia's office.

The nursing home manager nodded at her drawer, where Toni knew she kept a box of dog treats especially for Archie. 'May I?'

'Sure. He's earned it—plus we're going for a run on the beach when we leave here, so we'll burn it off,' she said with a smile.

Archie, knowing from long experience what was coming, sat beautifully and offered a paw.

Julia grinned, rubbed the top of his head and gave him a treat. 'I love the fact you visit us on Mondays. It really sets our residents up for the week, not to mention the staff.'

'He loves it, too,' Toni said. 'I assume you wanted to talk to me about a couple of residents?'

'Yes.' Julia took three files out of her drawer. 'I think Liza is brewing a UTI. I did a dipstick test this morning, and although it wasn't conclusive I'd like to nip any infection in the bud before it becomes full-blown.'

Toni knew that urinary tract infections could cause additional confusion in elderly patients, making dementia worse; and they were more frequent in elderly patients who sometimes refused to drink enough and weren't that mobile. 'OK. Do another dipstick test in the morning and let me know the results. I'll flag it up at the team meeting tomorrow and see what everyone's schedule looks like. Either I'll come out tomorrow myself and see them, or I'll get one of the doctors to come out; we won't wait until our scheduled weekly visit on Thursday.' Toni checked the notes. 'This is potentially her fourth UTI in three months, so I'd like to look at giving her a lower dose of antibiotics long-term as prophylaxis.' As a nurse practitioner, Toni was able to prescribe antibiotics rather than having to consult one of the GPs, which made life a lot easier.

'Agreed.' Julia, as the nursing home manager, was also a qualified geriatric nurse and Toni knew she was good at picking up early signs. 'And I'm also a bit concerned about Renée. I've noticed she has a bit of a tremor when she holds a mug, and she's been a little bit off with everyone for the last couple of days.'

'You think her lithium levels might need rebalancing?' Toni asked, knowing that Renée was bipolar; lithium levels in Renée's blood needed to be checked regularly, to make sure they weren't too high and the drug was doing its job properly. A tremor was often one of the first signs of a problem, along with a change in mood.

Julia nodded. 'Again, I'd like to catch it early if we can.'

'I'll take a blood sample now and drop it in to the surgery on my way back,' Toni said. 'We've missed the bloods pick-up for today, but I'll pop the sample in the fridge overnight and it'll go in tomorrow's batch. We'll ring you as soon as the results are through.'

'Thank you.'

She washed her hands, and went to see the charge nurse to pick up a syringe, a plaster, a phial and a label. Renée was a little more scattered than usual and kept wringing her hands. 'They don't like me in here, you know,' she confided. 'They're going to tell me to leave.'

Toni knew from experience that when Renée was worried, she'd keep circling back to the same fears and no reassurance would work for longer than a couple of minutes; it just needed a couple of days for her lithium levels to get back in balance and her mood would change and her worries would disappear. So instead Toni gently asked if Renée would mind her taking a blood sample, then after her agreement changed the subject to the weather and how pretty the sunset had been last night.

Thankfully, the distraction worked and she was able to take the sample, then reassured Renée a little more before going to see Julia again to collect Archie.

'Even before we get the test results, from her behaviour I'm pretty sure you're right and her lithium levels are out of balance,' she said. 'But we need the numbers to fine-tune the dosage, and although I can prescribe a few things this is a medication I'll have to talk to one of the GPs about.'

'OK. Until we get the results back, we'll keep reassuring her and changing the subject so she doesn't get too anxious,' Julia said. 'Thanks, Toni. It's appreciated.'

'No problem. One of us will come out to see you to-morrow,' Toni said, 'and Archie and I will see you next Monday afternoon.'

'She's a smashing girl, Toni,' Mr Fellowes said. 'She used to work in a big London hospital. We're lucky to have her.'

The nurse practitioner had come here from London, too? And it was unusual to move from a hospital to a general practice. Had she been burned out, in London? Ben wondered. Or had there been some other reason why she'd come here? Even though they'd clashed, Ben had been very aware of her—and, despite his intentions never to get involved with anyone again, he found that she intrigued him.

Mr Fellowes went on to answer the unspoken question. 'She came home to help her sister look after their grandmother when she became ill. Lovely woman, Betty Butler. Her girls did her proud.'

Which sounded as if Toni and her sister had been brought up by their grandmother. Which was none of his business, Ben reminded himself. He wasn't going to ask what had happened to her parents, or why her grandmother had needed looking after, or if her grandmother was still around. It was nothing to do with him.

'She'd do anything to help anyone, our Toni.'

Which told him that the nurse practitioner was kind as well as being popular. He felt another twinge of guilt. Maybe he'd overreacted a bit about the dog. Or maybe he'd overreacted because he'd noticed the colour of her eyes and his awareness of her had spooked him slightly because he hadn't noticed small details like that about anyone for the last two years.

'That's good to know,' he said neutrally, and guided the conversation back to the ulcer on Mr Fellowes' lower leg that refused to heal.

Toni dropped the blood sample into the surgery. She wasn't sure if she was more relieved or disappointed not to see the new GP again, which unsettled her slightly. If he was a hotshot London doctor like Sean had been, he was the last person she wanted to spend time around. And yet there was something about him that drew her.

She shook herself, and drove to the car park by the beach. She changed into her running shoes, slung a bag over her shoulder with two bottles of water and a bowl for the dog, then clipped his lead on and took him to the dog-friendly side of the beach before letting him off the lead again so he could bound along the sand.

The tide was halfway out; she followed the dog down to the shoreline, enjoying the freshness of the slight breeze coming off the sea and the swishing sound of the waves against the sand. Running produced the usual endorphins; by the time they'd run along the shore and then back to the car park, she was feeling much less grumpy than she had after her run-in with Ben Mitchell.

She picked up a home-made apple pie at the beach café and a sausage for Archie, then clipped the dog into his harness on the back seat and drove to her sister's house.

Stacey greeted her with a hug. 'Perfect timing. The kettle's hot.'

'Lovely. I'm dying for a mug of tea. And I brought pudding.' Toni kissed her sister and handed over the apple pie. 'How's my best niece?' she asked, lifting Scarlett out of her bouncy chair and giving her a cuddle.

Scarlett giggled and plastered a mushy kiss to Toni's cheek. 'Tee-to!'

Scarlett-speak for Auntie Toni; Toni was so glad she'd stayed in Norfolk and had the chance to watch her niece grow up instead of going back to London, when maybe she would only have seen her sister once a month and missed all the important milestones in her niece's development.

'How's your day been, Stace?' Toni asked.

'Good. We had toddler group this morning, and Mary brought her guitar in. Then we went for a picnic in the park. How about you?'

'My usual Monday afternoon at The Beeches,' Toni said. 'Archie brought a smile to a few faces.'

'That's good. Though it must be bittersweet for you, going back and knowing Gran isn't there any more,' Stacey said softly.

Toni nodded. 'It is. And I know you miss her, too.' There was a lump in her throat. 'She would've adored Scarlett.' Except Betty Butler had died from pneumonia, the month before Scarlett was born. In some ways Toni had been relieved, because at last her grandmother was out of pain and confusion; but in others she'd been devastated. Another link to the past severed. If only Betty hadn't developed dementia. If only their parents hadn't died. They would all have loved Scarlett so much. And it must be even harder for her sister with all the might-have-beens.

'Yes.'

Hearing the slight crack in her sister's voice and knowing they were sharing the same regrets, Toni changed the subject. 'The new doctor started at the practice today.'

'What's he like?'

Toni wrinkled her nose. 'Your age, I'd say. Tall, dark and grumpy.'

'Not handsome?'

'I didn't notice.' It was a slight fib. Ben Mitchell was very nice-looking. Or he would be if he actually smiled. And his eyes were the same green as the sea on a spring day. Not that she should be focusing on that.

'But *grumpy*?' Stacey shook her head. 'I can't imagine Ranjit offering a place to someone grumpy. Someone like that just wouldn't fit in at the practice.'

Ranjit Sidana, the head of the practice at Great Crowmell, was one of the nicest-natured men either of them had ever met, always full of smiles.

'We clashed a bit.' Toni rolled her eyes. 'Over Archie. He didn't approve of the dog being at the surgery.'

'Maybe it was first-day nerves,' Stacey suggested. 'You know what Gran would've said. Give him time to settle in before you judge him.'

'I guess.'

'So what do you know about him? Is he married? Single? Any children?'

Toni heard the hopeful note in her sister's voice and sighed inwardly. 'I have absolutely no idea. All Ranjit told us about him was that he's moved here from London.'

'Like you did.'

'From another practice, rather than a hospital.' And the reason why he'd moved from the capital to a quiet country practice was none of her business. 'Even if he isn't involved with someone, I'm really not interested,

Stacey. You don't have to hope that he's a potential date for me. I don't want to date anyone.'

Stacey squeezed her shoulder. 'You know I worry about you being alone.'

'I'm not alone. I live in the same village as the best sister and brother-in-law and niece in the world, I have plenty of friends locally, and I have Archie to keep me company at home.'

Stacey raised an eyebrow. 'Thank you for the compliment, but you know what I meant. Surely you'd like to share your life with someone who says more than just "woof"?'

Toni laughed. 'There's an awful lot to be said for talking to someone who doesn't answer back.'

As if to emphasise her point, Archie wagged his tail and licked Stacey's hand and then Scarlett's foot, making the little girl giggle.

'I swear you trained him to do that on purpose.' But Stacey was smiling. 'Just don't let Sean the Smug put you off finding happiness with someone else. Not all men are like him.'

'I know they're not.' But she hadn't managed to pick anyone who felt right before him, either. 'I'm doing just fine on my own, Stacey. I live in my favourite place in the world, I love my job, and I have my family and friends nearby. I don't need anything else.'

'Hint taken, and I'll stop nagging,' Stacey said.

For now, Toni thought. She knew her sister's motives were good, but her life really was just fine as it was. Toni felt very much part of the village where she'd grown up and she had absolutely no regrets about coming here from London. She had a great life; she didn't need to date someone.

She didn't need to prove her judgement to herself, either. Of course she knew that not all men were as selfish and demanding as her ex. But if she was honest with herself she knew that the two men she'd dated before him had been just as single-minded and just as selfish as Sean. Sometimes she wondered if she subconsciously picked men who just couldn't give her love and security so it wouldn't break her heart when things went wrong. She'd already lost too many people who really mattered at too young an age. Sean had given her an ultimatum: dump her grandmother, or be dumped. That one had been very easy, and she was done with ultimatums.

Single and happy. That was her. And that was the way she intended to stay.

'Let's get you back down in your chair, Miss Beautiful,' she said to her niece, 'and I'm going to help your mummy cook dinner.'

'Din-dins,' Scarlett said, and beamed.

CHAPTER TWO

ON TUESDAY MORNING, Ben was in early for the weekly team meeting. 'I made brownies,' he said, taking the lid off the tin and putting it in the centre of the table.

'Thank you. Good choice,' Ranjit, the head of the practice, said with a smile.

Everyone except Toni took a brownie; Ben sighed inwardly. Obviously he'd annoyed her enough that she was going to ignore his peace offering. Well, he'd had it with women who were snippy. He'd put up with it from Karen—until he'd learned the bitter truth—and he wasn't going to bend over backwards to please Toni Butler.

Once they'd gone through the morning's agenda, Ranjit asked, 'Is there anything that anyone wants to bring up?'

'Yes—we need someone out at The Beeches today, please,' Toni said. She looked at Ben. 'That's the local nursing home. Forty beds; and they're set up for patients with dementia. We need to follow up Liza's UTI and Renée's lithium levels.'

'Can you do the follow-up for us, Ben?' Ranjit asked. 'It'd be useful for you to meet Julia and her team.'

'Sure.' He looked at Toni. 'Do you do a regular practice visit, Nurse Practitioner Butler?'

'Toni,' she said.

Oh. So she was thawing slightly. Good. He wouldn't go out of his way to make friends with her, but a decent working relationship would be good both for the team and for their patients.

'Our practice's regular visit is on Thursdays, though obviously we pop in whenever we're needed as well.' Her grey eyes were very clear. 'I visit The Beeches on my Monday afternoons off with Archie. He's a therapy dog. I bring him to the surgery with me on Monday morning because I go straight from here to the nursing home.'

'A therapy dog.' He hadn't expected that.

'No doubt you disapprove of that, too,' she said.

He blew out a breath. Maybe he'd asked for that, because he'd reacted badly to the dog yesterday. But she'd been snippy with him, too. 'No. I've seen studies showing that having a pet visiting can really help elderly people, especially those in residential care.'

'Exactly. It helps the residents—even a small observational study by the manager at The Beeches last year showed that a visit from Archie helps with the residents' moods and helps with their social interaction with the staff as well as each other. It gives the residents something to talk about other than their illness, and even the ones who don't really hold a conversation any more smile when they see him. The residents all really look forward to Mondays. And obviously it's done in a supervised environment, we know that none of the residents is allergic or afraid of dogs, and we're very aware of infection control. There's a policy at the home as well as here.'

She'd just covered everything he'd brought up yesterday. Clearly what he'd said still rankled. He knew what he needed to do. 'I apologise,' he said, 'for snapping at you yesterday.'

She inclined her head in acknowledgement. 'But you don't like dogs.'

Now she'd brought it up… 'No. Obviously I'd never hurt one, but I wouldn't go out of my way to spend time with one.'

'I get that not everyone's a dog person,' Toni said. 'But Archie is a genuinely nice dog. He's passed a very thorough assessment—he can be stroked and handled by anyone and he'll take treats gently and wait patiently. Plus he doesn't jump up, paw people or lick them too much.'

And Ben could guess exactly why that was part of the assessment. 'Because elderly people have very frail, thin skin.'

She smiled at him, then. A genuine smile. And Ben was shocked to realise that it made him feel as if the room had just lit up. This wasn't good. He didn't want to be attracted to anyone. His life was on an even keel again and he wanted it to stay that way.

He needed to keep his thoughts on his job. 'All right. I'll go to the home at lunchtime, as soon as my surgery finishes,' he promised.

'Thank you.'

Now she was smiling rather than scowling at him, Toni Butler was seriously pretty. She didn't wear a ring on her left hand, but that meant nothing; she could still be in a serious relationship with someone without being married. He wasn't going to ask and start the gossip mill working, either. She was his colleague. End of. And, even if she was single, he'd learned his lesson the hard way. Relationships were just too fragile, too easily broken. Like his heart. He'd only just finished putting himself back together after Karen and Patrick's betrayal, and he had no intention of setting himself up for a repeat of all that heartache.

Toni was always a little bit suspicious of people who didn't like dogs. She didn't understand that mindset. But she knew she hadn't really given Ben Mitchell a chance; she'd let herself react to him as if he was like Sean, expecting her to do things his way with no discussion, so she'd been combative with him rather than trying to find common ground, the way she normally would.

Of course not all men were like her ex.

But Ben was as self-assured as Sean had been, something that instinctively made her wary. Plus he was the first man since Sean who'd made her look twice. When he'd smiled back at her in the staff meeting and lost that brooding look, he'd been breathtakingly beautiful—green eyes, dark hair that flopped over his forehead, and an incredibly sensual mouth. He could have rivalled any film star. She really hadn't expected to be so attracted to him.

But she knew that romantic relationships never worked out for her, so she had no intention of acting on that attraction. A good working relationship was all they needed. End of.

After his shift, Ben tapped the address of The Beeches into his satnav and headed out to see the patients.

When he introduced himself to Julia, the manager, she said, 'Ah, yes. You must be the new doctor at the practice. How are you settling in?'

'Fine, thanks. Nurse Butler said you had a patient who needed to be seen about a possible UTI, and it made sense for me to come and introduce myself because I'll be seeing you on some of the regular Thursday morning visits,' he said.

'Good call. Thank you.' She smiled at him.

'I'd also like to say hello to Renée, even though her blood test results aren't back yet,' he said.

'Of course. Toni's filled you in on all the patients' histories?'

Yes, but it was useful to go over it again in case he'd missed anything. 'I'm happy for you to tell me whatever you think I need to know,' Ben said.

After he'd seen the two patients Toni had been worried about, Ben made time to meet the charge nurse, who was responsible for the drug round, and introduced himself to all the residents who were in the lounge.

'I agree with you about Renée. We'll review her medication as soon as her bloods are back and ring you,' he said to Julia in her office at the end of his visit. 'And I agree with Toni that we should give Liza a low dose of antibiotics for the next six months to put a stop to the UTIs. I'll get the prescriptions sorted out so they'll be ready for collection later this afternoon.'

'Thank you,' Julia said. 'Nice to meet you, Dr Mitchell.'

'Ben,' he said with a smile.

Once he'd sorted out the prescriptions and some admin back at the surgery, he headed for the supermarket on the way home to pick up a couple of pints of milk. As he walked into the chiller aisle, he saw Toni putting a bottle of milk into her trolley.

'Hello,' he said.

'Hi.'

No dog, he noticed. But of course dogs weren't usually allowed in supermarkets, so he stopped himself asking something clueless. Instead, he opted for polite small talk. 'Doing your weekly grocery shop?'

'My neighbour's, actually,' she said. 'Shona came off her bike awkwardly three weeks ago and broke her arm.'

'That's kind of you to do her shopping.'

Toni shrugged. 'She'd do the same for me. Great Crowmell is the kind of place where people look out for each other.' She smiled. 'Right now she has Archie sprawled all over her lap, enjoying having a fuss made of him.'

The dog. She was very much a dog person, and he really wasn't. 'Uh-huh.'

She bit her lip. 'You and I rather got off on the wrong foot yesterday. Look, if you're not busy this evening, why don't you come over for dinner? I'm a reasonable cook.'

Awareness flickered through him, and he stifled it. She wasn't asking him to dinner because she was attracted to him. She was asking him because she was trying to get their professional relationship onto an even keel. Which would be a good thing, and he'd accept purely on that basis. Because he really wasn't interested in starting a relationship with anyone. Karen had hurt him deeply. He wasn't letting anyone that close again, even if Toni was as nice as she seemed. 'Thanks. Dinner would be great,' he said.

'You're welcome to bring your partner, too, and any children,' she said. 'Just let me know how many I'm cooking for.'

Partner and children. Not any more. It had left a huge hole in his life that he tried to fill with work and studying. It hadn't worked, which was why he had moved here, hoping that a fresh start would help. He pushed the thought away. 'Just me.'

'It's just me and Archie at my place.'

So she was single, too—and clearly not in the market for a relationship. He was glad that they'd cleared that up. Established boundaries. 'OK. Can I bring pudding?' Then he remembered her refusal of his brownies. 'Um—that is, do you eat pudding?'

She grimaced. 'Ah. You must've noticed I didn't take one of your brownies this morning. Sorry, it wasn't anything personal.' She gave him a rueful smile. 'My sister says I'm weird, because I'm about the only person in the world who doesn't actually like chocolate cake.'

Funny how that made him feel so much better to discover that she hadn't been snippy with him; she just didn't like brownies. 'Noted. And I'll make blondies, next time,' he said.

'Thank you. And yes, please to pudding.'

'As long as it's not chocolate,' he confirmed.

'Absolutely. Is there anything you're allergic to or don't eat?'

'Allergies? Spoken like a true medic.' He couldn't help smiling back at her. 'No allergies, and I eat anything.'

'Good. I'll see you tonight then. About seven?'

'I'll be there.'

She gave him her address. 'It's on the edge of town, but there's plenty of parking in my road.'

'You're not that far from me. A walk will do me good,' he said. 'See you at seven.'

Sean had always said she was too impulsive.

Maybe he had a point, Toni thought as she finished buying Shona's groceries. But she was going to have to work with Ben Mitchell. It made sense to make sure their working relationship was a good one, for their patients' sake. But she was feeling ever so slightly guilty about being judgemental towards him yesterday. OK, so he'd annoyed her with his attitude towards Archie; but she could almost hear her grandmother saying softly, 'Walk a mile in someone else's shoes before you judge them.'

She hadn't done that at all.

So the very least she could do was to cook dinner for the man and help him settle into the community.

She bought ingredients for dinner, dropped off Shona's groceries and put them away for her, and took Archie out for a run before making a start on dinner.

At precisely seven o'clock, her doorbell rang.

Ben stood there with an armful of gifts. 'I bought a lemon tart and raspberries for pudding. I hope that's OK.'

'Perfect, thank you—I'm baking salmon with pesto, so the lemon will pick up the basil,' she said with a smile.

'I forgot to ask if you prefer red or white wine, so I've played it safe.' He handed her a bottle of wine.

'Lovely. New Zealand Sauvignon blanc is my favourite,' she said.

'And—well, I was brought up to take flowers if someone invites you to dinner,' he said.

'Thank you. They're beautiful,' she said, accepting the sunflowers. 'Come through to the kitchen and I'll pop them in water and sort out a drink.'

'Thanks.'

'I should warn you that Archie's in the kitchen. But if you'd prefer me to put him in the garden while you're here, I will.'

Toni was clearly trying to make an effort to accommodate him, Ben thought. So maybe he needed to do the same. 'It's fine. Though I didn't grow up around dogs and I don't have a clue how to behave around them, so you'll have to give me some pointers.'

He knew he'd done the right thing by the way she smiled at him—the real full wattage instead of the polite and more subdued version, and it lit up her eyes, too; it made his heart miss a beat.

'Thank you. Come and say hello.' She ushered him into the kitchen, where Archie sat in his basket, wagging his tail and clearly desperate to bounce over and greet their visitor, but at a signal from Toni he stayed exactly where he was.

'He's very well trained,' Ben commented.

'He is,' she agreed. 'And he'll stay there until I tell him he can come and say hello to you. If you feel uncomfortable, just let me know. Springers are usually pretty bouncy and exuberant—and Archie is definitely springy when he gets the chance—but they're also very kind, biddable dogs who just love to be with people.' She looked at him. 'If you hold your hand out to him, he'll sniff you, and then you can stroke the top of his head. As a therapy dog, he's used to elderly people with thin skin, and being around very young children who might be nervous or unpredictable. So he's very, very gentle.'

'You work with children as well?' Ben asked, surprised.

'I go into the school on Wednesday mornings,' she said. 'We're there to help the reluctant readers, the ones who are too nervous to read out loud in front of the class. They come and read to Archie.' She grinned. 'The head teacher thought it was a completely bonkers idea at first, when I suggested it.'

Yup. He thought it was bonkers, too. But the passion in her eyes as she talked about her work drew him.

'But we've seen the shyest and most hesitant little ones really grow in confidence since they've been reading to Archie. They all improved their reading ages by several months in the first six weeks alone.' She smiled. 'As a reward for good behaviour, two of the children get to sort out his water bowl and mat. They love doing that, so it's a really strong motivator.'

'Reading to dogs.' He shook his head in amazement. 'I had no idea that was even a thing.'

'There are quite a few schemes with therapy dogs,' she said. 'Archie loves it, and so do the kids. If he falls asleep, I tell them it's not because he's bored—it's like when someone reads them a bedtime story and they go all relaxed and sleepy.'

Ben was beginning to see what made Toni Butler tick. His patients and his colleagues had all sung her praises; now he could see why.

'OK.' He took a deep breath. 'I'll stroke him.'

'Stay, Archie,' she said softly.

The dog stayed where he was and let Ben stroke the top of his head. Exactly what Toni had promised: Archie was a sweet, kind, biddable dog with soft, soft fur and big, soulful amber eyes.

'Studies show,' she said, 'that blood pressure goes down when someone pets a dog. And in times of stress dog-owners experience less cardiovascular reactivity.' She looked rueful. 'Though I'm guessing if you're not a dog person...'

'It's probably still the same,' he said.

'Dinner is in five minutes. Would you like a glass of wine?'

'That'd be lovely,' he said.

Her kitchen was very neat and tidy; and there were

photographs held to the door of her fridge with magnets, of herself and Archie with various groups of people, all smiling. It was clear that she led a full and happy life.

Dinner was scrumptious: salmon baked with pesto, new potatoes, asparagus, baby carrots and roasted courgettes. Karen hadn't been keen on cooking; and Ben hadn't bothered much since his marriage had broken up because cooking for one was so lonely. He'd almost forgotten what it was like to share a meal with someone, except when his parents and his sister had invited him over and then tried to matchmake because they wanted him to be happy again.

But this was his new beginning. He and Toni could be friends as well as colleagues. He damped down the burgeoning thought that maybe she could be more.

'This is really lovely,' he said.

'And—apart from the salmon, obviously, and the pine nuts in the pesto—everything is homegrown. I love June because the garden's just brilliant.'

'You're a gardener?' He hadn't expected that.

'Not as good as my grandmother was. But that's why I moved here rather than to one of the fisherman's cottages near the harbour—it means I have a garden for Archie, and I've got space for a small vegetable patch. I got my brother-in-law to haul some railway sleepers for me to make raised beds.'

'So have you been here for very long?'

'At this cottage, for two years. But I grew up in Great Crowmell,' she said. 'My parents died in a car crash when I was twelve and my sister Stacey was fourteen, and Gran swept us up and brought us to live with her. Before that, we used to stay with her every summer. We'd spend whole days on the beach and thought we were in paradise. We lived in London, and that tiny bit of sand you get on the banks of the Thames every so often just wasn't enough for us. We loved it here, where the sand went on for miles.'

'You grew up in London?' He looked at her in surprise.

'In Highgate, when my parents were still alive. Then, when I trained as a nurse, I lived in Victoria and worked in the emergency department of the London Victoria hospital.'

'So you went back to the bright lights?'

'Something like that.'

'So what made you come back?' He knew the question was intrusive as soon as it was out of his mouth, because she flinched. 'Sorry. You don't have to answer that.' And then maybe she wouldn't ask him why he'd moved, either.

'No, it's fine. I came back because Gran became ill.' She looked at him. 'She had dementia. Stacey went to college here and stayed after she finished—she's a dressmaker—but it wasn't fair to leave all the looking-after to her, so I came back to support them both. I found a job at the practice, and I moved in with Gran so she didn't have to go into residential care for a few more months.' She shrugged. 'Gran didn't hesitate when we needed her, and we didn't hesitate when she needed us. I just wish she'd been here to meet Scarlett—my niece. She's fourteen months old.'

Now Ben understood why Toni's life had undergone such a sea change, why she'd switched from working in a big London hospital to this small general practice in the country. 'You never wanted to go back to London after your grandmother died?'

She shook her head. 'I love the pace of emergency medicine and knowing that you can make such a huge difference to people's lives, and I always thought I'd go back to it after Gran died. But then I discovered that actually I like working in the practice more than I do at a hospital. It's cradle to grave medicine. You know your patients, you can watch the little ones grow up and blossom, and because you know their family history you've got a lot more chance of working out what your patient feels too awkward to tell you in a consultation. Plus my family is here—and I really missed Stacey when I was in London.'

There was a slight shadow in her eyes; or maybe he'd misread it, because it was gone again within an instant. He had a feeling that there was another reason why she hadn't gone back to London after her grandmother's death, but he wasn't going to pry. It was none of his business. Plus asking her would leave himself open to questions, and he didn't want to talk about Karen and Patrick.

'That's why I chose to be a GP rather work in a hospital,' Ben said. 'I like working in a community.'

'Where were you before here?' she asked.

'London. Chalk Farm. We lived not far from Primrose Hill, so I was lucky enough to be able to do my morning run in the park there—the view of the city is amazing.'

'It sounds as if you miss it.'

'I do.' But he didn't miss the misery that had dragged through the last few months of his marriage, or the two years of loneliness since. He'd put it down to pregnancy hormones and he'd tried his best to be supportive and understanding. And then, just before the twenty-week scan, Karen had dropped the final bombshell; and he'd realised that the reason they hadn't been getting on was nothing to do with hormones and everything to do with guilt...

'There are good places to run, here. And if it's low tide you really can't beat running by the edge of the sea. If you're lucky, you might even see some seals,' she said. 'Why did you move here from London?'

The question he'd dreaded: though it was the obvious one and he should've found an anodyne answer for it by now. Except there wasn't one.

Because my wife fell in love with my best friend and broke my heart along with our marriage. Not that he wanted to discuss that. It had taken him nearly two years to get past it, and he didn't want to dwell on it now.

'Do you have family in the area?' she asked.

'No. Sometimes you just need a change,' he said. 'This seemed like a nice place to live.'

And the best way to distract Toni from asking anything else, he thought, would be to switch the conversation back to her dog. 'So what made you decide to train Archie as a therapy dog?'

'When Gran went into the nursing home, one of the other residents used to be visited by her dog, and seeing the dog always made Gran's day brighter. After she went into the home, I got Archie to keep me company. The manager at the care home suggested training him as a therapy dog and bringing him to The Beeches. I looked into it, and I think we both enjoy it.'

'That's good.' He kept the conversation neutral until pudding.

'Oh, now this is sublime. Thank you so much.' She ate the lemon tart with relish. 'Lemony puddings are the best—and it's the perfect pairing with raspberries.'

'Agreed.' He couldn't help smiling. 'So you're a foodie?'

'Guilty as charged,' she said, smiling back. 'I'm really interested in nutrition, and because I'm in charge of the diabetic patients I was thinking about trying to do something to teach them to tweak their favourite dishes to make them diabetic-friendly. And I'd quite like to do the same for our cardiac patients. So maybe I could run a cookery class or maybe develop a section on the practice website to help with meal plans and recipes.'

'That sounds good. The diet and exercise routines that work best are the ones you enjoy, because you stick to them,' he said.

'I've already gathered that you're a foodie, too; do I take it from the brownies that you're a cook as well?' she asked.

'I'm reasonable,' he said. Karen had left all the cooking to him, and he'd enjoyed it, finding it relaxing. Though he hadn't bothered much since she'd left him for Patrick. Cooking for one felt too lonely, and the brownies were the first cakes he'd made in months.

'Maybe we can work together on the project?' she suggested.

The previous day, Ben had disliked Toni and he hadn't been able to work out why everyone else seem to adore her. Now, he could see exactly why they did. Her warmth, her bright ideas, the way she tried to include everyone.

If he was honest with himself, he was attracted to her as well as liking her. But he had no intention of acting on that attraction. He wasn't setting himself up for things to go wrong again.

But colleagues and friends—he could do that. With pleasure.

'I'd like that,' he said. 'Do we have regular clinics for our diabetic and cardiac patients?'

'Diabetics, yes—that's me on Thursday mornings,' she said.

'It might be worth asking them for suggestions of dishes they'd like us to help them tweak. And maybe we could look at regular clinics for our cardiac patients and do the same with them.'

'Great idea.' She smiled at him. 'I'll work up a proposal, we can fine-tune it together, and then we can talk Ranjit into it.'

'Deal.'

Shaking her hand was a mistake. Awareness of her prickled all the way through him. He was going to have to be very careful to keep things professional.

Part of him knew he ought to make an excuse when she offered him coffee. But he was really enjoying her company and it was too hard to resist.

He liked her living room, too. The large window looked out over the salt marshes, and there were watercolours of what he guessed were local scenes on the walls—a stripy lighthouse, bluebell woods, and a sunset over the sea. She had a small TV in one corner, a large bookcase with an eclectic mix of novels and medical textbooks, and a speaker dock for her phone. And there were lots of framed photographs on the mantelpiece: with another woman who looked so much like her that she had to be Toni's sister, with a couple he assumed were her parents, and with an elderly woman he guessed was her grandmother.

Archie trotted into the room behind them; when Toni sat down, the dog sat with his chin on her knee, looking imploringly up at her.

'All right, then.' She lifted her hands and the dog hopped up lightly, settling himself on her lap. She gave Ben a rueful smile. 'He's too big to be a lapdog, really, but he's sat on my lap like this ever since he was tiny.'

Just to prove the point, the dog closed his eyes and started snoring softly.

Ben was shocked by how at home he felt here, how relaxed. His own—rented—accommodation was really just a place to eat and sleep and store his things, and his house in London hadn't been the most relaxing place for the last year he'd lived there. But here... Here, he felt a kind of peace that had escaped him for a long time. And how unexpected that it was in Toni's company—and that of her dog. He wasn't sure whether it reassured him more or scared him. Maybe both.

'I ought to make a move,' he said. 'Can I wash up, first?'

'No, you're fine.'

'Then thank you for dinner.'

'Thank you for pudding,' she said, gently ushering the dog off her lap and standing up.

'See you tomorrow morning.'

'Afternoon,' she reminded him. 'Wednesday mornings during term time is Archie's session at infant school.'

'Enjoy your reading,' he said.

'We will.'

He looked at the dog and took a deep breath. 'Bye, Archie.'

The spaniel, as if realising that Ben couldn't quite cope with making a fuss of him, gave a soft and very gentle 'woof'.

And all the way home Ben couldn't stop thinking about Toni Butler's smile.

He was really going to have to get a grip.

CHAPTER THREE

TONI ALWAYS ENJOYED her reading morning at the school and the enthusiasm of the children; but on Wednesday she couldn't get Ben Mitchell out of her head. She still had no idea why he'd moved from London to their little village on the coast; she had a feeling that it had something to do with the fact that he was single, but she wasn't going to pry.

Because then she would have to admit to the mistake she'd made in dating Sean—a man who only cared about himself and appearances. Sean might be a brilliant surgeon, but he didn't have a scrap of empathy and he was utterly selfish when it came to his personal life. How on earth had she missed that for so long, let herself be blinded to it by his charm?

Well, she knew the answer to that one. Probably because he was so charming. She'd been completely bowled over by him, by the dinners out and weekends away and surprise bouquets of two dozen deep red roses. But it wasn't just being spoiled; she'd done her best to spoil him back, surprise him with good tickets to a show. She'd enjoyed his company. They'd had fun together. And everything had been fine until her grandmother fell ill; then, Toni had found out the hard way that Sean's charm was all surface and he wasn't prepared to support her or put her needs first. She'd been so sure he was The One that his ultimatum had shocked her to the core. She'd fallen out of love with him very quickly after that.

Funny, she'd disliked Ben almost on sight when he'd criticised Archie, assuming that he was another man like Sean—the hot-shot and very self-assured doctor from London who threw his weight around. Yet he'd apologised for being short with her and he'd made an effort with Archie, even though he wasn't a dog person. He'd tried to meet her halfway.

Sean would have expected her to put the dog in the garden as soon as he arrived. Then again, Sean would have objected to a single dog hair sullying the pristine gorgeousness of his overpriced designer suit.

She shook herself. This really wasn't going anywhere. As she'd told her sister, she didn't want a relationship. Didn't *need* a relationship. She liked her life as it was. Ben was her colleague; he might become her friend, but that was all she could offer him. She wasn't risking her heart again.

And focusing on work was the only reason why she'd talked Ben into spending his lunch break with her at the harbour to sit on the wall, eating chips and discussing their plans for the project on patient nutrition, she told herself.

'I hope you can see the irony,' Ben said. 'Two medical professionals discussing nutrition for two particular groups of people—'

'—while stuffing our faces with one of the very things we'll ask them to avoid,' she finished. 'Totally. We're utter hypocrites.' She ate another hot, salty chip with relish.

'But you're right about the chips.' He did the same.

'They're more than worth the long run I'm going to take after work tonight to burn them off.'

His eyes were exactly the same greeny-blue as the sea in the harbour, and they crinkled at the corners. For one moment of insanity, Toni was tempted to lean forward and press a kiss to his mouth.

Then she realised that he was looking at her mouth. He looked up to meet her gaze, and her breath caught. Was he leaning towards her, or was it her imagination? She felt her lips parting involuntarily, and panicked. This wasn't a good idea. Yes, Ben was physically gorgeous and he made her laugh for the right reasons—but they'd be crazy to act on this attraction. She couldn't think about him in romantic terms.

Before they could do anything stupid, she shifted her position on the wall. There was a sudden slash of colour in his face, so she was pretty sure he'd been thinking the same thing. He'd been tempted as much as she was, and had come to the same conclusion: that even if sitting together right now felt like a date, it wasn't. This had to be work and nothing else.

'So did Archie fall asleep this morning when the children read to him?' Ben asked.

She was relieved that he'd let her off the hook and changed the conversation to something safe. 'Yes—and when one of them got a bit stuck and stopped, he opened his eyes. I explained that meant he couldn't wait to hear the next bit, we untangled the difficult word together, and everyone was happy.'

'Sounds good. So do you work part time at the practice?' he asked.

'Given that I'm off on Monday afternoons and Wednesday mornings, you mean? No—we're open from eight until six, and until eight on Thursday evenings. I stay the whole day on Thursday, so that makes up my official thirty-seven and a half hours per week.'

'What about the nutrition project? If we do it as a course, that will take another couple of hours a week.'

She shook her head. 'That's not work. That's giving something back to the community.'

Which was what she did on her Monday afternoons and Wednesday mornings off, too. Toni Butler was definitely one of the good guys. Ben couldn't understand how he'd managed to clash with her at all on Monday.

But this wasn't about his feelings towards Toni. This was work.

Together, they finished the plan to pitch to Ranjit.

And then Ben asked what had been bugging him. 'What's in the bag?'

'Yesterday's fish. A little treat for Archie, who absolutely loves fish,' she said.

'So the entire village is in love with your dog?'

'Pretty much.' She grinned. 'The dad of one of my Wednesday readers owns the fish bar. So every time I come in he gives me a bit of yesterday's fish for the dog. Just as Fluffy—the headmistress's cat—gets a regular delivery.'

Ben had liked the closeness of his community in Chalk Farm, but Great Crowmell was in another league altogether.

'So everyone knows everyone here,' he said.

'And looks out for everyone, too. It's an amazing place to grow up in.' She smiled. 'Sometimes I found it a bit frustrating when I was a teenager—if I was going to a party and I tried to buy a bottle of wine or something, the shop assistants all knew how old I was and refused to sell it to me, and Gran would hear about it on the grapevine before I even got home and then she'd tell me off. But on the flip side it means that when it's icy, none of the elderly people in the village has to go out and risk a fall because someone will go and pick up their shopping or post letters for them; and, if you break your arm, like my neighbour has, there are people who are more than happy to help by driving you wherever you need to go.' She smiled. 'I guess some people would find it a bit stifling, with everyone knowing everyone else's business, but Stacey and I love it here.'

Ben remembered her telling him why she'd moved here at the age of twelve. 'Losing your parents so young must've been really hard.' He couldn't imagine how it would feel to have grown up without his parents.

She nodded. 'But Gran was here, and everyone in the village was really supportive. It's nice that I can still talk about my parents with people who remember them— and about Gran. It means that the three of them are still with me, in a way.'

'What made you go to London for your training?' he asked.

'I was a teenager. Although I love it here, when I was eighteen I kind of wanted the whole bright lights city living thing. And I'm glad I went. It gave me a lot of experience, especially in the emergency department.' She paused. 'What about you? Did you train in London?'

'Yes. I grew up there.'

'You must miss your family.'

'I do. But I wanted to get out of London.' He'd needed a fresh start, away from the people who'd hurt him so badly. Ben hadn't just lost his wife and the baby he'd thought was his, he'd lost the man who'd been his best friend for almost half a lifetime, since they'd met on their first day at university. His best man, who'd been in love with Ben's wife all along.

Why hadn't he seen that?

He'd thought that Patrick didn't like Karen very much but put up with her for his sake. He hadn't had a clue that Patrick had fallen in love with her the very first time he'd met her, and the three years Patrick had spent in Edinburgh immediately after the wedding had been all about putting some space between them. Ben hadn't had a clue that his wife had fallen for Patrick, either. Patrick, the hot-shot surgeon everyone loved working with because he did his best for his patients and for his team. The man who worked one day a week in Harley Street—but always *pro bono*, for children with cleft palates or facial disfigurements. The man who made everyone's life brighter by just being there.

'Ben?' Toni looked concerned.

'Sorry. Wool-gathering.' And nothing was going to drag his thoughts out of him. He'd make something up if she asked him anything more. Instead, he switched the conversation back to their nutrition project.

Later that afternoon, they pitched the idea to Ranjit.

'Brilliant,' the head of the practice said. 'If you do a class, where would you hold it?'

'Hopefully the high school, so we can use their ovens,' Toni said. 'If not, the village hall. Or we can start with a blog or something on the website, and then maybe talk one of the local chefs into doing a demo for us. Actually, that'd be a good fundraiser for the village hall, so I'll bring that one up with the committee.'

'And that would open it up to all our patients,' Ben said. 'People who want to maybe eat more healthily but they've read so much confusing stuff on the internet that they don't know what they should be focusing on.'

'Let me know if you need anything from me,' Ranjit said.

'It's my diabetes clinic tomorrow,' Toni said. 'I can talk to my patients about it and see what they'd like us to do.'

Ben smiled. 'Once you get an idea, you really don't hang about, do you?'

'Life's very short and I'm a great believer in seizing the day. When I'm old, I won't look back and have regrets about all the things I wish I'd done.' She had a few regrets, but she pushed them back where they belonged. You couldn't have everything you wanted, and she was grateful for all the things she did have. Wanting more was just greedy.

Over the next couple of weeks, Ben felt that he had really settled into Great Crowmell. He'd got used to his new routines and his team mates at the practice; and, although he missed the stunning views over London from Primrose Hill on his morning runs, he discovered that he really liked the beach, hearing the swish of the waves against the sand and the cry of the seagulls.

On the Monday evening, he made blondies for the team meeting in the morning. This time, at the meeting, Toni took one of the cakes with her coffee. 'Oh, wow. These are amazing,' she said.

How bad was it that he felt utterly gratified?

Worse still, when she smiled at him, his heart skipped

a beat. Part of him felt as if he was thawing out, coming back to life; but part of him was unsure.

He was really going to have to keep a grip on his emotions. She'd made it clear that she was interested in dating him, but he knew he couldn't trust his judgement. Although he realised Toni wasn't the sort to hurt someone deliberately, neither was Karen and she'd still hurt him.

He was still brooding about it when he saw his last patient of the day, Courtney Reeves. She was seventeen, and was in the middle of doing her A-level exams. He guessed that she wanted to talk to him about anxiety management, because she'd refused to tell the receptionist what was wrong when she'd made an appointment.

'What can I do for you, Courtney?' he asked.

She bit her lip. 'I'm in a mess.'

'OK,' he said. 'Do you feel you can talk to me about it? Or would you prefer someone else to be here with you when we talk? Your mum?'

'I… I can't tell my mum. Please don't tell my mum.' She burst into tears.

Ben handed her the box of tissues on his desk. 'Anything you tell me is completely confidential. Your medical records are completely private,' he reassured her. 'The only time I will talk to someone else about you is if I think you're in danger, but I'll always talk to you about that first.'

'I've got a place at Cambridge,' she said. 'If I get my grades.'

'And that's where you want to go?' he asked. Or maybe her parents were putting pressure on her to go there and she was finding the extra stress hard to handle.

'I do.' She looked miserable. 'But I've messed it all up.'

He waited until she was ready to start talking. Eventually, she rubbed her eyes. 'I… There was a party. I had too much to drink. I did something really stupid.' She swallowed hard. 'It was a month ago.'

Now he could guess exactly what was wrong. She'd had unprotected sex with someone. 'And now your period is late?' he asked quietly.

She nodded. 'I caught the bus to Norwich and bought a test and did it in the loos at the library—if I'd bought one here someone would've told my mum.'

'And it was positive?' he checked.

She nodded. 'And I don't know what to do. I know I should've got the morning-after pill but I didn't want my mum to know I'd been so stupid and had unprotected sex, and then it was Monday and it was too late.'

'Have you told anyone else?' he asked. 'Is there a counsellor at school you can talk to?'

'Just my best friend. She made me come to see you. She's waiting outside for me.'

'You've got a really good friend there, and you've done exactly the right thing in coming to see me,' Ben said. 'OK. So you've done the test and it's positive. Do you have any other early pregnancy symptoms?'

'Morning sickness, you mean? No. I feel fine. Just that I missed my period. I thought it was because I was stressed over the exams, but I'm always regular. Always.'

He looked at her. 'I'm not judging you, Courtney, but as you didn't use a condom it's possible that you might have picked up an infection, so it might be a good idea to do a swab test.'

'An STD, you mean?' She shook her head. 'It was the first time, for both of us. And I know that for definite.'

'Have you told your boyfriend?'

'And ruin his life as well as mine? How can I?' she asked. 'He's supposed to be going to Oxford.'

And he didn't want the hassle of a baby? Not that Ben would be mean enough to ask. 'Let's talk about your options,' he said. 'If you want to keep the baby, we can start your antenatal care now.'

'I don't want the baby,' she said. 'I'm too young. I'm just not ready for this.' Her face had lost all its colour. 'But the idea of having a termination... That's...' She grimaced. 'I do Biology A-level, so I know right now it's a tiny bunch of cells, not an actual b...' Her voice tailed off. 'I hate this, Dr Mitchell. I don't know what to do. Whatever I do feels wrong. Someone's going to get hurt. I don't...' She shook her head in anguish, clearly unable to speak because she was fighting back the tears.

'It's a hard decision,' he said. 'And you don't have to make it right away because it's still very early in the pregnancy. You have options. If you don't want to keep the baby but you don't want a termination, you can have the baby adopted and take a gap year between now and university. Or I can refer you to the hospital or clinic for assessment if you feel you'd rather have a termination. Whatever you decide, Courtney, the main thing is you're not on your own. We can support you here at the practice.'

'My mum's going to be so angry.' Courtney dragged in a breath. 'She had me when she was seventeen and she's always regretted it. I mean, I know she loves me, but if she hadn't had me her life would've been so different. I've heard her talking to people when she thinks I can't hear. If she hadn't had me, she wouldn't be a single mum. She would've gone to university and travelled the world and got an amazing job.' She shook her head.

'And now I've done exactly the same thing she did. She's going to be so disappointed in me.'

'When she's got over the initial shock of the news,' Ben said, 'she might be the best person you can talk to about it. She's been in your shoes, so she knows exactly how it feels.'

'I've let her down,' Courtney said. 'I've let everyone down. And I was supposed to be going to study medicine. How can I possibly be a doctor when I've done something like this?'

'You're human. And plenty of medics I know have had an unplanned pregnancy.' His ex-wife's pregnancy hadn't been planned, either, and he was a medic. Not that it was appropriate to talk about that to Courtney.

'You need to talk things over with your mum,' he said. 'There's no rush. You have plenty of time to make a decision. Think about what you want. And if you'd like me to be there when you tell your mum, or if you'd like someone else you know from the practice to be there, we can arrange that.'

Another tear leaked down her cheek. 'You'd do that?'

'Of course I would. We want to help you, Courtney. You're not alone.'

She looked as if she couldn't quite believe it.

'Find out when's a good time for your mum, and we'll make an appointment to talk to her together,' he said. 'It's all going to work out.'

By the time she left his consulting room, Courtney looked a lot happier. But Ben couldn't stop thinking about Karen. She must've been just as dismayed when she'd realised that she was pregnant. Courtney at least knew who the father was; for Karen, it had been more complicated. Her fling with Patrick had happened while he was away on a course. Given the timing, as soon as she knew she was pregnant she'd realised that there was a strong chance that the baby was Patrick's. She'd panicked, not knowing what to do and not being able to talk to Ben about it because he was part of the problem.

The truth had come tumbling painfully out the day she'd got the appointment for the twenty-week scan.

He blew out a breath. It was pointless making himself miserable about it and wondering where he'd gone wrong. Karen had told him he hadn't done anything wrong. She'd just fallen in love with Patrick. They'd both fought against it, not wanting to hurt him—but then he had been sent away on that course, Patrick had taken Karen to a show in his place, and the emotions had spilled over into kissing and that single night in Patrick's bed.

Although they'd kept apart after that, the guilt and worry had eaten away at Karen, and the upcoming scan had been the last straw. Not wanting to lie to Ben any more, she'd told him the truth. Told him that she wanted Patrick. And, even if the baby turned out to be Ben's, she'd fallen out of love with him and she wanted to make her life with Patrick instead.

Ben had been horrified. What if the baby *was* his? What then?

But Karen had been adamant. Either way, she didn't want to be married to Ben any more. If the baby was his, they'd come to some sort of access arrangement, but she didn't want to live with him for the baby's sake. It wouldn't be fair on any of them.

As for finding out who was the baby's father, she'd done some research on the Internet. She'd found a non-invasive test, based on a simple blood sample from her and a mouth swab sample from himself and Patrick.

The sample would analyse the cell-free foetal DNA in her blood—avoiding the risk of miscarriage that could be caused by an invasive test such as chorionic villi sampling—and it would compare genetic markers between the baby's DNA, Patrick's and Ben's. Five thousand of them, so the test would be conclusive.

And so they'd all done the test. Karen had stayed at her mother's for the two weeks it took for the results to come back, not having any contact with either Ben or Patrick until she knew for sure which of them was the father. Ben hadn't wanted to see Patrick, to hear his excuses—plus he didn't trust himself not to be so overwhelmed with emotion that he'd actually punch his ex-best friend.

Those two weeks had been the longest of his life. The seconds had dripped by like treacle. Although they knew that a court of law wouldn't recognise the test, instead asking for a post-natal DNA test for final proof, everything Ben had read about the procedure and the results told him that there was a probability of ninety-nine point nine per cent of inclusion and one hundred per cent of exclusion. That was more than good enough for him.

At least Karen had told him the results face to face. She'd actually given him the results sheet so he could see it for himself.

Patrick was the baby's father.

And Ben's world had imploded.

He'd lost everything. His wife, his baby and his best friend.

He tried to push the thoughts away and finished writing up his notes.

There was a rap at his door.

'Yes?' he called with irritation.

The door opened. 'Ben, I was wondering—' Toni began.

'What now?' he snapped—then hated himself for being so rude. It wasn't her fault and he shouldn't take it out on her. 'Sorry,' he muttered. 'I didn't mean to snap at you.'

'What's wrong?' she asked.

'Nothing.'

'Uh-huh,' she said. And he didn't blame her for not believing him.

'I get that you might not want to talk,' she said, 'but right now you look like crap. Why don't you come running with me? It'll make you feel better.'

Part of Ben wanted to tell her to mind her own business, because he was just fine—except he wasn't fine. And he knew that Toni had a point. The endorphins from going for a run would help his mood, and the sheer mechanics of running, putting one foot in front of the other, would clear his head. Plus it would be nice not to be alone with his thoughts. 'OK,' he said finally.

'Get your running stuff and meet me in the car park outside Scott's Café in half an hour,' she said.

When he drove into the car park, Toni was already there, dressed for a run, leaning against her car with the dog sitting patiently next to her.

Remembering the other night, he put out his hand; the dog took a sniff and then licked his hand. Instead of feeling repulsed, Ben felt warm inside, which he hadn't expected. Comfort from a dog. He would never have guessed that was possible.

'No talking. Just run, when we're on the beach, because I think you need this,' she said, and led the way down the wooden steps to the dog-friendly end of the beach. She let Archie off the lead and began running when the dog raced off.

It had been a long, long time since Ben had run with anyone. And he was truly grateful that Toni didn't push him to talk. The tide was out, and they just ran, both adjusting their stride so they were running side by side. There were other dog-walkers on the beach; Archie bounded up to one or two, whose owners clearly knew Toni and put up a hand in acknowledgement as they passed.

They ran all the way to the dunes, where she stopped. 'Hydration break,' she said. Obviously this was something she did a lot with Archie, because her small backpack held bottles of water and a bowl for the dog. She poured a bowl of water for the dog first, then looked at Ben. 'Did you remember to bring some water?'

'I forgot,' he admitted. His thoughts had been too full of the past.

She handed him a bottle. 'Here you go. It's a new bottle and it's chilled.'

'Thanks.'

She waited until he'd finished drinking before she asked softly, 'Do you want to talk about it?'

Yes and no. Part of him wanted to bury it, but part of him knew it was better to let it out before the memories turned even more poisonous and made him miserable. He blew out a breath. 'This is all in confidence, yes?'

'Of course.'

'One of my patients is pregnant—it wasn't planned and she was pretty upset about it. And I guess it stirred up a few memories for me.'

She waited, not interrupting or asking questions. Just as he did with patients when he wanted to give them the space to talk, knowing that eventually they would fill the silence.

'My wife—ex-wife—was pregnant,' he said quietly. 'Two years ago. The pregnancy wasn't planned.' He had to swallow the lump in his throat. 'And the baby wasn't mine.'

She reached over to squeeze his hand briefly. 'That's a tough situation.'

'It was a mess.' Which was the understatement of the year. It had broken him.

'Had you been married for long?' she asked.

'Five years. I'd just started getting broody. I was thrilled when she told me she was pregnant. I was really looking forward to being a dad. But it all went wrong.' He gave her a wry smile. 'But I guess we both made a mistake. I wasn't the one she really wanted.'

'So how did you find out?'

'She told me, when she got the appointment for the twenty-week scan. She didn't want to lie to me any more. So we did a prenatal paternity test.'

Her eyes widened. 'CVS?'

'No. We didn't want to do anything invasive. It was a blood test for her and mouth swabs with me and…' What would she say if he told her who the other man was? His best friend, the man he'd loved like a brother?

But he didn't want her pity.

He shrugged. 'The other guy. Nothing I could say or do would change what happened. Karen and I had a long talk that night, and she admitted they'd had a fling while I was away and the timing meant she wasn't quite sure who the father was, him or me. What I'd thought was pregnancy hormones making her snappy with me—it wasn't that at all. She felt guilty and angry with herself, and she couldn't help taking it out on me.'

'That's tough for both of you.'

He nodded. 'When I found out, I was so hurt and angry. And the DNA tests showed that the baby wasn't mine. That broke me a bit. But talking to my patient today has made me think about what my ex went through. She was in a mess. The baby was going to change everything. And she did love me when she married me. It was just...' He shrugged. 'She fell out of love with me and in love with him.'

'Did he love her?'

Ben nodded. 'He always had. He tried to fight it for my sake.'

'So you were friends?'

He might as well tell her the whole sorry truth. And if she started pitying him, he'd walk away. 'Yes. He didn't seem to like her very much and he always seemed to avoid her. It never occurred to me that there might be another reason why he did it—like that film my sister, Jessie, watches every single Christmas, where Andrew Lincoln stands in the doorway with those oversized flashcards and tells Keira Knightley that he'll always love her, even though she's married to his best friend.'

He grimaced. 'Jessie always said that was so romantic—but it really isn't. Not when you're on the other end of it and you realise that everyone's lied to you. And *everyone* gets hurt. That's not love.' He looked away. 'After Karen and I got married, Patrick moved to Edinburgh for three years. He told me it was for the sake of his career—but in hindsight I realise that it was actually to put some space between himself and Karen. To keep her out of temptation's reach. But it happened anyway.'

'It sounds like one of those situations where, whatever happened, you were all going to get hurt,' she said gently, taking his hand and squeezing it briefly. 'That's rough.'

He risked a glance at her. There was definitely sympathy in her eyes—but to his relief there was no pity. 'Yeah.'

She waited, giving him a chance to spill the rest.

So he did.

'The baby wasn't mine, so there was no fight over custody. She went to be with him, and we tried to sort everything out without making it any worse than it already was.'

'Did you stay in your house?' she asked.

He nodded. 'Until we managed to sell it. Then I rented somewhere near the surgery where I worked. But I got sick of facing all the pity and then all the matchmakers who were so convinced that if they found Ms Right for me everything would be OK again. That's why I jumped at the idea of coming here. It meant a new start, where nobody knew what had happened.'

'I can understand that,' she said, sounding heartfelt. 'And what you've just told me will stay strictly confidential, I promise you.'

He believed her. 'Thank you.' He gave her a wry smile. 'It's pretty much put me off the idea of marriage and relationships.'

'Hardly surprising. If it makes you feel any better,' she said, 'I'm not very good at picking Mr Right, either.'

'No?' He hadn't expected that. He'd already worked out that Toni was very capable.

'When Gran was first diagnosed with dementia, my ex said that Stacey and I should put her straight in a nursing home. He pretty much gave me an ultimatum—if I came back here to help Stacey look after Gran, we were through, because he didn't want to live in a backwater and he didn't want to have to drive to the middle of nowhere every time he wanted to see me.'

Now he understood those brief shadows in her eyes when she'd talked about London. 'That,' Ben said, 'is incredibly selfish. Especially as I'm guessing he knew that she looked after you when your parents were killed and you grew up here.'

'Exactly. It wasn't a difficult choice.' She smiled grimly. 'I told him that he needn't bother giving me an ultimatum because we were through anyway. And it took him all of half a week to replace me.'

'What an idiot,' Ben said.

She laughed. 'Yes. He was a total stereotype: the epitome of an arrogant surgeon. I should've listened to the theatre nurses who said he was vile to work with.'

'I know the sort.' Patrick was a surgeon, too. But he wasn't arrogant. He was one of the good guys. Which made it hurt even more: how could such a nice guy betray him like that? Ben still didn't understand. 'You're worth more than that.'

'You bet I am. But, actually, I like my life as it is. I love my job, I love being part of this community, and my closest family live nearby. Wanting anything more would be greedy.'

'I should be grateful for what I have, too,' Ben said. Instead of wishing things were different and that he'd been enough for Karen.

'You've got a great job, you're finding your place in a brilliant community, you've got the sea on your doorstep and right now the sun is shining. It doesn't get better than this,' Toni said.

He lifted his empty water bottle in a toast. 'I would drink to that, so just pretend there's some water left.'

She smiled. 'Come back for dinner, if you like, and we can make that toast with wine. It won't be anything fancy, though. Just whatever's in the fridge or I can dig up from the garden.'

'You cooked for me last time, so it's my turn. Plus it will prove I'm capable of making more than just cake.'

'As friends,' she said.

'As friends,' he agreed. Which was the sensible thing to do. Even though regret twinged through him, because in another time and in another place they might have been more than just friends. Much more.

'Then thank you. That will be lovely. Archie can keep Shona company,' she said. 'And I'll bring pudding. You don't have to worry about allergies or food dislikes—absolutely anything is fine by me. Well, except chocolate cake, but you know about that already.'

'I do indeed. Let's run back to the car.' He paused. 'And thank you for listening, Toni. I think I needed to let that out.'

'Any time,' she said. 'And if you don't want to talk to a human, you can borrow Archie. He won't talk back or ask awkward questions, though he might decide to wash your face.'

And the sweetness in her smile made him want to hug her.

Except they'd just agreed this was a friendship only. He wasn't going to cross the line and spoil it.

CHAPTER FOUR

BACK AT HER HOUSE, Toni showered quickly, popped next door with Archie and made Shona a mug of tea and a sandwich, then collected some strawberries from her garden and a tub of salted caramel ice cream from her freezer before driving over to Ben's house.

Ben had clearly showered and changed into jeans and a T-shirt when he'd got home, and it made him look younger than he did at work—and much more approachable. Though, now he'd told her about his past, she knew she needed to keep her distance. He could offer her friendship and nothing more.

'Hi.' She handed him the strawberries and the ice cream. 'Bit of a cheat, I'm afraid.'

'Are these home-grown strawberries?' he asked.

She smiled. 'Picked just before I walked out of the door. You can't get much fresher than this or have fewer food miles.'

'And Scott's ice cream. Moira told me on my first day that it was the best ice cream in town; I've tried a few flavours and this one is my favourite. Thank you.'

'Archie loves the doggy ice cream, too,' she said. 'It's really more like frozen yoghurt, so there's no added sugar to wreck his teeth.'

'I'm still getting my head around the concept of ice

cream for dogs,' he said. 'Come in. Can I get you a glass of wine?'

'I drove over—so the ice cream didn't melt—so no, thanks—just water for me.' She sniffed appreciatively. 'Something smells nice.'

'The sauce is home-made,' he said, 'but I'm afraid the ravioli and flatbread aren't.'

'I won't hold it against you. I love ravioli and flatbread,' she said.

Ben's house was neat and tidy, but it felt more like a show house than an actual home. There was nothing personal on display; in the kitchen, there were no notes or photographs stuck to the fridge door with a magnet. Her fridge had pictures of family and friends, her shopping list, recipes she wanted to try cut from magazines. She hadn't let Sean's behaviour isolate her from the rest of the human race; but, then again, he hadn't betrayed her in the way Ben's wife and his best friend had betrayed him.

If you'd been hurt that much, it was only natural that you'd see your home as a place to sleep, not a place to live. And she'd be very foolish to think she could change the way he felt. He was being polite, but it was obvious to her that he'd shored up all his barriers, not letting anyone close. It felt as if he regretted confiding in her. So it was time to back off, make it clear she was offering him friendship and expecting nothing more. 'Are you busy next weekend?' she asked.

'Yes. I'm keeping up with my professional development,' he said.

Studying? 'In that case, can I tempt you out to play on Saturday?' she asked. 'Just it's the nineteen-forties weekend.'

'Nineteen-forties weekend?'

'You might have seen the posters around the village. Everyone dresses up, all the local businesses join in, and so does the steam train in the next village. And there's a nineteen-forties-themed dance in Great Crowmell Village Hall on the Saturday night. All the proceeds go towards the cost of running events for the local kids over the summer holidays.'

Ben thought about it. Dressing up, a steam train and an evening dancing. It sounded a lot less lonely than the whole weekend spent doing an online course.

'The food is themed as well,' she added. 'So you'll have the delights of corned beef and Spam sandwiches, lentil sausages, homity pie and dairy-free cakes. Oh, and the fish bar is going to have a pop-up stall—on the grounds that fish and chips weren't rationed—and a local brewery is doing the bar. Beer, cider and old-fashioned lemonade.'

'That sounds good. Where do I get a ticket?'

'For the steam train, you buy one at the station. But I can organise your ticket for the dance,' she said with a smile.

'Thanks. Let me know how much I owe you.'

'Will do. And, if you fancy baking some scones to a wartime recipe, the Village Hall committee would love you for ever.'

The penny dropped. 'You're on the committee, aren't you?'

'Yup,' she confirmed. 'We do all sorts of things. There's a dog show later in the summer.'

'Why do I get the feeling that was your idea?' he asked wryly.

She grinned. 'It wasn't, actually, but I'm organising

it this year, so Archie isn't allowed to enter any of the classes. He did win the classes for Waggiest Tail and Most Handsome Dog last year, though. If he hadn't, I think there would've been a riot in the infant school and the nursing home. I can just see them now, chanting, "Archie has the waggiest tail!"'

He couldn't help smiling. Toni Butler made him feel light at heart. She really was a ray of sunshine. Why on earth had her ex given her that stupid ultimatum instead of following her here and applying for a surgeon's post at one of the local hospitals? It wouldn't have been that arduous a commute; in fact, it would probably have been a shorter journey to work than he'd had in London.

But that was straying into dangerous territory.

Yes, he'd confided in Toni, but he didn't want to risk getting closer, even though at the same time he yearned for that closeness. Despite his reservations, he found himself asking her to stay just a bit longer—for two cups of coffee after dinner—and he refused to let her even look at the washing up.

'I'd better get back,' she said at last. 'I need to pick up Archie from Shona, and I promised to wash her hair for her this evening. Until it happens to you, I don't think you realise how much you can't do when you break your arm; even though it's not her writing hand, there are so many things she finds tricky. And being in plaster during the summer…' She wrinkled her nose. 'Really not fun.'

'Poor woman. Let me know if I can do anything to help,' he said.

'Bake me that dozen scones,' she said. 'I'll email you the wartime recipe.'

'Great. Enjoy your reading morning with Archie at the school tomorrow.' He saw her to the door. 'And thank you for today. For listening and not...' He shrugged awkwardly. 'Not judging.'

'Any time,' she said. 'That's what friends are for.'

It suddenly struck him that she was right: they had become friends over the last couple of weeks. And it warmed him all the way through. Even though a little voice in his head was whispering that he'd like her to be more than his friend...

The following week, on the Saturday morning, Ben made scones to the wartime recipe that Toni had sent over—which, to his surprise, included grated carrot. He made two dozen, and they'd cooled by the time Toni came to pick him up.

'*Two* dozen? Thank you, you superstar,' she said with a smile. Then she looked him up and down. 'And you look pretty much perfect, as a nineteen-forties village doctor—pleated trousers, checked shirt, Fair Isle sleeveless jersey, fedora and a tweed jacket.'

'Thank you. I hired my costume, though obviously the stethoscope is modern.'

'You hired your costume from Moira's cousin?' she guessed.

'Yes. You look very nice, too.' She was wearing a pale blue cotton tea dress decorated with bright red peonies, cream sandals with a strap around the ankle and a low kitten heel, and her hair was put up in a neat roll. Her lipstick matched the peonies on her dress, and Ben really had to fight the urge to kiss her.

'Thank you. Stacey made the dress for me.'

'Is she coming today?'

'Definitely. You'll get to meet her later. Shall we go?' she asked. 'We just need to drop these off at the village hall, and then we can head down the coast to catch the train.'

They dropped off his scones and her mini homity pies, then parked on the outskirts of the next town round the coast and walked to the train station.

The streets were absolutely crammed with people, and the only cars that were parked in the High Street were vintage ones. A couple of policemen arrested a spiv who was offering people watches from the inside of his jacket; servicemen in uniform walked alongside Land Girls carrying baskets of eggs and old-fashioned milk cans; and several children were dressed as evacuees, carrying a teddy and a gas mask box and with labels tied around their necks. The shops and cafés had all joined in, with sandbags piled outside the doors and brown tape stuck to the windows in cross formation; even the window displays were vintage, from sweets to clothing to groceries. There was bunting everywhere, pop-up stalls offered to do vintage make-up and hair, and in a corner of the village square a stage was set up for singers to perform using an old-fashioned microphone.

'This is amazing,' he said. 'How long has this event been going?'

'A couple of decades, now. It started with a few steam railway enthusiasts setting up a weekend, not long after Stacey and I moved in with Gran, and it just snowballed, with more people joining in every year. Gran used to love this. And we loved going with her, because she used to tell us all her childhood memories and about what life was like growing up in wartime, and we'd look through all the old photo albums—from Mum's childhood as well as Dad's.' She took his hand. 'Come on. Let's go and get our tickets for the steam train.'

There were soldiers and sailors everywhere, women sporting fox fur tippets that Ben rather hoped were fake, others wearing overalls with scarves tied round their heads, and men dressed as the Home Guard. The train was crammed with people, and the carriages were vintage with a corridor for the guard and two bench seats per compartment that stretched across the whole width of the compartment and a metal and rope netting shelf above the seats for luggage.

'Room for two,' the guard said, and made everyone squash up. He grinned at them. 'We can seat six a side. And remember there's a war on.'

Toni insisted that Ben have the window seat, and he was stunned by the glorious view of the sea across the cornfields.

'This is quite an experience. I can't ever remember travelling on a steam train before,' he said. 'I loved all the stories about trains when I was small, but we never went anywhere like this as a family.'

'My mum and dad loved it. Steam trains had been phased out in favour of diesel by the time my parents were born, but Gran remembered being on a steam train when she was younger and she and my grandad used to take us on this one when we were small,' Toni said.

'When I was a kid and my favourite books talked about the trains making a "chuff-chuff" sound, I thought it was just the story, but they really do make that sound. It's amazing,' he said.

'And look, you can see the steam coming past the window,' she said.

There was a faint smell of sulphur in the air, which Ben assumed was from the coal. And it really did feel as if he'd gone back in time.

At the end of the line, there was a small funfair with old-fashioned steam gallopers and swing-boats, and stalls with old-fashioned games.

'Going to win me a coconut, Dr Mitchell?' she teased.

When he won her a coconut first time and presented it to her with a bow, she laughed. 'You've done this before, haven't you?'

'No. But I played cricket a lot when I was younger.'

'Remind me to introduce you to Mike, who runs the village cricket team,' she said.

The tea tent had notices everywhere telling people not to waste sugar as it was on ration, and there were old-fashioned cakes on sale.

'This is great,' Ben said. 'I haven't had this much fun in...' he paused '... I don't know when.'

'Good.' She smiled at him, and again his heart skipped a beat.

Back in Great Crowmell, once they'd dropped her car at her house and were walking towards the harbour, she grew more serious. 'Are you sure you're all right about meeting Stacey, Nick and Scarlett? I mean—I understand if it'll be too...' She paused, as if trying to find the right word.

Ben knew what she meant. He'd thought he'd be a dad, and then it had been taken away from him. Being around a small child would remind him of what he didn't have.

'It's fine,' he reassured her, though he appreciated the fact that she'd thought about what he'd told him. 'Remember, I treat babies and small children at the surgery—and parents who bring their babies with them.'

'Just as long as I'm not ripping the top off the scab.'

'It's fine,' he said.

And when he met Stacey, he liked her immediately;

she was as warm and kind as Toni. Their grandmother must've been a really special woman, he thought.

'Ice creams are on me,' Nick said, leading them towards Scott's.

'I keem!' Scarlett crowed happily from her very old-fashioned pram.

'It's borrowed,' Stacey told him, having clearly noticed his glance at the pram. 'It's amazing what's survived from seventy years ago. This is the kind of thing our great-grandmother would have used—though I have to say it's way heavier than Scarlett's pram and it doesn't fold up, so it'd be a nightmare to try and put this in a car.'

'I've never been to this sort of fundraising thing before,' Ben said. 'And to think that the whole village is involved—well, several villages—is incredible.'

'It's a good community, here,' Stacey told him.

Which he was really beginning to feel part of, thanks to Toni. And here, where nobody except Toni knew his past, he was finally healing. The bleak emptiness that had stretched out in front of him in London didn't feel quite so bleak any more. He met Toni's neighbour Shona properly, too, and Toni made a point of introducing him to the cricket club captain, Mike.

Weirdly, Ben felt more at home here than he ever had at Chalk Farm. How was that even possible?

At seven, they headed for the village hall, which had been thoroughly decorated with bunting, sandbags and tape on the windows. Inside, there were trestle tables for the food, covered in white tablecloths, and with vintage china cake stands and dishes for the food.

'So the community has all come together for this?' Ben asked. 'All the food is donated?'

'We all either grew up here and benefited from the generosity of people in the past, or we've got kids who use it now. The village hall organises stuff for all age groups and as I mentioned, the money raised means we can run events for the kids free during the summer holidays, and keep everything else down to a reasonable cost,' Toni explained. 'So whether it's the toddler group, the senior citizens' afternoon tea dances, or youth club evenings, which can be anything from a talent competition through to self-defence classes and archery lessons, there's something for everyone.' She looked at him. 'Surely you had stuff like this in London?'

'Not really,' he said.

'Well, there you go—another benefit of living here,' she said.

Just about everyone in the room wanted to talk to Toni, he discovered. And she made sure she introduced him to everyone in the village he hadn't met yet, finding common interests so they had something to talk about, and he wasn't left standing around on his own, feeling awkward.

When the music started, Ben said, 'May I have this dance, Miss Butler?'

'Sure,' she said. 'Though I should warn you that I have two left feet and your toes might regret you asking me.'

'Or maybe they won't. Follow my lead,' Ben said with a smile.

It was nice that Ben had joined in, Toni thought. He'd made scones, he'd hired a costume, and now he was going to dance with her—so very unlike Sean's reaction to the nineteen-forties weekend. When Toni had suggested that he join her family at the event, he'd balked at the idea of wearing anything other than designer jeans and a high-end brand shirt, let alone something vintage. In the end, he hadn't been able to join them because he'd been called to the hospital to treat a complication in one of his patients; but Toni suspected that he'd got someone to make that call rather than say straight out that he didn't want to go.

She expected Ben to be a slightly better dancer than her, but she wasn't prepared for him to be absolutely brilliant, spinning around and leading her on the floor in a way that made her feel as if she could actually dance instead of being her usual hopeless self.

'You're amazing!' she said when she caught her breath. 'You're a dark horse, Ben Mitchell. Where did you learn to dance like *that*?'

'Let's say I had a misspent youth,' he told her with a grin.

And, now he was relaxed and laughing, he was utterly gorgeous, Toni thought. No wonder he was attracting admiring glances from every woman in the room. He was definitely making her own heart go pitapat. Which was crazy, because she knew he didn't want to get involved with anyone. But, just for tonight, maybe she could dream.

'You had dance lessons?'

'Jessie did,' he said.

His sister, she remembered.

'She needed a partner, so I was the obvious choice.'

Because he was her big brother, looking out for her? That didn't surprise Toni. Ben Mitchell was the sort of man who would've asked his little sister's shy and geeky best friend to the prom so she wasn't left feeling awkward and alone. Kind. Thoughtful. A huge contrast to

Sean—how could she ever have thought Ben reminded her of her ex? It might have seemed that way at first but, the more she got to know him, the more she liked him. 'So she learned to do the jive and stuff like that?'

'All the ballroom dances and all the Latin ones,' he said. 'Jessie took all her exams and got gold medals.'

'And so did you?' she guessed.

'To support her,' he said, glossing over the question.

So clearly he'd done well but wasn't the sort to boast about it.

'Our teacher really liked big band music and nineteen-forties dances,' Ben said, 'so she taught us the jitterbug and the Lindy Hop as well.'

'The jitterbug? Now that's *way* above my pay grade,' Toni said, laughing.

'You might be surprised. Let's give it a go.'

He talked her through some of the steps—and, the next thing she knew, she was actually dancing the jitterbug with him, twirling round and actually going in the direction she was supposed to go instead of the complete opposite. And it made her feel as if she was flying.

Though, if she was honest with herself, it wasn't just the dance moves that made her feel so good. It was Ben himself.

Which was dangerous. She knew she wasn't good at relationships, and he was understandably wary. She needed to be sensible.

'I loved that,' she said when the song was over. 'I've never been able to dance anywhere near as well as that before.'

'Who are you and what have you done with my little sister?' Stacey teased, coming over to them with her arm wrapped round her husband. 'Toni, I've never seen you that co-ordinated before. That was amazing.'

'I'm not taking any credit for that. It was all him,' Toni said, gesturing gracefully towards Ben.

'You could be a professional dancer, Ben,' Stacey said.

Ben laughed. 'I'm happy with my current job, but thank you for the compliment.'

'Very much deserved. Dr Mitchell, please may I have the next dance?' Stacey asked.

'Sure.' He held his hand out to her. 'Are you two joining us?'

Nick looked at Toni and shook his head. 'I can't do what you do, Ben—and I value my toes! You and I are going to queue up at the bar and sort out a round, Toni.'

'Perfect,' Toni said, tucking her arm through Nick's.

'Can we get you a beer, Ben?' Nick asked.

'That'd be great, thanks. I'm not fussy what you get,' Ben said. 'And the next round is mine.'

'I like him. He's a nice guy,' Nick said when they were in the queue.

'Don't you start,' Toni warned. 'Or did Stacey prime you to say that?'

'Hey. You're my baby sister-in-law. I worry about you nearly as much as Stacey does,' Nick said.

'I love you, too, big brother-in-law,' Toni said with a smile. 'But I'm fine as I am. Really. You don't have to worry about me.'

In between the odd sip of beer, Ben danced with quite a few of women in the hall—including a virtuoso display with one of the local dance teachers, which had everyone standing around them in a circle, clapping and cheering as they executed amazing spins and turns.

'That man,' Stacey said to Toni, 'is something else.'

Toni knew that tone well. 'He's my colleague,' she reminded her sister.

'And I've seen the way he looks at you. He likes you.'

'Strictly as a friend,' Toni said firmly. And she wasn't going to admit to that wobble in her stomach when he caught her eyes across the dance floor and smiled at her.

'Give him a chance, Toni.'

Toni hugged her. 'I love you, and we've had this conversation a lot of times. We're going to agree to disagree, OK? I'm not good at choosing men, and Ben has his own reasons not to want to get involved. We're friends. End of.'

She signalled to Ben at the end of the dance. 'Want to come and get some food?'

Between them, they got a selection of sandwiches, scones and a couple of the mini homity pies Toni had made earlier.

'So what exactly is a homity pie? A kind of quiche?' Ben asked, looking at the open-topped pies.

'Sort of. Eggs and onions were scarce in the war, so the filling's mainly potato and leek with a chopped apple, one egg and a little bit of cheese,' she said.

'Making do. Yeah. It took me a while to get my head round the idea of putting grated carrots in scones,' Ben said.

'Sugar replacement plus added moisture. Which I guess we still do today; think of carrot cake,' she said.

'So where did you get the recipes?'

'One of the village hall committee has an original wartime recipe book that belonged to her grandmother, so we use that.' She took a bite of one of his scones. 'These are wonderful. If you were in the market for a relationship, between your dancing and your cooking I think you'd have a queue of women a mile long wanting to date you.'

Ben looked at her. He wasn't in the market for a relationship. But if he was, he didn't want a queue of women a mile long. He wanted just one woman.

Toni Butler.

But she'd made it clear she wasn't looking for a relationship and they were just friends.

He wished she hadn't put the idea of relationships into his head when the music turned slower and he ended up dancing with her again; this time, they were cheek to cheek and he could smell the fresh floral scent of her shampoo and feel the warmth of her body in his arms.

He tried mentally naming all the muscles of the body in order from the *triceps surae* to the *occipitofrontalis*, but it didn't switch his attention away from her. So in the end he gave in to the demands of the music and his heart and just held her, swaying with her.

When he pulled back slightly, her pupils were huge and her mouth was slightly parted. All he would have to do was tilt his head slightly and his lips would touch hers. His mouth tingled and his heartbeat was skittering around.

Could he?

Should he?

Was it his imagination, or was she staring at his mouth, too? Did she want him to kiss her? Like that day when they'd sat on the harbour wall, eating fish and chips, and he'd nearly kissed her.

The temptation was too great, and he was about to

lean forward and kiss her, just once, when the song ended and the band struck up another fast dance.

'I think your fan club awaits,' she said with a smile.

What could he do but dance the Lindy Hop with the next woman who asked him?

And his dance with Toni turned out to be the last slow dance of the night, so he had no more excuses to pull her back into his arms.

'Can I walk you home?' he asked, really hoping that he wasn't blushing and sounding as bashful as a teenager. 'I mean, I know you're perfectly capable of seeing yourself home, but...'

'That'd be nice,' she said. 'Thank you.'

And somehow on the way home his fingers brushed against hers. Once. Twice. The third time, he let his fingers cling to hers. And by the end of the road they were holding hands. They weren't discussing it or even acknowledging it, but they were definitely holding hands.

At her garden gate, she said, 'Will you come in for a coffee?'

He could be sensible and make an excuse.

Or he could follow the urging of his heart. To look forward instead of back. To consider the enticing possibility of a future.

'Thank you. I'd like that,' he said.

Archie was thrilled to see them and leaped round the kitchen.

'Sit,' Ben said.

To his surprise, Archie actually did what Ben asked.

He held out his hand, let the dog sniff him, then rubbed the top of the dog's head. Archie rewarded him with the gentlest of licks.

'He likes you,' Toni said, and the approval in her voice warmed him all the way through.

'He's a nice dog. And he's gone a long way to—well, making me a bit nicer.'

She smiled and let the dog out into the garden. 'It wasn't that you were totally horrible; we just had a few crossed wires and we got off to a bad start.'

'Thank you.' He smiled back at her. 'Did you enjoy the dance?'

'I always do—but you made it special for me, this year. I've never danced like that before.'

'Seriously? It isn't just family teasing that you can't dance?'

'No. If you ever go to a dance aerobics class with me, I'm the one who's doing all the right moves—but in the wrong direction,' she said with a grin. 'I'm infamous for it. And the men in Great Crowmell only dance with me if they're wearing steel toecaps.'

'You were doing just fine with me.'

She looked at him, her gorgeous grey eyes darkening. 'Can we do that again?'

'The jitterbug?'

'The other one.'

The slow dance. The one that had made his heart beat in a crazy rhythm. 'Sure,' he said. 'We need some music. Let me find some on my phone.'

The next thing he knew, their coffees were ignored and she was in his arms, swaying with him to the soft, slow song.

And this time, when he pulled back and saw the glitter in her eyes, he gave in to the temptation that had been tugging at him all evening and let his mouth brush against hers. Once, very lightly, skimming across her skin.

He felt as if he were going up in flames.

And then her arms tightened around him and she let him deepen the kiss.

He had no idea how long they stayed locked together in the middle of her kitchen, just kissing.

But then reality seeped in.

He hadn't been enough for Karen.

There was no reason why he would be enough for Toni, either.

What was he doing? If this carried on, they were both going to get hurt. Much as he wanted to scoop her up and carry her to her bed, it would be a really reckless, stupid thing to do.

This was meant to be his new start, and he was in severe danger of messing everything up.

They needed to stop this.

Now.

He pulled away. 'Toni. We shouldn't…' He dragged in a breath. 'I need to go.'

Reality crashed in as if Ben had just thrown a bucket of icy water over her.

What had she been doing, letting herself get carried away like that? She knew he didn't want a relationship. He was still licking his wounds after what had happened in London—when his wife had had an affair with someone who was supposed to be his friend, and the result had been a baby that wasn't his.

Maybe in another time, another place, it could have worked out between them. She liked him and, from the way his sea-green eyes had turned almost black, his pupils enormous, she could tell that he liked her.

But this was the wrong time for him; and she'd had enough of making mistakes and falling for Mr Wrong.

Better to keep things strictly platonic.

'Sure,' she said brightly, and squashed the urge to suggest that instead they could act on the pull between them, get it out of their systems and then go back to being strictly colleagues. That was way too reckless and it was so obvious that they would both end up hurt. She was rubbish at relationships. They needed to keep things simple. 'See you at work,' she said.

Once he'd gone, she curled up with her dog.

They'd done the sensible thing, Toni knew. The right thing.

So why did she feel so miserable about it?

'This is ridiculous, Archie,' she told the dog. 'I'm rubbish at relationships. I didn't see past Sean's Mr Charming act—even though I knew Gran and Stacey didn't think that much of him, I made excuses for him and didn't let myself see how selfish he was. The two before him were nearly as bad. And the three guys I've dated since I moved back were all nice men, but there just wasn't a spark between us.' She sighed. 'Am I just an idiot who only falls for awful men?'

Ben Mitchell wasn't an awful man. Far from it. He wasn't selfish. But she was definitely attracted to him every bit as much as she'd been attracted to her last Mr Wrong.

Though Ben was complicated. Vulnerable. He'd been badly hurt and he'd made it clear that, although the attraction was mutual, he didn't want to get involved with anyone.

'Gran would say it would all come out in the wash,' she said. 'Tomorrow we're going for a run at the beach and everything will be fine.'

But even saying it out loud wasn't quite enough to convince herself. She had a feeling it would be really awkward, the next time she saw Ben. How were they going to fix this?

CHAPTER FIVE

TONI SLEPT BADLY that night, full of guilt and longing, and cross with herself for being wet.

'Common sense and sea air to blow the cobwebs out. That's what we need,' she said to the dog.

And then she would throw herself into the rest of the nineteen-forties weekend, meeting up with her sister again and enjoying spending time with people she loved most. She was so, so lucky. She had nothing to whine about and she needed to stop being so self-indulgent and longing for what she couldn't have.

She walked the dog down to the harbour and up to the beach, then went for a run along the shoreline. The sound of the sea and the fresh air did their usual trick of rebalancing her.

'Sausage?' she asked Archie as they reached Scott's Café.

The dog woofed softly in agreement.

She hadn't bothered grabbing more than a banana before they went out, and the café was dog-friendly, so she went in to order a latte, a bacon sandwich and one of the sausages the café kept especially for dogs.

And of course Ben *would* be sitting there in the corner.

So had he, like her, felt antsy enough to need a run to clear his head? Was he as confused as she was?

What should she do now? Give him space, smile and sit in the opposite corner of the café? Or go along with the whole friends and colleagues thing, treat him just as if he were one of the other medics at the practice, sit with him and pretend that kiss had never happened?

She wasn't the dithery sort. What on earth was wrong with her?

He looked wary and confused, too.

That settled it. She'd be professional—and she had Archie as a buffer.

'Hi. Have you been out for a run?' she asked brightly.

'It's the perfect start to a Sunday morning,' he said. And either he was better at pretending than she was, or that kiss had affected him a lot less. 'Obviously you've been for a run, too.'

'Yes. We've just ordered breakfast,' she said.

'Me, too. If Archie is allowed to sit in the café, you're both welcome to join me.'

So they really were going to manage to pretend that kiss last night hadn't happened? They could keep their good working relationship and she hadn't messed it up? That was a relief; and at the same time there was a sneaking sensation of disappointment, too, because it meant that kiss would stay a one-off. And that kiss had awoken all sorts of feelings she'd thought she'd buried. Desire. Need. A coil of lust snaked through her.

She reined in her wayward longings. 'Thanks. That would be good.' She looked at Archie. 'No scrounging, Arch. You've got your own order.'

'I noticed they had sausages for dogs on the menu,'

Ben said with a smile. 'I'm assuming it's a regular order for Archie?'

'It is,' she admitted.

Ben's bacon sandwich arrived first.

'Don't let it get cold by waiting for us,' she said, gesturing to him to eat.

'Or we could go halves until yours arrives?' he suggested.

'No, it's fine.' She smiled at him. 'Enjoy.'

He was halfway through the sandwich when he said to her, 'My knee feels warm.'

She groaned, knowing exactly what her dog was doing. 'Give it two minutes and your knee will be wet as well. Sorry.'

'Can I give him a little bit of my sandwich?'

For someone who was a self-confessed non-dog person, Ben had really thawed out towards Archie. 'Sure. But make him sit nicely for it, and he only gets the very last bit when you're done.'

He smiled. 'Got it.'

She could feel the dog inching forward towards Ben under the table. 'Sorry,' she said again.

'It's fine,' he said with a grin and when Archie sat nicely and took the corner of the sandwich very gently from Ben's hand, 'Your dog,' Ben said, 'is definitely winning me over.'

Was there something more in Ben's expression, or was she seeing what she wanted to see?

'That's good,' she said carefully, playing it safe.

They made small talk until her sandwich arrived, and she sliced Archie's sausage for him. Then she looked at Ben and couldn't help smiling. 'Right now you've got the same expression on your face as one of my Wednesday readers.'

Rather than being offended, he laughed. 'Yeah. I guess I know how they feel. Being dog monitor for the day.'

'Feed him the sausage. It's very gratifying. You can get him to do tricks for a piece of sausage—sit, lie down, offer you a paw.' She paused. 'Dare you.'

He tried it.

And Toni thoroughly enjoyed watching the surprise on Ben's face, followed by pleasure as the dog obeyed every single command.

'You're right. It's very gratifying. Like feeding a baby.'

Instantly the shadows were back in his eyes. And she knew why. The baby that wasn't his.

He would've made such a great dad.

And it was hard to come back from a situation like that, to learn to trust again. No wonder he'd moved away from London; a fresh start in a place that held no memories would help him get over it.

But was she the one who could mend his broken heart?

She only seemed to pick the kind of men who were so selfish that she ended up walking away. Sometimes she wondered whether it was because, deep down, she was scared of losing her heart to someone and then losing them the same way she'd lost her parents and her grandmother; by constantly picking Mr Wrong, it meant that she was the one to leave instead of the one who was left behind, sad and lonely. But, if she was honest with herself, she was still lonely anyway.

And Ben was nothing like her exes. That made him more dangerous. If she trusted him with her own heart, would he keep it safe? Or would he be the one to end up walking away, leaving her desolate?

'I'd better let you get on,' he said when she'd finished her sandwich. 'I have an online course sending me nagging emails. See you tomorrow.'

Even though part of Toni wanted to give him a hug and tell him that not all women were like his ex and he would find someone to love him as he deserved, she didn't. This was a public place and Ben was quite a private man; although he'd been open in the practice meeting about why he was wary of dogs, he hadn't told anyone except Toni about his ex or the baby, and she had no intention of betraying his confidence. 'See you tomorrow,' she said.

But as they walked out of the café they could see a small boy standing on the patio, crying and guarding his arm, with an elderly couple who were presumably his grandparents looking very anxious and clearly trying to persuade him to let them look at his arm.

'That's Jake Flowers,' Toni told Ben, recognising the little boy. 'He's not one of my Wednesday readers, but I went to school with his mum and he's in the same class as some of my readers. Hi there,' she said brightly, going over to them. 'Jake, did you hurt your arm?'

He nodded. 'I fell over. It really hurts.'

'He won't let us touch it,' the elderly woman said.

'I'm a nurse and Ben is a doctor,' Toni reassured her. 'Maybe he'll let us help.' She turned to the little boy. 'You know Archie from school, don't you? He helps some of your friends with reading.'

Jake nodded.

'He thinks Dr Ben and I can help your arm feel better. Will you let us look at it, to stop Archie worrying about you?'

Jake nodded, still a little reluctantly, but stopped guarding his arm.

Ben gently examined him. 'I think when you fell over you dislocated your elbow, Jake. The bones slipped out of place, and that's why it hurts. I can pop it back in for you, so it will stop hurting.'

Though the procedure of fixing the dislocation would really hurt for a brief moment, Toni knew. She needed to do something to distract the little boy so he didn't tense up in anticipation of it hurting and make things worse.

'Tell you what,' she said to Jake. 'To stop Archie worrying, while Dr Ben puts your elbow back in place, can you tell him a joke?'

'I don't know any jokes,' Jake said. His lower lip wobbled.

'What's that, Archie? You know one?' She pretended that the dog was whispering in her ear. 'That's a good one! Jake, what do sea monsters eat?'

'I don't know.'

Toni smiled. 'Fish and ships!'

The little boy smiled, despite himself.

'Oh—he wants your grandad to help him tell the next one.'

The old man looked taken aback, but to her relief he went with it and crouched down next to the dog, pretending that the dog was whispering in his ear, too. 'That's a good one, Archie! What did the sea say to the sand?' he asked.

Jake shook his head.

'Nothing—it just waved!' Jake's grandfather said.

Ben made one swift movement, and Jake cried out—and then he looked surprised. 'Oh! It's stopped hurting. Thank you, Dr Ben.'

'My pleasure. And you were *really* brave. Archie's going to bring you a special sticker from me on Wednesday,' Ben said, 'when he comes to help with reading at your school.'

Jake beamed. 'Really?'

'Really,' Ben promised.

'Thank you so much,' Jake's grandmother said. 'We came down for the nineteen-forties weekend and we thought we would take Jake to the sea and give Lee and Sally a few minutes to themselves, this morning. I feel so bad he fell over and hurt himself.'

'These things happen,' Ben reassured her. 'If his mum and dad had been with you when he fell over, it would probably still have happened.' He examined Jake's arm. 'It looks fine to me. Jake could do with a bit of infant paracetamol because his elbow will still be a little bit swollen and sore for a while, but his arm should be fine. If he's not using his arm as normal by lunchtime, it's worth popping in to the hospital for an X-ray, but I think you'll be just fine.'

'Thank you so much,' Jake's grandfather said. 'I don't know what we would've done if you hadn't been here.'

'I'm glad we could help,' Ben said. 'And don't worry about it happening again. It's probably a one-off. He just needs to be a little bit careful for the next week or so. Archie has got one more joke for you, Jake,' Ben added, and pretended to listen to the dog. 'How do you make an octopus laugh?'

'I don't know,' Jake said.

'With ten tickles!'

The little boy giggled; Ben smiled and stood up.

He was fabulous with children, Toni thought. He would've been an amazing dad. She hoped for his ex's sake that the man she chose, the baby's biological father, would be as good a dad as Ben would've been.

'Enjoy the rest of the nineteen-forties weekend,' Ben said to Jake's grandparents. He smiled at Toni, and headed for his car. Toni said her goodbyes to Jake and his grandparents, and then walked back home with Archie before changing back into her nineteen-forties costume and going over to her sister's.

'Ben not with you today?' Stacey asked.

'He's studying,' Toni said.

'OK.' Stacey looked at her. 'I liked him very much.'

'You've already told me that, Stace,' Toni said with a smile. 'Remember, he's my colleague.'

'You weren't looking at each other like colleagues yesterday,' Stacey pointed out.

No. But she'd got that very badly wrong, hadn't she? 'It was probably just the shock of me managing to dance without bruising someone's toes,' Toni retorted. 'Let's go and see the sights.'

To her relief, Stacey didn't quiz her any further about Ben. And it *was* fine: they were colleagues, and that was that.

CHAPTER SIX

BEN LOOKED AT the screen and sighed. Normally he loved doing professional development, keeping his knowledge up to date and learning about new things that would help his patients. Just today he could hardly concentrate.

And he knew why.

Toni Butler.

Toni, with her lovely grey eyes, her sweet, sweet smile and her amazing warmth.

If he was honest with himself, he'd gone for that run on the beach because he knew that she often went there and he'd been hoping to bump into her 'accidentally'. And then she'd walked into the café.

It would've been so easy to suggest spending the rest of the day together and catching up with his studies that evening. He even liked her dog, which had been a huge surprise to him.

But his head was all over the place. He wasn't in love with Karen any more, but he was still healing from what had happened. When he'd said to Toni that rewarding her dog with slices of sausage for performing tricks was as gratifying as feeding a newborn, it had brought all the regrets flooding back.

He ought to move on.

He wanted to move on.

But Toni had been hurt, too. By a man who sounded as if he'd been full of charm on the surface but deep down was utterly selfish. Ben knew that he wasn't like that, that he would treat her the way she deserved to be treated. But the nagging doubts were in his head. Could he trust again? He didn't think that Toni was the cheating type; then again, he hadn't thought that Karen would cheat on him, either.

Guilt was nagging at him, too. He'd pretty much put a wall of misery between himself and his family, and he'd moved here and let that wall harden. Seeing how close Toni was to her sister made him realise how much he missed his own sister. He'd always enjoyed spending time with her, and it wasn't fair to push Jessie away.

On impulse, he picked up the phone.

Jessie answered within three rings. 'Ben! How are you?'

'Fine. You?'

'Fine, but I miss you. Have you settled in, yet?'

'Yes, I think so.'

'So can we come and see you?'

He loved his family, but his parents had never been particularly good at emotional stuff and he knew he'd end up squirming and wishing he hadn't invited them. 'My place is quite small. Maybe just you, Kit, Kelly and the baby?' His nephew, and Ben was guiltily aware that he hadn't been supportive enough to his sister, because seeing the baby brought back all the might-have-beens.

'Great. It'd be lovely to have a weekend by the sea. How about next weekend?'

'Sorry, I'm rostered on for a shift at the surgery on Saturday.'

'The weekend after?'

'I'm studying.'

'Ben.' Her voice was full of disappointment. He'd dangled a promise and then cut it off.

He didn't really have a valid excuse to put her off any longer. And, actually, it would be good to see his sister. 'The week after that?'

'Put it in your diary now. I can't wait. I've missed you,' she said again.

'I've missed you, too,' he admitted. 'There's a nineteen-forties fundraising event here at the moment. There was a dance in the village hall last night—the jitterbug, the Lindy Hop, the lot.'

'Oh, Ben. I wish you'd said. I would've loved to go to that.' She paused. 'Did you dance?'

'Yes. And I dressed up.'

'Good.' She sighed. 'Oh, Ben. I've really missed you.'

'I've missed you, too,' he said softly. 'But I needed to get out of London.'

'After what Karen and Patrick did, you needed a fresh start, I know. And I understand. I just wish you were nearer,' she said 'So have you settled in OK? It's been so hard to get hold of you.'

'Sorry. I've just been a bit busy,' he said. 'I'm doing fine. Really. My new team is great. And our nurse practitioner has a therapy dog. He's a sweetheart and he was very handy today as a distraction when I needed to put a small child's dislocated elbow back in the right place.'

'GPs don't work on Sundays, and you're not a dog person,' she said. 'So what were you...? Oh! Are you dating the nurse practitioner? What's her name?'

'No. We're colleagues, and we just happened to be at the beach café at the same time. I'm very far from being ready to date anyone, and we're not right for each other anyway. There's no chemistry between us.' It wasn't strictly true, but he needed to head Jessie off before she got too hopeful that he'd finally moved on. He was definitely getting there, and he was beginning to think that maybe Toni was the one who'd help him trust again, but it was still early days. 'I'd better let you get on. See you a week on Friday—and I'll speak to you before then.'

'All right. And I'm glad you called, Ben.'

'Me, too.'

'Love you,' she said softly.

'Love you, too.'

On Monday, Ben went to the surgery armed with dog treats.

'Who are you and what have you done with the scary doctor who disapproves of my dog?' Toni teased.

'A reformed man who has been through impromptu aversion therapy,' Ben retorted. 'And less of your cheek, Nurse Practitioner Butler, unless you want me to organise a dancing demonstration at the village hall with you as the star turn.'

'Bring it on,' she said. 'I don't mind making a fool of myself, if it raises funds. But your toes might want a word with your mouth later for suggesting it.'

Ben couldn't help grinning. He really liked this woman. If only he could be enough for her. But he couldn't quite let himself believe that he'd be enough for anyone. 'You keep her in check, Archie,' he said, and ruffled the fur on the top of the dog's head.

Every single one of his female patients that morning commented either on his dancing or his scones, and half the men mentioned that their partners were nagging them to take dancing lessons.

And, just like that, Ben realised that he really had become part of the community. He'd been here a month, but it felt as if he'd been here for ever. He *belonged*.

Toni brought the goodies for the Tuesday morning practice team meeting—a light, fluffy orange drizzle cake—and he handed her an envelope. 'Would you mind making a special delivery for me on the way to your reading class tomorrow, please?'

'To Jake? Of course. He'll be thrilled that you remembered his sticker,' she said.

'What's this?' Bill, one of the other doctors, asked.

'Jake Flowers. We'd both gone for a run on Sunday and ended up at the beach café,' Toni explained. 'Jake dislocated his elbow and Ben put it back into place.'

'Not just me. It was teamwork,' Ben said, 'because you and Archie kept him distracted so he didn't tense up.'

'That's what the practice is all about,' Ranjit said. 'Talking of teamwork—how's the new meal plan for the website coming along?'

'Is this Ranjit-speak for "bring samples"?' Toni teased.

He laughed. 'Yes, and in return I'll tweak my mum's recipe for *chana masala* for you.'

'Oh, now, I want samples of *that*,' Janice, one of the other doctors, said.

'We could have a practice pot-luck dinner,' Toni suggested. 'We each bring a dish, but we make sure we tweak it to suit diabetics or cardiac patients, and we use the recipes on the practice's website. Ranj, your garden's the biggest. Would you host it?'

'Done,' Ranjit said. 'We'll set a date and if we sort out between us beforehand who's doing mains, who's doing sides and who's doing dessert, it won't be like the antenatal pot-luck lunch I once went to when every single person brought tuna pasta salad!'

The team at his last practice hadn't really socialised much outside work, apart from the annual Christmas lunch, Ben thought. Here at Great Crowmell, it was very different. And he really, really liked it.

On Wednesday, Toni sent him a text suggesting lunch by the harbour when he'd finished morning surgery and she'd finished her reading session. And he thoroughly enjoyed sitting on the harbour wall, looking at the boats and the salt marshes, while they ate their wraps from the deli.

'Jake was absolutely thrilled that you remembered his sticker,' Toni told him.

'Good. It's important to keep promises to children,' he said. 'How's his arm?'

'Absolutely fine. Apparently it was a bit sore on Monday. But he told his teacher about Archie's wonderful jokes, and everyone in the class wanted to hear them— so I'm going to need some new ones before I run out. And, as you were so good, I'm going to beg for a couple of new ones from you every Tuesday from now until the end of term.'

'I have friends who work in Paediatrics,' he said. 'I'll get some from them so you've got a stock.'

'Brilliant,' she said.

Friends and colleagues.

That was what they'd agreed.

And they had a great working relationship.

Except Toni wanted more. He'd really come out of his shell over the last few weeks and become part of the heart of the community. Was he finally ready to move on from the heartbreak of his past? Or should she back off and give him more space? Was she just making the same mistake over again—except this time she'd chosen someone lovely but unobtainable, instead of having surface charm that hid the kind of man she didn't want? Would he ever let anyone close—and, if so would it be her?

So many unanswered questions.

And there was nothing she could do to change things. She just had to be patient. Which she was finding more and more difficult to do.

Part way through Friday afternoon she had a phone call that left her reeling. 'Hey, Julia. How are you? Do you need one of the team to come out to see a resident?' she asked when Moira put the call through.

'No. I'm sorry, I've got some bad news for you. Because she was such a close family friend and you made a point of spending time with her every week, even on the days she wasn't well...' Julia dragged in a breath. 'I'm afraid there isn't a way to cushion this. Ginny passed away in her sleep last night.'

Ginny, her grandmother's best friend, had been almost a second grandmother when Toni had been growing up, and the news brought back all the sense of loss Toni had felt when Betty had died.

'Thank you for telling me,' she said. 'I'll call her son later to give my condolences to her family.' It was hard on the staff, too, when a resident died. 'And I'm sorry for your loss, as well.'

'Thank you. I just wanted to tell you the news myself today, as I knew you were fond of Ginny.'

'I was. She was fond of Archie, too. She always smiled when we walked in.'

'I know. I'd better let you get on. I'm sorry it's sad news.'

Toni held herself together for the rest of her shift.

Her next patient was a teenager who had been having chest pains that his mother thought might be due to exam stress, but Toni gave him an X-ray to check that there wasn't an underlying problem that hadn't been diagnosed yet; thankfully, it was normal.

'I think your mum is probably right—the more worried you get, the more your muscles can tense up as part of the "fight or flight" response. That's why you feel a bit sweaty and dizzy as well, Darren,' she explained. 'Exercise can help—swimming, cycling, going for a walk—because it helps release tension and it gets your brain to produce serotonin. I can give you some websites with some online courses that could help you.'

'So it's not my heart?' Darren asked.

'It's not your heart,' she confirmed. 'But I'd like to see you in a couple of weeks to see how you're getting on and if your symptoms are any better. If they're not, we can try some medication to help with the symptoms. Avoiding caffeine can help, too—caffeine can disrupt your sleep and speed up your heartbeat, and when you're tired it's hard to control any anxious feelings. So switch to decaf coffee and herbal tea, and stay away from energy drinks and fizzy drinks.'

He bit his lip. 'But I need the energy drinks to help me concentrate for my exams.'

'Getting enough sleep will help you concentrate more,' she said. 'Try a warm bath before bed, or a hot milky drink, putting a bit of lavender on your pillow. It's worth having a look at different things to help you relax—and make sure you switch your phone or any other screen to night mode so the blue light doesn't affect your sleep.'

'Mum says I shouldn't look at a screen for an hour before bed,' Darren said.

'That would be preferable,' Toni said, 'but at this time of year it'll probably worry you more if you don't read things before bed. See what you can manage, and we'll review everything in a fortnight. Though obviously if you get chest pains again and they're worse, it's worth calling in to the emergency department for more tests.'

She booked him in on her computer, saw a couple of patients for smear tests, a couple more for blood pressure checks, and yet more for their regular six-monthly medication reviews—and then finally her shift was over.

She finished typing up her notes, made sure her desk was clear, then took a deep breath and walked out of the door.

Ginny's death had really knocked Toni for six. Right at that moment it was hard to put one foot in front of the other. Hard to breathe. She missed her grandmother so much—Betty's warmth, the way she had of putting a positive spin on everything, the way she could always make things better with a hug. Losing Ginny brought back all the sadness of losing her grandmother.

And right now Toni knew she was letting her grandmother down by moping and being miserable. Ginny was at peace, now, no longer lost in a world of confusion and fear. Plus Toni knew that she and Archie had helped to bring a bright spot in Ginny's last days.

Find the bright side. Toni could almost hear her grandmother's voice echoing in her head.

Although there didn't feel as if there was a bright side.

One foot in front of the other, she told herself. But, as she walked down the corridor, her vision was blurred by tears, and she stumbled.

'Toni? Are you—? No. Stupid question. Of course you're not all right,' Ben said.

She hadn't even noticed him in the corridor. 'I'm fine,' she lied.

'You're crying,' he said gently, 'and your eyes are puffy enough for me to know you've been crying for a while. You're not fine at all. Look, why don't you come back with me? I'll make you a cup of tea—and you can stay for dinner. You don't have to talk. I'll give you space.'

His kindness broke her. 'Archie...'

'Will be fine and he won't mind waiting a little bit longer for his dinner,' he said firmly. 'I'll drop you home after we've eaten. Did you drive in this morning?'

'No, I walked,' she said.

'Then that makes things easy. Come on.'

He drove her back to his house, keeping the radio on low. Just as he'd promised, he didn't push her to make meaningless small talk—or, worse still, spill what was in her heart. He made her a cup of tea that was way too strong and too sweet, but she drank it anyway, recognising the fact that he was trying to comfort her and not wanting to make him feel awkward.

And it did help. Just knowing that he was there, understanding that she felt bad, and he was taking care of her in a practical way by cooking her dinner and making her a drink—with no pressure to talk until she was ready. He didn't even push her to talk when he served dinner at his kitchen table.

'Take one mouthful,' he coaxed. 'Just one mouthful and you'll feel better. I promise.'

She forced herself to take a mouthful. And another. And then somehow she'd managed to clear her plate.

'Thank you,' she said. 'That was really good. And you were right. It did help.'

Unlike Sean, Ben didn't gloat about being proved right. He just gave her one of those almost shy smiles that made her heart do a backflip. 'Any time.'

'I'll do the washing up.'

He shook his head. 'There isn't much. I'll do it later. I think right now you need a hug.'

'I do,' she admitted.

And how good it felt to have the warmth of his arms enveloping her, the clean citrus scent of his shower gel filling her senses.

'Talk to me, Toni,' he said softly. 'Tell me what's in your head, even if it's a jumble. Let it out. It's not going any further than me, I promise. And maybe saying it out loud will help.'

She closed her eyes and rested her head on his shoulder. 'Ginny died—one of the residents at The Beeches.'

'The one who doesn't talk?'

'Yes. She was my gran's best friend. She lived just round the corner, and she was like a second gran to me and Stacey. We used to go to hers from school if Gran was at work, and she helped us when Gran was first ill. Then she got ill, too. I know I should be glad that she's at peace now instead of being lost and confused, but...' Her words trailed off.

'It's brought back the loss of your grandmother?' he guessed.

'Yes. And Ginny was sort of the last link to her.'

His arms tightened around her, and she was seriously grateful that he understood her so well.

'That's hard,' he said.

'I miss her, Ben. I miss my mum and my dad.' Then she remembered when she'd talked to Sean about it and how dismissive he'd been. 'I'll pull myself together. Just ignore me. I'm being boring and selfish.'

'It's not selfish or boring at all,' he said. 'You're allowed to feel, Toni. You're allowed to grieve.'

So very different from the way that Sean had seen things.

'In the weeks I've known you I've seen for myself that you're one of the nicest, kindest, most unselfish women I've met. Don't be so hard on yourself.'

He meant it. And it did actually make her feel better, knowing he understood how she felt and wasn't judging her as harshly as she judged herself. 'Gran always taught me to look on the bright side.'

'She was right. There's always a bright side. Sometimes you have to look really hard for it, but it's there.'

'I know. I'm being wet.'

'No. You're human,' he said gently.

She willed the tears to stay back, not wanting to howl her eyes out in front of him.

She had no idea how long they stood there, just holding each other; but then somehow his cheek was against hers, and she was remembering how it felt to dance with him, and then her mouth was touching the corner of his lips. The next thing she knew, they were kissing—really kissing—and it felt as if he'd just lit touch-paper.

They were both shaking when he broke the kiss, and he looked stricken. Guilty.

'Toni, I'm sorry. I shouldn't have done that. I don't want to take advantage of you.'

'You're not. I think I started it.' She couldn't help laying her palm against his cheek, and he twisted his head so he could press a kiss into her hand.

'I just wanted to make you feel better, the way you did for me when I had a tough day,' he said.

'You have. You fed me. You got me to put one foot in front of the other and move, and I really appreciate it.'

His sea-green eyes were almost black, his pupils were so huge.

And she couldn't resist reaching up to steal another kiss.

He looked haunted. 'Toni. This isn't fair of me. Neither of us is in a place to start a relationship.'

'I know. But right now,' she said, 'I need to celebrate life.'

This was a really bad idea.

His head knew he ought to find an excuse, something that wouldn't make her feel bad. Right now she was vulnerable, grieving—and this was a knee-jerk reaction, a need to make herself feel alive while she was facing the grim reality of death.

He wasn't going to take advantage of her, even though his heart was screaming out to him to kiss her, make her feel better, make them *both* feel better.

Then she laid her palm against his cheek again. 'I need you, Ben,' she whispered. 'Make it better. Please.'

And then he was lost.

How could he say no? How could he leave her miserable and hurting?

'Are you sure about this?' he asked, while his common sense was still just about clinging on.

'Very sure,' she said.

And then there was only one thing Ben could do: to dip his head again and brush his mouth against Toni's. Softly. Gently. A kiss of warmth and promise.

Then he repeated it again, this time taking a tiny nibble of her lower lip, coaxing her into a response. When she slid her fingers into his hair and kissed him back, he relaxed, knowing this was going to be all right.

She broke the kiss.

'If you change your mind at any point, that's OK. Because I've never bullied a woman in my life before and I'm not going to start now.'

She reached up and stole a kiss back. 'Thank you.'

He wanted to behave like a caveman and his pulse was leaping crazily. 'Except I don't have a condom.'

'I do,' she said. 'In my handbag.' She fetched it and took his hand. 'Take me to bed, Ben,' she whispered.

The look in her eyes made him so dizzy with desire that he could barely think straight. But he lifted her hand, pressed a kiss into her palm and folded her fingers over it.

'Come with me,' he whispered back, and led her up the stairs to his bedroom. He closed the curtains and snapped on the bedside light; then he pulled her back into his arms and kissed her lingeringly.

She was still wearing her nurse practitioner's uniform of navy trousers and a navy tunic with white piping. With shaking hands, he undid the buttons of her tunic and discovered that she was wearing a lacy bra.

'That's one hell of a view,' he said, his voice husky with wanting her.

'Thank you.' She dipped her head in acknowledgement.

He slid the tunic off her shoulders and hung it neatly over the back of the chair; then he unzipped her trousers and let them slide to the floor so she could step out of them.

'You're wearing too much. We need to do something about that,' she said.

He smiled. 'I'm in your hands.'

'Good.'

She undid his tie and then the buttons of his shirt, very slowly, one by one. He could feel the pads of her fingertips stroking the skin of his abdomen, warm and soft and very, very sure of what she was doing; it made him catch his breath as a wave of desire surged through him.

She unbuttoned his trousers and nudged the material over his hips so they fell to the floor; he stepped out of them, he dipped his head again and brushed his mouth lightly against hers in the sweetest, gentlest kiss. Within a nanosecond the kiss had turned so hot that his bones felt as though they were melting.

She was shaking when he broke the kiss.

'The way you make me feel—it's like when you dance with me, as if I'm walking on air,' she whispered. She rubbed the pad of her thumb along his lower lip. 'You're beautiful. Everything about you.'

Desire licked down his spine. 'That's how you make me feel, too.' He traced the lacy edge of her bra with the tip of one finger. 'Just gorgeous. You blow my mind.'

He slid the straps of her bra off her shoulders, kissing her bare skin before unsnapping her bra and letting it fall to the floor between them, then dropped to his knees and teased her with his hands and his lips and his tongue, stroking her skin and kissing her until she was quivering.

And then it was her turn to touch him, to kneel down next to him and let her fingertips skate over his pectorals and down over his abdomen, taking it slowly and deliberately, learning the texture of his skin with her fingertips and just how and where he liked being touched.

'My turn again,' he whispered, and did the same to her.

Then he picked her up, pushed the duvet to one side and laid her down against the soft pillows. He kissed his way down her body, paying attention to all the hidden parts: the curve of her elbow, the soft undersides of her breasts, until she was murmuring with pleasure.

Then he knelt back and worked his way upwards from her ankles, touching and kissing and nuzzling until she tipped her head back against the pillows and fisted her hands in his hair.

'Ben, this is killing me,' she murmured.

He wanted this first time to be for her; so he teased her with his mouth and his hands, stoking the waves of pleasure until her climax finally hit and she cried out.

When he shifted up the bed to lie beside her, she curved her fingers round his shaft, stroking and caressing until he arched against the bed and gasped with pleasure.

Then she undid the little foil packet and rolled the condom over his shaft, then shifted to straddle him.

'Now,' she said, and lowered herself onto him.

'Toni,' he breathed, and pushed up to meet her.

She felt amazing.

He laced his fingers through hers as she moved over him.

This should've been awkward and a bit clumsy; instead, it felt so right. Perfect. He was completely in tune with her, in a way he'd never expected.

As he felt her body tightening round his, he released her hands, sat up and wrapped his arms tightly round her.

Their climaxes hit at the same time, and he jammed his mouth over hers.

She kissed him back, wrapping her arms just as tightly round him.

As the aftershocks of his climax died away, he lay back and let her climb off him.

'I need to deal with the condom,' he said. 'Don't go anywhere.'

When he came back to bed, he wrapped her in his arms.

'Sorry. I didn't mean to…' Her breath shuddered.

'You have absolutely nothing to be sorry for,' Ben said, stroking her face.

'Apart from abandoning my dog.'

'You've just made him wait a little bit longer for his dinner. And he loves you so he won't hold it against you,' he said. 'I would ask you to stay, but is there anyone who could feed Archie and let him out?'

She grimaced. 'I need to go home.'

'OK. I'll drive you home now.'

'Sorry. I feel as if I'm being selfish and ungrateful and—'

He cut off her words by kissing her. 'Stop apologising. We can think about this and overanalyse it another time. Right now, you need comfort. Help yourself to whatever you need in the bathroom.'

'Thank you.'

While she sorted herself out in the bathroom, Ben got dressed; and then he drove her back to her cottage.

'Thank you for bringing me home. Would you like to come in for a cup of tea?' she asked.

Was she simply being polite and hoping that he'd refuse? Or did she really want his company but also didn't want to impose on him by asking him to stay?

The sadness in her grey eyes decided him. 'I'd love a cup of tea.'

Archie greeted them ecstatically when they walked into the kitchen.

'I'll make the tea while you sort out his dinner and what have you,' Ben said.

'Thank you.' She let the dog out and refilled his water and food bowls. Archie scoffed his dinner in what seemed like three seconds flat, then came to sit at Toni's feet, curling in close to her as if he recognised that she needed comfort.

'Is there anyone you need to call?' Ben asked, placing the mug of tea in front of her.

'No. I'll text Stacey in the morning. Thank you.'

'Is that photograph on the fridge of your grandmother?' he asked, gesturing to the snap of a middle-aged woman standing next to a sandcastle on the beach, with a much younger Toni and Stacey.

'Yes. I would have been about six and Stacey was eight at the time. It's one of my favourites.' She smiled. 'So many happy memories.'

And bittersweet, because they couldn't be shared with her grandmother, he guessed.

'I learned baking at her knee, too,' Toni told him. 'I loved my mum dearly—like Stacey, she was amazing with a needle and she was a costume designer for one of the West End theatres. But when it came to cooking, it was legendary that my mum could burn water. My dad had to do all the cooking, and he wasn't that brilliant at it, either.' Her mouth curved. 'We ate a lot of sausages, chips and baked beans. And salad. It was one of the reasons we always loved coming to Gran's—it meant we got perfect roast dinners and home-made apple crumble with proper custard.'

It made Ben feel slightly guilty that he'd pushed his

family away, of late. He had something that Toni clearly missed so badly, yet he'd taken it for granted. 'It sounds great.'

Toni smiled. 'Gran would have liked you.' Though she hadn't liked Sean, saying that he was too full of himself. Toni had told herself that it was simply a case of them rubbing each other up the wrong way—but eventually Betty had been proved absolutely right about Sean.

'I'm sorry,' Ben said softly, 'that you've lost so much in your life.'

'It happens,' she said. 'And I'm trying to focus on the fact that I did at least have a good relationship with my parents, my gran and Ginny, even if I didn't have them for as long as I would have liked. Not everyone's that lucky.'

That was true. Ben's own parents weren't good at the emotional stuff and they hadn't known how to support him when Karen had dropped her bombshell. But he loved them, and he loved his sister—and Toni had made him realise it was time to make more of an effort instead of taking them all for granted.

'Just remember that you and Archie helped to make Ginny's life happier in her last few months,' he said.

'I know. It's still going to be hard, walking in there on Monday afternoon.'

'I'll go with you, if you want me to arrange cover for my shift,' he said.

She shook her head. 'Thank you, but I need to pull myself together and face this.'

He went over to her chair and wrapped his arms around her. 'OK. But I'll cook for you on Monday night, or we can go to a dog-friendly pub with Archie and have dinner, so you don't have to worry about cooking.'

'That's kind,' she said.

He didn't feel kind, where she was concerned.

He felt all kinds of things that he was still trying to get his head round.

They spent the rest of the evening on the sofa, with the dog curled up between them, watching reruns of old comedy shows on television. When Toni started yawning, Ben kissed her forehead. 'I'd better let you get some sleep.'

'Ben—I know it's a lot to ask, but would you stay tonight?' she asked.

Spend the whole night with her.

Just to comfort her? Or was this the next step, heralding a change in their relationship—a move from friends to lovers to dating properly?

And was he ready to move on from the past?

Then again, even if he wasn't, how could he resist the entreaty in her face? She clearly didn't want to be alone. He knew how that felt.

'OK. I'll stay,' he said softly.

CHAPTER SEVEN

BEN WOKE WHEN sunlight filtered through the cotton curtains. He was spooned against Toni, with his arms wrapped around her; it would be oh, so easy to close his eyes again and go back to sleep. Except he had a shift at the surgery this morning and he needed to get up.

He also needed to talk to Toni, but that would have to wait until later today. It wasn't a conversation he wanted to rush.

This was the first time he'd woken in bed with someone since he'd split up with Karen. The first time for years that he'd woken in bed with someone other than Karen. In some ways, it felt strange and uncomfortable; in others, it felt good—because it was Toni. He liked her. A lot. He liked her warmth, the way she always saw the good in things. His world had felt a lot brighter since she'd been in it.

He kissed her shoulder. 'Toni. Wake up.'

'Hmm?' She shifted around to face him and her grey eyes widened in apparent surprise; and then she smiled at him, clearly remembering last night. 'Good morning.'

'I'm due at the surgery,' he said, 'so I need to go home and change.'

'Of course.'

He tucked a strand of hair behind her ear. How soft and silky it was. 'Can I see you this afternoon? Maybe we could take Archie for a run on the beach.' He paused. 'And talk.'

'That would be good.'

'See you outside Scott's Café at two?'

'I'll be there,' she promised. 'Can I get you some breakfast before you go?'

He glanced at the clock on the bedside table. 'Thanks, but I need to get going. I have to be at the surgery by half-past eight.'

'OK.' She stroked his face. 'Thank you for staying last night.'

'No problem.' He paused. 'Are you OK?'

'I will be,' she said. 'And you have patients to see. They're more important.'

Typical Toni, not putting herself first. He stole a kiss. 'They're not more important than you, but I do have to go. I'll see you later. Close your eyes.'

She laughed. 'Because your clothes are in a heap on my floor? In the circumstances—'

'—I shouldn't be shy,' he finished. 'Weirdly, I am.'

'Then I'll close my eyes, shy boy,' she teased.

Ben climbed out of bed and dressed swiftly. 'See you at two,' he said.

'I'll see you out. I need to let Archie out anyway.' She looked at him. 'What's sauce for the goose is sauce for the gander, you know.'

'I'll see you in the kitchen,' he said.

Which meant he was the one to get the canine greeting of a slow tail thump, a luxuriant stretch as Archie climbed out of his basket, and a wet nose shoved against his hand to say hello.

A month ago, he would have flinched and moved away from the dog.

Now, enjoying the experience, he scratched behind the dog's ears. 'Good morning, Archie.'

Archie licked him in greeting, and Ben smiled.

Toni joined him a few moments later, clad in a short fluffy dressing gown. 'Are you sure I can't get you coffee and toast to go?' she asked.

'I'm sure. I'll grab a banana and a coffee at the surgery,' he said, and kissed her lightly. 'See you later.'

Ben Mitchell was definitely on the side of the angels, Toni thought as he closed the front door behind him. He'd helped her to function yesterday when grief had sideswiped her. He'd stayed, last night, when she'd needed someone to hold her.

So where did they go from here?

He'd said that they needed to talk, and he was right.

The night of the dance, he'd kissed her and they'd both backed away, both panicked by their pasts. But the attraction between them was still there, and it wasn't going away any time soon. It wasn't just a physical thing. She liked him. More than liked him. And she rather thought it was mutual, or else he would either have made an excuse not to stay last night, or persuaded her to go and stay with her sister.

She'd barely dated since she'd split up with Sean; there just hadn't been the spark with the few men she'd gone out with, and they'd agreed to keep things platonic. And she knew Ben hadn't dated since his ex had left. Was he really ready to take a risk with her?

Their conversation that afternoon needed to be frank and honest, even if it hurt. They needed to know what each other wanted; trying to second-guess would only make things harder.

She called Stacey with the news about Ginny— leaving out Ben's involvement—and then called next door to see if Shona needed anything, caught up with all her chores, and was sitting with Archie outside Scott's Café at five minutes to two.

Ben had changed into jeans, a T-shirt and running shoes, topped with a pair of sunglasses. He looked absolutely gorgeous and Toni's heart skipped a beat.

'Hi.'

Was he going to greet her with a kiss?

Her stomach clenched with disappointment when he didn't.

OK. So this was obviously going to be a 'Dear Jane' conversation. He'd tell her that he was the one at fault, not her, and he'd ask her to cool things between them back to their previous professional relationship.

She braced herself. 'Shall we go?' she asked brightly.

'Sure.'

She waited until they were on the designated part of the beach before she let Archie off the lead. Though that meant she didn't really have anything to do with her hands, once she'd put Archie's lead into her beach bag.

Ben still hadn't said anything, so she was guessing that he was trying to find a nice way of telling her that he didn't want to take their relationship further.

When they got to the dunes, he said, 'Hydration break?'

Which was just what they'd done the day he'd had the case that had brought his past back to haunt him. 'Sure. I brought an extra bottle of water.'

'And I brought strawberries,' he said. 'They're washed and hulled. And grown locally.'

'For a moment I thought you were going to say you picked them yourself.'

'Not quite. I picked them up from the farm shop on the way back from work,' he said.

'OK.' How horrible that they were reduced to small talk. But she didn't know what else to do. 'Did you have a good shift?'

'Yes. Did you have a good morning?' he asked, equally polite.

'Yes.'

He took her hand and laced his fingers between hers.

Here it comes, she thought. *It's not you, it's me...*

She couldn't bear it. She would rather be the one to call it quits, the one to walk away. 'I'm sorry about last night,' she said.

'Don't apologise. You were upset. Of course I wasn't going to just leave you on your own. I'm glad I could be there for you.'

'As my friend.'

'That's why we need to talk,' he said softly.

'I understand. You're not ready for—'

Ben cut off the rest of her words by kissing her.

Once she was stunned into silence, he said, 'I wasn't expecting this thing between us. I thought I was still licking my wounds after Karen. But there's something about you I can't resist, Toni. I know it's not fair of me to ask you to start dating me properly. I'm still working things through in my head. But the feelings I have towards you just aren't going away.' He paused. 'But it's your call. I know you've been hurt before. But I would never give you an ultimatum like Sean did. I'd never want you to stop being who you are. I'm not like your ex, and I know you're not like mine. Do you think we could give it a go?'

She felt her eyes widen. 'Are you…asking me out?'

He nodded. 'I feel as if I'm fifteen years old again, not thirty-five. I'm terrified you're going to say no—and I'm also terrified that you're going to say yes and I'm going to make a mess of it.'

'You already know I have a habit of picking Mr Wrong,' she said. 'With the good guys, there's no chemistry.'

'I think there's chemistry between us,' he said softly.

'That's why this whole thing is so confusing. You're not like the men I usually date—and I wasn't looking to start dating someone.'

'So we both think this might be a mistake,' he said.

She nodded. 'Except you're right. There's chemistry between us, and it isn't going away any time soon.'

'So let's see how it goes,' he said. 'Maybe we should keep it just between us, for now, until we know what's happening.'

She grinned. 'It's pretty hard to keep things quiet in a small village. But OK. We'll see how it goes—and try to keep it just between us.'

'Good.' He leaned over and stole a kiss. 'So what sort of things do you like doing?'

'Apart from walking or running on the beach?' she asked. 'I like music. I'm hopeless at dancing, though.'

'You just need practice,' he said. 'How about the theatre? Cinema?'

'Yes to both, and anything from Shakespeare to stand up to sci-fi. Not gory stuff, though,' she said, 'or all-out weepies. You?'

'Same as you, and I prefer drama to comedy. I really hate slapstick,' he said. 'But I love bad puns.'

'How about sport?' she asked.

'I'd rather play than watch it,' he told her. 'You?'

'I'd rather not watch or play,' she said. 'Except for throwing tennis balls, if you can count that as sport.'

He grinned. 'And I'm guessing you get a fair bit of practice at that.'

'I do indeed.'

'Museums?' he asked.

'Yes. And art galleries,' she said. 'Especially if there's a nice café.'

'Maybe we can make a list of places we'd like to go,' he said.

'Good idea. My idea of the perfect day,' she said, 'is just taking Archie somewhere for a really long walk. It doesn't matter whether it's by the sea, in the forest or in a park.'

'That sounds good to me,' he said. 'So how about we go to the cinema tonight and take Archie exploring tomorrow?'

'That would be perfect,' she said with a smile. 'Let's walk a bit further.'

This time, they walked hand in hand. The tide was out, so it took a while to reach the sea; when they finally reached the shoreline, they both took off their shoes and paddled in the shallows, while Archie galloped through the water, splashing them both.

'Sorry,' she said.

He smiled. 'He's having fun. And so am I.'

'Me, too. Though we do need to keep an eye on the tide,' she said. 'Once it turns, it comes in fast—and if you're the wrong side of the channel you can get caught out.' She raised an eyebrow. 'I remember Stacey once went to the beach a couple of villages down with some of her mates, and they left their clothes on the sand while they went swimming—but they didn't leave their stuff far enough up the slope. The sea came in when they were too busy having fun to notice and washed all their clothes away.'

'As the tide's so fast, is there any kind of warning signal?' he asked.

'Yes. There's a siren,' she said.

'That's good to know.' He smiled at her. 'This place is amazing. I'm glad I moved here.'

'I have no regrets about moving back here from London,' she said.

They walked a bit further, then a teenager in a group at the edge of the water started yelling. 'My foot! It really hurts!'

'Are there jellyfish locally?' Ben asked.

'I haven't heard any reports so far this summer, but it's been warm enough for jellyfish,' Toni said. 'Or maybe he might have stepped on broken glass or the sharp edge of a can.'

She whistled to Archie and they hurried over to the teenagers, who were coming out of the water.

'I'm a doctor and Toni is a nurse practitioner. Can we help?' Ben asked. 'What happened?'

The boy was white-faced. 'I was just mucking about in the water, and something hurt my foot. It's *burning*.'

'Can we have a look?' Ben asked.

The boy nodded, and sat down; Ben sat down beside him and took a look at his foot. 'It doesn't look as if you've stood on glass or anything sharp, but there is a tiny spot of blood on your heel, which suggests to me it's some kind of puncture.'

'It feels as if it's burning,' the boy said again. 'All the way up my leg.'

'It might be weever fish,' Toni said. 'I haven't heard any reports of them for a while, but they bury themselves in the sand, and if you stand on them the spines are really sharp—plus they contain venom.' She grimaced. 'Sorry to tell you this, but if it was a weever fish the pain will get worse over the next half an hour.'

'It's bad enough now—I don't think I can walk on it,' the boy said, grimacing.

'We need to get the spines out of your foot. Archie, sit,' she told the dog, who sat perfectly still while Toni rummaged in her bag. 'What's your name?' she asked the boy.

'Ollie,' he said.

'OK, Ollie. I've got tweezers in here. Can one of your mates run up to the lifeguards' hut and ask them to get some hot water ready? Tell them we think you stood on a weever fish. I'll get the spines out of your foot, Ollie, and we'll help you up to the lifeguard. But in the meantime I need you to talk to Ben about your medical history— any allergies, any medication.'

She busied herself taking the tiny spines out of Ollie's foot with the tweezers, while he told Ben that he wasn't on any medication, he was allergic to fabric plasters, and his foot really, really hurt.

'I'm going to have to squeeze your foot now to make it bleed, so the blood washes the venom out,' Toni said. 'I'm sorry. It might hurt a bit.'

Ollie clenched his fist. 'That's OK. Do it.'

He winced as she squeezed the puncture site, but didn't make a sound.

'What we'll do now is give you some paracetamol to help with the pain, and then we need to put your food in really hot water for half an hour,' Ben said. 'That will break down the poison and increase blood flow to the site of the sting, to help it heal.'

'So my mates aren't going to have to pee on my foot or anything?' Ollie asked.

'No,' Ben reassured him, 'and you don't need to put vinegar on it, either. You're best not covering up the wound, because that could risk the puncture getting infected.'

'You'll be fine by tomorrow. If you find the area around the site really swells up, your chest hurts or you can't breathe properly, or you feel lightheaded or start throwing up, you need to go straight to hospital or ring for an ambulance,' Toni said.

'And keep an eye on the wound—not just for swelling. If it gets redder or there's any sign of pus, come straight to the surgery and we'll give you some antibiotics,' Ben said.

'Got it,' Ollie said. 'And thank you for helping. You're not even on duty.'

'It's all part of being a medic,' Ben said. 'You never just leave people when you can help.'

They helped Ollie walk back towards the lifeguard station, and his friends met them halfway back.

'The lifeguards are getting the hot water ready,' one of them said. He looked at Toni and Ben. 'And I told them you're a doctor and a nurse.'

'Archie isn't allowed on that side of the beach,' Toni said, 'so I can't go any further with you.'

'I'll go to the lifeguards with Ollie and fill them in,' Ben said. 'See you at the café?'

'Good idea. All the best, Ollie.' She patted the teenager's shoulder.

'Thanks again for helping me. Even if it did hurt,' he said.

'No problem. Take care,' Toni said.

Ben came into the café twenty minutes later. 'It looks as if he'll be fine. He knows to look out for signs of complications.'

'Just as well we were there,' Toni said.

'Yes.' Ben made a fuss of Archie. 'Do you want a coffee or something cold?'

'Coffee would be great, thanks.'

There was a soft woof from Archie and Ben laughed. 'I'm sure you'd love a sausage, but I bet you've already had one today.'

'He has and, even though he was brilliantly behaved while we were treating Ollie, he's not having another or he'll get fat,' Toni said firmly.

'Tomorrow,' Ben promised the dog in a stage whisper.

When he returned with a coffee, they pored over the screen on his phone to see what was showing at the local cinemas.

'There's a pop-up cinema in the grounds of the local stately home,' Ben said. 'I quite like the idea of watching a film outdoors. If we can get tickets, shall we go?'

'*Mamma Mia*. I love that film.' She smiled. 'Are you sure it's not too girly for you?'

'It'll be fun. I haven't been to an outdoor cinema in years,' he said.

A couple of minutes later, their tickets were booked.

'The website says there are food stalls, so all you need to bring are fold-up chairs or a blanket to sit on,' he said.

'I have some fold-up chairs and blankets, as long as you don't mind a few dog hairs on them.'

He laughed. 'I don't mind dog hairs. So if I pick you up at seven, we've got plenty of time to set up our chairs, have something to eat, and then enjoy the show,' he said.

'Sounds perfect. See you at seven,' she said.

At seven, Ben walked up the path to Toni's door. He wasn't sure whether he felt more nervous, excited or scared. All three at once, maybe. Even though he and Toni were colleagues and had become friends, this was their first official date. The first time for the best part of a decade that he'd dated someone who wasn't Karen. He wasn't even sure that he remembered any of the etiquette of dating. When to hold her hand, when to kiss her. What to wear, even: was he dressed right? Too formal, too casual? He'd opted for jeans and a light sweater, given that they were spending the evening outdoors. Would Toni think he was taking her for granted and not making an effort to dress up in something a bit smarter?

It felt as if he was fifteen again, gauche and shy. Which was crazy.

Why was he making such a big deal of this? Toni was lovely. Or maybe that was why: because he suspected that she could matter. A lot.

He pulled himself together and knocked on Toni's door. She answered, wearing a pretty top, a skirt and high heels. She looked absolutely gorgeous and his mouth went dry from pure desire. He couldn't actually speak, for a moment, and had to clear his throat. *Idiot*, he told himself. *Speak to her.* 'You look—' He stopped, unable to find the right words. He didn't want her to think he was gushing, but he also wanted to tell her how beautiful she looked. 'You look fabulous,' he said, knowing it sounded lame.

'Thank you.' She grinned, suddenly looking younger herself. 'So do you.'

Funny how it made him feel more relaxed. 'Thank you. Are you going to be warm enough?' he asked. 'Once the sun goes down, it will be chilly, especially as we won't be moving about.'

'I have blankets to snuggle under,' she said, indicating the bag by her side. 'And two fold-up chairs.'

'Brilliant. Let's go.' He took the chairs and the blankets from her and carried them to his car, then drove to the stately home in the next village. The car park was full; clearly the pop-up cinema was popular and they'd been lucky to get tickets.

Once they'd found a place to set up the chairs, they queued for pizza and hot chocolate. 'The food's my treat,' she said, 'because you bought the cinema tickets.'

'It's our first date,' he said, 'so shouldn't this be my treat—especially as it was my idea?'

'Which century are you living in, Dr Mitchell?' she teased, giving him a sassy grin.

'Point taken,' he said dryly. 'And thank you.'

Although the film wasn't really his thing, Ben enjoyed sitting under the stars with Toni, with a fleecy blanket tucked round them and her fingers twined through his. It had been years since he'd last held hands with someone at the cinema and he was surprised by how happy something so simple and so small made him feel.

'Thank you. I really enjoyed tonight,' she said when he dropped her home and walked her to her front door.

'Me, too.' He kissed her softly. 'Can I see you tomorrow?'

'I'd like that.'

'Let's go somewhere we can take Archie,' he said.

'That'd be brilliant.' She paused. 'Um—I…'

'It's our first official date,' he said, 'so I'm just going to kiss you goodnight.'

She stole a kiss. 'I like your old-fashioned courtesy. Even though it kind of makes our relationship the wrong way round.'

'Spending the night together before we started dating?' he asked.

She groaned. 'Does that make me a bit of a tart?'

He wrapped his arms around her. 'No. You're lovely. But I want to do this properly now. I want us to get to know each other better before we go to bed together again.'

'To be sure we're doing the right thing?' At his nod, she said, 'Me, too.' She kissed him. 'See you tomorrow. I'll have a think about where we can go.'

In the end, they took a picnic and went further down the coast to Brancaster.

'It's like Great Crowmell in that the tide comes in really quickly, and a few people have been stranded while they were exploring the wreck,' she told him. 'But as long as we keep an eye on the sea, we'll be fine.'

The beach stretched for miles, and Ben really enjoyed walking hand in hand with Toni, barefoot in the warm shallow water, with the dog splashing about in front of them.

There was something magical about the place, with the bright blue sky contrasting sharply with the pale golden sand, and the light of the sun on the waves lapping against the shoreline looked almost like fairy dust.

After Karen had left, Ben had been so sure he'd never get involved with anyone, let alone fall in love. But here, on the gentle East Anglian coast, he felt different—because Toni was beside him. Right now, the world felt filled with brightness and hope, an adventure to revel in.

And every moment of the day felt special—everything from the warmth and brightness in Toni's grey eyes, through to the fun of finding pretty shells on the beach, buying ice creams from the kiosk by the car park and sharing a picnic on the dunes. Ben couldn't remember when he'd last felt this carefree—this *happy*.

When the tide started to come in, they headed back to the car.

'I've had such a great day,' he said. 'And I know it's selfish of me, but I'm not ready for it to end just yet.'

'Me neither,' she admitted.

When she met his gaze, it felt as if his heart had exploded

'Toni.' He stroked her face, then rubbed the pad of his thumb along her lower lip. She caught his thumb gently between her teeth, and his pulse kicked up a notch. He leaned forward and kissed her, and it felt as if fireworks were going off around him, massive starbursts full of joy.

When he broke the kiss, he was trembling. And so was she.

'I want to show you something,' she said.

He nodded, and she drove them further up the coast. The sun was starting to slip down the sky.

'I thought this was the east coast so you'd see the sun rise over the sea?' Ben said.

'This is the only west-facing beach in Norfolk. The

sunsets here are amazing,' Toni said. 'Stacey and I used to love it when Gran took us here. I wanted to share it with you.'

They found a space on a bench on the cliff top and watched the sun slide lower. The huge red ball cast a plume of red light across the silvery blue sea, and Ben slid his arm around Toni, with Archie curled by their feet.

'I used to like watching the sunset from Primrose Hill when I was in London,' Ben said. 'You had the whole city spread out in front of you with all the amazing colours in the sky. But this is amazing.' It wasn't just the romance of the sunset, though. *She* made him feel amazing.

'Do you miss London?' she asked.

'I grew up there, so I do miss it a bit,' he admitted. 'But I'm coming to love Great Crowmell. The people, the place, and it's wonderful to live so near to the sea.' He looked at her. 'My sister's coming to visit, the week-end after next.'

'Uh-huh.'

'I was wondering if maybe you'd like to meet her.'

Her eyes were very clear. 'As your colleague?'

'Or as my girlfriend.' The words were out before he could stop them.

Her eyes widened. 'So we'd be official.'

This was it. The moment to prove to himself that he could move on, 'Official,' he said.

And her answering smile made the world feel full of wonder.

CHAPTER EIGHT

MONDAY WAS HARD for Toni, walking into a building full of memories.

Ben sent her a text at lunchtime.

Thinking of you this afternoon. Here if you need me.

Toni had no intention of calling him, knowing that he would be busy seeing patients; but she really appreciated his support.

When she arrived, everyone at The Beeches was subdued, and even Archie couldn't get a smile out of Julia.

'Days like these, I hate my job,' Julia said.

'Hey,' Toni said, giving her a hug. 'You've made a real difference to the residents' lives. You've got nothing to reproach yourself for.'

'And death goes with the territory, I know. It's like when you work in the emergency department and you know you can't save everyone, no matter how hard you work and how much effort you put in.'

'I brought you these from my garden,' Toni said, handing her a bunch of golden roses. 'These were Gran's favourite. And they smell amazing.'

'Bless you. Sunshine in a vase,' Julia said.

The residents were all talking about Ginny, all missing her; though petting Archie seemed to help some of them relax a bit more. After her therapy dog session at the nursing home, Toni took Archie for a run on the beach before heading back to her house, needing the endorphins to lift her mood. Ben had left her a second text.

Hope things were bearable. Let me know when you want me to pick you up. Dinner at a dog-friendly pub or I'll cook for you.

She called him. 'Hi. I'm home.'

'How are you doing?' he asked.

'A little bit sad,' she admitted. 'Julia gave me a photograph that one of the staff had taken of Ginny with Archie, a few months back.'

'That's nice. Something to hold onto—good memories,' he said. 'When do you want me to pick you up?'

'To be honest, I don't really want to go anywhere,' she said. 'I'm not quite in the mood for socialising.'

'Then I'll bring dinner to you, if you don't mind me taking over your kitchen. Half an hour?' he suggested.

'That'd be nice,' she said.

She splashed her face with water. Ben was so much more thoughtful than any of her exes had been. Sean couldn't cook, so he would've demanded to go out for dinner—and he would've sulked at her refusal. Ben completely understood how she felt and he'd come up with a perfect compromise.

Why on earth had Ben's ex fallen for someone else? Toni wondered. She couldn't understand it. If he had some deep character flaw, it would've shown up by now. Even the most practised charmer couldn't keep up the pretence all the time, and Ben wasn't a charmer. He was genuine.

He turned up with an armful of sweet-scented stocks. 'It's a kind of cheer-you-up thing,' he explained.

'Thank you. They're my favourites. I love the scent.'

'I'm glad you like them.' He gave her the cheekiest wink. 'I thought the in-your-face pink ones would be perfect for you.'

'Because I'm loud?'

'Because you're bright and lovely,' he corrected, and kissed her lightly. 'Right. Dinner is in ten minutes.'

'Seriously? What did you do, buy fresh pasta and a jar of sauce?'

'Yes to the fresh pasta,' he said, 'and it's from the deli, so I know it's the good stuff. No to the sauce. By the time you've got those flowers in water, dinner will be almost done.'

'Can I do anything to help?'

'Put the salad into a bowl,' he said.

By the time she'd arranged the stocks in a vase, and shaken the bag of salad leaves and the tomatoes into bowls, dinner was ready.

'It smells amazing,' she said.

'Scallops and linguini in garlic and lemon sauce,' he said. 'A nice recipe for our diabetics, if you take out the Parmesan.'

She tasted a forkful. 'You could've been a chef. I think you'd give the posh Michelin-starred place at Little Crowmell a run for its money.'

'Thank you. I've just always liked cooking,' he said. 'It relaxes me. I'm planning a barbecue for when my sister and her family come to stay.'

'I'll make pudding,' she said. 'What do they all like?'

'I do know Jessie will do anything for cheesecake.'

'That's easy, then,' she said.

'And bring Archie with you,' he said casually.

'Really? Would that be OK with your landlord? Because you could always have your barbecue here if it would be easier.'

'Unless Archie is going to dig a massive hole in the lawn or chew a chair leg, my landlord will be fine about him visiting,' he said.

She grinned. 'Then I'll bring a tennis ball and a chew with us. He'll be on his best behaviour—and so will I.'

'Good.'

'I really appreciate what you've done for me tonight,' she said. 'You've made a horrible day so much better.'

'You're my girlfriend,' he said softly. 'Of course I'll be there to support you.'

Maybe she'd actually found Mr Right this time, Toni thought. Someone who made her pulse beat faster but who wouldn't make her miserable.

He didn't stay that night, but they managed to sneak in another date during the week—a comedy show in a tiny theatre in Norwich where they held hands through the whole show and just laughed for a couple of hours, forgetting their worries, and then back at Toni's house they sat outside to watch the stars with Archie sprawled at their feet.

'So you like museums if they're about science,' she said.

'Clocks, space and rocks make my nerdy heart happy,' he said. 'I particularly like the display in the Natural History Museum where there's a massive fulgurite.'

'Which is, in English?' she asked.

'Lightning that has struck the earth through sand and turned it to glass—I guess it's a kind of fossilised lightning,' he said.

'Fossilised lightning? Wow. The best I can offer there is to take you back to the stripy cliffs at Hunstanton to find fossils,' she said. 'Or West Runton, where they found a mammoth in the cliff.'

'You are so on.' He smiled at her. 'So what kind of museums do you like?'

'Textiles,' she said promptly. 'I love the V&A. All the pretty dresses. It's my favourite place in London, and Stacey and I sometimes snatch a day there together.'

'I should have guessed, given how perfect you looked on the nineteen-forties weekend.'

She could tell by his expression that the compliment was genuine, and it warmed her from the inside out. 'Thank you.' She paused. 'What about nature reserves, that kind of thing?'

'The nearest I've been to that in London is walking in one of the parks or alongside the Regent Canal,' he admitted.

'In that case,' she said, 'I know exactly where we're going at the weekend.' She refused to be drawn on the subject until they'd arrived and she'd actually parked the car—this time without Archie accompanying them.

'A seal trip?' he said, seeing the board in the car park.

'This is one of the best bits of Norfolk,' she said. 'It's the biggest colony of grey seals in England—and at this time of year we might be lucky enough to see some common seal pups.'

'That's amazing—I've never actually seen seals that close before,' Ben said when they were on the boat, his eyes wide with wonder. 'They're gorgeous. They remind me of Archie, with those big eyes—except his are amber rather than dark brown.'

'And he's not *quite* as big as the grey seals,' she said with a grin. 'An adult male could be ten times his weight.'

'Remind me of that, next time he plonks himself on my lap,' Ben teased.

He was really relaxed with her dog now, Toni thought. Which was good, because that could've been a real sticking point.

But part of her still worried. Her relationships had all collapsed before. What was to say that this one would last? Would she find herself falling in love with Ben, and then he disappeared, like her exes? The fear brought an edge to her delight in their burgeoning relationship, but she couldn't find the right words to talk about it with him, not without sounding pathetic.

He was right to have insisted on taking a step back from the night when he'd comforted her and stayed. Taking things slowly was a good move. And she could maybe keep a tiny bit of distance between them, protect her heart until they were sure where this was going. Neither of them wanted to face the heartbreak from their past again; and if things went wrong it could make life seriously awkward at work. Even though they were both professional and would always put the needs of the patients first, team meetings would definitely be a source of tension.

So when he kissed her goodbye on her doorstep that night, even though part of her was tempted to ask him to stay, she let him go.

Time. They just needed a little time.

* * *

The following week flew by; and early on Friday evening Ben opened his front door to his sister, brother-in-law, niece and nephew.

'The sea air definitely agrees with you, Ben,' Jessie said, hugging him. 'You look happier than I've seen you in years.'

He was—and it was all thanks to Toni. She'd helped him to see the bright side of life again. 'Yeah, yeah,' he said. But he was smiling. 'I'm being lazy and not cooking tonight; I thought we could eat fish and chips on the harbour wall, and then go for a walk by the sea.'

'After the squash on the tube this week in London,' Kit said, 'and the traffic on the M25, that sounds amazing.'

'Bring your stuff in, and we'll go. You must be starving,' Ben said. He showed them to their rooms, then took them down to the harbour. He ended up introducing his family to a dozen or so people while they ate their chips.

'You've really settled in,' Jessie said approvingly.

'It's pretty good here,' Ben said. 'I really like my team. We're having a pot-luck dinner at the head of the practice's house next weekend.'

'That sounds like fun. Maybe I should suggest doing something like that with my team at the lab,' she said thoughtfully.

Jessie, Kit and Kelly all loved the beach; Josh fell asleep in the baby carrier Kit was wearing.

'Can I come and stay in the summer, Uncle Ben, and can we make a huge sandcastle?' Kelly asked.

'And collect shells,' Ben said. 'We can do that tomorrow morning, too, if you like.'

'Yay!' She hugged him. 'I love you, Uncle Ben. You're the best uncle in the world.'

'I love you, too. And you're the best niece in the world,' he said. It made Ben feel a pang of guilt that he'd abandoned his niece, too, by letting his own misery get in the way. He needed to make it up to her.

'I wish you still lived near us in London,' Kelly said wistfully.

'I've missed you, too, Kelly,' he said, and hauled her up to sit on his shoulders. 'But you can all come and see me any time you like. Plus I can still read you a bedtime story over a video call. We'll make it a regular thing. Every Monday evening.'

'I love you,' she said again.

'You're going to meet a very special dog tomorrow. One of the people I work with has a therapy dog who loves reading time, and he'd like to meet you.'

'Would this dog happen to belong to the nurse practitioner?' Jessie asked, her tone deceptively mild.

'My colleague Toni, yes,' Ben said, trying to keep his voice casual.

'Hmm,' Jessie said. 'Colleague.'

He sighed. 'All right. She's my girlfriend, too, but we're taking things steady and getting to know each other.'

'I'm glad you've moved on,' she said.

'I'm in the process of doing that,' he said softly. 'There's still a bit of me that's scared it could all go wrong. And she's been hurt in the past, too.'

'Maybe you'll be good for each other.'

'Maybe.' It was so hard to trust again. To let himself relax and take the risk of falling for Toni. To believe that this time it wouldn't go wrong.

On Saturday morning, Ben took everyone to the beach again. They made a massive sandcastle, to Kelly's delight, and collected a pocketful of really pretty shells.

'I'm going to make a magic mirror,' Kelly said, 'and stick the shells around the edge.'

'Great idea, Kelly,' he said with a smile.

'And I'm going to wish—no, I can't tell you that, or it won't come true.'

Ben knew what he wished for. But, like his niece, he wasn't going to tell anyone, because he really wanted it to come true. For him and Toni to be together and have a happy-ever-after. For it to work out this time. For him to be *enough* for Toni, the way he hadn't been for Karen.

Meeting Ben's sister. Part of Toni was panicking about it. Supposing Ben's family didn't like her? Then again, Sean's family had loved her, and look how badly that had turned out. All she could do was be herself. And she really ought to tell Stacey that she and Ben were more than just friends —though, given the indulgent smile on her sister's face, Toni had a feeling that Stacey already knew.

She clipped Archie's harness into the seatbelt, then drove over to Ben's house.

When he opened the door to her, his smile warmed her all the way through.

'Thanks for coming,' he said, and stole a kiss. 'Come and meet everyone.'

'Okay.'

'Toni, this is my sister Jessie, my brother-in-law Kit, my niece Kelly and my nephew Josh,' he said, shepherding her through to the kitchen where his sister was chopping a salad.

'Lovely to meet you,' Toni said with a smile.

'Everyone, this is Toni, and her dog, Archie,' Ben said.

'Lovely to meet you, too,' Jessie said.

'I've brought pudding,' Toni said. 'Vanilla cheesecake—home-made—and strawberries that I picked from my garden just before I left.' She handed Ben two plastic boxes and a bottle of wine.

'I love cheesecake,' Jessie said.

'I love strawberries,' Kelly added shyly.

Josh simply cooed from his father's arms and pointed at the dog.

'Would you like to come and play with Archie in the garden, Kelly?' Toni asked. 'He's been looking forward to meeting you.'

Kelly looked at her mother.

'We'll both come and we'll leave the men to finish making the salad,' Jessie said.

Meaning Jessie would be able to ask questions without making it awkward for Ben, Toni thought.

'OK,' Ben said. He stroked Archie's head. 'And, yes, I'll make sure we save a sausage for you.'

Archie gave a soft woof of appreciation.

'That's something I'd never thought I'd see,' Jessie said. 'Ben isn't a dog person.'

'He's kind of got used to Archie being around,' Toni said. 'Sit, Archie, and give Kelly a high five.'

To the little girl's obvious delight, the dog sat nicely and lifted his paw.

'That's so cool!' Kelly said, looking thrilled.

'Ben said he's a therapy dog. How does that work?' Jessie asked.

'We do a session once a week at the nursing home, where basically he sits and lets them make a fuss of him and talk to him. Having him around is brilliant for the residents, because having a canine visitor gives them something to focus on apart from their illness. Plus studies show that making a fuss of a dog brings down people's blood pressure, so it's good for them physically as well as mentally,' Toni said. 'The team at our nursing home say that Archie helps with more than just the residents' moods; they tend to interact more with each other and the staff after they've seen him. So he's really good for them. And he enjoys his work.'

'That sounds lovely,' Jessie said.

'It's nice to give something back—it's the nursing home where my grandmother was when her dementia meant she needed more care than my sister and I could give her. Her best friend Ginny, who was kind of like a second grandmother to me and my sister when we were growing up, ended up being cared for there, too. And once a week we go to the local infant school and the reluctant readers read to Archie. I know that sounds a bit airy-fairy,' Toni said with a smile, 'but it's brought their reading age on by an average of three months in the last term. They stop worrying so much when they read to him, and it helps them focus.'

'That,' Jessie said, 'is amazing.'

'It's lovely to be able to make such a difference. And Archie loves it, too. He's a very sociable dog.' Toni paused. 'Ben told me you're a research chemist.'

Jessie nodded. 'I'm a biochemist. I've just gone back after maternity leave and I'm working on a new cancer drug at the moment.'

'That's wonderful,' Toni said.

'I'm so glad Ben's settled in. He keeps telling me he's fine, but I've been worrying about him,' Jessie said.

'Seeing him for myself has made me feel a lot better. He looks a lot more relaxed.'

'He's a good man, and everyone in the village has responded to that,' Toni said. 'And I think this place is good for him, too.'

'Did he tell you about…?' Jessie bit her lip, looking awkward.

Toni guessed what Jessie meant. The thing that had driven Ben away from London. 'His ex falling for his best friend and them having a baby while she was still married to Ben, yes. That was pretty rough on him.'

'It pretty much broke his he—' Jessie stopped and gave an over-bright smile. 'Hey, Ben.'

'As it's warm out here, I thought you might like a drink,' he said, nodding at the tray he was carrying, which contained a pitcher of home-made lemonade and glasses.

Jessie blushed. 'Thank you. Sorry. I wasn't gossiping.'

'You're my little sister and you worry about me, I know. But I'm fine. I'm moving on,' he said gently, and ruffled her hair.

Jessie didn't bring up the subject after Ben had gone back to the kitchen, so they chatted while Kelly threw the tennis ball for Archie, who brought it back, dropped it at her feet and wagged his tail hopefully at her until she did it all over again.

By the time that Ben and Kit emerged from the kitchen together, ready to start the barbecue, Jessie and Toni had become firm friends.

Once the food was ready, they ate out in the garden, with Archie waiting patiently for his share of sausages and chicken to cool. And baby Josh—who'd woken briefly to eat puréed chicken casserole and mashed banana—was asleep in his pram.

'You're so lucky, living by the sea,' Jessie said. 'Have you always lived here, Toni?'

'Since I was twelve—my grandmother brought my sister Stacey and me to live with her after our mum and dad were killed in a car crash,' Toni said. 'I trained in London and worked in the emergency department at the London Victoria, but I moved back here when Gran became ill and needed support. But it's a wonderful village.' She smiled. 'And Ben has the entire village falling at his feet since the nineteen-forties weekend. Half of them were bowled over by his baking and the other half by his dancing.'

'I wish I'd known about it,' Jessie said. 'It sounds like a lot of fun.'

'It is. Come next year,' Toni suggested. 'Ben told me he went to dance lessons with you. Maybe you can do a demo of the jitterbug for us at the village hall.' She gave Jessie a sidelong look. 'You could always give me a demo now...'

Jessie laughed. 'I'm a bit out of practice.'

'Go on, love. You're fabulous,' Kit said.

'Please, Mummy? Please, Uncle Ben?' Kelly asked. 'And I can dance with Daddy.'

'What about Toni?' Jessie asked.

'Don't ask me to dance. I have two left feet. Archie and I can give you marks—just like in *Strictly Come Dancing*,' Toni said with a grin. 'I think you should earn your cheesecake, Jessie.'

Ben found some music on his phone, and the four of them danced a very energetic jitterbug. Toni clapped when they had finished. 'I award both couples a perfect ten,' she said. 'What about you, Archie?'

The dog barked softly twice.

'That's Archie-speak for "me, too",' Toni said.

'But you're not getting away without dancing,' Ben said, and took her hand.

'Me and Archie will be the judges now,' Kelly said.

So what could she do but join in? Ben led her round the garden and, just like the first time she'd danced with him, she felt as if she was dancing on air. Everything melted away, as if it was just the two of them, while the sun began to set.

For a moment, she thought he was going to kiss her. His sea-green eyes were dark and deep with emotion. But then the music ended and Kelly started clapping, breaking the spell, and Josh woke up and began crying.

Kit lifted the baby out of the pram. 'Bath and a change for you, young man, and then some milk.'

Toni was thrilled when Jessie asked her if she'd like to feed the baby. 'I love babies,' she said. 'I have a fourteen-month-old niece. It's been fabulous seeing her grow and change.'

Ben looked at the two parts of his life colliding. Seeing Toni cuddling his nephew felt odd. And then he realised why: he didn't feel as if he had to insulate his heart any more. Seeing his girlfriend holding a baby didn't remind him of what he'd lost; instead, it gave him hope that he was finally moving on.

After Toni had fed the baby and handed him back to his mum, she ended up reading a story to Kelly, with the little girl sitting on her lap and Archie's head on both their knees. When the little girl's eyelids started to droop and the spaniel's eyes were closed, she said gently, 'I think I need to take Archie home to bed now, Kelly. He's really tired. But we've had a lovely time with you all today and we're both very glad we met you.'

'Can you come back tomorrow? Uncle Ben is taking us on a steam train,' Kelly said.

Toni smiled. 'Thank you for asking me, and although I'd love to join you I'm afraid I can't because I'm seeing my sister tomorrow.'

'She can come, too,' Kelly said.

Toni ruffled her hair. 'Another time. That's a definite date.'

Once she'd said her goodbyes, Ben saw her to the door. 'Thank you for coming today.'

'I've had a wonderful time. I like your family very much.'

'It's entirely mutual.' He kissed her. 'I'll call you later.'

'OK.' She snatched a last kiss. 'Have fun at the steam train tomorrow.'

Jessie waited until Kit was putting Kelly to bed before tackling Ben. 'She's lovely. And so is that beautiful dog.'

'He's a therapy dog. He's trained to be like that.'

'I liked Toni a lot. She's kind, she's sweet and she's great with Kelly. I know it's early days,' Jessie continued. 'But I saw the way you look at each other. And Kelly was going to say a last goodbye to Toni and Archie, but she said you were kissing Toni so she thought she'd better come back.'

'I didn't even hear Kelly coming into the hallway,' Ben admitted.

'You've got it bad,' Jessie said with a smile. 'I gather you've told her about Karen and the baby?'

He nodded.

'I'm glad. I liked her a lot. She was telling me about the therapy dog work. That's such a lovely thing to do. She's definitely one of the good guys.'

'And she's been hurt before,' he said. 'By someone who sounds as if he was incredibly selfish. So we're taking things slowly.' He and Toni hadn't exactly taken things slowly so far, he thought, trying to hold back the colour that threatened to rush into his face. But they were dating properly now. Getting to know each other. Seeing where this thing took them—and if he could finally let go and learn to trust again.

'I think,' Jessie said, 'you might be just what each other needs.'

And he had a feeling his sister was right.

CHAPTER NINE

'YOU MADE A real hit with my sister,' Ben told Toni on Monday evening, when they'd taken Archie for a long walk on the beach.

'I liked her very much, too,' Toni said. 'Kit seemed lovely—and Kelly and Josh are adorable.'

'So,' Ben said, 'are you.'

Which thrilled her to her bones, and they walked back down to the harbour with their arms wrapped around each other.

On Thursday, it was Ginny's funeral; although it was good to share memories with Ginny's family and friends, it also made Toni really miss her grandmother and her parents, and by the time she got home she felt really flat and miserable. Even a cuddle with Archie wasn't enough to fill the empty spaces.

That evening Ben brought dinner round to Toni's — for Stacey, Nick and Scarlett, too.

Stacey gave him a hug. 'I know I'm not supposed to know anything about what's going on between you two, but I'm glad you and Toni have found each other.'

'Me, too,' Ben said softly.

On Saturday it was the practice's pot-luck dinner. Ranjit had a trestle table set up for the food and plenty of chairs; although Toni and Ben arrived separately, they managed to sit together in the garden.

Ben had brought lemon-glazed chicken and sweet potato wedges; and Toni had made a lemon tart with an almond pastry base, supplementing it with fruit from her garden. By the time everyone from the practice arrived, the table was groaning.

After dinner, Toni instigated a round of charades that had everyone enjoying themselves, from the younger children through to the teenagers as well as the entire practice team. When Ranjit put some music on, Ben ended up giving everyone an impromptu dance lesson. And at the end of the evening Ben insisted on walking Toni home.

'I really enjoyed tonight,' he said. 'Our team is lovely, and so are their families.'

'Plus we've got loads of recipes now for our patients. I'll need to run them all through one of the nutrition sites so I can work out the calories, fat, carbohydrate and protein content,' she said, 'but I think we've got a really good base for our meal plans now.'

'I'll send you the photographs I took of all the dishes,' Ben said.

'Thanks. A picture might be the thing that persuades someone to try making a dish,' she said.

At her doorstep, she asked, 'Would you like to come in?'

'Very much,' he said. 'I want to dance with you again.'

'You sort out the music, and I'll pour the wine.'

Swaying with her to a soft bluesy track, with their arms wrapped round each other, made Ben feel at peace with the world. And it was a wrench saying goodnight to her. He was oh, so close to asking her if he could stay. But he knew that rushing things wasn't the way forward. He still needed time to learn to trust. To put the past behind him. To be sure that he could give his heart again.

On Wednesday, Toni's eyes were sparkling when they took Archie for a run on the beach. 'Stacey texted me earlier to see if you're free on Sunday. She and Nick are hiring a boat on the Broads. Would you like to come with us?'

'The Norfolk Broads, as in the Bowie song?' he asked.

She smiled. 'Absolutely. They're actually medieval peat diggings which filled up over the years to make a series of lakes and channels. The scenery is amazing, and so is the wildlife. I know you enjoyed the seals, so I thought you might enjoy this, too.'

'So is this an official date with your family?' Like the barbecue had been with his sister.

'If you want it to be,' she said.

He thought about it. This would be the next step. And when he was with her like this, just the two of them and her dog, he felt so light of spirit. Would it change things if they went public? Would *she* change?

He decided to take the risk. 'Official. OK. That's good with me.'

'We're leaving at about ten. We're taking sandwiches for lunch and stopping for dinner at a pub on the way home, if that's all right with you.'

'That's great.'

She smiled. 'Then I'll pick you up at ten minutes to ten.'

'I'll be ready,' he promised.

On Sunday, when she picked him up, Ben wasn't that

surprised when he discovered that Archie was coming, too; but he was surprised to discover that the dog had a lifejacket.

'I had no idea they made lifejackets for dogs,' he said.

'The same as for small children,' Stacey told him with a smile, and he saw that Scarlett, too, had a special lifejacket.

Nick and Ben took turns steering the boat while Toni and Stacey took turns cuddling Scarlett and pointing out all the wildlife to her—coots and moorhens on the water, along with the ducks, huge swallowtail butterflies in the bushes, and even a bright blue kingfisher swooping down.

Ben watched Toni cuddling her niece, patiently teaching her new words and clapping when she got them right.

She was so good with children. She'd make a brilliant mother.

But he'd thought that about Karen, and look where that had got him.

He pulled himself up sharply. It was time he put the past to rest. To draw a line, put it behind him and focus on the good—on his new life here, in a little seaside village full of people who were prepared to open their hearts to him, instead of brooding.

'You're quiet,' Toni said, coming to join him at the front of the boat while Nick went to see his wife and daughter.

'I'm fine,' he fibbed.

'Are you feeling a bit seasick or anything?'

'No.' He didn't want to tell her how ridiculous and self-indulgent he was being. He wanted her to enjoy the day. 'Show me what you were showing Scarlett. I'm a city boy at heart so I know absolutely nothing about flora and fauna.'

To his relief she didn't push him. Instead she did what he'd asked. 'OK. See all those water grasses at the edge of the Broads? Sedges have edges, and reeds are round. The reeds are the ones that are harvested and dried to make roofs for the thatched cottages around here.'

'Right.'

'And those black birds swimming over there are moorhens and coots.'

'What's the difference?' He frowned. 'I've heard the saying "bald as a coot", but they don't actually look bald.'

She laughed. 'No, they're not. I've no idea where that saying comes from.'

'Maybe it's the same as "bald eagle",' he said, 'so it's to do with having white feathers?'

'Maybe,' she said. 'The coots have the white bills and the moorhens have the red bills. The way to remember which one is "moorhen, more colour".'

Ben thoroughly enjoyed the journey, seeing the windmills and the waterways and the stunning range of flora and fauna. But even more he enjoyed being close to Toni and her family.

That night, when she dropped him home, he waited a moment before opening the car door. 'Are you doing anything next weekend?'

'I don't think there's anything in my diary. Why?' she asked.

'I was thinking, it might be nice to go away for the weekend. If you can get time off on Friday afternoon, maybe we could have a weekend away.'

'A romantic mini-break? That sounds wonderful.'

'Abroad, maybe. Except, even if you have a pet passport, I'm not sure that it'd be fair to take Archie on a city break.'

She looked thoughtful. 'It's the school summer holidays now, so I probably can't get him into the boarding kennels at this short notice, but I'm pretty sure Stacey will have him to stay. Though I'd rather check with her first before you book anywhere.'

'Sure,' he said. 'Let me know, and then I'll book somewhere. Can I surprise you?'

'That,' she said, 'would be lovely.'

Stacey was happy to look after Archie for the weekend, so Ben booked a weekend away, refusing to tell Toni anything more than what the temperature was likely to be and what she'd need to pack. He managed to keep the surprise of where they were going until they checked in at the airport and it was obvious from the check-in desk.

'Vienna? How lovely,' she said. 'I've never been there before.'

'I believe it's all about cake, chandeliers and coffee,' he said with a smile. 'I thought we could just wander round the city, visit art galleries and gardens and old palaces, and have plenty of stops for coffee and cake.'

'That sounds perfect—really romantic,' she said.

And it was. The hotel was gorgeous, converted from an old palace, with high ceilings, chandeliers and marble floors, and a view from their window over the park.

'I thought we could maybe start with the Sisi Museum in the Imperial Apartments,' Ben said. 'I think there's an exhibition of Empress Elisabeth's clothes.'

Toni was thrilled that he'd remembered her love of costume museums. 'That sounds fabulous, but won't you be a bit bored?'

He smiled back. 'Not with you.'

Toni was enthralled by the displays and the paintings. 'This replica of Sisi's wedding dress is incredible. And that gown in the painting with the stars in her hair—that's stunning.'

'So would you dress up in something like that?' he asked, intrigued.

'Maybe.' She smiled at him. 'I can imagine you dressed up as a nineteenth-century aristocrat, in a tail coat and a white cravat.' Mischief danced in her eyes. 'And a top hat.'

He grinned. 'A top hat to me means Fred Astaire.'

'But I'm no Ginger Rogers,' she said. 'If I tap dance with you, your toes would be sulking for the next decade.'

He laughed and stole a kiss. 'Don't be so hard on yourself.'

Though Ben was hard on himself, she thought. He blamed himself for his wife's betrayal, thinking he hadn't been enough for her. And that wasn't fair. Here in Vienna, would the magic of the city work on him, the way it was working on her?

Toni had brought a little black dress with her and they ate at the hotel's Michelin-starred restaurant that night before strolling through the city centre with their arms wrapped round each other, charmed by the string quartets and opera singers on every corner.

'This is such a treat,' she said. 'Fabulous food, beautiful architecture, those gorgeous dresses in the museum and this wonderful music. I don't think I've ever heard buskers as amazing as this before.'

'Me, too. And you're the perfect person to share it with.' He smiled. 'And now we're going to have a twilight tour of the city.'

He helped her up into a *fiaker*, one of the horse-drawn carriages that lined up near the cathedral, and sat with his arm round her as they drove through the cobbled streets. The carriage driver pointed out places of interest as he drove them round the city. Places where Mozart and Beethoven and Haydn had lived, the Parliament building, the Hofburg Palace and the Opera House.

'Imagine being here nearly two hundred years ago,' she said, her expression wistful, 'and driving in one of these carriages to the theatre, then hearing Beethoven's Ninth played for the very first time...'

'Funny you should say that,' he said. 'We have tickets for a concert tomorrow night. It's not Beethoven's Ninth, but something I hope is special.'

She smiled at him. 'I'm with you. Of course it'll be special.'

And the ice that had surrounded his heart for the last few months finally cracked. Right here, right now, Ben thought, he couldn't be any happier. The empty spaces inside him began to feel full of light. Vienna was called the city of dreams as well as the city of music. Would his dreams of the future finally start to come true with Toni?

That night, Ben waltzed barefoot with Toni in their suite, before undressing her slowly, carrying her over to the bed and making slow, sweet love with her. It was the first time they had made love since that night when she'd been so desperate for comfort; but this time was all the sweeter because it was just for them. No past, no sorrow to get in the way—just the sheer joy of being together.

And there was no awkwardness the next morning when she woke, warm and comfortable in his arms: just closeness and sweetness and looking forward to the rest of the weekend.

'So is it the first time you've been to Vienna?' she asked over a breakfast of good coffee, freshly squeezed orange juice and amazing pastries.

'Yes. You?'

She smiled. 'Yes. And I'm so glad we're going to explore it together.'

'I thought we could do the art galleries today—and have a wander through the gardens, as it's so sunny outside,' he said.

'That sounds perfect.'

And it was: Toni thoroughly enjoyed walking hand in hand with Ben in the public gardens, discovering that they liked the same kind of art, and taking selfies with the fountains of the Belvedere Gardens behind them, and the massive white palace with its green copper roof reflected in the lake.

They stopped at one of the oldest cafés in the city for coffee and cake.

'Vienna is famous for the Sachertorte,' Ben said. 'We really ought to try it.'

'Is there a non-chocolate version?' she asked hopefully.

'That's the whole point of it. Chocolate overload, and it's meant to be amazing—even you might like it.'

'How about a compromise?' she suggested. 'I try a forkful of yours, and you try whatever I choose.'

'Deal,' he said with a smile.

It took her ages to choose a cake from the huge selection in the glass-fronted cabinet, but eventually she chose Esterhazy torte, a stripy layered confection of almond meringue and buttercream.

The melange coffee, the Viennese version of a cappuccino, was perfect—but the cake wasn't. 'Sorry. It's much too rich for me. I know I'm a heathen,' she said ruefully.

But she enjoyed feeding Ben a forkful of her own cake, watching his sea-green eyes widening in bliss. Seeing the curve of his mouth and remembering how it felt against hers.

'That's sublime,' he said. 'Though I have to admit I prefer mine.'

'Stacey would agree with you,' she said.

'They sell smaller versions of the big *tortes* in the shop, here,' he said. 'Maybe we can take one back for her.'

'Great idea.' She smiled at him. 'I'm so glad we came here, Ben.'

The day got even better, with a wander round the Gothic cathedral with its mosaic tiled roof where Mozart had got married, a stroll through the streets, and then a quick traditional dinner of schnitzel with potato salad.

'I really hope you like this,' Ben said as they reached the tiny concert hall.

'This is amazing,' Toni whispered as they took their seats. The room was gorgeously baroque, from the ornate floral decoration on the walls through to the stunning Venetian glass chandelier. Better still, the musicians were all wearing period dress. She could just imagine being here two hundred years ago, as she'd said to him the previous night in the *fiaker*.

'This is where Mozart himself played to selected audiences,' Ben told her, and he held her hand throughout the performance, his fingers warm and sure around hers.

Toni recognised the music as some of Mozart's most famous: *Eine Kleine Nachtmusik*, along with the *Dissonance* quartet that he'd dedicated to Haydn. The musicians were superb and it would've been a treat in any concert hall, but here it was even better. And she really, really loved the costumes. She couldn't have imagined a more perfect evening.

'That was so special. Thank you,' she said when the concert was over.

What was even more special was sharing the sheer joy of the music with Ben.

As they wandered back to the hotel, their arms wrapped around each other, Toni was pretty sure she was falling in love with Ben. With this thoughtful, gentle man who also never hesitated to do the right thing, the man who had pushed himself to overcome his wariness of dogs to make friends with Archie, and who made her world feel like a better place.

Not that she was going to spook him by telling him. Not yet. She knew he still needed time to get over the collapse of his marriage; but she hoped that spending time with her and her family was helping him to do that.

It was raining the next morning, but the weather couldn't spoil their mood. 'Perhaps we should do something indoors this morning,' Ben said. 'How about the rest of the Imperial Apartments and the butterfly house?'

'Sounds perfect,' Toni said.

She enjoyed wandering around the Imperial Apartments; and then they headed for the butterfly house. The tropical interior with its waterfall, pond, bridges and palm trees was gorgeous; and there were hundreds of butterflies flying freely, of all colours and sizes—from blues to bright orange, vivid red to yellow. Toni was fascinated by the huge owl butterflies with their enormous spots like an owl's eye in the middle of their wings, resting and feeding from a peach on one of the tables.

'This feels magical,' she said. 'I've never been anywhere like this before.'

'It's amazing,' he agreed. 'And I'm so glad I'm here with you.'

His smile made her feel as if the weather outside was bright sunshine rather than pouring rain. They'd become closer over the last couple of days, more in tune with each other, and Toni was convinced that Ben really was the one for her. That she could trust him with her heart, and know he'd be there for her—just as she would be there for him.

Finally they travelled back to England and went to pick up Archie from Toni's sister.

'We brought cake to say thank you for looking after Archie,' Toni told Stacey, handing her a beautifully wrapped package.

'I recognise the name on the packaging. This isn't just cake,' Stacey said, her eyes widening. 'It's the best chocolate cake in the world.'

'I did try a forkful of Ben's,' Toni said, 'but I much preferred the Esterhazy torte, all almond and buttercream.'

Ben laughed. 'I'm with you, Stacey. Every cake I tried in Vienna was chocolate-based, but this one was definitely the best.'

'Thank you.' Stacey hugged them both.

'We brought you some chocolate as well,' Ben said. 'The little ones shaped like kittens are for Scarlett. And there's some proper Viennese coffee.'

'You really didn't have to spoil us quite so much,' Stacey said. 'We've loved having Archie for the weekend. I'm your sister, Toni, and I know you'd do exactly the same for me if it was the other way round.'

'We just wanted to bring you something nice,' Toni said. 'And we saw butterflies.'

'Look, Scarlett.' Ben showed the toddler his picture of the owl butterfly that had landed on his hand.

'Oooh!' Scarlett said, beaming and pointing at the butterfly.

'Maybe we can go and see some butterflies together,' Ben said. 'As a family.'

Toni glanced at her sister, and was gratified to see the warmth of her smile. And she knew exactly what her sister was thinking: *This time, you've found Mr Right.*

Life didn't get any better than this, Ben thought. He hadn't been this happy in years. He loved his job, he loved his morning run on the beach—and he was definitely falling in love with the nurse practitioner and her dog.

But in the middle of the week, he and Toni were watching the sunset from her garden when her phone beeped to signal an incoming text.

She glanced at the screen. 'Nothing important. It can wait,' she said.

But Ben had glanced at the screen at the same time, more out of habit than nosiness. The problem was that he'd seen the message—and he'd seen who it was from.

Sean. Her ex. Why was he texting her, and especially with that kind of message? It was a couple of years since they'd broken up, and Ben knew that Toni had been hurt by the split. She certainly hadn't mentioned staying in touch with her ex.

Though he could hardly demand to know why Sean was texting her, or why she even still had his number on her phone, because that reeked of paranoia. He knew Toni wasn't like Karen; but, despite that, he couldn't stop that tiny little seed of doubt creeping into his mind. Was he making the same mistake all over again? Was he trying so hard to convince himself that the future was bright that he was missing something?

Of course not. He was being utterly ridiculous.

But the thought wouldn't go away, and he ended up making a feeble excuse and going back to his own home instead of staying at Toni's that night.

Had something happened? Toni wondered. Ben had been really quiet that evening.

Or maybe he was just tired.

She made herself a cup of tea, and turned her attention to the text she'd ignored earlier.

Can you call me? I miss you.

She rolled her eyes, not believing a word of it. It was more likely that either Sean had sent it to her by accident, or he had some kind of event coming up where he needed to schmooze for the sake of his career, and he'd just split up with someone and wanted a reliable plus one to step into the breach.

She could ignore it, but that might mean he'd take her silence as meaning that he needed to make some kind of charm offensive. She really wasn't interested.

Quickly, she typed a reply.

Assume you sent that text to me in error. Toni.

He didn't text her again, so she assumed her guess to be right. Obviously Sean, being Sean, couldn't be bothered even to acknowledge her texts—because then he would have to acknowledge he'd made an error, and Sean could do no wrong in his own eyes.

She'd had such a lucky escape. She was so grateful that Ben wasn't like that. He had at least opened up to her and talked. He listened to her. And, after Vienna, she felt that he was the one she could commit to—and he would be just as committed to her.

Over the next few days, life felt just about perfect for Toni. She was really in tune with Ben, both at work and outside it. They'd worked on the new practice website pages between them and had received a lot of compliments from their patients, as well as more suggestions of recipes to tweak. And she was very close to the point where she was ready to go public to everyone, not just their families, with the fact that she and Ben were a couple. There were some moments when she felt as if he was holding something back, but she thought she was probably just being paranoid and stupid.

And then on Wednesday morning she woke up feeling odd.

Her breasts were sore and she felt a bit queasy. And one mouthful of coffee for breakfast made her gag.

If any of her patients had come to see her with those symptoms, she would've suggested that they do a pregnancy test...

She shook herself. Of course she wasn't pregnant. She and Ben had taken precautions.

But she knew that the only one hundred per cent form of contraception was abstinence. Considering that she gave a talk every year at the local high school on that particular topic...

She counted back mentally to the date of her last period, and went cold.

It was eight weeks ago.

Surely she'd made a mistake? Maybe there was another reason why her period was late.

Except she couldn't think of one.

Eight weeks. Which meant that conception would've been six weeks ago. Around the time that Ginny had died. She'd been upset, and she and Ben had ended up making love for the first time. Had they taken precautions? She couldn't remember. She couldn't think straight.

The chances were that she wasn't pregnant and this was just a blip in her cycle. But the only way to put her mind properly at rest was to do a pregnancy test.

No way could she buy a test from anywhere in Great Crowmell, because speculation would go round the village like wildfire. She'd have to go somewhere else to buy it, somewhere that nobody knew her.

It was just as well that Ben hadn't stayed here last night, because until she knew one way or the other about this she really couldn't face him.

Term had finished, so she had a free morning instead of taking Archie to the infant school for their reading session. If she drove into Norwich, she'd be able to pick up a pregnancy test, do it, and be back in Great Crowmell before her afternoon shift.

Archie had clearly picked up that something was wrong, because he sat as close to her as he could, as if trying to comfort her.

'It's all going to be fine, Arch,' she reassured him.

It had to be.

She drove to the city, parked, bought the test, and headed for the public toilets in the library building.

Thankfully it was too early for it to be busy, so she didn't feel guilty about staying in the cubicle while she waited for the test to finish working.

According to the packaging, she'd have the results within three minutes. She'd bought a digital one so there could be no mistake, no squinting at the little screen to see if there was a faint line.

The hour-glass symbol flashed at her to let her know that the test was working. But the seconds seemed to stretch on and on. How was it that time could fly by while she was at the beach with her dog, yet now it dragged? She kept staring at the screen, willing it to change and willing it to tell her what she needed to know.

Three minutes of limbo.

Three minutes that went on and on and on.

Three minutes of…

Pregnant.

Adrenalin flooded through her, making her hands shake, and she dropped the test stick.

When she picked it up again there was a figure on the line below the words: *3+*—meaning that it was more than three weeks since conception. Which tied in with what she'd half suspected: she'd become pregnant the day of Ginny's death. When she'd thought she was celebrating life with Ben, they were actually making a new life together.

What now?

What now?

The question echoed like a heartbeat.

Sitting there locked in a public toilet cubicle wasn't going to help. She'd have to face this and think about the possible ways forward.

Carefully, she slid the test back inside the box, then replaced the box in her handbag.

One foot in front of the other.

She washed her hands, then walked down to the cathedral. Maybe here she could get her thoughts together. She went over to the huge openwork metal globe where a couple of candles were already lit, put some money into the offering box and lit a candle for her mother, her father, her grandmother and Ginny. The huge, soaring space of the building helped to still some of the turbulence in her head; she walked quietly over to the door that led to the cloisters, and then out into the green space in the centre where the labyrinth lay.

Walking a labyrinth was a good way to meditate. Putting one foot in front of the other, following the twists and turns of the pattern and knowing it was a continuous path rather than having dead ends to baffle her, helped. And, by the time she reached the centre, her thoughts had settled enough that she knew what she wanted to do.

This baby was hers and Ben's. Toni understood now the bittersweetness that Stacey must have faced during her pregnancy with Scarlett, knowing that their parents and their grandmother weren't there with them physically to cuddle the baby and share their joy. But at the same time she knew she'd see bits of them in her baby, just as she saw them in her niece Scarlett—a smile, an expression, the curve of her face. Little traits that went from generation to generation, love that was passed down through the years. And they'd always be there in her heart.

One thing was for definite: although this baby wasn't planned, it was wanted. She was going to keep it.

And she wanted to share the baby with Ben. He was

the kind of man she knew she could trust, who would be there to support her dreams, and he would always be there in the tough times. More than that, he made her heart beat faster, made her feel as if the sun was shining even on a drizzly day. He was nothing like the selfish egotists she'd dated in the past.

But how would he feel about an unplanned pregnancy?

He'd been here before, and it had all gone horribly wrong.

This time round, the situation was a little different. He knew she wasn't seeing anyone else, and he'd know for sure that he was the father. But this pregnancy was still going to bring back bad memories for him—memories of rejection and loss.

She had absolutely no idea how he'd react. She knew he'd wanted to make a family; he'd told her that he'd been broody and looked forward to being a father. Had that changed, because of Karen's affair? Would he see this as a second chance, a way for everything to be right, this time round? Or would it totally mess with his head? Would it heal the hurt, or make it worse?

She'd have to find the right words to tell him.

What if he didn't want to make a family with her?

Toni dragged in a breath. Stacey and Nick would be there for her, she knew, and she was sure that Jessie would want to be involved in the life of her niece or nephew.

But Ben…

It was the one area where she wasn't quite sure of him. He'd want to do the right thing, she was sure—but the personal cost might be too high. She didn't want to hurt him, but she was scared that this might be the point where it would all go wrong between them.

She sat in the cathedral grounds for a while longer, taking strength from its peace and serenity. And then she drove back to Great Crowmell in time for her afternoon shift. Though before she saw her first patient she texted Ben.

Can you meet me outside Scott's after work, please? We need to talk.

CHAPTER TEN

Can you meet me outside Scott's after work, please? We need to talk.

BEN STARED AT the message Toni had sent him.

He had the strongest feeling that something was wrong, but he had no idea what. Clearly it was something big enough for her to want to talk about it face to face.

Yes, sure, he texted back.

He'd thought that things were going well between them, that they'd grown closer since their weekend in Vienna, but had he been deluding himself? Had she changed her mind? Even though he tried to ignore it, the thought went through his mind: was it anything to do with the text she'd received from Sean and never mentioned? Was he making a fool of himself all over again?

He focused on his patients for the rest of the afternoon, putting his worries in the back of his head, but the worries all rushed back when he arrived in the car park outside Scott's Café and Toni was sitting on one of the benches without Archie.

She never came to the beach without her dog.

Had something happened to the dog? No, surely not.

She wouldn't have said they needed to talk. She would've told him if Archie was ill or hurt—or worse.

'Hi. Where's Archie?' he asked.

'At home. I came straight here from work.'

So whatever the problem was, he was pretty sure now that it was about them.

'Want to walk?' he asked.

She nodded, and they headed out to the dunes—but she didn't hold his hand, the way she had done for the last couple of weeks or so. And he had a nasty feeling that if he tried to hold her hand right now, she'd pull away. It was as if there was some kind of invisible force-field round her, keeping him at a distance. She didn't talk, either. This really, really wasn't like her.

When they got to the dunes, he stopped and looked her in the eye. 'What's wrong, Toni?'

Her beautiful grey eyes were filled with anguish, and she took a deep breath. 'There isn't an easy way to say this.'

She wanted to call a halt to their relationship? So he'd been right to be paranoid, and that text from her ex really had been the beginning of the end. It felt as if he'd been sucker-punched, but he wasn't a coward. 'Tell me straight, then,' he said, trying to keep his voice as neutral as possible so he didn't put any pressure on her.

He was expecting to hear the words 'I can't do this any more,' or 'it's not working'; what she said instead shocked him so much that he couldn't quite take it in. Had she *really* just told him that, or had he misheard?

'What did you just say?' he asked, needing her to repeat it so it would sink in properly.

'I'm pregnant,' she said.

It felt as if all the air had been sucked out of his lungs.

He'd been here before and it had ended so badly. He knew Toni hadn't been dating someone else secretly, but he could still remember seeing the anguish on Karen's face and hearing the words tumble out, the horrible truth. A little voice in his head whispered, *Here we go all over again. How do you know you can trust her? How do you know that text was innocent when she's never talked to you about it?*

He shoved the thoughts away and tried to focus on the facts.

Toni was pregnant.

With his baby.

How could it have happened, when they'd taken precautions?

Well, of course he knew the science of it. He was a GP. He knew that there was always a tiny chance that contraception would fail, even if you were careful. The only one hundred per cent guaranteed form of contraception was abstinence.

Right at that moment, he didn't know what to say. What to do. His brain just wasn't functioning. There weren't any words in his head, just white noise: as if it had suddenly become winter and a storm had sent the waves crashing onto the shore.

But he had to say something. He couldn't just stand here in silence, watching her wilt visibly before him.

He opened his mouth, intending to ask her if she was all right, but what came out was, 'I need time to think.'

Toni thought she'd prepared herself mentally for Ben having difficulty with her news, but she really hadn't. That wasn't just shock on his face, it was absolute horror.

He was going to let his past get in the way of his future. What had happened to him was horrible, yes, but she'd never given him any reason to think she would cheat on him. And she really resented the fact that he was treating her as if she'd behaved in the same way as his ex, when she hadn't.

Which meant that she'd managed, yet again, to pick Mr Wrong. He didn't want to make a family with her. She'd fallen for someone who didn't want her. Someone who'd maybe seen her as his transition partner rather than his for ever partner. And who wasn't ready even to talk, let alone have a real relationship. She was going to have to be brave.

She took a deep breath and willed her face and her voice to stay as neutral as possible. She wasn't going to let him know how much this hurt. 'OK. You need time to think. I'll give you that. Call me when you're ready to discuss things.'

And then she turned away before he could see the tears filming in her eyes, folded her arms round herself, and began to walk away from him.

One foot in front of the other.

She could do this. She was strong. She'd survived worse emotional trauma in the past.

But, oh, this hurt. A deep, visceral pain of rejection.

You need time to think. I'll give you that.

The words echoed in Ben's head, over and over again.

Toni was walking away from him, just as Karen had. Except it wasn't the same thing at all. Karen had walked away because she'd fallen in love with his best friend; Toni was walking away because he'd pushed her away.

That wasn't what he wanted.

At all.

But it felt as if the beach had turned into set concrete, and he was stuck there. Worse still, it was as if someone had superglued his lips together. He couldn't open his mouth to call out to her, to ask her to wait. All he could do was watch her walking quickly away. And he hated himself for it.

Time seemed to stop.

Eventually he made a decision. He couldn't stay here. He needed to get away and think. To go home to London and take stock.

He took his phone from his pocket and called Ranjit. The head of the practice was sympathetic, and promised to sort out a locum to cover Ben's absence.

His next call was to his sister.

'I'm heading out to my aerobics class,' she said, 'but I'll be back by the time you get here. Of course you can stay. Stay as long as you like.' She paused. 'What's happened?'

'Tell you when I see you,' Ben said.

'OK. Drive safely.'

'I will,' he promised.

He drove home and packed a bag.

And then, just before he left, he texted Toni.

Sorry. I'm going back to London. I'll call you.

Once he'd got his head straight. He felt bad about hurting her, but he needed to think, and he couldn't do that here.

Selfish, stubborn and stupid.

That was Ben Mitchell.

How could he think that it was history repeating it-self? How?

Toni wanted to grab his shoulders and shake him until his teeth rattled. Though she knew it wouldn't make him any more likely to talk to her.

And the text he'd just sent her made her even angrier. Sorry? If he was really sorry, he wouldn't be walking away from her in the first place. He wouldn't be going back to London. And he certainly wouldn't be vague. *I'll call you.* When? This year, next year, sometime, never?

What was very clear was that she'd been very wrong indeed about Ben Mitchell and commitment. He didn't want to commit to her and their baby. Yet again, she'd picked Mr Wrong.

'You selfish, stubborn, *stupid* man,' she said through gritted teeth, and Archie woofed softly as if in agreement.

On the way back to London, Ben's phone rang; the display on the car's hands-free system told him it was his sister. Thinking she was probably wanting to know what time he was likely to arrive, he answered, 'Hi, Jessie.'

'Ben.' Her voice was high and breezy with panic. 'Are you still coming? It's Josh. He—he—he's in hospital.'

'Hospital?' Ben repeated, shocked. 'What's happened?'

'Kit gave him his dinner and then he just went red and stopped breathing. Kit called the ambulance and gave him CPR. The paramedic said it was anaphylactic shock. Oh, God, Ben. What if he—if he…?' She couldn't get the word out.

He knew what was going through her head. What if baby Josh died? 'He's going to be fine,' he said reassuringly. 'Many, many more infants survive anaphylaxis than die from it. Plus he's in hospital, so he's in the right place if there's another emergency. I know it's frightening, but I promise you the stats are all on your side. I'm about halfway to London now—tell me which hospital you're in and I'll let you know when I'm close.'

Her words were barely coherent but he worked out that she was at Muswell Hill Memorial Hospital.

'I'll be there soon. Is Kelly with you?'

'No. Kit's mum met us at the hospital and took her home.'

'That's good. And Kit's with you?'

'Yes. He came in the ambulance with Josh and Kelly. Oh, God, Ben, if I hadn't gone to aerobics tonight—'

'It would still have happened,' he told her gently. 'I'll be there soon. I love you and it's going to be fine, Jessie. I promise it's going to be fine.'

Anaphylactic shock. That meant Josh had a severe allergy to something. It had happened after Kit gave him his dinner, so the most likely culprits were nuts, milk, eggs or shellfish. And Ben could give his sister and brother-in-law all kinds of advice to help them keep Josh safe in the future.

It felt as if it took for ever to get to London, but when the satnav said he was fifteen minutes away from the hospital he used the car's hands-free system to text Jessie that he was nearly there. Finally he parked the car and headed for the Emergency Department.

'My nephew, Josh Harford, was brought in with anaphylactic shock this evening. I've driven straight here from Norfolk. Can you tell me if he's still in your department, please?' Ben asked the receptionist.

She checked for him. 'He's just been moved to the

children's ward,' she said, and directed him to the paediatric department.

That was a good sign: it meant the baby was out of immediate danger, though Josh would probably be kept in overnight for observation and maybe for most of the next day.

At the paediatric department, the reception team directed him to Josh's bedside.

He rounded the corner and saw them in the little bay: Jessie and Kit with their arms wrapped around each other, and their free hands clearly holding Josh's.

'How's Josh doing?' Ben asked. 'And how are you both holding up?'

'Oh, Ben.' Jessie dissolved into sobs and he held her close, resting one hand on Kit's shoulder for comfort and support.

'It was all my fault,' Kit said. 'I gave him scrambled egg for his dinner. I thought it'd be nice and soft because he's been teething, and... Oh, God. Then he went red round the mouth and his face started swelling up, and he was having trouble breathing.' Kit was shaking. 'Thank God that work sent me on that first aid course the other month. I rang 999 and, by the time I'd done that, he was unconscious and I had to give him CPR. I thought we were going to lose him. I thought our baby was going to die.' Kit dragged a hand through his hair. 'I'm never going to forgive myself.'

'You weren't to know that he was allergic,' Ben told him. 'I'm assuming the paramedics gave him an injection of adrenalin?'

'And an oxygen mask, and a drip,' Kit said.

'That was all to help him breathe and sort out his blood pressure,' Ben said, reassuring him. 'I'm guessing Josh is going to be in here overnight and possibly tomorrow for observation.'

'I think that's what they said,' Kit said. He raked his hand through his hair again. 'Nothing the nurses tell us stays in my head, and they're so busy I can't keep bothering them. I just see Josh there and it's like a fog. I don't know what to do.'

Reassurance, Ben thought. That was what they needed. Reassurance.

'You're going to be just fine, aren't you, Josh?' he said gently.

The baby was asleep, but Ben was happy with the figures he could see on the machine next to the bed. 'I know right now it feels like the end of the universe, but Josh is in the right place and you're all going to get through this. I know what all those figures mean on that machine and I promise you it's all good.'

He could see Jessie and Kit both visibly relax as he spoke. 'Sit down,' he said, 'and I'll talk you through everything.' He held their hands. 'Ask me to repeat anything I say if you can't remember. It's fine. And I'll write it all down for you in a minute,' he told them. 'OK. Egg is one of the big four foods that can cause severe allergic reactions in children. The very first time Josh ate something with egg in it, he might have had a milder reaction to it. Given the age he is, the red face and swelling could look like normal teething symptoms rather than an allergic reaction,' he said.

'But this time, when he ate the egg, his immune system recognised the allergen and overreacted big-time. Hence the rash, the swelling and the breathing difficulties. He'll be fine, and before he leaves here the team will give you an auto-injector with adrenalin that you'll need to keep with him all the time, and a written emergency plan so anyone who might be looking after him knows what to do if it happens again.'

'Oh, my God. Are you telling me this could happen again?' Jessie asked, looking terrified. 'He could stop breathing like that and his heart could stop again?'

'If he accidentally eats something containing the allergen, then yes, his system will overreact to it again,' Ben said. 'But if that does happen then you'll know exactly what to do. And you'll have the adrenalin to use straight away, so it won't be quite as scary. When you leave here, you'll be given an appointment with your GP or an allergy specialist, and they'll do some tests to confirm that Josh is allergic to eggs and to check his reaction to any other of the big allergens, too. And your GP can give you advice on how to help Josh avoid allergens in future.' He paused. 'Actually, I can do that. I've got leaflets I give to my patients. I'll print out some copies at your place tonight, so anyone who looks after Josh will have the information to hand, too.'

'I'm so scared, Ben,' Jessie said, her teeth chattering.

'Of course you are. It's terrifying, seeing your baby lying there with an oxygen mask. But it's going to be all right. They know what's wrong and they know how to treat him. Josh isn't going to die. He's going to recover from this.' He looked at Kit. 'You're both going to have to be really strict about the food he eats, but he'll be fine. Anaphylaxis is seriously scary, and I can't imagine what a nightmare it must be to have to give your own baby CPR.'

'It…' Kit was shivering. 'I thought he'd die.'

'But you gave him CPR. You saved his life,' Ben said.

'You saved him, Kit,' Jessie echoed. 'If it wasn't for you, he would have died.'

'But I was the one who gave him the egg in the first place—the thing that made him nearly die.'

'You weren't to know. It could just have easily been me,' Jessie said.

'Or anyone else who looked after Josh. Your parents, mine, a family friend.' Ben looked at them. 'And I bet neither of you has eaten anything tonight.'

'I couldn't face anything,' Kit said.

'Me neither,' Jessie admitted. 'And I haven't put the sheets on the spare bed for you or—'

'It's fine,' Ben cut in gently. 'Josh is going to get through this, but I'm guessing neither of you want to leave him for a second, so I'm going to go and get you both something to eat and a hot drink. No arguments. You need to keep your strength up so you can support Josh.' And each other, he thought.

When he got back from the canteen with sandwiches and hot drinks, Kit and Jessie were clinging together, watching their infant as he slept.

'I know neither of you normally takes sugar, but right now I think you need it,' Ben said, handing them in the drinks. 'Josh is doing just fine. I want you to eat and drink now. No arguments.' He tried for humour. 'Doctor's orders.'

They'd both lost the grey tinge of anxiety, he was glad to notice.

It took him two hours, but eventually he persuaded Jessie to let him drive her home. And she only agreed because Kit was staying with Josh and because Ben pointed out that at least one of them needed to get some decent sleep to support Josh when he was discharged next day.

Ben sorted out the spare room, making Jessie go and rest even though he suspected she wouldn't sleep very much. It took him a long time to get to sleep, too, because the way Kit and Jessie had been together in a crisis had really made Ben think about what he wanted from life. He wanted the same warmth and closeness and utter trust in each other—true love.

And he wanted it with the mother of his baby. The woman he'd treated incredibly badly because he'd let his past get in the way. Of course that text was innocent. She hadn't told him about it because Sean meant nothing to her any more. Ben knew he'd been incredibly stupid and hurtful, and he needed to make amends.

It was too late to call her now, but he'd call her tomorrow. Or, better still, he'd go back to Norfolk and have that conversation face to face. Because being here in a familiar bit of London, just round the corner from the place he'd called home for so long, had made him realise that this wasn't home any more.

Norfolk was home.

With Toni.

If she'd give him the chance to make it up to her.

The next morning, he drove Jessie to pick up Kelly from Kit's parents, then took them to the hospital to see Josh. The baby was sitting on his dad's lap, bright-eyed, and he gurgled with joy when he saw his mum—setting Jessie in tears again, but this time they were happy tears.

Finally, just after lunch, Josh was discharged, and Ben drove them all home. He stayed long enough to be sure they'd settled in and would call him if they had the slightest worry, then headed back to Norfolk.

Ben knew Toni would be at work. It wouldn't be fair

to call her and have a conversation at the surgery, but he definitely needed to talk to her. To apologise.

In the end, he texted her.

Coming back from London. Please can we talk this evening?

She still hadn't replied by the time he was almost back in Great Crowmell and he stopped off at a shop to buy flowers.

He couldn't blame her for being angry with him. He hadn't been fair to her; he'd let her down when she'd needed him most.

Would she give him a chance to explain, or would he end up making everything worse?

In the end he drove straight to her house. Her car was parked outside, and the windows were open, so he was pretty sure that she was home.

He rang the doorbell.

A couple of minutes later, she opened the door; she stared at him, but said nothing. And there was a world of hurt in her eyes.

'I'm sorry,' he said, and tried to give her the flowers.

She leaned against the doorjamb with her arms folded, refusing to accept them. 'You're sorry.' Her voice was completely neutral and he didn't have a clue what was in her head.

'I'm sorry for a lot of reasons. I'm sorry I hurt you, I'm sorry I wasn't supportive when I should've been, and I'm sorry I was such an idiot,' he said. 'I let the past get in my way, and I shouldn't have done.'

'Yes. Because I'm not Karen. I've never even *met* your best friend—ex-best friend, whatever you want to call him—let alone had a fling with him.'

'I know.' He took a deep breath. 'I'm ashamed of myself. I should have supported you properly. What you told me was a shock, but it must've been a shock to you as well.'

'Uh-huh.' She didn't move.

'Can I come in?' he asked. 'Please?'

'Yes,' she said. 'But, just so we're clear, giving me flowers isn't what I want. It's not about gifts and throwing money at a problem—that's the sort of thing that Sean would've done.'

'Sean.' He was going to have to admit to that, too.

She stood aside and let him walk into her kitchen. Archie was there, but he didn't rush up and bounce about, the way he usually would. He stayed in his bed, looking mournful, and Ben felt even more guilty.

'These aren't a proper apology,' he said. 'I bought them because I know you like flowers.' Sweet-smelling stocks, roses and gerbera; to his relief, this time she accepted the flowers, but she didn't put them in water. She placed them on the draining board, folded her arms and looked at him.

'The apology...' He blew out a breath. 'I hardly know where to start. I'm completely in the wrong.'

'Yes.'

She wasn't going to make this easy for him; then again, he didn't deserve it to be easy.

'I let my past get in the way,' he said again.

'And I don't understand why.'

'Because of Sean.'

She frowned. 'What about Sean?'

'He texted you.'

Her frown deepened. 'And you think a text equates to having a fling?'

'No, of course it doesn't. But I couldn't stop myself wondering why you didn't mention it to me.'

'Because there wasn't anything to mention.' She shook her head in what he guessed was a mixture of frustration and exasperation. 'Why didn't you ask me about it, if you were that worried?'

He squirmed. 'Because I thought I was being paranoid and ridiculous.'

'You *were* being paranoid and ridiculous.' She rolled her eyes. 'I have no idea why he texted me. His text asked me to call him and said he missed me, which is utter rubbish. I thought either he'd texted me by mistake, or he was trying to schmooze me, because maybe he needed a plus-one at some event to help boost his career and he thought I might help him out—and, by the way, if that'd been the case I would've said no. I texted him to say I assumed he'd messaged me by mistake, and he never replied.'

'Seeing as I'm being ridiculous and paranoid, I might as well say the rest of it.' He had nothing else to lose. 'Why would you still have his number in your phone?'

A muscle worked in her cheek. 'Because,' she said, 'I changed my phone a couple of months before I met you. The phone shop transferred all my data across for me, and something went wrong so they ended up duplicating all my contacts. They said it's something to do with the way numbers are stored on a phone and on a SIM card and they couldn't fix it. I'd just have to delete the numbers I didn't want any more. I must've deleted his number off one of them but not the other, so when the techies messed up my data it ended up back in the list. I meant to tidy everything up but it's one of those jobs I kept putting off.'

The explanation was simple and completely plausible, and Ben felt even worse. 'Sorry.'

'And now you can give me a good reason why I shouldn't ask you to leave.'

'Because I'm an idiot,' he said, 'and because I need you.' That wasn't enough. He owed her total honesty. 'This scares me stupid, Toni, but I love you. My world's a much better place with you in it. I should've told you that when you told me about the baby, instead of letting everything get in the way and stomping off to London. And I wanted to tell you last night when I got back from the hospital—'

'Hang on. Hospital?' she interrupted.

'Josh ended up in the emergency department. Kit gave him egg and it turns out he's allergic to them. He had anaphylaxis,' Ben explained.

She looked shocked. 'Is he all right now? How are Jessie and Kit?'

Typical Toni. He'd hurt her and she had every right to be furious with him, yet she was putting other people first. 'He's fine. He's home now. Jessie and Kit are a bit wobbly but they're getting there. I gave them the anaphylaxis leaflet from the surgery so they've got everything written down, and I said I'd go with them to Josh's appointment with the allergy team because it'll be a lot to take in.'

'I'm glad he's OK,' she said.

'I'm so sorry I hurt you,' he said. 'Can I rewind to yesterday and say what I should have said? What I want to say.'

She looked wary. 'OK. But I'm still reserving the right to throw you out.'

'Absolutely,' he said. 'The news was a huge shock,

but I shouldn't have said what I did. I should've thanked you for being brave enough to tell me so soon, because I'm guessing you'd only just found out, too, and it was a huge shock to you as well. And I want to apologise again, just in case I say anything over the next few minutes that hurts you, because I'd never want to do that. What's important is *you*. Are you all right?'

Then her face crumpled and she started to cry. Archie rushed over to her, shoving his nose into her hand in a gesture of doggy comfort. And Ben took a risk—he closed the distance between them and wrapped his arms tightly round her, holding her close, until she'd stopped shaking. Then he wiped away her tears with the pad of his thumb. 'Tell me about the baby,' he said softly. 'How did you find out?'

'I couldn't face my coffee at breakfast and my breasts felt sore. And then I counted back and realised my last period was eight weeks ago.' She dragged in a breath. 'Wednesday was my morning off, and it's school holidays so we didn't have reading group. I drove to the city to buy a pregnancy test and did it in the loos at the library.'

So nobody locally would know or guess.

'I think… I think it must've happened the day Ginny died. When we…' She bit her lip. 'I can't remember if we used a condom.'

The first time, at his house, they had. But in the middle of the night, when he'd been curled round her in her bed… 'I can't remember, either,' he admitted. 'I just wanted to comfort you. The rest of it's a blur.'

'I know the baby wasn't planned. And I know this must be hard for you, because of what happened with your ex.'

'That was a totally different situation. And I know

I let that get in the way, but I had time to think about it yesterday and realised what an idiot I was being.' He stroked her face. 'Have you had time to start coming to terms with it? Any idea about what you want to do? Because, whatever you want, whatever you need, I'll support you. No pressure. You're the one who's important here, Toni, and I'll be guided by you.'

'Thank you.' She swallowed hard. 'I want to keep the baby. I'm clear on that. But I know this is going to be hard for you.'

'What's harder,' he said, 'is knowing that I hurt you, and I promise I'll never do that again. I should've just asked you. Been honest with you about what was in my head.'

'I'd never cheat on you.'

'I know. And I'll do my best to give you everything you need. I'll support you through every step of your pregnancy. Every bit of morning sickness, every single antenatal appointment, and I'll be right by your side all the way. Even when you're in transition and you crush my hand and yell at me.'

To his relief, she gave him a wry smile. 'I'll hold you to that.'

'Good. We've got a lot of things to work out,' he said, 'but the important thing is that we work them out together.'

But was he saying that because he wanted to be with her—or was this all for the baby's sake? Toni wondered. Was he doing what he thought was the right thing, or doing what he really wanted to do?

There was a big difference, and she didn't want him

to be with her out of duty. She wanted him to be there because he loved her.

'So what made you change your mind? Yesterday, you walked out on me. Today, you're back.'

'Yesterday, I was very stupid and I let my past get in the way. Yesterday, I watched my sister and her husband at their baby's bedside after Josh had stopped breathing. I saw how much they were a team, how they were there for each other—and I realised that was what I want. A real partnership. Love and liking and respect, the whole lot all bundled in together. And I want it with you.'

Could she believe him?

'What do you want, Toni?' he asked.

He'd asked her straight out, so she'd be honest with him in return. This might turn messy, but at least they'd both know exactly where they stood. It might be painful, but better that than quietly wishing and hoping and watching things turn pear-shaped because she hadn't had the courage to speak out when she should've done. And she never wanted to go through the misery of yesterday again.

'I want,' she said, 'to live with someone who loves me and who loves our baby. Someone who wants to be a family with me.' She looked him straight in the eye. 'What do *you* want, Ben?'

'I want to be a dad to our baby,' he said. 'And I want to be with you. Be a family with you. I want to make a future with you and our baby, if you'll have me. I'm not perfect and I'm going to get things wrong in the future. I'll do and say the wrong thing sometimes. But I'll never deliberately hurt you. And I'll do my best to talk to you instead of hiding away in my head. I'm scared that I won't be enough for you—like I wasn't for Karen, otherwise she wouldn't have fallen for Patrick. I know that makes me paranoid and ridiculous, but I owe you total honesty.'

'I thought you'd gone away because you didn't want commitment. I thought I'd picked another Mr Wrong.'

'Mr Wrong-headed, perhaps,' he said. 'But I do want commitment. I want everything, Toni, and I want it with you. If I'm enough for you.'

'You're enough for me,' she said. 'Just for the record, I wasn't expecting to fall in love with you. I didn't even like you, the first day I met you. I thought you were unreasonable and grumpy, and I was prepared to ignore you as much as I could.'

'I wasn't expecting to fall in love with you, either. You have one hell of a glare,' Ben said. 'And you refused my brownies.'

'I hate chocolate cake. Even posh, award-winning, super-special Viennese chocolate cake,' she said.

He smiled. 'But you tried it anyway because I asked you to.'

'You danced with me without complaining that I hurt your toes.'

'You didn't hurt my toes. You're perfectly capable of dancing, whether it's a waltz or a jitterbug.' He grinned. 'As long as you're being led by someone who knows what they're doing.'

'Like you.'

He stroked her face. 'Teamwork. We're good together, Toni, at work and outside. And all I could think about on the way back from London was you. I don't belong in London any more; I belong here, with you and our baby and Archie. This is where my life is. Where I want to be. You want commitment? You've got it. Because I love you,

Toni Butler. I love everything about you and my world's a better place with you at its centre. And I really want to marry you. Not because of the baby, because of you.'

He loved her.

Just the way that she loved him.

This time, she'd found the right man. One who wasn't going to let her down or give her ultimatums. One who'd actually commit to her.

'I probably should ask you somewhere a lot more romantic. I maybe should've asked you in Vienna, in the middle of all the butterflies—because that's when I realised how much you make my world feel full of colour,' Ben said. 'But I want to be a family with you and Archie. I want to make sandcastles with our children and look for shells. I want to run on the beach with our dog at sunrise, and treat our patients, and be a proper part of this community. I want it all, and I want it with you. Will you marry me, Toni? Be my love, my life?'

'What do you think, Arch? Should we say yes?' she asked.

The dog gave a single woof.

'I agree,' she said with a smile. 'I love you, too, Ben. Yes.'

EPILOGUE

Ten months later

BEN STOOD IN the porch of the huge flint-built church at Great Crowmell with Toni at his side; he was carrying their daughter, Elizabeth, while she was carrying their son, Max. The twins were fast asleep; the godparents—Jessie, Kit, Stacey and Nick—were waiting inside with his parents, toddler Josh and a host of their friends. Archie had special dispensation to be at the christening, just as he had at the wedding, and was sitting under the watchful eye of Kelly.

'You're beautiful, Mrs Mitchell, and I love you very much,' he said, stealing a kiss. 'Are you ready for this?'

'Ready.' She smiled at him. 'Let's go and join our family and friends. And then we can get this party started...'

* * * * *

A NURSE TO TAME
THE ER DOC

JANICE LYNN

MILLS & BOON

To Dr. Jay Trussler, for his insight into
working for a major music festival.

Thanks for the tour, the stories,
and for answering all my questions.

CHAPTER ONE

YES! NURSE TAYLOR HALL mentally pumped her fist in the air as she looked across the Rockin' Tyme music festival medical tent at the tall man wearing a "Medical Staff" T-shirt and navy shorts.

Yes. Yes. *Yes.*

Her body had noticed a man.

Sure, the current tingles were just sparks of physical attraction, but as she'd thought good old-fashioned lust a thing of the past at the age of twenty-five, Taylor cherished the incoming zings.

She wasn't dead inside after all.

Her ex hadn't accomplished quite as much as she'd given him credit for this past year. Thank God.

Seeming to sense someone was watching him, the medical staff hottie glanced up from the clipboard he'd been studying and met Taylor's gaze with eyes so brilliant she questioned if they were colored contacts. She was positive she'd never met him, but recognition flashed in his baby blues and a huge smile lit his face.

Wow. Just wow.

Awareness sparks burst into blistering red-hot flames.

Crazy that something as simple as physical attraction could make her feel so ecstatic, especially since she wasn't interested in a relationship, but Taylor credited the heat as a sign she was healing. She truly had progressed from the beaten down woman she'd been at her divorce a year ago.

Of course she had. She was a strong, independent woman who didn't need a man to hold her hand. She held her future. No one else.

The job interview she'd gone to earlier that day had been yet another sign of how far she'd come. She'd moved on from the past and was taking charge of her life in new and exciting ways.

Curious at the man who'd awakened her libido when she'd been so oblivious to the opposite sex for so long, she took in his features. He wasn't the most handsome man she'd ever seen, not even close to her ex's Hollywood perfect good looks. But there was something about this guy that had drawn her attention the moment she'd stepped into the Rockin' Tyme music festival medical tent, which was abuzz with activity.

His shoulder-length, sun-kissed brown hair, pulled back with a rubber band, and skin told a story of someone who loved to be outdoors and spent a lot of time doing so. Someone who didn't worry about his outward appearance, but who'd been blessed with natural good looks. Friendly face and eyes, great smile, nice body, and if he was who she thought he was, he was Amy's friend.

Her bestie had never liked Taylor's ex.

Amy had said she would know Dr. Jackson Morgan when she saw him. Everything inside her had "known" this man—or sure wanted to.

Taylor smiled at the hunk standing twenty or so feet away. Would he think her certifiable if she walked over to thank him?

He immediately put his clipboard down on the table in front of him and crossed the tent. Had he read her mind and was going to say, "You're welcome."?

Ha. She'd hug him for real.

She fought back another smile and told herself to get a grip. Just because her body suddenly remembered it was female, it didn't mean she would dare act on those zings. After the raking over the coals Neil had put her through, she had planned to avoid men forever. Not all men were like Neil. She knew that. But no matter how many sparks and tingles, no matter how excited she was that her insides weren't dead, when it came to men, her brain warned her to steer clear.

Men weren't worth the trouble.

Once upon a time she'd thought she needed one. The last year had taught her she was just fine without one.

Better than fine.

"Taylor, right?" He grinned, causing happy lines to fan out from his eyes.

Great smile, she thought again as she nodded. Genuine, not calculated. A smile that radiated as much from his eyes as his mouth.

"I'm not a crazy stalker." He chuckled. "Amy Sellars told me to be on the lookout for you."

Another wave of disappointment that Amy wasn't there hit Taylor. Not that Amy could help it that her grandmother had fallen and broken a hip two states away, but Taylor had really been looking forward to catching up with her best friend. Amy had come to Louisville last summer immediately following the finalization of Taylor's divorce, but that seemed forever ago, and Taylor hadn't done much more than cry.

Tears for lost dreams and tears of happiness that she'd escaped Neil's controlling, abusive hands.

"Amy has a picture of the two of you on her fireplace mantel," the medical staffer continued. "I recognized you immediately."

Taylor knew the photo he spoke of. She had the same one displayed at the tiny apartment she'd leased following moving out of Neil's sprawling showplace. The photo was a close-up following her and Amy's nurse pinning ceremony. Their smiles had been huge, as had their dreams for the future.

Her university roommate had tried for years to get Taylor to work the infamous annual festival that took place in her hometown. Taylor finally had and now Amy wasn't even in town.

Agreeing to work the music festival had been more about spending time with her friend than the generous sum she'd be paid for her three twelve-hour shifts. But the extra pay wasn't a bad thing.

Still, if her job interview that morning had gone as well as she thought, they'd soon have lots of catch-up time.

If all went according to plan, she'd be living with her former roomie yet again. Amy had tried to get Taylor to relocate last summer, but Taylor had needed to put her life back together on her own. She'd needed to stand on her own two feet. It would have been too easy to let Amy take over and just have gone through the motions.

Which was what Taylor had done her whole life.

Gone with the flow. Done what had been expected. First with her parents and then with Neil. She'd never stepped outside the boundaries they'd set. Not until she'd left Neil and filed for divorce.

She was a work in progress but was happy with the woman emerging from the wreck she'd been. She was still peeling back the layers of years of toeing the line, but most mornings she liked the person staring back at her in the mirror.

"Amy was excited you're working the festival."

Taylor's attention zoned back in on the man who was studying her. The man who'd been inside her friend's apartment.

Was Amy dating him? She hadn't said so, but her friend had been enthusiastic when talking about him. She'd gotten the impression Amy had been hinting at a possible romance between Taylor and the doctor during the music festival, hints Taylor had ignored because she'd not been interested in a man since long before her divorce. She had no plans for a relationship and, even if she had, she'd just as soon have her fingernails ripped out as to get involved with another doctor.

He held out his hand. "Jackson Morgan."

He'd introduced himself without using his medical title, something her ex would never have done. Kudos for that.

"Nice to meet you, Jackson." Taylor returned his smile, shook his hand, and marveled at the tingles of awareness that shot up her arm at the warmth of his hand.

Men sworn off or not, the guy was electric.

"My friends call me Jack," he commented as she pulled her hand free from his.

"Jack." Taylor let the name roll off her tongue. "You're the hotshot traveling emergency medicine doctor Amy works with at Rockin' Tyme each year."

"My reputation has preceded me yet again." His eyes danced with mischief.

Taylor tried to recall what her friend had said but couldn't pull up much. She'd thought Amy matchmaking when she'd gone on and on about the doctor they'd be working with at the festival. Taylor had been excited about seeing her best friend, not about meeting a man. What had Amy said?

"Good looking, funny—can't wait for you to meet him. Think you'll really like him. He's the best."

"Nothing bad," she admitted, smiling at Jack. If he and Amy were an item, then good for her friend and even better for this guy. Any man would be lucky to call Amy his own. If he was good to her friend then, doctor or not, Taylor would hug him for a totally different reason than the one that had hit her upon first seeing him.

"Good to know she's not talking smack about me." He glanced around the medical tent, his gaze skimming over the cots along a far side where a group of workers was chatting. "I'll miss her being here. Hated to hear about her grandmother."

"That makes two of us. She convinced me to sign on and now she's not here." Following his gaze out the open flaps of the tent, she took a deep breath. "I can't help but wonder what she's gotten me into."

"No worries. She made me promise to take good care of you."

Taylor's gaze cut to his. "Oh?"

He grinned, and his eyes crinkled. Wow, such a great smile. "At least a dozen times—and that was just this morning."

Taylor smiled. Her friend always had looked out for her.

If only Taylor had listened better.

Jack working as a traveling doctor must create relationship problems. "Do you get to see her often?"

"I see Amy several times a week," he answered, looking a little surprised at her question. "I liked Warrenville so much I temporarily relocated here a couple of months ago to fill in for a doctor on an extended medical leave."

"Oh." Had her perky friend influenced that decision? Good for Amy. Taylor was happy for her but why hadn't Amy told her? Maybe her friend had been afraid of jinxing whatever was happening. Still, that Amy hadn't mentioned their relationship made Taylor sad as once upon a time they'd shared everything.

Then again, hadn't she put on a face for her friend for years? Not wanting Amy to know the truth behind her miserable marriage?

"Have you met the rest of the crew?" Jack asked, drawing her focus back.

Taylor shook her head. "Do you already know each other?"

"Mostly," he admitted. "There are always a few new people, but most of us come back each year. It's a tradition. A lot of the staff are locals, but some do travel. It's a good bunch who work the medical tent. You'll enjoy hanging with us."

Either way, it was just for a few days so she'd survive. She'd survived worse. Besides, wasn't she all about new life experiences and stepping outside the box she'd lived in for so long?

"How did you get involved with the festival?" she asked, glancing out the front of the medical tent to the "oasis" that was located about a hundred yards away. Fake palm trees planted in a huge sand pit with splash pools for play and cooling down during the hot July heat.

This was definitely a new life experience.

"Music festivals are in my blood. My grandparents were hippies and actually met at Woodstock." Grinning, he made a peace sign with his fingers. "I've been going to festivals since before I could walk. My parents thought I'd grow up to be a musician—or a gypsy," he added, chuckling. "But medicine called me. Since I left med school, I've worked numerous festivals every year so it's a balance of work and play. Makes me feel I've evolved from those days of driving across the country with a car load of buddies with nothing on our brains except good music and good times."

"Sounds like fun." Taylor couldn't imagine the carefree trips he was describing. Her strict parents had barely gotten by and Taylor had had her first job at fifteen. She'd been working ever since. Even then, there'd never been money or time for cross-country road trips to soak up the sun and music. For a short while early in their relationship she'd felt happiness and a sense of peace with Neil. After their wedding, nothing had been carefree during those torturous two years.

"The best." Jack grinned, but something was off in his smile as he looked back out over the festival. "Let me give you the low down on how things will run the next few days in the tent and introduce you to the others."

Taylor was scheduled to work Thursday and Friday from four a.m. to four p.m. and on Sunday from four p.m. to four a.m. on Monday.

"We're on the same work schedule," she commented, spotting Jack's name on the schedule near hers.

"It's not a coincidence," he admitted, grinning. "Amy and you are purposely on the same schedule as mine. Didn't see a reason to change it when Amy cancelled at the last minute. How else can I keep my promise if you and I are on different schedules?"

"How indeed?" At least she was guaranteed a friendly face during her shifts because Jack seemed to always smile. He was the most laidback person she'd encountered in a long time. Maybe ever. "Do most of the crew sleep or participate in the festival activities during their down time?"

"A mixture. Most take in a few concerts. But some hang around the camping area or leave the farm to check out local attractions."

"Is that how you fell in love with the area?"

He hesitated a minute, then said, "Amy had a lot to do with that."

If she'd had any doubt, there was her confirmation that there was something between her friend and Jack. She fought back a fresh twinge of disappointment that he was taken, reminded herself he was a doctor and she wasn't interested anyway. Plus, she truly was pleased for Amy. She'd just met Jack and she already liked him.

"I'm happy for you."

He stared at her a moment, then his eyes lit with surprise. "Not sure what Amy told you…" he chuckled as he continued "…but we're just friends. I'm sure she feels the same."

Heat flooded her face. Just friends. "Oh."

"You thought she and I were more?"

Oh, good grief. Her face burned. Her ears burned. Could the ground just please open and swallow her now?

"Well, you did mention you were at her apartment," she reminded him, trying to explain why she'd thought what she had.

"At a party she threw for a co-worker." His eyes

danced with merriment. "Nothing nearly as exciting as what you were imagining."

"Too bad for you. Amy is a great catch." All true, but even as she said it she had to remind herself yet again that she was not interested in becoming involved, especially not with someone in the same profession as Neil. No way.

"I agree," Jack assured her. "Amy has been talking with my best friend for the past couple of weeks. Nothing would make me happier than if the two of them continue to hit it off."

Amy hadn't mentioned the best friend either. Had Taylor and her bestie really grown that far apart over the past few years? She'd been so wrapped up in trying to make her marriage work and ashamed of the situation in which she'd found herself that she'd not invested time into their friendship. Yet Amy had always been there any time Taylor had called, like when she'd finally filed for divorce.

Guilt hit her. She'd do better. Lots better. It had taken her the past year to build a foundation of who she was, who she wanted to be.

"So, nothing between the two of you?" she double-checked, just to be sure she'd understood correctly.

"Friendship."

"I'm sorry." She really was. Amy was the best person she knew and deserved the best of everything. Maybe Jack's friend would prove to be worthy.

"I'm not."

"Why's that?" Her gaze locked with his and her breath caught. His eyes sparkled like sunshine dancing across lake water.

"Let's just say—" he was looking at her as if she were the sweetest soda pop he'd ever wanted to taste "—I've been looking forward to meeting you."

Awareness filled Taylor. Awareness that had nothing to with anything except good old-fashioned girl meets boy. Good grief. Her body didn't seem to care about his taboo medical credentials and her ban against men.

Eek. Maybe she shouldn't have been quite so ecstatic about her libido's revival.

When Taylor's brow lifted, her expression cautious, Jack chided himself for his admission. If he wasn't careful, she was going to think he really was a stalker.

Was it considered stalking if her best friend had talked about her so much Jack had been looking forward to meeting her for weeks?

Longer.

She'd caught his eye years ago the first time he'd seen her photo. Something in her eyes, her smile had called to him. He'd been sad to learn she was married. When Amy had mentioned her divorced best friend was coming to work Rockin' Tyme, he'd been intrigued, wondering if the real deal would intrigue him as much as her photo.

She did.

Taylor Hall was a beautiful woman. Thick almost platinum blonde hair, golden brown eyes, pouty lips, and a body he had to force himself not to think about. She was easily one of the most beautiful women he'd ever seen, but it was something in her eyes that had snagged his attention years ago and refused to let go even now that he'd met her in person.

He suspected that although her outside packaging was beautiful, the real beauty was hidden away like a secret treasure.

Jack introduced her to the crew, all of whom were

friendly but really brightened when he told them she was Amy's friend.

"Shame Amy's not going to be here this year," one said, giving her hand a hearty shake.

"Sorry to hear about her grandmother," another commented.

Robert, a paramedic from a couple of counties away, grinned, stuck his hand out to Taylor, and eyed her in much the way Jack probably had.

"Tell me I'm the luckiest guy on the planet and you're single?"

Jack's gaze immediately shifted to Taylor's to see how she'd respond to the man's blatant flirting.

Eyes wide with surprise, she eyed him, then laughed softly. "I'm single."

Looking upwards, Robert made a thankful gesture.

"But not looking for a music festival hook-up, if that's what you mean by lucky."

"A pity," Robert said, eyeing her with a huge grin. "You and I could have had a lot of fun."

Jack liked the paramedic, but currently he wanted to throttle the guy. "Ignore Robert. The sun gets to him real quick and he talks out of his head."

Taylor laughed. "That explains a lot."

"Besides, certain staff interactions aren't encouraged."

Robert eyed Jack as if he'd grown an extra head, and no wonder. "Never heard of it being discouraged, not here."

There had been romances pop up between staff. Jack himself had met a few interesting women over the years that he'd enjoyed getting to know. But he didn't want Robert having the wrong idea about Taylor.

She was off limits.

Next thing you knew, Jack was going to be beating his chest and acting like a fool. Shaking his head, he chuckled. "Okay, Casanova, back off and let me introduce her to Duffy."

He and Duffy had worked numerous events together and he genuinely liked the fifty-something travel nurse who craved adventure almost as much as Jack.

"Duffy Reynolds is who you need to see if you have questions and I'm not around."

"Or you could ask me," Robert volunteered, earning a glare from Jack. "I'd be happy to help with any questions. Or to give a tour of the grounds."

Glancing toward Jack first, Taylor smiled at Duffy and ignored Robert's comment. "Nice to meet you."

Once he'd shown her their "twenty-bed" operation, he asked, "You checked out the stages?"

She shook her head. "When I arrived, I went straight to the main medical tent, registered, then came here."

"You camping?"

She nodded. "Amy and I had planned to tent together with maybe a trip to her place for showers and refreshing ourselves if the shower lines were too long. I'm camping solo now."

"Don't let Robert hear you say that or he'll offer to share his tent."

Her gaze lifted. "He was just teasing."

"Don't you believe it," Jack warned. "You so much as give him a smile and he's going to be all over you in hopes of a festival fling. If that's not what you want, steer clear."

"Noted."

Jack eyed her a moment, waiting for her to elaborate or say something further. "Is that what you want, Taylor?"

"A fling with Robert?" She shook her head. "I came to spend time with my best friend, not to have a fling."

"That'll make my job of keeping you safe easier."

"He's dangerous?"

Feeling guilty he'd given her that impression, Jack shook his head. "No. Just making sure I keep my promise to Amy to watch out for you. She wouldn't be happy if I let someone break your heart while you're here."

"There is that," she agreed, studying him. Smiling, Taylor's eyes narrowed. "Why do I get the feeling you're way more dangerous than Robert ever thought of being?"

He laughed. Yep, she was onto him.

"Come on, let's walk around the grounds before it gets too crowded. People will be pouring in over the next twenty-four hours as this party gets started."

Taylor had to admit she was impressed at the organization of the event. There were three main stages and several smaller ones. The five-night event offered everything from big-name pop stars to small-time local bands hoping to make it big someday. There were huge rows of food vendors and a shopping village made up of tents offering their wares. There was a comedy tent, a dance party tent, sponsored by a popular music television station, and a dozen more entertainment tents. Some tents were huge commercial numbers with electricity and some having generator-run air-conditioners even. And people. People were everywhere.

"It already looks crowded," she mused, taking in the multitude checking out their surroundings prior to the first show kicking off. "How many more are expected?"

"They're expecting about a hundred thousand attendees. By this time tomorrow night this place will be packed."

Taylor nodded. She'd expected most of the festival-goers to be college-aged kids. Most were, but there was a huge variety of ages represented, even some young parents with two or three kids in tow and some who appeared to be older than Taylor's parents.

"Most of what we'll see in the medical tent will be dehydration and intoxication, but there's always a mix of other things thrown in just to keep things interesting."

Taylor knew security screened for drugs, but that where there was a will there was a way. Amy had told about some of the patients they'd seen over the years. Unfortunately, there had been a few overdose deaths.

"From what Amy's told me, boredom shouldn't be an issue."

He laughed. "Boredom is what I hope for at these events."

Taylor glanced his way. "Oh?"

"Boredom means everyone is having fun with no worries."

"Ah." Glancing out over the happy, energetic crowd, she nodded. "Then that's what I'm going to hope for, too. Boredom."

But glancing toward the man walking beside her, who was telling her about the different tents and upcoming acts as they made their way over to the main medical tent, Taylor suspected boredom was the last word she'd be using to describe the next few days.

CHAPTER TWO

TAYLOR FROWNED AT the pile of poles and canvas, then went back to studying the instructions. She was a highly skilled ICU nurse. She could put together a tent. No problem.

Well, okay, some problem.

Mainly, that every time she put one pole end in the designated loop it would pop out when she tried to put in the other end. What she needed was—

"You need help with that?"

Taylor jumped, then looked up at Jack. She started to tell him she had it, because she would figure it out and hadn't she made great strides in not depending on a man for anything?

But common sense won out, so she smiled and said, "Um…yeah, I do. I've got a tarp down for a moisture barrier, got my tent all spread out like these say…" she waved the instructions "…but that end doesn't want to stay in that loop thingy when I put in the other side."

Jack's lips twitched. "The loop thingy?"

Before she could say more, he bent down, threaded the pole back into the end loop just as she had. But when he bowed the pole and hooked the other side, the pole behaved and didn't slip out on the other end.

"Well," she mused, putting her hands on her hips, "you made that look easy."

"It's all in how you handle the pole."

Taylor's cheeks heated and she ordered her mind to get out of the gutter.

"Um…yeah…well…" She hemmed and hawed, then brushed her palms down her shorts. "Thank you for your help."

"Anytime."

His grin was cocky as all get-out. "Anything else I can help with?"

"I feel guilty you had to help with that," she admitted. A strong independent woman should have been able to figure out how to put up a tent, right?

"Wasn't any trouble. I was on my way to my tent to grab a drink."

"Your tent?"

He gestured to the tent next to hers.

Next to hers. Seriously? The medical staff parking/camping area located behind the main medical tent wasn't that big. What were the odds?

He was offering help, but that hard-won independent streak refused to be silent. "Grab that drink and check on me in a few minutes, if that's okay."

"Be glad to." His eyes danced with what she could only describe as happiness. How could any one man radiate so much positivity?

Trying to ignore the fact that Jack was a tent away, that if she coughed, sneezed, or made any other weird noises, he'd hear, Taylor pulled the air mattress from its box and placed it inside the tent. She hit the battery-operated control button and was relieved when the unit blew up perfectly. Within minutes she had her bed made and her bag to one side. The tent was large enough that both she and Amy could have set up their air mattresses, so with just the one she had floor space.

"Everything going okay?" Jack asked when she climbed out of the tent.

"So far," she told the man sitting in a fold-up chair facing in her direction.

He held a refillable drink container and a protein bar. "You know it's killing me not helping, right?"

"White knight syndrome?"

He shrugged. "Momma taught me to be useful syndrome."

Taylor laughed. "Fine. You can help."

Immediately he rose, set his water bottle down on his much sturdier appearing table than the one she'd just pulled out of the back of her car.

"I take directions well."

Taylor arched her brow. "A man who takes directions well? I thought those were the things of unicorns and fairies."

He winked. "Try me and see."

Taylor gulped back the thoughts that ran through her mind. "Well, I've got to set up the canopy tent. Amy said to be sure to put it as close as possible so it would help shade my sleeping tent."

"Yep, otherwise your tent will be hot as Hades in the daytime."

She pulled out the canopy tent her friend had left in her living room along with the other camping items for Taylor to pick up on her way to the festival. "Let's see if we can figure this out."

The canopy tent was easier to set up, and not just because Jack was helping.

Well, maybe because he was helping. Certainly, it was more fun and had gone faster.

"What's next, ma'am?"

"The table?"

He lifted the folding table from where she'd propped it against her car and set it up beneath the canopy tent, which had been scooted partially over the entrance of the smaller tent she'd be sleeping in.

Holding up a lightweight tarp she'd pulled from a duffle bag that contained at least one more, Taylor said, "I found the tarp with the tent and used it as a moisture barrier per Amy's instructions, but was I supposed to do something with these?"

"Amy usually attaches them to the sides of the canopy to create shade and keeps one to put over her tent if the weather doesn't co-operate and it decides to flood."

Taylor wrinkled her nose. "If it decides to flood, I'll be sleeping in my car."

Jack laughed. "You wouldn't be the first person to do so. Just set an alarm so you don't overheat after the sun comes up. It gets too hot fast inside a vehicle." He took one of the tarps and began attaching it to the canopy. "With Amy canceling, I'm surprised you decided to camp rather than stay at her place."

Trying to mimic how he was hanging the tarp, Taylor began attaching a second tarp to another side. "She insisted that rather than go back to her place I stay here and enjoy my first music festival."

"Really?" He looked incredulous. "This is your first music festival?"

"Hard to believe I've been missing out on this all these years." Giving him a wry look, she spread her arms to indicate the festival just beyond the main medical area.

Together they worked to attach the third tarp, leaving the fourth side open. "Since this is your first music festival experience, I'll make sure it's a good one so you'll want to come back."

Butterflies danced in Taylor's belly. "Oh?"

"Since neither of us are on duty tonight, you want to watch the shows with me?"

Ha. Was this a trick question or what? Wander around by herself or sit next to a charismatic man who had awakened her dormant hormones? Hmm…hard decision.

It should have been a harder decision given his profession.

Still, she was smiling when she said, "I'd love to."

Taylor could get into music festivals. Or maybe it was the man beside her she was into. Glancing over at him, she couldn't help but think how fortunate she was to have him there this week since Amy hadn't been able to attend. Otherwise she might really have packed up and gone to Amy's.

Amy had texted earlier to make sure she'd arrived, and everything was okay. She'd not mentioned her unexpected reaction to Jack but had said everything was great.

Maybe if Jack were anything other than a doctor, she'd give in to the heat, let herself have a free pass life experience.

She wrapped her arms around her knees and looked back toward the stage where a band with a current chart-topping song had kicked off the festival an hour before and was still jamming out.

Around them others on blankets were watching the show and others danced along to the tunes, some dressed similar to Taylor's shorts and T-shirt, some in costumes, some in not much of anything at all.

"Having fun?"

She smiled at Jack and nodded.

"The band is awesome, isn't it?"

Again, she nodded. She didn't really follow any particular band, but did enjoy singing along with the radio from time to time. The band playing really was good.

When the group on the main stage finished, Jack turned to her. "You want to stay here until the next band, move to a different stage, or go find something to eat?"

Her stomach growled. "Eat?"

He packed up the blanket they'd been sitting on into a backpack that he slung over his right shoulder. "What are you hungry for?"

"What are my options?"

"Anything from burgers to a meat and three. There seems to be vendors who offer just about anything you can think of. Why don't we walk around for a while and see if anything catches your eye?"

"Or my nose," she added, taking a sniff of the air. Something sure smelled good.

He laughed. "Or that."

They ended up getting bowls of jambalaya from a Cajun food booth and standing at one of the chest-high tables set up near the row of vendors.

"This is good," she enthused, hoping she didn't have food on her face or between her teeth.

He'd already finished his. "Yep."

Feeling self-conscious under his watchful eye, she asked, "Are there any particular bands you're hoping to catch tonight?"

He named one she'd heard of but couldn't recall the

names of any of their songs. Sadly, she felt as if she'd been living under a rock since graduation. Before that, even.

She had been. She'd gone from toeing the line for her strict parents to toeing the line for Neil. She'd spent the last year learning to make decisions for herself, learning she didn't need to have anyone's directions or approval for the choices she made. If she messed up, so what? It was her life to live.

"That okay with you?"

She nodded. "Sounds good."

"If there are any particular shows you want to see, speak up and we'll go. I'm game for whatever."

"Duly noted." Game for whatever. He had no clue as to what ran through her mind at his innocent comment.

Or maybe, with the way his eyes danced, his comment hadn't been so innocent.

"How is it you've never been to a music festival?" He leaned across the table to stare into her eyes and, again, she wondered if perhaps he'd read her mind and knew more than she thought.

She shrugged. "Just not that lucky, I guess."

"I'm glad you're at this one."

"Me, too."

His grin shined brighter than the sparkly dance ball a few hundred yards away and Taylor really was glad she'd agreed to work the festival, that she'd gotten away from Louisville, and that she'd met Jack.

Because she was in charge of her life now, was making changes, reaching for new adventures, taking chances, had given herself permission to make mistakes as long as they were mistakes she'd chosen to make.

Her gaze connected with Jack's, her heart speeding

up as she wondered if she'd choose Jack as her next new adventure. If she could give herself permission to take a chance that he'd be her next mistake.

Because becoming involved with a man, any man, would be a mistake.

Becoming involved with Jack would be a big one. Colossal.

Taylor didn't sleep well that night. Not that her bed wasn't semi-comfortable. It had been. The night air wasn't nearly as sticky and hot as she'd expected either. The temperature had almost been cool.

What had kept her awake had been the noises around the festival. Obviously, she and Jack had been the only people in the entire place who had wanted to sleep. Then again, there weren't that many inside the event grounds who would be getting up at four a.m. to go to "work" either.

Donning a pair of khaki shorts and a T-shirt, she pulled her hair up into a ponytail, then slipped out of her tent.

Her gaze immediately went to Jack's tent. In the dim moonlight and lights coming from the festival, she could see he was up. He gave a little wave.

Taylor's stomach grumbled. Whatever Jack had going on his portable stove smelled a lot more mouth-watering than the breakfast bar with which she had planned to start her day.

"I made extra," he told her in a low whisper.

Although there was noise coming from beyond the other side of the main medical tent, the medical staff camping area itself was relatively quiet other than crickets chirping and the early morning crew slowly making their way out of their tents.

"Thanks," she mouthed, taking the plate. "Hey, this is good."

He grinned. "Did you think it would taste bad?"

She shook her head. "Smelled too good for that. Just wasn't expecting it to be amazing."

They finished up, cleaned up their mess, then headed to the main medical tent. When they got inside, they checked in, were given that day's mandatory medical staff T-shirt and would change each day. Guys changed T-shirts in the main area. Taylor fought—and lost—to keep her eyes from soaking up the rippling of Jack's muscles. As he pulled his T-shirt down over his six-pack, his gaze met hers and he grinned, as if he knew she'd been watching him and had liked what she'd seen.

"I, uh, need to put this on," she mumbled, turning to go to one of several enclosed areas in the tent where any private examinations would take place inside the main medical tent. She quickly stripped off her T-shirt and replaced it with the designated one.

She crammed her removed shirt into the backpack she'd brought with her and returned to where the others were waiting for a staff member to drive them to the medical tent.

When they arrived, Jack reached up to take Taylor's hand to assist her off the golf cart. It might have been before the crack of dawn, but that didn't stop the zings that shot up Taylor's arm at holding his hand. Zings shot and her heart kaboomed.

"Thank you," she murmured, cramming her fingers in her pocket the moment he let go. How was it possible to go from completely dead inside to so very aware? Had her body just saved years' worth of sexual nothingness and was unleashing it all at once?

And why, why, why, why couldn't he have been anything other than a doctor? To give in to Jack's smile would mean ignoring not only her man aversion but also her decision that never ever would she get involved with another doctor.

At the medical tent they switched with the night shift and took over the few cases currently being treated. Taylor reviewed a case of possible food poisoning and an intoxication patient. As the sun came up and the hours passed, the temperature soared. A steady trickle of people came in with various complaints.

Two young girls came into the tent. One asked for a bandage for her leg as she'd tripped and skinned her knee.

Taylor started to register the girl and do minor wound care, but Duffy waved her off. "I've got this one."

While Duffy was cleaning the girl's grazed leg, another two young women came in. One was almost completely supporting the other.

"She started passing out but never completely did, but she's talking out of her head, like she did something, you know, but she didn't do anything," the patient's friend gushed, not pausing for breath as Taylor helped them over to a vacant cot.

"I was flipping out," the woman continued. "I wasn't sure she was going to make it here and then what was I going to do?"

"I'm just really hot," the barely coherent patient said, her hand on her temple. "And my head hurts."

"Name?"

"Cindy Frazier," the friend answered. "We're nineteen. I'm Lori. We're from Maine."

Maine? That was a long way to travel for a music festival, Taylor thought as she got Cindy registered.

Taylor ran a thermometer over her forehead.

Eek. One hundred and five degrees Fahrenheit.

She glanced around to see who was free and could grab an ice pack. Everyone was with someone except Jack.

"Dr. Morgan?"

Odd to call him that when in her head he was Jack. He glanced up from his clipboard, his blue gaze meeting hers.

"I have a hyperthermia case. Temp is one-oh-five. Can you grab an ice pack and ice water, please, while I finish checking vitals?" She supposed she should have offered to get them and let him take over with the patient, but Jack didn't balk, just rushed to get the needed supplies.

Cindy moaned and clutched at her stomach.

"Are you feeling nauseous?"

Eyes squished closed, she nodded. "I may throw up."

Jack stepped up, handed Taylor the items she'd requested. "I'll get an emesis pan and anti-emetic."

Taylor wrapped the ice pack collar around the girl's neck.

"That's cold!" she complained, shivering.

"We have to cool you down. You got too hot and you're dehydrated, that's why you're feeling so bad."

Jack was back, and handed the plastic pan to the girl. He bent to shine a penlight into Cindy's eyes, then her nose and mouth. He listened to her heart and lung sounds.

"She's tachycardic."

Taylor opened the bottle top then handed the girl the

iced water. "I want you to get as much fluid in you as you can."

"I'll throw it up."

"Maybe not, but if you do, use the pan if you can. Just drink." She glanced at Jack. "You okay with me starting the cold IV fluid and putting the anti-emetic in?"

"You took the words out of my mouth."

She checked the girl's veins and frowned. Dehydrated, Cindy's veins were poor at best. Still, Taylor had always prided herself on being good at accessing veins and hopefully would hit her mark the first try, despite not having much to work with.

Gathering her supplies, Taylor then cleaned her IV site with an alcohol pad while Jack finished examining Cindy, including rechecking her temperature.

"Still one-oh-five."

"Is that bad?" Lori asked, wringing her hands as she watched them work on her friend.

"It hasn't gone up, so that's a good thing," Taylor assured her, breathing a sigh of relief when the IV catheter slid into Cindy's vein perfectly. "Once we get these cold fluids in, her temp should drop."

If not, they'd put her in the ice tub.

"I feel like I can't breathe," Cindy gasped, putting her hand to her chest.

"It's going to be okay, Cindy." Jack sounded calm as he continued to assess the girl, watching her closely. "Just take slow, deep breaths."

Cindy visibly took a deep breath.

As Taylor taped the IV line to Cindy's left hand, she fought breathing deeply herself as Jack's voice was so hypnotic.

"Your temperature will start dropping any minute,"

Jack assured their patient. "Once that happens, you'll slowly start feeling better."

Jack's soothing voice made Taylor feel better as she grabbed the anti-emetic to go into the IV. Lots better. How could he be so calm when the girl's situation really could turn dire if what they were doing didn't work?

"I'm scared," Cindy admitted, bursting into tears, which caused her friend to also burst into tears.

"Look at me, Cindy."

The young woman lifted her tearful gaze to Jack's. He took her hand in his and gave it a squeeze. "It's okay. You're okay. We're doing all the right things to get your temperature down and we'll keep you here until you're feeling okay. You're going to be fine."

"Phew," Lori sighed in relief, sniffling as she plopped down onto an empty cot next to Cindy's. "She's not the only one who's scared. I've heard about people dying at music events but never thought about it possibly happening to someone I knew. She had me terrified when she started blacking out."

Taylor leaned forward to inject the medication, but before she could administer it, Cindy's body tensed. Taylor grabbed for the emesis pan, but lightning fast Jack had it to the woman's mouth, making it just in time.

"Oh, no," her friend groaned as Cindy heaved her stomach contents into the pan. "This is bad. I know it is."

"It's not uncommon for someone with hyperthermia to throw up." Taylor injected the anti-emetic into the IV solution. "The nausea should calm down soon, too."

Fortunately, it did.

Due to the degree of Cindy's hyperthermia, Taylor stayed with her, closely monitoring her vitals over the next thirty minutes.

Jack came and went as he checked other patients who'd come in for care. Most were minor issues, thank goodness.

As Taylor checked Cindy's temperature yet again, Jack walked up behind her.

"What is her temp now?"

"Ninety-nine."

"That's awesome," Jack praised, placing his hand on Taylor's shoulder. "Almost back to normal."

Relieved at how Cindy was responding to their treatment and wondering at how her own temperature had just spiked at Jack's innocent touch, Taylor nodded.

He gave her shoulder a squeeze before his hand fell away.

Gracious. Had he felt it, too? The sparks that flew when they touched? Or was she just crazy and imagining things in the midst of patient care?

Cindy finished off her water.

Reaching to take the bottle, Taylor gave a thumbs-up. "Want another?"

Although her color and disposition had greatly improved, the girl still looked weak. "Will it help me get back to normal quicker?"

"You may not feel yourself for a few days but, yes, hydrating well is vital," Jack answered, then listened to Cindy's chest again. When he removed his stethoscope from his ears, he grinned. "Heart rate is down to eighty-eight."

"Is that good?" Lori asked. To give the girl credit, she'd stayed by her friend's side, encouraging her to drink more water and holding her hand during the times Cindy got overly emotional.

Taylor chatted with Cindy for a few minutes, then left

her to rest on the cot with Lori watching over her so she could help with other patients now that Cindy was stable.

"Great job there," Jack praised when she joined him at a triage table, where he was attending to a new patient.

"Thanks. I'll take this one from here so you can check on the other patients," she offered, knowing the tent was hopping with patients who probably needed his attention.

Their gazes met. Taylor's belly flip-flopped.

Jack rose from where he sat. "Thanks."

The new patient looked worn out, hot and couldn't give any specific symptoms, just that she felt exhausted. Taylor took her information, checked her vitals—all of which were normal—then put her on a cot and went to get her water.

When she got back, the girl was sound asleep.

"Well, okay, then," she said, picking up the clipboard with the girl's information and making a note.

"We'll have some who do that." Jack walked up beside her to watch the girl sleep. "They'll come to medical just to take a break from the hyper-stimulation and to cool down."

"It's a whole different world from anything I've ever known," Taylor admitted.

"Just wait until we watch the shows tonight. Last night will seem tame."

She shot a curious look his way. He planned on them going to watch the shows together again?

"The costumes, the people, the vibe in the air." His excitement came through, creating its own vibe. "Tonight people will have found their bearings and will be more relaxed. There will be more booze, drugs, sex, more everything."

More. Her cheeks heated. "Oh."

"No worries. Most are here to have a good time. We're here to make sure they do it without any lasting problems."

His grin was so infectious Taylor's breath caught.

Apparently, it didn't matter that Jack was a doctor and she'd sworn the profession and men off forever.

Now that her body had remembered it was young, healthy, full of hormones, it refused to be ignored.

Not only refused to be ignored but demanded attention. Jack's attention.

Why not? an inner voice asked. It wasn't as if anything that happened this week would go beyond the music festival.

Maybe she could—should—forget an outside world existed and just go with the flow. Wasn't that what she was trying to do? Step outside her comfort zone?

Jack Morgan was way outside her comfort zone and would be one humdinger of a life experience.

CHAPTER THREE

BATHING HAD NEVER felt so good.

Taylor had had to wait in line over half an hour to get into the shower, but the wait had been worth it. To have washed the dust from her hair and put on clean clothes felt amazing.

When she went back to the medical camping ground, Jack, Duffy, Robert and a few others were playing guitars in front of Jack's tent. Duffy was singing a country song about wild women and drinking too much.

Taylor grabbed her chair and joined the group. Listening to their song, she brushed out her hair, then braided it into a French braid, twisting a band around the end. When she'd finished, her gaze collided with Jack's.

He'd been watching her. With more than casual interest.

Then again, there was nothing casual about the sparks that had flown between them all day.

He winked and, heart kerthunking, she winked back.

Something she'd never done. Her ex hadn't been the kind of man one winked at. Neil hadn't been playful or fun. Ever.

Jack was playful and fun.

At some point he'd gotten a shower, too. He looked

refreshed in his navy shorts and T-shirt while he plucked the strings of a rather beat-up, well-loved-appearing guitar, keeping perfect tune with the others.

Having no musical talent, Taylor was impressed.

She was even more impressed when Duffy's song ended and they started playing another. This time Jack did the vocals. His voice was a raspy baritone that reached inside and tugged at her very being.

The man had a beautiful, unique timbre.

A beautiful, unique everything.

She wanted to close her eyes and just listen to his voice, but her eyes refused to be denied the privilege of feasting on the image of him strumming along on his guitar while he sang.

When the song ended, Taylor clapped and gave a self-conscious whistle. Another first. This stepping outside one's comfort zone thing wasn't so bad.

Actually, it was kind of fun.

"I think you have a groupie," Duffy teased.

"Never had a groupie before," Jack mused, his smile aimed at Taylor. "But we are at a music festival, so I'm game."

"Can't say I've ever been a groupie," Taylor admitted, knowing her cheeks were pink but that a silly smile was on her face. "Maybe I'll settle for being an avid fan, rather than a full-fledged groupie."

"Far less fun. Stick with the groupie," Robert suggested, gathering a few laughs.

"Avid fan is more my speed," Taylor admitted, feeling a little self-conscious that all the men's attention was now on her rather than their music. "Don't stop playing on my account. I was enjoying listening."

"You play?" Duffy asked, offering her his guitar.

She shook her head. Maybe she'd add guitar lessons to the growing list of things she'd tried since her divorce. So far she'd taken art classes, cooking classes, exercise classes, and was taking a foreign language course online. Not necessarily to expand her horizons but to figure out things she liked and enjoyed rather than be an extension of her parents, then Neil.

"You sing?" Robert asked.

She gave him a dubious look. "Not if I want to keep any of you as friends."

A few chuckles sounded.

"We're not a picky crowd, so feel free to join in at any time. The more the merrier."

Duffy launched into another song, but Taylor didn't know the words so joining in wasn't an option even if she'd wanted to give it a try.

After a few more songs Robert stood, stretched, and announced he had plans to meet a cute little nurse who was working in the main medical tent. The others left one by one, leaving Taylor and Jack.

"Do you really not play or sing or you just didn't want to show up us guys?"

"Ha," Taylor snorted. "Believe me when I say I did you a favor by keeping my mouth shut."

Jack's gaze dropped to her lips. "A shame. I'm positive I'd enjoy hearing you sing."

"You only say that because you've not heard me do so," she assured him, thinking she'd never be comfortable enough to sing in public.

"You don't sing, you don't play music, and this is your first music festival." His gaze searched hers. "What do you do in your free time, Taylor?"

Good question. One that two years ago she'd have

answered with do everything she could to keep her husband happy, spend all her time trying to somehow be good enough so that perhaps their failing marriage would morph into what she'd once dreamed it would be. A year ago she'd have answered with cry and try not to dwell on the mess she'd made by not really knowing the man she'd married in a whirlwind while thinking she was the luckiest girl alive that a handsome plastic surgeon wanted to marry a plain Jane like her.

Thank goodness she'd never given in to his wanting her to not work but stay home. As his wife, she'd gone part time, but had kept working. The ICU, her patients had been her solace. Other than her work, she'd had no life, no being Taylor, just Mrs. Dr. Neil Norris.

"I run." One of the habits she'd picked up immediately following her divorce.

"Competitively?"

She snickered. "Hardly. I run for me, to relieve stress, for exercise, to clear my head."

She'd started on a whim of wanting to be healthy but running had quickly become her therapy. She spent the time working through the past, how it had molded her, how she was determined to break those molds and forge herself into a person she liked. Neither her indifferent parents nor Neil got the final say on who she was.

"So you work, sleep and run." Jack frowned. "Not a very exciting life you're describing, Taylor. Surely there's more?"

"I never claimed I led an exciting life." She crossed her arms as she stared back.

"What else, Taylor?" he pushed.

Glancing down at the green grass beneath her tennis

shoes, she shrugged. "I have all the usual hobbies people have." She did. Now. "I sculpt."

She'd signed up for the sculpting class after seeing an ad she'd come across on social media but had loved it from the first moment she'd felt the clay between her fingers.

Jack's brow lifted. "As in statues of naked men?"

Taylor rolled her eyes. "That's such a guy question."

His lips twitched. "But is it true?"

"A couple of times," she admitted, her face warm and getting warmer at how his eyes twinkled.

"In the name of art, right?" he teased.

Smiling, Taylor didn't bother to explain she'd been oblivious to the men who'd posed during her art class. She could barely recall what they'd looked like. What she'd enjoyed had been the feel of the clay beneath her fingers as she'd taken nothing and transformed it into something.

Much as she'd done with her life.

Nothing to something.

"I'd like to see some of your work."

Unless he saw the piece she'd brought to give to Amy, it was unlikely. Until recently, she hadn't wanted anyone to see her work as too much of her was caught up in it.

"Or if you got the urge to work while here and needed inspiration…" His tone teased.

Yeah, had Jack been the model, she seriously doubted she'd have been oblivious. Looking at the man was like looking at the most interesting piece of artwork she'd ever encountered, beautiful, intriguing, and full of character.

Meeting his gaze and feigning excitement, she

couldn't resist saying, "You really think Robert would do that for me?"

Jack laughed. "I'm sure you could convince him."

"I don't know," she said, trying to sound unsure. "There's that nurse he was meeting when he took off earlier."

"There is that." Jack's gaze stayed locked with hers, both of them smiling, Taylor feeling really good on the inside.

This, she thought. This was fun. Light and held no real meaning. Just a man, a woman, and good old-fashioned physical chemistry.

Was the new Taylor the real Taylor, okay with starting something with Jack—a doctor, for goodness' sake!—when she knew they'd go their separate ways when the music festival ended because she didn't want a relationship? Not that she suspected he did either, just that she didn't want a man in her life. She had too many things to still learn about herself.

"Hungry?"

Starved, and not for food. She wanted what she saw in his eyes, in what being near him hinted at within her body.

Did that mean she was okay with a meaningless fling?

Or maybe she just wanted to learn what Jack could teach her about herself?

He propped his guitar against his chair and stood. "I have sandwich stuff. You want to eat with me or grab something from a vendor?"

"You don't have to feed me." Was she talking food or sex? Or both? "I brought food."

His lips twitched. "Something more exciting than ham and cheese?"

"Does such a thing exist?" she asked with feigned seriousness, eliciting a laugh.

While he pulled out his sandwich supplies from his cooler, Taylor dug through her supplies to find a plastic container of cookies she'd made, thinking she and Amy would gobble them up.

When she set them on his table, he stopped what he was doing and helped himself to one.

"Hey, these are good."

He sounded so surprised that Taylor laughed.

"You didn't mention anything about being a good cook," he accused.

"I'm not, but I can bake cookies."

During her classes, she'd discovered she found cooking so-so but enjoyed baking. She'd mastered basic skills but had thrown herself into spending more time at her sculpting class.

"They're good," he repeated, reaching for another.

She slapped at his hand. "Didn't your mother make you wait until after dinner before having dessert?"

His gaze lifted to hers and, grinning, he shook his head. "My mom would have been the first to encourage me to have the good stuff first because life is short."

Taylor's brow rose. Wow. "Sounds fun."

And very unlike her older parents who hadn't planned to have children, hadn't wanted them, but had been stuck with her all the same.

"But not very nutritious," Jack added wryly.

"There is that."

Jack spread a blanket on the ground a good distance back from the stage. He and Taylor could have made their way closer, but closer to the stage meant more crowded. No way could they have seen from their sitting positions.

Taylor's arms were wrapped around her knees and she was watching the band as if they were the most fascinating group she'd ever seen. Her head bobbed ever so slightly to the beat.

"Our little jam session may fail to impress you now that you've seen this."

She glanced toward him. "Not likely. You were good."

"Glad you thought so."

Still looking his way, she asked, "Did you ever want to play music professionally?"

He chuckled. "Probably the same as every other kid who played an instrument dreams of being a rock star. But if you mean was I ever in a band then, yeah, a few over the years."

"What happened?"

"I wasn't that good, and I fell in love with medicine."

Her expression became thoughtful. "A musician or a physician. Interesting choices."

"Maybe if I'd been better at the music there wouldn't have been a choice." He shrugged. "Once I was exposed to medicine, there wasn't a choice. I knew that's what I was supposed to do."

Not once had he ever regretted that decision. Sometimes life threw things at you to point you in the right direction. In his case, life had hit him over the head—heart—to steer him down the right path.

"I'm glad you get to play from time to time and have both in your life."

Ready to shove the past back as far away as it would go, he took a drink. "I enjoy life."

A true statement. He'd dealt with what had happened

years ago to Courtney and had spent years making atonement. It was all he could do.

"Not many people can say that," Taylor mused, her voice sounding almost wistful.

He turned toward her. "Can you?"

She took a long time answering, but finally nodded. "I am enjoying life very much. Thank you."

The emotion in her voice, almost surprise, at her answer did funny things to Jack's chest.

He reached over, took her hand into his and gave a reassuring squeeze. "I'm glad you're enjoying life, Taylor."

He was also glad that rather than pull her hand away, she laced her fingers with his and shot a grateful smile toward him. As if maybe she'd meant right now, this very moment, was what had made her say she was enjoying life.

That he played a role in her happiness.

A humbling thought.

There was something fragile about Taylor. Something that brought out a protectiveness that left him feeling a bit lost.

In the past, if he'd felt an attraction to a woman and that attraction was reciprocated, he'd acted without hesitation. Lord knew, he was no saint. Far, far from it.

Taylor felt an attraction to him. He was sure of it. Although there was a hesitation on her face at times, she hadn't really tried to hide her interest. But there was a vulnerability in her eyes that had him second-guessing himself. He didn't do vulnerable in his personal relationships and sure didn't want to feel protective of someone he was destined to walk away from.

Still, what he wanted to do was lean over and kiss Taylor. They wouldn't be the only couple at the concert making out. Kissing would be tame compared to some of the amorous sessions that happened around the festival.

But most of those making-out sessions were just chemistry playing out between young, healthy couples.

Just?

What was it he thought was between Taylor and him should he kiss her, if not *just* chemistry?

He didn't do relationships that weren't just physical chemistry. Not ever.

Well, once, but never again.

CHAPTER FOUR

IT HAD BEEN a long time since Taylor had been on a date.

Years.

The last dates she'd been on had been with Neil.

Neil, who had been perfectly put together, clothes always perfectly arrayed and wrinkle free, appearance always perfectly groomed, hair always perfectly styled.

Neil, who had always taken her to the nicest restaurants, to premier shows in Louisville, to only the best of the best. Taylor had taken that to be a sign of him trying to impress her. In reality, it had only been Neil being Neil and wanting to show off his possessions to the world. He thought *he* deserved the best of the best, that the entire world revolved around him.

She'd been the envy of her fellow nursing students because the hospital's most eligible bachelor was besotted with her, bought her clothes and jewelry to wear to events with him. If only they'd known the only person Neil had been besotted with was himself.

She still wasn't sure what had attracted Neil to her. He'd wanted to change everything about her. Maybe he'd wanted a doll to bend and shape into what he wanted her to be. She'd played that role well for her parents. Letting him take over had been easy. When he'd decided she was who he'd wanted for a wife, she'd thought she was the luckiest girl alive. Plain her the wife of a renowned plastic surgeon who wanted to give her things and show her off to the world.

They'd been the envy of all their friends—Neil's true purpose.

To Neil, she'd been a possession. A piece added to his collection to be seen and not heard. Had she not caught him cheating, she might still be in her oblivious bubble of living her life on eggshells.

"Whatever you're thinking, stop."

Taylor glanced toward the man next to her. A man who was wearing shorts and a T-shirt, and whose pulled-back long hair was unkempt in a sexy sort of way—a man who had a shadow on his face where he needed to shave, and whose blue eyes were fringed with thick, dark lashes.

A man who made her stomach flip-flop. Jack seemed comfortable with who he was and didn't need to impress anyone.

Which felt like a breath of fresh air.

"Deal," she agreed, inhaling deeply, determined she would push thoughts of Neil far from her mind. These days, she rarely thought of him, but meeting Jack seemed to have triggered a plethora of comparisons.

"Good." Jack studied her. "I was beginning to think I was going to have to visit medical for crush injuries. Quite a grip you have there."

Relaxing her hold, Taylor glanced at where their fingers were interlaced. She liked his hands. Strong, capable, clean but not professionally manicured and softer than hers. Had she been clamping down or holding on for dear life?

She glanced back up. "Sorry."

Eyes locked with hers, he lifted her hand to his lips and pressed a kiss against her fingers. "You're forgiven."

Taylor's stomach bypassed flip-flops and went into full out Olympian gymnast gold medal mode. Wow. If she'd thought his touch caused zings, his lips were powerhouses.

"That was easy," she pointed out, wondering why she was tempting fate. "Not making me beg for forgiveness?"

Neil would have made her grovel.

Ugh. She didn't want to keep comparing Jack to Neil, but perhaps it was inevitable.

Jack's eyes were locked with hers, his expression serious, his hand warm around hers. "Forgiveness isn't on the list of things I want you to ever beg me for."

Taylor's insides quivered. She swallowed the lump in her throat and turned back toward the stage and pretended to watch the band.

All her brain could process was that Jack had kissed her fingers, had implied he'd like her to beg him for... for what?

Sex.

If she was willing, he wouldn't make her beg.

Heaviness plagued her chest, making breathing difficult.

She'd been over-the-moon giddy that her body wanted him, but the reality was she'd only had sex with one man and she'd been married to him.

Maybe that's why Neil had married her.

Because she'd refused to sleep with him, saying she was saving herself for marriage. His ego had liked it that he'd been the only man she'd been with. Or maybe it was the challenge of possessing what he'd been denied.

"What's his name?"

"Who?" she asked, glancing toward Jack.

"The man you keep thinking about."

She winced. Obviously, she sucked at hiding her emotions. "I'm sorry."

"Your thoughts aren't good ones."

She glanced down at their hands. "Was I squeezing your fingers again? Sorry." She lifted her gaze to his. "I'd never intentionally hurt you."

He gave her hand a gentle squeeze. "Despite the fact we just met, I know that about you."

"How?" she asked, her voice catching in her throat and coming out hoarse.

"The same way you know I'd never intentionally hurt you."

She nodded. Which was crazy. She didn't know him, and you'd think she knew better than to ever trust a man again.

Perhaps it was because he was Amy's friend, but she believed the cause ran deeper.

Restlessness overtook her and she needed to move.

"Can we walk for a bit?" She stood, brushed off her shorts. "I need to move."

As the band was still playing, surprise darkened the blue of his eyes. "Then we'll move."

He shook out their blanket, put it in his backpack, and took her hand back into his. They walked in silence, making their way through the crowd. When they reached the fence along one edge of the festival grounds they turned and made their way back toward the stages. The show they'd been watching had finished and the crowd was thinning to head to one of the smaller stages.

"Sorry I made you miss the last of the show."

"Not a problem. I'd rather have been with you."

"Yeah, right," she snorted.

"Really."

She glanced toward him, saw genuine concern on his face. "Thank you."

"For?"

"Being so nice."

One corner of his mouth tugged upward, digging a dimple into his cheek. "Well, I did promise Amy to take care of you and make sure you had a good time."

Taylor stopped walking. "Is that what this is?"

"This?" He looked confused.

She lifted their raised hands.

An odd noise, almost a snort, came from deep in his throat. "Amy is a good friend, but I wouldn't become romantically involved with someone for her sake."

He shook his head as if to clear the very idea from his mind.

Taylor arched her brow. "Romantically involved?"

A repentant sort of grin on his face, he shrugged. "I guess that was presumptuous."

"Is that what's happening here?" she pressed, needing to hear him verbally confirm what was happening. "Us becoming romantically involved?"

He searched her gaze. "You tell me. Is that what you want?"

Refusing to look away, she held his gaze, determined to make sure he understood who her core being was. "I don't sleep around."

Sex, or even thinking about sex, just hadn't been an issue until she'd met Jack. She'd not really thought about or tried to figure out what she, the Taylor she was morphing into, wanted regarding a sex life because she'd thought she wouldn't have to deal with that until way into the future.

"Good," he said. "Neither do I."

"No, I mean I really don't." She paused, tried to figure out how to explain, feeling it imperative she make him understand. "It makes me old-fashioned, but the only person I've been with is my husband."

At Jack's look of surprise, she corrected, "My *ex*-husband."

His expression softened. "That you haven't slept around isn't a negative in my book, Taylor."

"But you wouldn't be opposed to us having sex?"

One side of his mouth hiked up, revealing a gorgeous dimple. "Is that a trick question?"

His response shouldn't annoy her, but for some reason it did. She pulled her hand free. "I want an honest answer, Jack."

"I gave you one." His expression grew serious. "Besides, you knew the answer when you asked."

"How would I know?"

"You knew the moment you walked into the medical tent and our gazes met," he pointed out. "I instantly felt a connection and you felt it, too. If I'm mistaken, tell me."

Taylor couldn't believe they were having this conversation in the middle of a crowd. They'd stopped walking. People thronged all around them, yet no one was paying them the slightest attention.

"You aren't wrong," she admitted.

He gave a low laugh. "Is that easier than saying you want me, too?"

"Even if I did, it doesn't mean we're going to act on

those feelings," she pointed out, even though she wondered if that's exactly what that meant. "I don't do that."

He didn't look upset at her answer, just asked, "Why not?"

Stunned, Taylor stared. "What do you mean?"

"Why don't you have sex?" he clarified.

Her face caught fire. She couldn't believe they were discussing her sex life—her lack of a sex life. "Because…"

"How long have you been divorced, Taylor?"

She'd told him the only man she'd been with was her ex-husband, but something in his voice, his eyes said he knew more than what she'd revealed about her past. What had Amy told him? That Taylor had screwed up her life by marrying a man who had been all shiny surface and no depth? That she was lonely and desperate?

She wasn't. This past year had been about healing, finding Taylor, not about replacing Neil. She didn't want to replace Neil. Not when she'd finally started discovering who she was and liking the woman emerging. The adult Taylor who didn't have to abide by her parents' heavy hand or be under her ex-husband's critical thumb.

She'd fight to protect that Taylor, would go to great lengths to keep any man from changing who was emerging from the dark cocoon she'd been encased in her whole life.

"A little over a year."

"And you've not had sex during the past year? Not even a rebound fling?"

She'd only thought she'd felt hot before. Now she burned so brightly she was surprised everyone wasn't whipping out their sunglasses to protect their eyes.

"You don't have to answer. I can see it on your face.

So again I'll ask, why haven't you had sex since your divorce? Are you still in love with him?"

"No." Unable to stand still, she took off walking, again, making her way through the throng of music lovers.

"Then why choose to be celibate?" Jack asked from beside her, obviously determined to finish their conversation.

"Not everyone has to go around having sex all the time, you know." She glanced his way.

His brow arched. "Is that what you think I do?"

"I don't know what you do. I just met you. Maybe you have a fling during every one of these music festivals and I'm just this festival's chosen partner."

"I haven't."

Why did his answer make her heart beat more wildly? Why did their conversation feel so important?

She tilted her chin higher. "But you have had flings?"

"Have I had mutually consensual and satisfying sex during a music festival?" Staring intently into her eyes, he nodded. "Yes. More than once. Is that what you want to hear, Taylor? That I have had a healthy, enjoyable sex life? Does my admission make me less in your eyes?"

Taylor realized they'd reached the other end of the festival grounds and were near the medical tent and the Oasis. The haven was practically deserted. Letting go of his hand, she took off running towards the Oasis and dropped down onto the sand.

The Oasis had called to her like some mystical mirage offering what she needed. For all her pushing, Jack hadn't raised his voice or seemed mad, more intent on pressing her to find answers within herself. As if he realized she needed those answers more than he did.

He didn't run after her but, hands in his shorts pockets, he strolled towards her, whistling a tune that sounded similar to one of the songs they'd listened to the band play earlier.

When he reached her, he didn't say anything, just sat down in the sand beside her, staring out toward the closest stage, and patiently waited for her to say something.

It was a long time before she found words. She marveled that he sat silently with her, giving her the time and space to get her thoughts together.

"One of the reasons I've not had sex in the past year is that I haven't *wanted* to have sex." She took a deep breath. "Not even a hint of wanting to touch or have sex." She exhaled. "Not until now." Another deep inhalation and exhalation because she might pass out if she didn't force herself to breathe. "You're the first person I've wanted to have sex with since my divorce, and I want you. A lot. I find that exciting and terrifying."

There. She'd said the words out loud. Let him think what he may.

"Is it wrong if I say I'm honored?"

His voice sounded so cocky and his eyes danced with such wicked pleasure that Taylor's hackles rose.

"Don't patronize me, Jack Morgan."

His eyes remaining locked with hers, he lifted her chin to make her look into his eyes.

"I want you, Taylor. A lot. More than a lot." The colored lights providing a soft glow around the oasis glittered in his eyes. "Hearing you say you want me too doesn't generate a single patronizing thought."

Staring into his eyes, seeing so much emotion reflected there, Taylor swallowed. "What does it do?"

"Makes me want to kiss you even more than I already did."

Jack wanted to kiss her.

She'd known that.

Still, his words thrilled her, made her want to jump up and down and dance around the sandpit like a giddy schoolgirl.

His words also made her want to take off running again. As far as her feet would take her because Lord help her at the things his admission did to her insides.

"We just met yesterday," she reminded herself as much as him.

His gaze held hers. "I haven't forgotten."

Her heart slammed against her ribcage so hard that surely he felt the impact of each beat. "It's too soon."

His thumb stroked across her jawline. "I know."

But even as the words left his mouth she leaned over and brushed her lips against his.

Oh, heaven. His lips were soft.

And *electric.*

It was barely more than a peck before she pulled back, searched his eyes, making sure the pounding inside her body wasn't deafening him.

It was deafening her.

Had he felt the same pleasure at the touch?

His held fell away from her face and he started to say something, but rather than let him she pressed her mouth against his again. This time she deepened the kiss and kept her eyes locked with his in the faint glow of the colored lights.

Those lights must be why a brilliant kaleidoscope flashed through her mind.

His lips were warm, undemanding, and yet nothing had ever demanded so much from her.

The kiss drew out every nerve ending, reached every

cell, refused to let any part of her be passive. Everything about him necessitated action.

He wasn't touching her anywhere except her lips, yet every part of her felt him. His eyes darkened to depths she wanted to topple into and drown within.

She knew she could push him away, could stand up and walk away, could tell him to stop at any point she wanted this to end, and he'd let her. She had entire control and the knowledge, the surety emboldened her to not do any of those things.

Instead, she got lost in the inky blueness that stared back, in the perfect pressure of his mouth against hers, tasting, caressing, tempting.

Jack wanted to kiss her.

He was kissing her.

She kissed him, not regretting that she'd leaned over and started this, but embracing this newly found freedom just as she'd embraced her body's initial reaction to him.

Jack made her come to life, awakening new and exciting parts of her she hadn't known existed.

Her heart raced, thundering like a stampeding herd. Her lungs struggled to get oxygen to her brain. She gave in to the escalating excitement at her core and kissed Jack with hunger.

With certainty.

Never had she felt so starved for what his lips gave.

Never had she felt the heat mounting inside her and pushing upward and outward.

Time faded. She had no idea how long they kissed, just that every breath she took was his, every sensation inside her started and ended with Jack.

Sweet, heavenly, laidback Jack who didn't mind giving her control of their kiss.

A group of teens came running onto the sand near them. Taylor pulled back.

Breathless, she stared at Jack in awe.

He grinned.

Amazed at the relief, the happiness that flooded her at his smile, she grinned back.

So that was what a first kiss should feel like.

Amazing and worthy of shooting stars and firework displays.

Jack made her feel good inside, made her feel alive, made her feel as if she was a whole woman, as if she knew exactly who she was and what she wanted from life.

She wanted to wrap her arms around herself and give herself a hug.

And maybe a high-five, too, that she'd kissed him and it had been perfect.

Holding hands, she and Jack went back to the main stage, spread their blanket, and watched the next act as if nothing monumental had happened between them. When the show finished they made their way to the medical staff camping area.

Taylor's heart kerthunked with each step they took into the campground, with each campsite they passed, drawing them nearer and nearer to theirs.

When they stood outside her tent, they paused, looked at each other, a thousand questions bouncing between them.

Jack's gaze glittered. "'Night, Taylor."

Disappointment hit that he wasn't planning to spend the night inside her tent.

She wanted him inside her tent.

Inside her. She wanted to loosen his hair from its

band and run her fingers through his silky locks. She wanted so much.

So much it stunned her.

"'Night, Jack," she whispered back.

A smile still on his face, he winked, then closed the distance to his tent.

Taylor watched as he unzipped the flap, glanced her way one last time, then disappeared.

Part of her wanted to throw caution to the wind and follow him, but another part wasn't willing to risk ruining the best night she'd had in a long, long time.

Maybe ever.

CHAPTER FIVE

JACK'S GAZE DRIFTED to Taylor yet again. It was early morning. The sun was just starting to rise over the hundred-acre Tennessee farm where the festival took place each year. Soon they'd wake a few who had spent the night in the medical tent, not due to any emergency but who'd partied too much and had needed to sleep it off.

Jack never minded that. Part of their job was to provide a safe place for festival goers.

Like the young woman whom Taylor was currently settling into the cot. A couple of friends had dropped her off, saying she wasn't acting right. Most of the patients they saw weren't in any real danger, but there were always those few.

"Busy morning," Taylor mused as she handed him the clipboard with her notes.

Skimming what she'd written, he nodded. "Each night of the festival brings a few more than the night before as the heat, booze, and lack of sleep kick in."

"Guess it's a good thing we're off tomorrow, eh?" she teased.

"Are you planning to stay at the festival tonight or go back to Amy's apartment?"

The surprise in her eyes said she hadn't thought about leaving the festival.

"What am I asking? This is your first music festival. Of course you're staying. Awesome bands are scheduled for tonight."

"Um…right." She smiled. "You know me and music so you may have to point them out."

His lips twitched. "That mean you want to hang with me tonight?"

"Yes." Relief shone in her big brown eyes. "Would that be okay?"

He grinned. "I'd say it'd be pretty amazing."

Her eyes brightened, and she smiled at him as if he'd just told her she'd won the lottery.

Refocusing his mind on the fact he still had a whole lot of hours to get through on today's shift, he glanced over again at the clipboard she'd handed him. Looked pretty run of the mill.

"Anything I need to know about our latest?"

Taylor shook her head. "She'll likely be fine in a few hours. Duffy is talking with her now to see if she knows what she took. During triage, she told me she didn't take anything, but he has a way of getting the truth."

Jack nodded. He'd seen Duffy work his magic firsthand. Unfortunately, there were times when a person didn't know they'd been slipped something, or they simply didn't know what they'd taken and no amount of talking could reveal it.

A long black-haired beauty flashed into his mind.

Sometimes the poison took hold and never let go.

He'd escaped.

Courtney hadn't…

Just as his eyes were about to close to the wave of pain

her memory triggered, a young man to Jack's left began violently trembling on his cot. An emergency medical technician had been doing the heavily intoxicated patient's intake, along with another who'd brought him into the medical tent.

Jack and Taylor were immediately at his side.

"Has he been given Narcan?" Jack asked, noting the man's blue lips as he lifted the man's eyelids to check his pupils. Pinpoint and no tracking.

"I injected him within two minutes of his arrival. He seemed to be stabilizing, his respirations picking up a little, heart rate, too. Then this shaking started and he looks awful."

"Give him another dose," Jack ordered, wondering if his thoughts of Courtney had somehow conjured the young man's turn for the worse.

"Pulse is thready—about fifty," Taylor told him, propping the guy's legs up. "Respirations ten."

Hell.

Glancing toward Taylor, he motioned to their crash cart. "I may need to vent him. Have everything here, just in case. This kid isn't going to die on our watch."

But it seemed he was going to give it a try.

The EMT called for an ambulance while they worked. Jeff would be shipped to the local hospital for care.

Just as Taylor got back with the crash cart, the kid's respiration rate dropped further.

If they could just keep him alive...

When Jack turned to Taylor, he didn't have to say a thing. Like the great nurse he'd already discovered she was, she was ready, gloved him up, then gave him the intubation tube.

Intubating patients wasn't something he did a lot of

at the events he worked, but he'd gotten a plethora of practice at the emergency room these past few months. The tube slid into place. Jack slid his stethoscope on, listened to make sure placement was correct as the man's chest rose and fell.

Glancing up at Taylor, he gave a thumbs-up.

"I feel as if I'm wearing half the farm."

Jack glanced at where Taylor sat on the golf cart. Strands of her hair had worked loose from her braid and flew about in the wind. A folded bandana covered the lower part of her face to save her from breathing in the dust kicked up from the golf cart. Dark glasses shielded her eyes from the bright sun. She wore the "Medical Staff" T-shirt she'd been given that morning and loose cuffed khaki shorts. A shiny sheen of sweat coated her skin, as did a layer of dust.

"So many jokes I could make," he teased, thinking she looked beautiful, if a bit tired. No wonder. The medical tent had been hell today. A total nightmare. Thank God it had calmed down about an hour prior to the end of their shift.

Taylor rolled her eyes. "You could, but should you?"

"Which is why I'll keep my farm jokes to myself."

"I appreciate that."

"You don't think you'd appreciate my farm humor?"

"Who knows? Maybe I would have even if they were *baa*-d."

He laughed at her play on farm humor.

"Either way, even if I have to wait in line hours to get a shower, I am taking one."

"Agreed." He was hot and sweaty himself. And somewhere between emotionally exhausted and exhilarated.

Today had been rough for more reasons than one. Which was why he normally didn't let the memory of Courtney into his head, ever.

Not that she was ever far away, it was just that he didn't consciously let thoughts of her take hold. Not like he had today.

"Wow. Don't you look as pretty as a Georgia peach?"

"Thank you." Taylor fought not to blush at Duffy's compliment. She wore a loose tie-dye sundress that tied around her neck and a pair of crisscrossed lace-up-her-legs sandals that she'd bought just for the weekend. For convenience's sake, she pulled her hair back up into its braid. Plus, her hair off her neck would be much cooler in the Tennessee heat. Because she was spending the evening with Jack, she'd brushed on a light coat of mascara and glossed her lips.

He didn't say anything, but his eyes told her he appreciated her efforts.

"You sure you aren't up for a festival fling?" Robert asked, his tone light, teasing. "A few whispered sweet nothings and you could steal me away from Amber."

"Yeah, yeah. You say that but I saw how you were following her around like a besotted puppy earlier today," Taylor teased back, not feeling threatened by Robert in the slightest. Not after how she'd seen how kind he was during patient care. The man had a big heart.

Robert looked sheepish at her claim. "She is a pretty little thing, isn't she?"

Taylor agreed. She'd met Amber earlier in the day. The woman was a tiny powerhouse of a nurse with bright eyes and a brighter smile.

Taylor's gaze shifted back to Jack, who was watching

her with those ethereal blue eyes. Despite the stressful day they'd had in the medical tent, he looked completely relaxed. He, Duffy, Robert, and a few others were sitting around. Jack's guitar was propped beside his chair so they'd probably been playing but were just chatting now.

While she put away her toiletries, Jack moved her chair for her to join them. The guys sat talking about past music festival adventures, trying to impress Taylor by upping each tale told. At one point her belly hurt from laughing so hard.

"The first gig I want to see starts at seven. You game still?" Jack asked, standing to put his guitar back in a beat-up case, then putting it in the passenger seat of his Jeep.

"I am," she agreed, conscious that the others were watching them. Ha. She imagined in this environment it wasn't difficult to pick up on romantic happenings during the festival.

Grabbing her sunglasses, a loose bag to toss over a shoulder, and a straw hat, she joined him and they headed into the main event area to find a spot as close to the stage as they could get and still spread their blanket.

"I'm surprised we haven't seen any injuries from people getting stepped on," she teased as they spread their blanket. Even though there was still a good forty-five minutes before show time, a crowd was already gathering.

He laughed. "You're right, but I don't recall having seen anyone with that particular complaint."

Once their blanket was spread, Jack offered to go and grab pizza and beer.

Taylor lay back, covered her face with her straw hat, and soaked up the late evening sunshine. It was hot, but not unbearably so. She must have dozed off because the next thing she knew Jack was back.

They ate, chatted, and Jack asked how she and Amy had become friends. By the time the show started, they were surrounded by festival goers.

Around them people were dancing and singing along. The band was one Taylor knew and soon, to her astonishment, she was singing along, too. Probably because the music was so loud no one could discern her voice over anyone else's anyway.

The group led into one of their most popular hits and the crowd went wild, cheering, screaming, and jumping up and down. Jack stood and held his hand out to her. Not sure what he intended, Taylor let him pull her to her feet.

The next thing she knew she was in front of him, dancing, his arm around her waist as they sang along with the band.

It might have been the beer. Or it might have been Jack's arms around her, but Taylor felt good.

Really, really good.

And free.

She'd never felt comfortable singing or dancing in front of others, but as she swayed to the beat and sang the words, she felt great.

The song ended, and another started. The crowd was really into the music and someone had started hitting a giant beach ball around.

When it bounced her way, Taylor tapped it back up into the air, thinking, *How fun*.

"Good hit," Jack praised, taking her hand into his then turning his attention back to the stage.

His hand holding hers stole all Taylor's attention.

Jack. That was the song she was interested in singing. In dancing to.

Jack.

Jack.

Jack.

He turned toward her and she realized she'd said his name out loud.

Caught up in the moment, she stretched forward and planted a kiss on his lips. A habit she seemed to be developing.

Surprise lit his eyes, then he grinned. "Enjoying yourself?"

"Immensely," she answered, then laughed and spun around. As she did so, a young man in his early twenties grabbed her hand, bowed, then spun her again.

Laughing, Taylor shrugged at Jack and let the man lead her in another spin, after which he handed her back to Jack and moved on to another nearby lady to do the same.

Taylor's gaze met Jack's. He was smiling. It struck her that Neil wouldn't have been. First off, she couldn't imagine him at a music festival. But if he had been and had witnessed her dance, he'd have accused her of flirting with the man, of egging on his attention. Despite her efforts to reassure him, she'd have paid the price for the young man's foolery.

Tension started tightening her neck muscles, but she shook it off. Neil was no longer in her life and never would be again. She wouldn't let him ruin the present or her future the way he'd tainted her past.

She squeezed Jack's hand. "Thank you."

Jack's brow lifted. "For?"

"Not being upset."

Genuine confusion shone on his face. "Why would I be upset?"

Exactly. He shouldn't have been.

Still holding her hand, he pulled her to him. "I want you to have a good time, Taylor."

"Because you promised Amy?"

"Amy who?" he teased, brushing his lips across her forehead.

Smiling from the inside out, Taylor laughed.

"Come on," he told her. "Let's dance."

They danced. And sang. And got caught up with the partying crowd around them. One band led into another.

Never in her life had Taylor let herself go and just let the music take over who she was and move her body. Never had she laughed so much, felt so much like she belonged to the beating rhythm of the crowd.

On a high, Taylor flopped down on their blanket and stared up at the night sky with awe and amazement at herself, at the music, at the fun crowd, at Jack.

Rolling over, she pulled her cellphone from her bag. "It's after midnight."

Lying down beside her, Jack asked, "You have somewhere you need to be?"

"Not particularly, but we've been up since before four this morning," she reminded him.

"You tired?"

"Maybe a little," she said, knowing he had to be exhausted. Just because she felt energized it didn't mean he wasn't tired. Not that he looked it but, still, she needed to be respectful of the fact that for him this wasn't all new and sparkly.

"Ready to go back to the campsite?" he asked.

She wasn't really, but logic said she should. "Whenever you are."

His gaze narrowed then he shook his head. "If you're up for it, we'll stick around for the next band."

It was almost three when they made it to their tents.

Taylor had wondered how they'd do this. If Jack would kiss her goodnight or if she'd kiss him again, and they'd go from there.

Other than when she'd kissed him earlier and his having kissed her forehead and hand a couple of times, they hadn't kissed, not really kissed, since the night before.

But rather than kiss her outside her tent, he squeezed her hand and whispered goodnight.

It had been, Taylor thought as she watched him go into his tent. A very good night.

The best night.

But it could have been better, a voice shouted in her mind.

It could have been a night where she invited Jack into her tent so she could kiss him as many times and ways as she wanted.

Because, despite her vow that she was fine without a man, she definitely wanted this one.

CHAPTER SIX

THE HEAT WOKE Taylor earlier than she'd planned. Using baby wipes, she cleaned the stickiness off her skin as best as she could, then climbed out of her tent.

"Good morning, Sleeping Beauty."

"Morning." She glanced toward Jack's tent, then smiled at the man who'd starred in her dreams. His hair was in its usual loosely pulled-back style. His T-shirt advertised a music festival she'd never heard of and his shorts were more colorful than her dress from the night before. He should look ridiculous, but instead he looked relaxed and gorgeous and perfect.

"Breakfast?" he offered. "I saved some."

She joined him beneath his canopy tent and took his offering. Eggs, bacon, and a couple of slices of buttered toast. The man knew how to camp.

"You're spoiling me."

"Gotta keep up your strength. We have a long day ahead of us."

Mouth full, she arched a brow.

"You're at a music festival, Taylor, and we don't work. As soon as you're through eating, we're going to go have fun."

"More fun than last night?" She hadn't thought there

were any bands playing until late afternoon, but perhaps she'd been wrong.

"Way more."

It was hard to imagine recapturing the carefree abandon she'd experienced with him the night before. However, today was a new day and she was game for whatever he had planned for them.

All in the name of new adventures and life experiences, of course.

Taylor eyed the little sand-filled sack dubiously. "I'm not sure about this."

"It's easy once you get the hang of it." As if to prove his point, Jack kicked his foot up to his side and hit the small sack a few times.

Behind her shades, Taylor's eyes narrowed at the ball being kicked around. "Let's go have fun, you say," she intoned, knowing she was about to try something else she'd never done. "Way more fun, you say. This is easy, you say."

Jack laughed and hit the sack to her.

She missed, picked up the sack, and tossed it to him. "I've changed my mind and think we'd be better off playing dodgeball."

He laughed. "You seemed interested until you found out they were playing with water balloons."

"Getting hit by a water balloon is appealing more and more," she mused as she missed the sack again. "In this heat, being doused with water would be a good thing, right?"

His grin was lethal. "That's what I was thinking."

His tone was both suggestive and teasing. Unable to

repress her smile, Taylor shook her head and tried again to hack the sack.

"You'll catch on. Here, let me show you." Jack put his hands on her hips, then guided her leg through a series of motions where the bag rested on the medial aspect of her foot.

"Now, let's try an inside foot delay. Just catch the sack. Don't worry about doing anything with it at this point." From about her chest height, he dropped the ball onto her foot.

It fell to the ground.

He walked her through the motions again. This time it rested on the inside of her foot. Over and over, he repeated his lesson until she was lifting her leg to catch the bag when he dropped it.

"You're doing great," he encouraged when she went several times in a row without missing. "Now, let's try with the other foot."

His patience amazed her and slowly she began to try to mimic the motions he walked her through time and again.

Soon a few others joined them on the grassy open area. Several others also had foot bags. Who knew people actually did this?

Before long, someone had music going and a foot bag challenge was on.

"Yeah, I'm sitting this one out." Taylor tossed the sand-filled ball back to Jack. "You've got this."

Waggling his brows, he and a half-dozen others kicked sacks around. After a few minutes only Jack and a guy named Will were moving to the beat, keeping their sacks in the air. A crowd gathered around them, chanting and urging them on.

"Go, Jack! Go, Jack!" she cheered, along with several others.

Will had his own cheer section, too.

"They're making this look too easy," a guy complained. "Someone get them a drink. We're going to add a new element to the competition to speed things along."

Two drinks showed up within seconds and were handed to Will and Jack.

Jack finished off his drink, keeping his sack in the air. Will did as well, but with kicks that sent the sack high into the air over his head, and he'd kick it back up from behind him, then repeat the motions, all while chugging his drink. His movements were so fluid he looked as if he'd done the trick a zillion times.

When he'd finished his drink, loud cheers went out.

Laughing, Jack caught his foot bag in mid-air and bowed. "You are the master."

The crowd clapped. Soon a group game started up of sacking it up.

"Come on," Jack encouraged, taking Taylor's hand. "You have to play, too."

Taylor wanted to say no. It's what the old Taylor would have done, claiming she just wanted to watch.

But she didn't want to just watch.

She wanted to do more than sit on the sidelines.

Even if she failed miserably.

She wanted to live. Not just exist but *live*.

The sack made it all the way around and Taylor managed to catch Jack's toss with the center of her foot and kick it to the person to her left without letting it touch the ground.

She was unable to hold in a big "Yes!" and do a little victory dance.

A giggly girl with flowers in her hair and an itty-bitty

bikini on her equally itty-bitty body missed her toss during the second round.

No one seemed to mind and they started back over at round one.

The few times Taylor recalled being involved in games, there had been such a competitive element she hadn't had fun. She wasn't even sure those games had been about having fun, just winning. That wasn't what this was about. The smiling, happy people around her just wanted to enjoy being alive and at the festival. Wow.

Taylor wasn't sure how long they played, but they did so until a midday comedy show drew several away. Taylor took a break to rehydrate and reapply sunscreen.

"Need help with your shoulders and the back of your neck?"

She started to tell him she had it, but only a fool would turn down Jack's offer. "Please."

Squirting a generous portion of lotion onto his palm, he then rubbed his hands together.

"I doubt that's needed today," she mused, appreciative, though he'd thought to warm the lotion prior to applying it. Jack was a thoughtful man. She liked that.

She liked him.

"You're probably right." He placed his hands on her exposed shoulders, running them slightly beneath the edge of her sleeveless T-shirt, then down her arms.

Goosebumps prickled her skin.

Um…yeah, she liked that, too.

Next he got her neck. "Turn."

Knowing it wasn't the heat that melted her insides, Taylor turned.

"Here." He carefully applied fresh sunscreen to her face, then smiled. "You're quite beautiful, Taylor."

Despite the lack of make-up and grooming, despite

the damage the sunshine and heat from the games had likely done, the way Jack was looking at her made her feel beautiful.

"Thank you." Her smile was as real as they got, coming from the inside out. "You need me to do you?"

His eyes sparkled.

"Apply sunscreen, that is?" she clarified, her lips twitching as she fought to keep a straight face.

"I'm good."

She bet he was. She didn't mean his lack of need for fresh sunscreen either.

A game of Ultimate Frisbee started and the others called them back over.

Taylor had never played with a foot bag but, thanks to Amy, she had played Frisbee on occasion during college. She wouldn't be performing any tricks, but she could hold her own by making decent catches and throws. It was one of the few team sports she had any experience with as her parents hadn't pushed for her to play as a child and she'd been busy with work and school once she'd gotten older.

About twenty people divided up into two teams. Skin versus shirts. Taylor was a shirt. Jack was not.

Watching him pull off his T-shirt had the same effect as him unleashing a secret weapon. One that left her slack-jawed and entranced.

The man had a beautiful body.

Taylor and the flower girl seemed on the same wavelength when it came to throws and they often made plays to each other.

Of course, Jack chose to try to block her catches. Tried and succeeded more often than not. Taylor attempted to reciprocate, but his reach outdid hers so he easily made his catches.

When their teams were tied nine each, Taylor decided to take matters into her own hands when Jack's teammates went to toss him the Frisbee for the winning point.

She leapt on him, wrapping her arms and legs around him.

Surprised, Jack caught her rather than the Frisbee, which landed a few feet away and rolled.

"Woo-hoo, looks like Jack caught more than he bargained for," one of the guys called out.

Another let out a wolf whistle.

"Are we playing tackle Frisbee or what?" another ragged, grabbing hold of his girlfriend's waist and pulling her to him for a kiss. "I'm all for a game of that."

Jack hugged Taylor, then let her slide down his body to stand, still flush against him.

Flush against Jack was hot.

Not because of the sun beating down on them. Or even because he was shirtless—although his damp skin was hot in more ways than one.

What was hottest was what she saw in his eyes, the way she felt his body tighten and his breathing hike up in intensity.

"You know this means war, right?" he teased, low and with a bit of a growl to his voice.

"Oops. Was I not supposed to do that?" she asked with feigned innocence, drawing a laugh from several of their teammates.

"Hey, baby, you can do that to me anytime you want," one of Jack's teammates offered.

"See what you started?" Jack accused with a laugh. "Now they're going to rewrite the rules and we guys don't stand a chance."

"Game on." A cute girl with a painted face, cat ears,

short blue denim cut-off shorts, and a bikini top, who was on Taylor's team, picked up the Frisbee and tossed it to another teammate.

"Here, I'm open," Taylor called.

"No, she's not," Jack corrected, bear-hugging her and lifting her off her feet.

But the guy who'd had the Frisbee had already tossed it and somehow, hiked up in the air in Jack's arms, Taylor managed to catch it, much to her amazement and the excitement of her teammates.

"We win!" She bounced around in Jack's arms, waving the Frisbee over her head. "We won!"

Jack tossed her back over his shoulder, bum in the air, and carried her over to his teammates. "What should we do with this one? Pretty sure she deserves punishment."

A few lewd suggestions went up.

"Put me down, Jack Morgan," Taylor demanded, laughing so hard she could barely talk, and lightly smacking his bottom.

"Be careful what you start, Taylor."

For that, she pinched his very nice bottom.

"Remember, you asked for this." He lifted her from his shoulders and put her on her feet.

His words echoed from her past and a surge of panic hit. Taylor braced, preparing to defend herself, if needed. Her heart beat hard and heavy and she fought wincing.

But all Jack did was lean in and pop a kiss on her lips.

A very sweet kiss that was much more a reward than punishment.

Taylor's muscles sagged with relief, relaxing from the tension that had overtaken her. She should have known, maybe she had, but old habits died hard.

* * *

Taylor was having fun. Jack could tell by the big smile on her face as they danced to the beat of his favorite band. The group hadn't started playing until almost midnight. The crowd was really big so they hadn't tried spreading the blanket tightly folded inside his backpack.

Just as well. He liked watching the gentle sway of her body.

He liked how she looked relaxed and was soaking up the music. There was no hesitancy in her eyes, just trust when she looked at him.

Except for that moment when they'd been playing Frisbee and her big brown eyes had filled with uncertainty and fear.

He'd instantly connected her tension to his thoughtless words.

Her ex had a lot to answer for.

Thank God that look had been fleeting in her gaze and she'd shaken it off as quickly as it had appeared. Jack wanted her trust.

Wanted to deserve it.

He also wanted her.

But no way could he act on that want without the other medical staff realizing. Not that any of them would care, but being seen leaving Taylor's tent or her leaving his would cheapen what was between them, make her no different from anyone else he'd ever met.

Taylor *was* different.

He'd known it the moment he'd noticed the photo at Amy's and been drawn to it. Amy had come over and commented about how much she missed her friend since she'd married, how she worried things weren't as great as Taylor pretended. Knowing she was married, Jack had immediately written off his interest, but he'd never forgotten the smiling woman in the photo.

Taylor was unlike anyone he'd ever known and the way he felt about her was completely foreign to him.

So he enjoyed the moment they were in and let it be enough. When the crowd jumped up and down in time to the music, he and Taylor jumped. When the crowd jammed, they jammed.

Through it all they laughed and smiled and laughed some more.

It was an amazing night.

An unforgettable night that he didn't want to end.

This was it. It was now or never.

Pausing outside her tent, Taylor swallowed the lump in her throat and turned toward the man who'd become so important in such a short amount of time.

"I don't want tonight to end," she whispered. "Not yet."

She wasn't sure what she expected, but something more than Jack standing still, staring at her, then closing his eyes.

"I want you, Jack."

His lashes lifted, revealing tormented blue eyes.

Uncertainty hit her.

"I…" She paused, not sure what to say. Not sure why he looked torn.

He rested his forehead against hers. "You have no idea how much it means to hear you say that."

She could hear in his whisper that what he said was true. Her words had affected him.

"But I'm not going in your tent with you."

Her heart pounded. Was she so terrible at seduction?

Should she have started kissing him rather than telling him what she wanted? Should she have just held his hand, unzipped her tent, and led him inside?

"Not because I don't want to," he continued. His voice was so low she could barely make out his words. "But because I want to so much."

Taylor wanted to flip on her phone's flashlight and put him in the spotlight so she could better see his face. "That doesn't make sense."

Yeah, her frustration was audible. Good. Let him know she wasn't happy about what he was saying.

"Perhaps not," he admitted, "but it's true all the same." Lifting his head from hers, he planted a kiss where his head had just rested. "Goodnight, Taylor. I'll see you in the morning."

Jaw a bit slack, she watched him go to his tent. Without looking back and giving her the wink she'd come to expect, he disappeared into his tent.

What?

He was just going to sleep now?

With no more explanation than that?

Forget shining her phone light in his face. She wanted to throw the device at him.

Part of her wanted to let herself into his tent and go for what she wanted.

Wasn't that what the past few days had been about? That he wanted to have sex with her?

If not tonight, then when? They'd work from four p.m. to four a.m. tomorrow night— technically, *that* night. Had he forgotten?

Or maybe as he'd gotten to know her he'd decided they were better as friends than lovers.

No. She'd seen how he'd looked at her. She'd felt how he'd touched her, how he'd kissed and held her.

Jack wanted her.

So why had he just gone into his tent *alone*? Was he trying to be noble? Save her from herself?

Her hands went to her hips and she glared at his tent.

What if she didn't want him to be noble? What if she didn't want to be saved? What if what she wanted was to have sex with a man just because she wanted to have sex? Because she wanted what his body offered? Because she felt physical excitement when she looked at him? What if she wanted to not overthink what was happening between them and just feel, just act, just do, and live in the moment?

She bit the inside of her bottom lip. She'd never been a seductress. Although Neil had initially thrilled at her lack of experience, he'd soon pointed out her shortcomings when it came to pleasing a man.

She should go into her tent and be done with this.

She should.

But she wasn't going to.

Because she wasn't the love-starved woman who'd married Neil. Neither was she the beaten-down woman who'd finally had enough and walked away from what she'd no longer been willing to bear.

She was a woman who was stronger, who was figuring out who Taylor was, what Taylor wanted out of life, and was determined to enjoy the journey to figuring those things out.

She didn't fool herself that Jack was anything more than a pleasant stop along that journey. One she'd look back on with fond memories and smiles and maybe even a few regrets.

Was she willing to let this moment pass and not take that next step? Not let him show her what she'd been missing out on for the first twenty-five years of her life? Because she knew sex with Jack would be nothing like anything she'd ever known.

A mosquito buzzed around her and she swatted it away.

Now or never, Taylor. Are you brave enough to go for what you want? Or live the rest of your life wondering what would have happened if you'd gone into his tent?

Have you shed enough of the insecurities of the past to march over to Jack's tent and do everything in your power to make memories rather than regrets?

CHAPTER SEVEN

IGNORING THE FACT Taylor hadn't budged from where he'd left her, Jack stripped off his T-shirt and shorts and lay down on top of his sleeping bag.

He closed his eyes, the surprised look on Taylor's face haunting him.

Haunted him because the surprise had been replaced with uncertainty and hurt.

He didn't want her to doubt herself, or that he wanted her.

But he'd had to step away while he still could.

He'd explain to her tomorrow why he'd had to make an abrupt exit.

The tent zipper gave way.

No.

Yes.

Jack's heart pounded so loudly everyone probably thought one of the bands had taken the stage again.

He propped himself on his elbows, staring across the dark tent at Taylor's silhouette, watched as she closed the tent flap, then, looking his way, stripped off her T-shirt and shorts.

Hell.

How he longed for light so he could permanently etch

into his mind the memory of what she looked like at this moment.

Darkness was good. He needed to send her away.

"What are you doing, Taylor?"

She didn't speak, just climbed in beside him and snuggled next to him on his twin-sized air mattress.

Her bare body pressed against his, which was only covered by his underwear, drove the nail home.

He could tell himself he needed to send Taylor away, but it was too late for that part of his brain to take control again.

Pulling her as close as their bodies would allow, he cupped her bottom, keeping her firmly against him as he covered her lips with his.

Sweet heavens. She tasted good.

He caught her soft sigh of relief and then lost himself in the desperation of how she returned his just-as-desperate kisses.

He wanted to see her, to know what was showing in her eyes as he ran his hands over her breasts, her hips, between her legs. But to turn on any sort of light would illuminate them to anyone walking by so he used his other senses to immortalize her.

The feel of her. The taste of her. The smell of her.

When she was ready, he donned a condom, maneuvered to where he was positioned just right, thrilled at how her fingers dug into his shoulders as he pushed inside, fought losing control at her soft whimper of pleasure as he moved his hips and she wrapped her legs around him, taking him as deep as he'd go.

Fighting to hold in his desire to roar, Jack brought her to the brink over and over until she desperately clung to him, quivering with her release, until his own body refused to hold back another moment and he lost himself.

His breathing hard, his chest feeling as if it was going to burst open, he collapsed on top of her. Then, worrying he was too heavy, he went to roll off, but she stopped him.

"Don't," she whispered. "Let me enjoy this for a little longer before you roll over to go to sleep."

Was she kidding him?

No way was he rolling over to go to sleep when she was naked and in his bed. But her words reminded him of how fragile she really was, of why he shouldn't have allowed what had happened to happen in a tent where they'd had to keep quiet, had needed to limit their body movements, had had to restrain the guttural reactions to just how good the other felt.

Because he had no doubt Taylor had felt good.

His own body tightened again. She'd wanted him to stay where he was, so she had no one to blame except herself when he started nuzzling her neck and running his hands over her body. Again.

Because that's what he wanted.

To touch her all over.

This time slower, surer, making it all about her, catching her moans with his kisses.

Jack wasn't sure what time Taylor had left his tent, but he woke alone, naked, and feeling a lot better than a man should feel who'd only slept a few hours.

At least, he thought it had only been a few hours. Stretching his arms over his head, he acknowledged that for all he knew it could be afternoon.

His tent was hot enough for it to be midday.

He dressed, unzipped the tent, and stepped out, immediately looked toward Taylor's tent. She was nowhere to be seen.

"Haven't seen her since early this morning."

Raking his hand through his hair, Jack turned toward Duffy. The older man sat in a chair, a soda in one hand and his cellphone in the other.

"'Bout what time would that have been?"

"You mean when I saw her sneaking out of your tent or when she left to go and shower?" Duffy stared at him with narrowed eyes. "Or later when she came back, put her stuff away, then took off almost immediately rather than talk with me?"

He met the older man's gaze and knew there was no point in denying any of the accusations in his friend's eyes. Instead of saying anything further, he opened his cooler and pulled out a drink, took a long swig, then went over to where Duffy was sitting.

"Take your pick."

Duffy's stare was uncompromising. "You going to hurt that girl?"

Of all the people to see Taylor leaving his tent, why had it had to be Duffy? Jack leaned back in his chair. "Not planning to."

"You like her."

"Yes, and you're right. I'll probably hurt her," he acknowledged. He was the first lover Taylor had had since her divorce and that made her even more vulnerable, made him want to protect her all the more, even when that meant protecting her from himself. "Then again, she may end up hurting me."

Duffy laughed. "Yeah, right."

Jack shrugged. "Crazier things have happened."

Duffy's brow lifted. "Never known you to get caught up enough with someone to be hurt. Not since Courtney."

Yeah, Jack wasn't digging this conversation. Not for a thousand reasons. Duffy knew him well. As well as anyone really. Hadn't Duffy played a major role in influencing Jack's decision to straighten his life out? To become a doctor?

"We agreed not to talk about Courtney years ago."

Scowling, the older man shook his head. "Can't say I recall ever agreeing to that."

"Perhaps it was an unspoken agreement, but I thought you understood."

"I understand a lot of things. Like that you never let anyone get close enough to care about them and I'm worried about whatever this is with Taylor."

"There are a lot of people in my life I care about."

"Not what I meant, and you know it. Let's talk about Courtney and then you tell me why I saw Taylor coming out of your tent."

Jack glared at his long-time friend. "Have you been drinking something besides soda this morning or just feeling philosophical about your own life choices and trying to project them onto me?"

Duffy's expression hardened, but rather than respond he just stared at Jack with cynical eyes.

Hell.

Jack stood from the chair, crushed his empty drink bottle. "I'm done with this conversation and don't understand why we're having it anyway."

"Because of what I saw this morning."

"Because you saw Taylor leave my tent? It wasn't a big deal." Jack rolled his eyes. "You've seen women leave my tent before, seen me leave women's tents before," he reminded Duffy, "and you'll likely see it happen again in the future. Not once have you felt the need to comment. Not once. Do us both a favor and don't start now because Taylor leaving my tent meant nothing."

Taylor hadn't meant to eavesdrop on Jack and Duffy's conversation, but hadn't been able to avoid doing so. Not with their close proximity and the absolute agitation rolling off Jack.

She'd not known quite what to expect when they first saw each other this morning, but this upset, almost angry-sounding man wasn't it.

She'd not been able to sleep and after she'd heard the four a.m. crew leaving the campground, she'd snuck out of his tent in the hope of being inside her tent before the returning night crew showed.

Except for Duffy, who must never sleep, she'd succeeded.

Not that she'd seen Duffy but, from what she'd just overheard, he'd seen her.

That's when it hit her that she really didn't care that he'd seen her. As Jack had once told her, she was a grown woman and could do as she pleased. She'd pleased herself quite well the night before. More than once.

She wasn't ashamed of that. Actually, she was quite proud she'd gone to Jack's tent and climbed into his bed with him. To have done so had been so unlike the woman she'd once been and she liked that change. Liked it that she'd taken the initiative to go for what she wanted.

She had no unrealistic expectations. Jack was right. Her leaving his tent had meant nothing.

She wouldn't pretend that it had or that she'd wanted it to.

Daring Duffy or anyone to tell her she'd been wrong, she lifted her chin and made her way toward them.

Duffy's gaze went beyond Jack to meet with hers.

Jack spun, spotted her and cringed. "You heard that, didn't you?" He shook his head with disgust, looking very unlike the laidback man she knew. "Why am I asking? Of course you heard that."

That her smiling, happy Jack was anything but threw Taylor. She took a deep breath, pasted a smile on her face and went toward where the men were.

"Heard what?" She walked right over to Jack, planted a kiss on his cheek as if it was the most natural thing in the world to do and her heart wasn't pounding out of her chest. She held up the bags in her hands. "You won't believe the cool things I bought this morning."

Duffy knew she'd been standing there, had heard, but the older man didn't call her bluff. Neither did he comment on the fact she'd kissed Jack's cheek.

Why had she?

Because she'd needed to touch him? To remind herself that he was real? Or had that kiss been an attempt to calm him?

Then it hit her.

She was behaving as she would have with Neil.

No matter what had been going on, she'd pretend everything was fine to keep the peace, not make a scene, defuse his anger.

Startled at the realization, she lifted her gaze to Jack's.

Happiness didn't fill her. Neither did trust or a sense of safety.

Anger. That was what filled her.

Anger that he'd immediately revealed this new side and she'd immediately fallen into old habits.

She dropped her bags at her feet. "Actually, I did hear your conversation, but I don't understand why you're upset that I heard. Like you said, it meant nothing. Not to either one of us." Okay, maybe that had been exaggerating the truth a bit, but it had sounded good. "At no point have I had any expectations that you wouldn't be sneaking into women's tents in the future, neither have I had any desire for you not to," she added for good measure. "So what does it matter that I heard things I already knew and had no problem with?"

Jack's jaw tightened.

Although he didn't come right out and do so, Taylor would swear Duffy gave her a mental thumbs-up for her change in attitude. Jack, however, didn't look so thrilled.

"We need to talk."

She rolled her eyes. "Isn't that what we're doing?"

"Not here. Not where everyone can hear."

She glanced around the mostly deserted campground. "I don't think anyone is paying us the slightest attention."

"I am." Duffy spoke up, raising his drink to her. "I'm enjoying the entertainment."

"You would," Jack accused, throwing the man a *butt out* look.

"You just say that because you know I'm right," the weather-beaten man accused.

"Right? About what?"

Duffy's gaze flickered toward Taylor.

Rather than answer, Jack raked his fingers through his loose hair, then sighed. "Yeah, I guess you are."

Taylor didn't stick around, instead walked over to her car and put her purchases inside with a loss of the sunshine she'd felt when she'd bought the colorful sundress and scarf.

What Jack had said didn't matter. It didn't change anything. She'd already known she was just a fling. That was fine. That's all he was, too.

What mattered was how upset he was with Duffy. How abrupt.

No one always smiled so it shouldn't bother her that Jack was irate.

But it did.

Because old feelings had pitted in her stomach and ruined everything.

"I'm sorry."

At Jack's interruption, Taylor didn't glance up from the book she was reading. Not long after she'd dropped her purchases off in her car, she'd grabbed her bag, a book, and had taken off until she'd found a semi-shady spot to while away the afternoon until it was time to report for her shift.

"For?"

"You know what for."

"It's not a big deal."

"Tossing my words back at me?" He squatted down next to where she sat on a blanket on the far side of the event area. "I guess I deserve that."

"You're giving me more credit than I deserve." She hadn't even realized that's what she'd done until he'd pointed it out.

"I'm not giving you nearly the credit you deserve," he countered. "Last night was amazing."

Trying not to let his words get to her, she nodded. "This morning not so much."

"I am sorry you heard that."

She shrugged. "Don't be. We both know it's true." She

took a deep breath, then continued. "And we are both okay that it's true. I'm just another festival fling for you and you're my post-divorce late rebound fling. We both got what we wanted and, like you said, it meant nothing."

He sighed, then gestured to her blanket. "Can I sit with you?"

Surprised that he'd asked, she nodded. "It's not as if you aren't going to see me in a few hours during our shift."

"I needed to talk to you before then. To tell you I'm sorry."

Her hands shook. She didn't want him to notice so she set her book on the blanket, wrapped her arms around her legs, and clasped her hands together. "I don't understand your need to apologize, because you just stated what we both already knew. But, fine, apology accepted."

He let out a long sigh. "I've ruined everything, haven't I?"

She didn't understand. "What is there to ruin, Jack? Last night was amazing. We work tonight and leave in the morning. End of story."

"I don't want us to end this way."

I don't want us to end at all.

Her eyes widened in surprise at her unexpected thought. She'd known from the beginning they would end, that whatever happened was temporary.

She swallowed to moisten her dry throat.

"I've had a great time with you, Taylor. The best."

She could feel her eyes starting to water and didn't want to cry, didn't even know why she was on the verge of doing so, just knew she did not want to let him see her cry. "Please, don't do this."

His brows formed a V.

"Don't say things you don't mean." Had her voice sounded a bit desperate? She'd been going for strong, independent, *I don't care*, not pleading. She straightened her shoulders, tilted her chin, and willed her persona to be nonchalant. "Don't pretend any of this was more than what it was."

Next to her on the blanket, his body tensed and his eyes darkened. "What exactly is it you think we had, Taylor?"

"A romantic interlude that rebuilt my confidence in myself as a woman, in my sexuality. You gave me my post-divorce rebound sex. It was great. I'm very appreciative."

His forehead creased. "Is that what last night was? You using me for sexual empowerment? That's why you came in my tent?"

It wasn't. Not really. But maybe it was better if he thought it had been since he seemed to take his knight in shining armor role a bit too seriously. She didn't want him feeling responsible for her. She'd known exactly what she'd been doing and she'd had no expectations of him beyond that moment.

"Like I said, I'm good with what happened last night and with our saying goodbye tomorrow morning." She was, wasn't she? Of course she was. "Thank you."

His jaw worked back and forth once, then, without looking her way, he said, "No, thank you. Too bad I had to restrain myself so much or I could have made your reintroduction to sex more memorable. Still, glad to be of service."

On that note, he stood and walked away.

Taylor watched him go, wondering at the growing ache in her chest with every step he took, but patting herself on the back that she'd held herself together so Jack wouldn't have to feel guilty.

The medical tent was hopping when Taylor arrived. She'd gone early, signed in and gotten that day's T-shirt, and opted to walk there.

She'd needed the exercise to ease the soreness from her muscles and she'd needed the time to decompress before she started her shift with Jack.

Jack.

Sweet, wonderful Jack who felt responsible for what had happened the night before. She'd seen it in his eyes.

She'd given him an out and he'd taken it.

Because she'd been right.

All they'd ever been was a festival fling.

For that fling, she truly was thankful. Meeting Jack, being with Jack, having sex with Jack had healed so much of her lingering insecurities.

He'd made her feel desirable, worthy.

She was desirable, worthy.

She wasn't cold. She wasn't frigid. She wasn't immune to men. She wasn't dead inside.

She was passionate, hot, full of feminine fire.

She could enjoy her body, enjoy being a woman giving herself to a man.

Sex with Jack had unlocked a part of her that had been caged up during her marriage. Maybe it had always been caged up, waiting to be unleashed.

Regardless of the ache at how they'd ended, she would always be grateful to Jack for setting her passion free.

CHAPTER EIGHT

"So, DID THE two of you hit it off?" Amy questioned Taylor over the phone.

It was late Monday afternoon and Taylor had only been home long enough to shower, unpack and take a short nap that had been cut short by another phone call. One that had made Taylor's day.

"I asked Duffy how things were going a couple of times," Amy continued, "but he never would give me a straight answer and neither you nor Jack, when I texted with him earlier, told me anything."

Jack hadn't told Amy anything that had happened.

"What did Duffy say?" she asked, her mind still wondering at Jack's silence. They'd parted on good terms overall. He'd apologized a few dozen times about what she'd heard him tell Duffy and their goodbye had been a bit awkward. But Taylor had no regrets about their fling or their goodbye.

"I told you that he wouldn't give me details beyond that everyone liked you and you seemed to be enjoying yourself." Seeming to catch on, her friend redirected her questioning. "What *could* he have told me?" Amy asked with giddy emphasis.

Someday she would tell Amy all about her adventure with Jack. Today wasn't that day. For now, what had happened between her and Jack was private, special and outside the ordinary.

For Taylor, he'd cut away the last of the weights that had held her down. She was ready to embrace her future.

"What Duffy should have told you is that he, Jack and I worked the tent together and I think they are both wonderful men."

Very true. They were both wonderful men. Both modern-day gypsies of a sort. Both very special in their own ways.

"That's it?" Disappointment coated her friend's words.

Taylor could picture Amy's expression. Her forehead would be scrunched with doubt. Again, she was grateful Amy couldn't see her face as she might see more than Taylor wanted to reveal.

"If you're asking if your matchmaking paid off," she said, deciding to just address what Amy really wanted to know, "maybe Neil immunized me forever, especially from someone who's also a doctor. You know how I feel about that."

She felt guilty for deceiving her friend but when she and Amy were face to face she'd make sure Amy knew meeting Jack had been a good thing.

A great thing.

A spectacular and marvelous thing.

"Now, tell me about this guy you're seeing?" Taylor injected a lot of pep into her tone. "Jack mentioned you were dating his best friend. Give me details."

Amy's giddiness was almost palpable over the phone.

"Dating might be presumptuous, but Greg is amazing. I want to be dating him."

"Jack seemed to think you two were an item already."

"Good to know," Amy admitted, sounding pleased. "But it's early days, especially as Greg doesn't live in Warrenville but about an hour away in Nashville. Long-distance relationships suck."

Yet another reason it was good she and Jack had ended when they had. Trying to keep up a relationship when they lived hundreds of miles from each other wouldn't have been any fun.

Not that they would have needed to have a long-distance relationship.

Taylor's stomach did an excited flip-flop.

Not for however long Jack would be working at the Warrenville emergency department.

"Speaking of long-distance relationships, I miss you," Amy told her. "How did your interview go?"

As thrilled as she was about the job in Warrenville, she was also a little nervous.

Because of Jack.

What they'd shared had been perfect, right? A beautiful interlude that had ended a little prematurely but which had otherwise been something from a fantasy.

Coming face to face with him day after day in the real world would dissipate their surreal experience. Then again, how much longer would he even be there before moving on to some other music festival or event?

"Really well." She'd barely hung up from the call when Amy's call had come in. "They offered me a position in the emergency room."

"What? Why didn't you tell me that first thing?"

"How could I? All you've talked about since we got on the phone is Jack." Ugh. Her tone had been a bit harsher than she'd meant it to. She wasn't anti-Jack by any means, but she did have reservations about being near him day after day.

"Sorry. I know I've gone on and on about Jack." Amy sighed. "I really thought the two of you would hit it off."

They'd hit it off all right. Like electric sparks that sizzled.

"Obviously I've talked about him to the point of ad nauseam. Sorry," Amy apologized. "Forget Jack. I can't wait until you get here! I'll get the spare room cleaned out."

Taylor was just as excited and wished she could pack her things and leave for Warrenville this very moment. Instead, she'd work out her notice first.

"It's time you moved away from that town and memories of Neil," Amy continued in a more serious tone. "He's not worth holding onto, Taylor. Surely you've figured that out by now."

"Memories of Neil could never hold me here." If anything, they'd drive her away. "And I'm certainly not holding onto him. I fought hard to rid my life of him and can't imagine circumstances where I'd ever let him or any man steal my joy."

"You go, girl!" Amy praised. "Thank goodness you finally saw the light."

Taylor nodded. She had, right? That's why she'd let Jack walk away, let him think he hadn't mattered, right? Not that he'd offered, but she'd not wanted more. Not really.

Sure, had she met Jack years ago, before Neil, it would

have been fun to have spent more time with him. The sex had been phenomenal. But she'd not been thinking long-term relationship. Neither had he.

"We'll have so much fun." Amy's excitement was almost palpable. "You moving here will be like old times. Plus, you'll be able to get to know Jack better."

"Amy, please don't push us together." Taylor took a deep breath. "Jack is a good guy. Thanks to you insisting that he babysit me, we watched a few concerts together, but it wasn't a big deal."

Liar, liar, pants on fire. Everything about Jack was a big deal.

Especially the sex.

Her pulse sped up just recalling how it had felt when she'd crawled onto his air mattress with him.

Taylor pushed back the memories. Rebound sex. Nothing more. Just rebound sex.

Very good rebound sex.

"And?"

"And nothing," she assured her friend. "Amy, we didn't even get to know each other well enough to exchange cellphone numbers. You're making something out of nothing."

True, yet not true. They hadn't exchanged numbers and yet she felt she knew him very well.

But the reality was that she didn't know Jack at all.

Taking the job in Warrenville meant having to come face to face with him again, but only for a short while.

Regardless, she'd never let another man prevent her from making the right choices for her. Taking the job in Warrenville and sharing an apartment with Amy was the right choice.

If Jack didn't like it that she'd be around, tough.

He could go work a music festival or something.

"Taylor starts orientation today. Isn't that great?"

Jack fought looking up from the chart he was finishing.

Thrilled her friend was relocating to Warrenville, Amy had talked about little else for the past month. Jack had been a bit blown away that Taylor would be in town, that he'd see her again, would get the chance to make up for his verbal blunder.

"Great," he agreed, and meant it. He was happy for Amy that her best friend was going to be close.

As for having his last two months in Warrenville interrupted by a beautiful blonde who'd turned his Rockin' Tyme experience upside down, well, worse things could happen.

Taylor was a beautiful, sexy woman with whom he'd had a great time. Other than her having overhead his conversation with Duffy and the fact they'd had sex at all, Jack had no regrets.

Duffy had been right that Taylor deserved better than a music festival affair, and Jack wasn't a man who could give that to her. Still, he believed the affair had been good for her.

He knew the sex had been. For him, too.

Best sex of his life.

Why hadn't Taylor told her best friend they'd gotten together at the music festival? Was she ashamed that she'd had sex with him?

If anything, she should be ashamed of what he'd said to Duffy. He was. He hadn't gone into Taylor's tent because he'd wanted to protect her. Instead, he'd cheapened what they'd shared with defensive words spat out at the man who knew more about him than any other person.

Taylor was in Warrenville. As she'd done from the beginning, she'd fascinated him. But Duffy had been right to question him.

Sure, mentioning Courtney's name had thrown his hackles up, just as Duffy had known it would.

Jack had enjoyed a lot of relationships over the years, but no one had interested him the way Taylor did.

No one had even come close. Not since Courtney.

Wild, fun-loving Courtney who'd been his soul mate at the tender age of seventeen.

She'd been his first.

He'd been her last.

His eyes blurred and he blinked to clear them.

He was a rambling man, would only be in Warrenville for two more months.

Taylor had been hurt in the past.

Whatever he did, he had to be certain not to add to that hurt. He'd watched her confidence grow throughout the week, knew it was telling that she'd come to his tent, and could kick himself for his words, meant only for Duffy's ears, as he'd watched her deflate.

He'd also been proud when she'd lifted her chin and put him in his place.

Glancing up from the desk where he sat, he realized Amy had still been talking. He hadn't a clue what she'd said, or had asked apparently as she seemed to be waiting for an answer.

"Jack, have you heard a word I've said?" Amy demanded, hands on hips and giving him an expression she usually reserved for uncooperative patients.

Fortunately, he was saved from answering by a new arrival. Not that Amy didn't give him a knowing look before she took off to triage the patient.

A knowing look with a big smile.

A look she'd given him multiple times since Rockin' Tyme.

Taylor made her way down the Warrenville Hospital hallway to start her new employee orientation early on Monday morning.

A month had passed since she'd worked Rockin' Tyme.

A month in which she'd ended her apartment lease, packed her belongings, given what she wasn't taking with her to charity, and moved to Tennessee.

No. Big. Deal.

She had this.

The move had been accomplished over the weekend and she'd semi-settled into Amy's apartment.

Now she had a week of orientation prior to starting work in the emergency department. Even then, she'd be partnered with another nurse for the first few weeks for training on the electronic medical record system and hospital protocol. Then she would be on her own.

She'd worked the intensive care unit since graduation, but had enjoyed her emergency room rotation while in nursing school. She wasn't worried about her nursing skills. She was a good nurse and would take good care of her patients.

Her only hesitation about the entire move was seeing Jack.

How would he take her being in Warrenville?

Would he even care? How much longer would he even be there? A few months at most.

A few months that would fly by.

Regardless, her butterflies at seeing him had been unfounded as she made it through her first day without bumping into him once.

As she lay in bed that night, she wasn't sure if she felt relieved or disappointed.

Disappointed, a voice inside her head whispered. Definitely disappointed.

CHAPTER NINE

To HAVE NOT seen Jack the day before, Taylor started Tuesday morning out by almost crashing into him first thing in the hospital hallway.

"Jack," she rushed out, hating how breathless she sounded as she stared up into eyes so blue they pierced her. Just as quickly, she averted her gaze.

How could she have forgotten how intensely blue his eyes were? How masculine he was and how every female bit of her responded to that virility?

Face it, Taylor. Your body recognized what a potent man he was from the moment you laid eyes on him and went from zero to a hundred. He woke you up inside.

"Sorry, I wasn't paying attention to where I was going," she told him, staring at where his almost neon-green scrubs brushed over the tops of his equally bright tennis shoes.

"Taylor."

Her name on his lips dried up all the moisture in her mouth, making her tongue stick to her palate. She couldn't look at him and not remember, not ache inside at how it had felt to be beneath him, over him.

He'd made her feel really good.

Get a grip, Taylor. It was just a fling. Rebound sex.

"I heard you were starting at the hospital," he continued, causing her eyes to drift upward.

His smile was full and dug indentations into his cheeks. No doubt if she looked into his eyes they'd be all sparkly and happy.

Part of her felt all sparkly and happy at seeing him, too.

"From Amy, no doubt." Not having been prepared to see him so early after not seeing him at all the previous day, before even making it to her Tuesday orientation class, she stumbled over her words. "For the record, I interviewed for this job prior to arriving at Rockin' Tyme, before you and I had met, and I was lucky enough to land the job." Acclimating to the fact that he stood a foot away, Taylor steeled herself and met his gaze. "My being here has nothing to do with you or what happened."

His smile didn't waver. "I understand."

Did he? She hoped so. Only she hoped he didn't understand too much.

Like how good it felt to see him and yet how part of her wished their paths had never crossed again so she could keep the memory of their night tucked away as something precious that had helped her along her path to discovering who Taylor was.

Trying not to stare, she reminded herself that she should get to orientation before they started without her or she lost her new job.

"That's good because, although it's good to see you—" definitely not a lie "—I don't want you to think I'm here because of you. I'm not." She gave a little laugh. She was rambling but wanted to make it clear that he shouldn't feel any type of obligation to her because of what had happened at Rockin' Tyme. "Honestly, considering, it would be simpler had we never seen each other again."

She pasted a cheery smile on her face. "But no worries. You'll be gone soon, right?"

Jack stared at the woman who'd haunted him for the past month.

Longer than that.

She'd haunted him since he'd first seen that photo in Amy's apartment.

Maybe a premonition of things to come?

He'd missed her.

Crazy.

They'd spent less than a week in each other's company and he'd missed her.

Taylor was here and for the next two months, they'd be working together.

Taylor kept her expression guarded. Despite the tension when they'd said their goodbyes, he hadn't thought she'd regretted what had happened, but regret was written all over her lovely face.

Of course she had regrets. Just as she'd likely been dreading their reunion. He'd been her rebound sex. Who wanted to come face-to-face with their rebound sex every time they went to work?

Lucky for her. Jack never stuck around any place too long and had already been in Warrenville much longer than anywhere he'd been since med school graduation. Soon enough he'd be out of here until next year's Rockin' Tyme.

The thought of leaving, of heading to the event in Daytona, should have his feet itching to get on the move. He loved his life.

Only he didn't like it that Taylor so obviously wanted him to hurry up and leave. Yeah, he didn't like that at all.

"Great to see you again, too." He gave a low laugh that echoed hollowly through him.

"Oh, I didn't mean…" Pausing, she winced, then gave a repentant little shrug. "Um…can we just start over? Hi, Jack."

She glanced up, met his gaze for the briefest moment before her big brown eyes filled with panic and she shook her head. "I've orientation this morning. Probably wouldn't look good for me to be late my second day to work. Nice seeing you, Jack."

Before he could get out another word she took off down the hallway at a pace meant to get her away from him as quickly as possible.

Watching her go, Jack scratched his head.

Seeing Taylor again hadn't gone anywhere close to any of the dozens of different scenarios he'd imagined over the past month.

"Hope you don't mind, but I invited company for dinner."

Even before Amy finished her sentence, Taylor guessed who she meant and wanted to throw her cellphone across the room.

No. No. No.

She needed to tell Amy everything and just be done with it so her friend would let up.

"I knew you had bought stuff last night to make something yummy for dinner," Amy reminded her, "so, I invited Jack over. I told him what a great cook you are."

Gripping her phone tighter, Taylor winced.

Oh, Amy, what are you doing?

"My cooking skills are mediocre at best. Call and tell

him you've changed your mind about the invite before I poison the poor man."

"But I haven't changed my mind," Amy insisted. "I'm almost home. Or maybe I should say we're almost home because he's following me. I just wanted to give you a heads-up so you could look your best."

"You know I was looking forward to a night with just you and me catching up, right?" Taylor sighed. "I think I'm going to put on my oldest, most ragged outfit and toss flour everywhere."

"We'll have plenty of time to catch up." Amy had the audacity to laugh. "And just remember, you make the mess, you have to clean it up."

In spite of having her evening plans completely changed, Taylor's lips twitched with a smile. "I thought it was if one cooks, the other one cleans."

"Is that how we used to do things?" Amy sounded amused. "Get to tossing that flour, then, cause we're almost there and if I'm busy cleaning the kitchen, that leaves you alone with Jack, right?"

Taylor sighed. How was she going to convince her friend to quit with the matchmaking?

Why was Jack going along with her anyway? Or did he realize that's what Amy was doing? Maybe he thought she just wanted to talk about Greg?

Maybe that did push Amy to keep trying. After all, wouldn't it be cool for two best friends to be dating two best friends?

But it wasn't going to happen. Not for her and Jack.

Taylor was making a new life for herself and that new life didn't include a relationship.

Especially not one with a man who was a doctor who she already knew wouldn't be sticking around long.

* * *

"This is really good," Jack praised, not surprised that Taylor was a good cook, and not because of Amy's glowing reviews. Long before that he had been sure Taylor could do anything she set her mind to do.

"Thank you."

Looking back and forth between them, Amy gave a big grin and asked, "So, Jack, who was your favorite act at Rockin' Tyme this year?"

Jack named the band that had been playing when Taylor had kissed him.

Although she'd been smiling and participating in the conversation, Taylor stared at her dinner plate as if she thought it might engulf the rest of her food.

"Although..." he named a band they'd danced and partied to "...gave a really good show, too."

Amy had grilled him multiple times at the ER about the festival, so her questions had to all stem around the fact that Taylor sat across from him.

If he moved his leg, no doubt it would brush up against hers.

He didn't move. It wasn't his place to purposely touch her if she didn't welcome his touch. But hell if he was just going to be complacent that she hadn't forgiven him for his stupid, careless words to Duffy.

"I'm still sad I missed it," Amy whined, her gaze going back and forth between Jack and Taylor.

"There's always next year. What about you, Taylor?" he asked, determined to pull her into the conversation. "You signing on for Rockin' Tyme next summer?"

Eyes wide, she shook her head. "Doubtful. I'll be busy."

Amy frowned. "Doing what?"

Taylor shrugged. "One never knows what life is going to throw at her. I mean, you had planned to go this year and that didn't happen."

"But you plan to sign up, right?"

Deciding to rescue Taylor from Amy's probing, Jack asked, "How is your grandmother, Amy? Still recovering nicely from her fall?"

Amy nodded. "According to my mother, yes. According to Granny, no. I'm planning to see for myself weekend after next."

Seeming surprised, Taylor's gaze lifted. "You're going out of town the weekend after this one?"

"Sorry. I just decided for definite earlier today. No worries. Jack will give you a good intro to Warrenville and keep you company. Won't you, Jack?"

Jack wanted to show Taylor Warrenville, but he didn't want to force his presence on her.

Like tonight.

He shouldn't have accepted Amy's invite. So why hadn't he said no?

Because he'd wanted to see Taylor.

It was for the same reason he said, "I'd love to if Taylor's not busy and wants to go."

"You did this, didn't you?"

Taylor watched as Jack ran his finger along the fluid lines of the sculpture. Although she loved the piece she'd given to Amy, causing her friend to gush on and on about how good it was, Taylor still felt insecure about her art.

"You don't have to answer," Jack assured her, still eyeing the piece. "I know you did. She's beautiful."

Her breath caught. "She?"

"It's a woman," he explained needlessly. "A woman dancing on the water."

Taylor doubted most people could look at the foot and a half piece and immediately see the sum of the lines and curves.

Stunned by his insight, she admitted, "I'm impressed you see that."

Glancing her way, he added, "It's you."

Her throat threatened to close. Jack saw too much. "I made the piece, yes."

His expression softened. "Not what I asked."

He knew. He looked at the piece and he knew, had seen the truth. Why did that make her feel both vulnerable and ecstatic?

Staring into his eyes, she confessed, "Some days I think she's me. Others, she's who I want to be, free and not afraid of anything, not even walking on water." With a half-smile on her face, she shrugged. "My reality is most likely somewhere between drowning and treading water."

As if he understood what she meant, he nodded again. "I'd like to see more of your work."

"Why?"

He gave her an odd look. "Because you're good and I'm interested in seeing what you've created."

"I've only done a few pieces." That she'd show anyone, at any rate. She hoped to get started again soon. Finding a local art studio where she could work was still on her list of things to do. "For the record, I don't think of it as creating something, more an unleashing of what's locked away inside the clay."

Jack studied her, making her feel exposed, like he could see deep inside her to her thoughts. Then again, hadn't she thought the same when they'd been at Rockin' Tyme? The man saw past her shell to what she had hidden inside.

"You're very talented," he finally said, and sounded sincere.

"See, Tay," Amy announced, coming back into the room from taking a bathroom break. "I'm not the only one who thinks you're amazing."

Eyes locked with Taylor's, Jack grinned. "Definitely not the only one. She is very talented."

Taylor's cheeks heated. Why did she get the impression he wasn't talking about art anymore?

Why did that excite her?

Because Neil had made her think she was abnormal and dull? Because, for all her therapy and growth, a part of her had believed him until she'd met the man running his finger lovingly over her sculpture?

She wasn't abnormal or dull. She was passionate and creative and still unpeeling so many buried layers of who she was, of who she wanted to be.

Just like with the clay, she was unleashing the real Taylor.

"Thank you, Jack." She didn't mean for his compliment regarding her sculpture either.

Eyes sparkling, his smile wrapped around her and threatened to pull her close. "You're welcome, Taylor."

Taylor fought gulping, turned away from him, but made the mistake of looking Amy's way.

Her friend was grinning from ear to ear. Ugh.

She really needed to be more careful or Amy was going to think she was onto something with her matchmaking.

Maybe if circumstances were different, she might give

in to the temptation she saw in Jack's eyes. She was in Warrenville to start fresh, not rekindle something that would be over almost as quickly as it started. She wasn't having a man and possible heartbreak interrupt the normal, happy life she was carving for herself.

Taylor didn't bump into Jack the following day at the hospital. Which gave her an emotional reprieve as she knew it was the last day of his three on, four off shift.

Unfortunately, Amy refused to let her enjoy that reprieve.

"A bunch of friends is getting together for dinner and drinks. I want you to meet them. Get ready and go with me."

Glancing up from where she was reading an article on antibiotic resistance, Taylor reminded Amy, "You don't have to invite me to go with you everywhere you go."

She didn't want to be antisocial, but she'd never operated on Amy's high level of social activity. Her friend had always been able to go, go, go.

"I know that and I don't." Amy's hands went to her hips. "You didn't hear me inviting you to go with me to my grandmother's, did you?"

Taylor rolled her eyes. "What I heard was you trying to throw Jack and me together, because he will be there, won't he?"

"Jack is my friend. Of course he'll be there." Amy gave a little so-what shrug. "Besides, you like him. I see it in your eyes when you look at him."

"I wouldn't be looking at him if you'd quit throwing us together," Taylor reminded her, putting her magazine down.

"Inviting you to go with me tonight has nothing to do

with those looks I see passing back and forth between you and Jack."

Taylor eyed her friend suspiciously. "I don't need to be babysat. A year ago maybe, but now I'm content spending time alone and just enjoying life."

She really itched to unpack her supplies, make a space in one corner of her room and get her hands wet with her clay.

Watching Jack touch her sculpture the night before had her fingers eager to mold and shape new pieces.

No, not pieces. One particular piece that was starting to take hold in her mind. She couldn't see it, just knew it was there, obscured from sight and necessary to be found by touch, necessary to be set free from the excess clay surrounding it.

"Yeah," Amy said, "except I don't see you enjoying life when you are sitting on the sofa, reading work-related articles."

"I've only been moved in a week," she said. "Should I have been throwing a party or out all night repeatedly during that time?"

"No, but you do need to quit hiding yourself away."

"Too bad I didn't hide myself away when I met Neil."

"Neil was an idiot, stuck on himself," Amy announced matter-of-factly.

Taylor snorted. "Agreed, and I married him. What does that say about my judgment?"

"That you should let me choose all future dates."

Taylor rolled her eyes. "You're under the assumption I want to date. I don't. I really am happy with where I am in life."

Mostly.

"Fine. You don't want to date and are happy with

where you are in life. Now, about dinner, because you have to eat…"

She'd lived with Amy throughout college. Her friend wasn't going to let her sit at home alone. "By going to dinner with you and your friends, what you mean is going to dinner with you and Jack?"

"Not just Jack and me. There will be others, too." Not looking one bit guilty, Amy laughed. "I always did say you were the smart one in our friendship."

Knowing Amy wouldn't relent, Taylor stood from the sofa, stretched, and wondered if she should change. "That's not how I remember it."

"Yeah, well, your memory might be a little foggy. Good thing you're here for me to remind you of all the fun times we used to have."

Dinner with friends consisted of several co-workers meeting at a local bar. There were nine in total, so their waitress pushed two tables together and pulled a chair to one end.

Jack took the chair on the end.

Taylor went to move to the opposite end of the table but, as luck would have it, everyone else was already in the process of sitting down.

Grinning at her foiled efforts, Amy took the chair opposite where she stood, leaving only one unclaimed chair.

Right next to Jack.

"If I didn't know better I'd think you were trying to avoid sitting next to me."

She sank into the seat and gave him a pert smile. "Good thing you know better."

He stared at her a moment, then offered, "I will move my chair to the other end of the table if you want, Taylor."

Quit being so nice, she wanted to scream. Instead, she shook her head. "There's no need for that."

The waitress took drink orders. Everyone up to Taylor ordered beer.

"A water with lemon, please."

"Ah, Tay, loosen up and have some fun," Amy encouraged.

Taylor just smiled at her best friend and was grateful when the waitress took Jack's order then left to get their drinks.

"Afraid to lower your inhibitions around me?"

First making sure Amy was caught up in her conversation with the phlebotomist sitting next to her, Taylor cut her eyes to Jack. "Should I be?"

"No." but the promises in his eyes warned otherwise. "Unless you're still upset with me about what I said to Duffy."

She shook her head.

"In which case, there's no reason why we can't be friends."

"Friends." Taylor let that sink in. Jack wanted to be her friend. "Is that what you want from me? Friendship?"

His gaze darkened. "Until a few days ago I thought I already had your friendship. Now I'm not sure."

"You did." Taylor sighed. "You do," she corrected, knowing it was true. How did she explain she'd enjoyed their tryst but didn't want to pick up where they'd left off? But that she feared her body wouldn't go along with that plan given half a chance?

The crinkles at the corners of his eyes fanned outward. "I'm glad. You have to admit we had a good time."

She couldn't deny it. Neither did she want to discuss their "good time" at a table of their co-workers, especially not as she could feel Amy's curious looks.

"Right. The concerts were great. I really appreciate you keeping me from going alone. Now, tell me about where you'll be headed for your next music festival."

Yes, she was changing the subject. To his credit, he let her.

"I don't have another until after my gig is up here in Warrenville. Then I'm off to Daytona for a country music weekend event."

"Country music?"

"Yep." He glanced around the bar where they were and stage-whispered, "In case you haven't noticed, we're knee deep in country in this place."

She had noticed the handful of couples out on the dance floor and the twangy music playing in the background.

"I didn't know you liked country."

"There's a lot you don't know about me." He grinned. "Yet."

"There's a lot I do know about you," she mimicked in a low voice. When she looked up, Amy had given up all pretense of conversation with the woman next to her and was watching them like a proud mother hen.

Straightening her napkin and ignoring Amy, Taylor asked, "So, which is your favorite? Country or rock?"

"I like and listen to both. Not sure I like one genre better than the other. Certain artists stand out more than others from both genres, but I really don't lean more one way than the other overall. What about you?"

"We've established that I'm not a big music buff."

"I thought we'd resolved that at Rockin' Tyme. You seemed to get into the swing of things." He grinned. "Literally."

She laughed. "Some random guy grabbing me and tossing me about a bit doesn't count as me getting into the swing of things."

Amy pounced. "I didn't hear about this random guy. Tell me more."

Taylor shrugged. "It wasn't a big deal. Jack and I were dancing and a fellow Rockin' Tymer wanted a turn."

"You danced?" Amy's eyes sparkled.

Feeling quite proud of herself, Taylor nodded. "I told you that I know how to have a good time. Why won't you believe me?"

Although she looked impressed, Amy shot back, "I keep waiting for you to show me."

"That's my cue if ever I've heard one." Jack pushed his chair back, stood, and put his hand out to Taylor. "Dance with me and show this skeptical lady what I already know."

Feeling pretty skeptical herself, Taylor arched a brow. "What's that?"

"That you know how to have a very good time."

CHAPTER TEN

TAYLOR STARED AT Jack's hand as if he were the Grim Reaper come to lead her down a dastardly path.

It wasn't a look Jack enjoyed seeing on her pretty face, but they needed to get away from the table and Amy's listening ears for a few. The dance floor offered that reprieve.

Rather than decline, she reluctantly put her hand in his, shot a glare toward Amy, who laughed, then let him guide her to the dance floor.

"You know the waitress is going to take orders while we're here, right?" she pointed out while following him to the far corner of the dance area. The other dancing couples didn't offer much shield from their co-workers' eyes, but at least their conversation couldn't be overheard.

"She'll come back," he said. "May I?"

"I think it's a given that you're going to since we're here to dance." She eyed him curiously. "Do you think this is a good idea with everyone watching?"

He wrapped his arms around her, letting his hands rest at her waist. At first she stood awkwardly against him, then sighed and put her arms around his neck.

Holding her again felt so good, so right.

"Let them wonder."

"Easy for you to say," she mused. "You're leaving in a couple of months."

He pulled back enough to look into her eyes. "You care what they think?"

She considered his question, then shrugged. "Only Amy."

"She approves."

Taylor snickered. "You think?"

He did his best to look innocent. "I've picked up on a few hints here and there."

Taylor rolled her eyes. "Observant of you."

"What about you?"

She arched her brow.

"Do you approve?"

"Of our dancing?" She shrugged. "I'm here, aren't I?"

"That you are," he agreed, pulling her closer as they swayed to the music. "You feel good, by the way."

She smelled good, too. A light vanilla with a dash of spice scent drew him in, making him want to inhale deeply. Cookies, he thought. She reminded him of fresh-baked sugar cookies.

"And," he continued, "I've missed you."

Her gaze lifted, but it wasn't a smile on her face. No, she was frowning. "How could you have missed me? We spent less than five full days together."

"Five great days that ended too soon."

She didn't look convinced. "What exactly did you think was going to happen Monday morning at the end of our shift? That we'd make plans to drive to see one another until the sexual chemistry fizzled out? You didn't know about my interview or that I might move here before your ER stint was up so I know you weren't planning to see me again."

"You think our sexual chemistry would have fizzled out?" He ignored the rest of her comments, because he didn't know the answers.

She rolled her eyes. "Be serious, Jack."

"I was. It's been over a month and the chemistry is going strong."

She missed a step, bumping her foot against his. "It is?"

"Do you really have to ask?" Jack held her close, fighting the urge to lower his head to where he could breathe in the scent of her hair, of her neck, see if she tasted of cookies, too. "I don't like this tension between us." Such an understatement. "I can't figure out if it stems from my comment to Duffy or Amy pushing us together or something I'm clueless about. Regardless, I want you, Taylor. I have from the beginning and that's not changed. Not for me."

"If you wanted me so much, why did I have to come to your tent?" Her eyes glittered with challenge and her chin tilted forward. "Why didn't you come to mine?"

He deserved her questions and she deserved the truth. "I was trying to do the right thing."

She snorted. "Guess I blew that all to pieces."

"So that you know the whole truth, I was afraid you weren't ready to take that step and didn't want you to have regrets." He shrugged. "Unfortunately, you do anyway and that's my fault for my careless comment to Duffy."

"Why does any of this matter now?"

"Besides the fact that we're going to be working the emergency department together soon?"

"There is that," she admitted.

"But more importantly," he continued, "it matters because I wasn't ready for our relationship to end and I don't believe you wanted it to either."

"We ended one night early," she reminded.

Jack had never had difficulties talking to women. Now wasn't the time to start, but he was struggling to tell Taylor how he felt, what he wanted.

"I think you misunderstand." He searched for the right words. "I didn't want us to end on Monday morning, Taylor. That's why I didn't come to your tent. Because you meant more to me than just another woman I met at a music festival. I was doing my best to make sure you knew that. I thought if we had sex, I'd never convince you that I wanted a relationship."

"I wanted you to come to my tent."

"I needed to do things the right way."

"Whose right way, Jack? Yours? Mine? Someone else's? Because what makes you think your way was the right way? Or what I even wanted? I'm tired of men who think their way is the right way," she ranted, her brown eyes narrowed to tiny slits. "Who says I wanted a relationship? What if I just wanted sex and for us to go our separate ways on Monday?"

She had a point. Still, it wasn't as if he was asking for forever. Just that he enjoyed her company and wanted more of it. Wanted more of her.

Was he was being selfish in wanting to pursue a relationship when he'd be leaving?

Then again, she wasn't saying she wanted more.

"What is it you want, Taylor? Friendship? Then we'll just be friends. If that's what you want, I'll respect your decision."

With all his heart he believed she wanted more than friendship. He felt it in her touch, in the way her fingers had found their way into the hair at his nape and toyed with it. "But, for the record, I want more than friendship."

Her feet were barely moving. "How much more?"

"I'm here for another two months."

"Beyond that?"

He inhaled. "Anything beyond that wouldn't be easy. Not with the way I travel." He exhaled slowly, not liking his next words. "Whatever happened would end when I leave Warrenville."

The song they danced to ended and another started. They continued to slow dance, but the tempo was more upbeat, matching the wheels turning in Taylor's head. He could see them spinning round and round, much as the other couples on the dance floor were.

"I miss you, too," she finally said. "But that doesn't mean anything is going to happen between us."

What she said registered and he laughed, pulling back and pretending to check her.

Taylor's hands stilled at his neck, where she'd been twisting his hair around her fingers. "What are you doing?"

"Checking for blood because I'm pretty sure that admission mortally wounded you."

She rolled her eyes, but the effect was lost as she was smiling. "Don't press your luck, Jack."

His arms already around her, his hands at her lower back, he hugged her. "In all seriousness, Taylor, I'm glad you miss me. I want you to miss me so much that, for the next two months, you can't stay away."

Her eyes took on a sparkle he'd not seen since Rockin' Tyme, other than when she'd been talking about her sculpting.

"Sounds a little creepy."

He laughed again. "There she is."

"Who?"

"The woman who captivated me during a music festival."

"Who do you think you had dinner with last night?"

"Someone who refused to let herself relax and enjoy being with me."

She closed her eyes. "Okay, I'll admit it. I don't want to want you, Jack."

"I know."

Her eyes opened. "Actually, the truth of the matter is wanting you at Rockin' Tyme thrilled me. It had been so long since I'd felt anything regarding the opposite sex. But now that I do feel, well, attracted…" she sighed, her warm breath caressing against the curve of his neck, "…it's inconvenient and doesn't fit with who I am or the life I want to make here. So, I want you but I don't like it."

There was so much sincerity, so much emotion in her voice it made his heart hurt for her. Made him want to protect her from ever adding to her leeriness or pain.

"We don't have to do this." Although convincing his body wouldn't be easy when she was melted against him so completely. "I was serious when I said we could be friends."

"I guess we'll see." She gestured beyond him. "The waitress has almost finished taking everyone's orders. We should join them."

Taylor wasn't sure who'd pulled what strings, but Amy was her orientation trainer. Amy had been an excellent nurse when they'd graduated. Her skills had only become more fine-tuned over the years since then and working with her was informative and enjoyable.

Working with Amy meant being on the same schedule as Jack.

Something Taylor was taking one day at a time.

Over a week had passed since their dance. A week in which she'd seen him more days than not, but always at work or in a social setting with others, sometimes just Amy.

Amy, who had bounced around with excitement and squeals of "I knew it!" when Taylor had confessed the truth about Rockin' Tyme.

Currently, Amy had gone to the lab to drop off a vial of blood she'd drawn as the phlebotomist had been tied up with another patient. She'd sent Taylor to assist Jack on a thirty-something man who had a laceration requiring closure.

Working with Jack was almost as awesome as working with Amy. He brought the same laidback professionalism to the emergency room that she'd gotten used to at the music festival. He didn't get overly excited no matter what drama was unfolding, but was always on top of things medically. He treated everyone, staff and patients, with care and consideration.

He really was a great guy and a gifted physician.

"You want to finish closing this wound?"

Surprised at his question, Taylor glanced up to see if Jack was teasing.

He wasn't.

She'd only sutured a few times and none over the past few years as the opportunity hadn't arisen in the intensive care unit where she'd been working.

Did she want to? Not really. Especially not with Jack

watching. But she wasn't going to say no to a learning opportunity and Jack was a great teacher.

With trembling hands, she took the needle holder from him.

Following the pattern he'd made along the man's gashed arm, she positioned the needle, then looked at Jack.

"Perfect," he reassured her as she pushed the curved needle into the man's anesthetized skin and out the other side of his wound.

Pulling the thread through, she released the needle, wrapped the ethilon around the tip of her needle-nosed holder multiple times, then tied off a knot. She repeated the knot-tying process several times. She wrapped one direction one time and the opposite the next, to make sure the knot didn't work loose as the man returned to his normal activities of daily living and increased tension was placed on the sutures.

"Beautiful stitch," Jack praised.

Glancing up, Taylor smiled.

"It is, isn't it?" she teased, pleased with both his praise and the suture.

She put the next three stitches in, getting faster with the last one.

"Excellent. Don't you think so, Ralph?" Jack asked their patient, who'd been talking a mile a minute about his logging business and how this same thing had happened a few years back.

Ralph glanced down at his closed cut. "Looks good to me. This mean I can go home now?"

Jack laughed. "Soon. Taylor is going to dress your wound, give you a tetanus vaccination, and print out wound-care handouts for you. When she's done, I'll write discharge orders. Then you can go home."

Taylor finished cleaning the man's more minor cuts and scratches. Really, the guy had been lucky. He'd been cutting timber and, unexpectedly, a tree had fallen near him. Some of the branches had left nasty cuts. The one on his left arm had been the worst and the only one requiring sutures.

"Nice job in there," Jack commended when she returned to the nurses' station where he sat with Amy.

"Thanks." She gave him a smile she hoped conveyed her true appreciation of his patience and praise. "It's been a while since I've sutured so I was nervous."

"You did fantastically. You can assist any time on my patients, Nurse Hall."

"Thank you, Dr. Morgan." She met his gaze, wondering how any woman could ever resist the shimmering joy in his eyes. How she'd ever thought she could resist?

"Listen to you two being all normal co-workers," Amy teased, standing up from the nurses' station where she'd been charting. "There's another new patient in Triage. I'll attend to him."

Taylor watched her go and fought sighing.

"She's persistent. You have to give her that," Jack mused, not sounding upset by Amy purposely leaving them alone.

"And as subtle as a ton of bricks."

"Speaking of which, this is the weekend she's out of town. She made me promise to make sure you didn't sit home alone."

"We both know what happened the last time she made you promise to watch out for me."

He shrugged. "I liked what happened last time."

She had, too, but that didn't mean it should happen again. Getting all tangled up with a man was not on the agenda of her new life. It just wasn't.

She glanced down to read the information on the patient Amy was triaging. A four-year-old with shortness of breath with suspected asthma. She pointed it out to Jack and he left to take a quick peek at the boy.

When he returned, he dropped in an order for a nebulizer treatment. "Amy took a verbal and has already gotten the treatment started. She said to tell you she'd let you know if she needed you."

Next to him at the nurses' station, Taylor studied Jack as he documented his physical examination of the child.

"Do you like kids, Jack?" The question popped out of her mouth as quickly as the thought had hit her. Her throat dipped somewhere in the vicinity of the pit of her stomach.

Pausing at the computer, he turned toward her. His eyes sparkled as he said, "All except the whiny ones."

"They're all whiny at one point or another, aren't they?" Grateful he hadn't seemed to read anything into her question, she continued, "Honestly, I'm not one to give thoughts on kids. I was an only child and have little experience with children outside nursing school or work."

"Only child? That makes you spoiled rotten, right?" he teased.

"Ha. Hardly, Mr. Also-an-Only-Child." She shook her head. "My parents were in their forties when they got pregnant with me. They'd not planned to have kids, so I was a surprise they didn't want and didn't know what to do with once I arrived. I mostly did what they expected of me, stayed quiet and kept to myself as not to disturb them too much."

If she ever had children, she'd make sure they never felt that way.

"That doesn't sound like fun."

"Fun was not a word in the Hall household."

"Poor Taylor."

"Don't mock me," she scolded. "I didn't say I had a bad childhood, just not a fun one. My parents were strict. Not quite military-school strict, but I imagine they got close. They weren't mean or cruel. I was always taken care of. Never without food, clothes, shelter, books to read. I certainly didn't have it bad. Just not the stuff of Normal Rockwell."

He studied her a moment, then confessed, "I was home-schooled."

"Really?"

He nodded. "We traveled too much for me to attend regular school so my mother provided my education. It was interesting, to say the least."

Taylor lifted one shoulder. "You went to med school so she must have done something right."

"She did a lot right and got lucky that I liked to learn and was a good student."

"I wasn't."

"Wasn't what?" he asked.

"A good student," she admitted, a little embarrassed that she felt compelled to do so.

"I find that difficult to believe."

"Oh, don't misunderstand. I made good grades," she clarified. "I just had to work really hard for them. Amy could party all night, go to class the next morning and ace a test. Not me. I had to put my nose to the books and learn the material inside out."

"Everyone learns differently."

"Yeah, some of us do things the hard way over and over." Glancing around the emergency room bay, which was rather quiet at the moment, restlessness overtook Taylor. "Guess I should see if Amy needs help."

"She's going to say she doesn't because she prefers you to be doing exactly what you are doing right this moment."

"What's that?"

"Talking with me."

Taylor sucked in a deep breath. "Jack."

He grinned. "I like it when you say my name."

"Yeah, well, I should say Dr. Morgan."

He shook his head. "No matter what happens, I'm always Jack to you. Always."

Amy left on Friday morning and Taylor's phone buzzed before ten a.m. with a text from Jack. She'd been up for a while, working on catching up on her laundry.

Staring at her phone, she sighed. *Oh, Jack. What am I going to do about you?*

She'd been clinging to what she'd overheard as an excuse to put distance between them. She recognized that just as she recognized the truth in what he'd said. She and Jack had no future together. Spending time with him set her up for heartache, but not spending time with him seemed impossible.

At least for as long as she was paired with Amy for orientation she'd be on the same work schedule as Jack. And, for at least as long as Amy had breath in her body, her friend seemed determined to push them together.

Jack's position at the hospital would be ending before long. Then she wouldn't see him. At all.

Just the thought of that made her heart squeeze.

Maybe she was only hurting herself by refusing him when she could be having sex with Jack. He missed her and wanted her. He'd told her so. Spending the next few weeks with Jack wouldn't derail her goals. She wouldn't depend on him or expect anything from him.

He was leaving. She knew he was leaving. She didn't want him to stay.

She'd be fine.

CHAPTER ELEVEN

TAYLOR'S HAIR WAS blowing about her face crazily as she and Jack rode in 'Jessica', his nickname for his Jeep. The sun beat down on top of her head. The radio was cranked up and could be heard over the wind noise.

Raising her arms above her head to let the wind blow through her fingers, Taylor laughed.

Jack glanced over at her and grinned. "Having fun?"

Between the air with the top off, the radio, and the engine, the Jeep wasn't conducive to having a conversation, so Taylor nodded her answer.

This was fun.

And a lot more relaxing than she'd have imagined.

They drove around on Tennessee back roads for more than an hour before Jack pulled over near a bridge.

"You want to walk down and play in the water?"

Taylor stared at him as if he'd lost his mind. "What?"

His eyes were full of challenge. "You heard me."

"I didn't bring clothes for playing in the water."

He waggled his brows. "Where's your sense of adventure?"

Good question.

"I was born with a genetic deficiency of that particular sense." But was working on developing it.

He laughed, grabbed his backpack from behind his seat, then climbed out of the Jeep. "Come on. If we hike just a short way, there's a cool waterfall. It's not big, only about six or seven feet, and flows down rather than being a straight drop, but it's a beauty with the way the water moves over the rocks."

"Do I even want to know how you know that?"

"I've been here before."

With a woman? she wondered.

Coming around to her side of the Jeep, he held out his hand. "One of the times Greg was in town, Amy, Greg, and I checked this place out. Amy is a treasure trove of off-the-beaten path places."

Taking his hand, she stepped out of Jessica. "Now I know why she's pushing us together."

"Why's that?" he asked, leading the way down the embankment to where the small river ran.

"So you'll quit being the third wheel on her dates with Greg."

He laughed. "You might be right."

Making it to the water's edge, Taylor took in the bubbling water with the big flat rocks scattered about. Small purple flowers grew along the banks, as did Queen Anne's Lace and Black-Eyed Susans. Beyond the bank was a field that led into woods. Everything in sight was absolutely gorgeous—the man included.

Tossing his backpack onto the grass, Jack kicked off his shoes and waded out into the water, which came just above his ankles.

"When will I get to meet Greg?" she asked as she sat down on the bank and began taking off her sandals. She had to at least dip her toes into the water. "I've been here a couple of weeks. They talk on the phone and text often enough, but I figured I'd have met him by now. He's only an hour away, right?"

"Amy would know better than me," Jack admitted. "But I imagine we've not seen him since you've moved in to give you two time to catch up. He'll probably drive up during Amy's next four days off. He was here almost weekly prior to your move."

She hadn't really thought about how her living at Amy's place impeded her friend's dating life. Amy had repeatedly invited her to move back in, but maybe her being there was an imposition?

"Good. I'm glad he's coming." Once she'd met him, she'd make herself scarce. "I need to make sure he's good enough for my best friend."

Holding his hand out to her as he waited for her to step into the water, he asked, "Turnabout is fair play?"

"Oh, Amy's not trying to make sure you are good enough for me. She gave her stamp of approval long before I'd ever met you." Taylor's eyes widened at how cold the water was. Her skin goose-bumped. "Wowzers, where are the ice cubes coming from?"

Jack chuckled. "This is fed from an underground spring about a mile from here and is a bit brisk when you first step in. You'll get used to it and it'll feel good in this heat."

The water temperature was definitely a direct contrast to the late morning sunshine, but Jack was right in that the longer she was in the water, the more she adjusted to the temperature.

A step ahead of her, Jack stopped walking, let go of her hand, and bent down to study the water in a semi-shallow spot where the creek bed was readily visible.

"Tell me you've not found a snake," she ordered, trying to see what he was looking at and not spotting anything. She took a step back, just in case.

"No, but it is possible we might see one. If we do, just don't panic. Odds are it'll be more scared of you than you are of him." At her look of alarm, he grinned. "No worries, Taylor. If anything tries to bother you, I'll rescue you."

"Yeah, yeah, but who's going to rescue me from you?"

He waggled his brows. "You have all the power where I'm concerned."

"What's that mean?"

"That whatever you say goes. That's why I haven't pushed this past week. Nothing will happen between us until you give the word that you're ready."

She was still pondering his comment when he reached down in the water and scooped up something with his hands.

Something that was alive.

"Don't throw that at me or I may never forgive you."

"I won't but come and see."

Taylor carefully made her way across the rocky creek bottom to stare into Jack's cupped hands.

"Is that a baby lobster?"

Looking up at her, he grinned. "I take it you've never seen a crawdad before?"

She shook her head. "Is that what that is?"

He nodded. "Technically, it's called a crawfish, but you won't hear anyone around here call it that."

"Those are claws, though, right?"

He nodded.

"Will he pinch you?"

Jack shrugged. "It's possible but in all my years of catching crawdads I've yet to have it happen."

"You've done this a lot?"

"Played in creeks catching minnows and crawdads? My whole life."

"Music festivals and catching crawdads. Sounds a little idealistic, Jack."

One corner of his mouth lifted. "At times."

Sensing there was something more behind his half-smile, she asked, "And at others?"

He shrugged. "Nobody's life is perfect, but I have no complaints."

"Our childhoods couldn't have been more different."

"I take it your parents never took you to a creek to catch crawdads and minnows?"

She shook her head. "This is my first time in a creek and you already know I had no clue what a crawdad was."

He held his hands out toward her. "You want to hold him?"

"What?" She stared down at the less than two inches long mini-lobster in Jack's cupped palms. "I'm afraid to."

"If he pinches, I promise to kiss you and make you feel better."

Heart pounding, Taylor's gaze lifted to Jack's and suddenly holding the crawdad didn't seem nearly as scary as continuing to stare into his eyes. It would be so easy to fall for him. To become so head over heels that her experience with Neil would seem like child's play. To let how wonderful Jack was sway her life views to where she just didn't care that in the long run he'd hurt her if she wasn't careful.

"Don't let him hurt me," she ordered, then scrunched her forehead. *And don't you either.* "How do we do this?"

"Cup your hands like mine and scoop water into your hands."

She did as he said, then looked at him expectantly.

"I'm going to hold my hands over where yours are cupped and put him into your hands." His voice held the same patience she saw him exhibit in the emergency room. The same patience he seemed to exhibit in all aspects of life. "Ready?"

She nodded. She could do this. Not that she'd ever known she wanted to hold a crawdad, but in this moment overcoming her fear seemed paramount. Did that directly relate to her fear of letting a man close enough to hurt her? To change who she was or impede the discovery of who she was?

He put his hands directly on hers, his skin cool from having been in the water, then moved his hands apart slightly to let the water and crawfish he held drop into her hands.

"Oh, my," she said, nervous she held the creature, but excited she was doing so.

"He won't hurt you," Jack reminded her.

She didn't take her eyes off the crawdad. "You're sure?"

"Ninety-nine percent positive."

Her gaze lifted. His grin was lethal.

"That doesn't make me feel better, Jack."

He laughed. "We should have brought cups to catch with. Crawdads I can do bare-handed. It's been a while since I've caught a minnow that way, though."

"I didn't know we were going to be doing this."

"Gotta be prepared for anything when you're with me."

"You could have told me that before I said yes to coming with you," she teased, then deepened her voice to intone, "Taylor, be prepared for anything, because you may end up standing in the middle of a creek holding something that looks like a baby lobster."

His lips twitched. "Would your answer have been different?"

Eyes locked with his, she shook her head. "No, not as long as this thing really doesn't decide to pinch me and not let go. That happens and you're on your own."

"If he does, we'll make him lunch."

"Um...no." Taylor wrinkled her nose, then glanced down at the creature in her palms. "Do people really eat them?"

"Many consider crawfish a delicacy."

"Doesn't look like much of a meal."

"Yeah," he chuckled. "One wouldn't be."

"You eat them?"

He nodded. "On more than one occasion."

Her gaze dropped back to the tiny creature with empathy. "Let's let this one go."

"Guess it's a good thing I brought lunch, then."

"You brought lunch?"

He nodded and gestured toward his backpack. "Drinks are in the cooler in Jessica, though."

"You're like a scout. Always prepared."

He chuckled. "Never a scout, but I've camped more than my share."

She arched a brow at him.

"Most of my childhood was spent in campgrounds. There were a few times we lived in actual buildings, but they were far and few between."

"You lived in tents?"

"Sometimes. Most of the time we had this pop-up

camper we pulled behind a mini-van my mother referred to as Bertha."

"That's where you get naming your Jeep?"

He gave her an incredulous look. "Have you never named a vehicle?"

She shook her head.

"Guess that's going to be another first for you, Taylor, because your car has to have a name."

"Yeah, well, my little sedan doesn't have Jessica's character. She'd be rather dull, I think."

"Your car is a female, then?"

She thought about it a minute, then nodded. "Definitely."

"Look, that one's a rabbit munching on a carrot." Taylor pointed to a group of puffy white clouds that contrasted starkly with the intense blue of the sky.

"I see the rabbit, but are you sure that's a carrot?"

She turned to look at Jack. "What else would it be?"

"A cigar. See the tiny puff of smoke coming off the end?"

"Okay, I'll give you that one." The clouds did look more like a rabbit smoking a cigar than one eating a carrot. "But, for the record, my rabbit was healthier than yours."

"You won't get any arguments from me on that one."

Something in his voice struck her and she turned her head to look at him in question.

Without looking her way, he admitted, "Both my parents smoked, which is why I lost my dad at too early an age."

"I'm sorry, Jack. What happened?"

"Heart attack in his late forties."

"You were young when it happened, then?"

"Fairly young," he agreed, but didn't elaborate.

"What about your mother? Is she still alive and smoking?"

"Mom quit smoking after Dad died. She decided she needed to live a healthier lifestyle. She traveled for a while but settled down. She runs a holistic hippie compound about an hour from here for anyone looking to find themselves. They grow their own food, make their own makeshift houses and live a mostly organic if isolated life."

Listening to him talk about his life made Taylor feel as if she were that rabbit in the sky, one that had fallen into another realm. "Really?"

"You think I can make this stuff up?"

"I can't imagine."

"I can take you there sometime."

She'd meant his childhood, but his offer caught her interest. "To meet your mother?"

"To see the compound," he clarified.

Taylor's face heated. She shouldn't have assumed he'd meant anything. "Oh, right. Sorry."

"You'd meet my mom, too, Taylor. She lives there."

"She probably wouldn't like me." The words slipped out of her mouth, revealing way more than what she should have.

"Why's that?"

"Sounds like she's very much a free spirit. That's not who I am. She'd find me plain and boring."

He rolled over onto his side to look at her. "She'd feel you were a kindred soul just waiting to break free from the confines of society and embrace your inner self."

His assumption pleased Taylor more than it should.

"That sounded rehearsed," she accused playfully, giving him a suspicious brow raise.

"You think?" He laughed. "I may have heard her say that a few times."

"About women you've taken to the compound?"

His gaze met hers and he shook his head. "I've never taken a woman to the compound."

"Oh." She stared into his eyes, marveling at how they perfectly matched the sky. "But you'd take me?"

He nodded.

She marveled at his answer, too. "Why?"

"Because you wanted to go. And for the record, you, Taylor, are the least plain and boring person I know."

Although Jack was enjoying lying on the blanket with Taylor, he was ready for a subject change.

"What about your parents? Are they alive? Do they live in Louisville?"

"They are alive. I used to see them a few times a year, but not since my divorce."

The pain in her voice gave any explanation needed. Her parents hadn't approved of her divorce. Had they cut her out of their lives? Or had she had to walk away from them along with her ex?

"I'm sorry."

Her voice breaking, she explained, "They thought I should stay with Neil. In their eyes, I should have appreciated how lucky I was to be married to a successful doctor no matter what he did."

"If you felt the need to leave, your parents should have helped you pack." And her dad should have kicked the guy's tail. Jack reached for her hand and gave it a squeeze. "What did he do?"

Taking a very deep breath, she shrugged. "He was himself. I just didn't see the real him until it was too late and I'd married him." She exhaled sharply. "I was a possession, meant to do as he said when he said, and should have been okay with his infidelity, among other things."

Jack winced. "He cheated on you?"

"Several times that I know of and who knows how many I never learned of?"

"He was an idiot."

Taylor laughed, but there was no pleasure in the sound. "Actually, he's a brilliant plastic surgeon and apparently does amazing work."

Something in her tone told its own tale. "He never operated on you?"

She glanced down at her moderate-sized chest. "Do these appear enhanced to you?"

Jack glanced at her breasts and fought gulping. "I found—find—your breasts just right."

Taylor snorted. "Well, he didn't and wanted to lift and enlarge them. He also offered to pad my bottom and freeze the fat in my thighs and make my nose smaller and my lips fuller and make my chin not so boxy and—"

Jack's finger went over her lips, stopping her words. "You're perfect the way you are, Taylor. He was the one who had problems. Not you. I'm glad you never let him take a knife to you."

Taylor sighed. "Sorry, I got on a rant, didn't I?"

"You deserve to rant. If a woman is unhappy with her body and wants to make changes, that's her choice and more power to her. So long as she is making the change for herself. But a man pushing a woman to change?" He shook his head. "A man should never make a woman feel she needs to make those changes because she's not good enough." He lifted her hand and pressed a kiss there. "You are good enough, Taylor. Way better than he ever deserved."

Better than Jack deserved, too.

"Sometimes I wonder if you're for real," she mused, eyeing him as if she thought he might disappear any moment.

Not sure what she meant, he waited for her to elaborate.

"You seem to know what to say to make me feel better about myself, to be justified in my outrage." She shrugged. "You make me feel better inside, Jack. Thank you for that."

Her compliment made him feel better inside, too. She made him feel better.

"You're welcome." He wasn't sure what else to say. He knew what he wanted to do. He wanted to hold her, kiss her, make love to her right here on a blanket in the middle of nowhere with a babbling little waterfall in the background.

But he'd told her she had the power, that he wouldn't push or do anything until she gave the word it was what she wanted. He wouldn't force himself on Taylor in any way.

So he settled for holding her hand and consoled himself that lying on this blanket, holding her hand in his, was more precious than all the kisses in the world from anyone else.

Which slapped him in the face yet again with the reality of how she affected him.

Taylor had been suppressed her whole life and had never been given the opportunity to just be. Whereas he'd grown up with no boundaries, with parents who'd encouraged him to step outside society lines, she'd been stuffed inside the box of others' expectations and forced to stay within those tight confines.

That she had so newly torn free of that box made her vulnerable, made making sure he did nothing to cause her to stumble and possible fall back into those confines all the more important.

For the next month he intended to help her rip down as many of those walls as possible. To show her the world from his perspective.

After his time was up in Warrenville, well, he hoped when she thought of him, she would smile and feel he'd made her world a little brighter place.

Taylor fiddled with her keys outside Amy's apartment door. "Thank you for today."

"You're welcome."

She'd had an amazing day. The best. Playing in water, cloud watching, a picnic, and then he'd taken her to a Japanese hibachi grill for a late sushi dinner, something else she'd never tried. The day had been filled with laughter, adventure, and light-heartedness.

"Will I see you tomorrow?" she asked.

"Do you want to see me tomorrow?"

He had to know she did. How could she not when their day had been so carefree? Making her feel as if she'd traveled back in time to play with him as part of his childhood?

What she was feeling for him was very grown up.

Very adult.

"Then you'll see me." He winked, much as he had on the nights he'd gone back to his tent, then left.

* * *

An hour later, as Taylor lay in bed, she stared at her ceiling in the darkness of her room, restless, mind racing, heart full.

Sleep wouldn't come.

No matter how long she lay there, she knew it was useless to keep trying.

Because she burned inside.

Burned that she'd not invited Jack inside the apartment. Burned with regret that she'd not invited Jack into her bed.

She wanted him.

Maybe she'd always want him.

He was that kind of man. Strong and virile, yet gentle and patient in a way that made her feel feminine and safe.

Safe.

Sweet, free-spirited Jack.

Inhaling sharply, she fluffed her pillow and rolled over. Calling him safe seemed hypocritical because it was the danger posed by him that had held her back when she'd first moved to Warrenville. That and not wanting him to feel obligated to continue being interested in her. More than anything, she realized she'd been afraid to risk falling in love with Jack.

Jack. Jack. Jack.

She couldn't let herself love him, but she couldn't help but want him.

CHAPTER TWELVE

"Did I wake you?" Jack asked, glancing at his fitness watch to make sure it wasn't earlier than he'd thought.

"Hmm, maybe," came Taylor's response. Sleep had her voice low and raspy over the phone line. Had him envisioning what she must look like and how he'd rather have wakened her.

"I'd ask if you had a late night, but I know what time I dropped you off," he mused.

"Needed my…" she yawned "…beauty sleep."

"Is that how you always look so amazing? Sleep?"

"Listen to you, Mr. Flatterer."

She was starting to sound more awake. An image of her stretching her body flashed into his head and he knew it's what she was currently doing. Arching her back and stretching her arms high above her head.

"It's after ten. I was going to invite you to lunch, but maybe I should call it brunch?"

"Brunch sounds good."

He could hear movement in the background, so she must have gotten out of bed.

"Ouch!" She let loose with a string of expletives that were so mild Jack fought not to laugh.

"We are going to have to enroll you in Cursing for Beginners because that was weak, lady."

"Yeah, well, I wouldn't be a lady if it was too brash, now, would I?" she shot back, eliciting another laugh from him.

"What happened?"

"I stubbed my toe against the coffee-table leg."

The coffee table?

"You were asleep on the sofa?"

"Mmm-hmm. I was too tired to make it to my bed."

"Our hike exhausted you that much yesterday evening?"

"Our hike was wonderful." She yawned again. "Let me shower, then I'll meet you somewhere for that brunch you mentioned. I'm starved."

"Okay if I just pick you up and we'll go together?"

She hesitated a moment, then, "Sure. Give me thirty minutes."

Thirty minutes. He could do that.

"Wear a bathing suit under your clothes."

"Huh?"

He could picture her baffled look.

"No questions. Just go with it."

"We going back to the creek?"

They'd had fun in the creek, but had never gotten into water any deeper than knee-high. He had something different in mind.

Smiling, he promised, "You'll see."

A knock at her apartment door.

She grabbed a big floppy bag into which she'd put her sunscreen, lip balm, cellphone, an extra set of clothes, and keys, and stepped out of the apartment.

Running his gaze over her, Jack whistled. "You must sleep a lot."

Confused, she furrowed her forehead.

"You truly are beautiful and if it's sleep..."

"Ah, I get your drift." She shot him a wry look. "For the record, I would have gotten more except someone called and woke me up this morning."

Spotting Jessica, she stopped walking and turned to look at him, eyes huge. "What are those?"

He grinned. "Kayaks."

"Kayaks?"

"I borrowed them and the trailer from Jeff." When she still looked clueless, he added, "He works in the lab."

Ah, that Jeff.

She continued to stare at Jack a bit in awe. "As in borrowed for us to get in and float around?"

He chuckled. "That's the idea so don't go all *Titanic* on me."

"Kayaking," she mused. "That'll be another first for me." Climbing into Jessica, she exhaled a deep breath. "Hope I don't ruin your day by totally screwing this up. I mean, I won't purposely *Titanic* Jeff's kayak, but what if I accidentally sink it? I've never been into sports or athletic kind of things. If this requires skills of any type, I'm going to disappoint you."

"The only way you'll disappoint me is if you let the voices in your head keep you from giving this a go," he told her. "I enjoy watching you do new things, showing and teaching you new things." He stood next to the passenger side of the Jeep, brushed his hand over her cheek and grinned at her. "Besides, I'm not worried. You've got this."

Jack really was good for her, so nurturing and positive. She'd been trying new things since her divorce but being with Jack made those new experiences seem like baby steps. Then again, she'd had to start somewhere, and baby steps had been huge at the time.

She flashed a big smile that she hoped conveyed how much she appreciated him, then ordered, "Get in Jessica, Jack. You promised brunch and I'm dying of hunger."

Laughing, Jack got in the Jeep.

"That was amazing!" Taylor gushed as she helped pull her kayak out of the river. They'd driven about thirty miles to a rather rundown-looking shack where they'd loaded up their kayaks and themselves on an equally rundown-looking bus without air-conditioning. Kayaks strapped down on top, the bus carried them, along with a dozen others, upstream and dropped them off for them to make their way back to the base where they'd started.

"You know I'm going to want to go again," she continued, amazed at how good her body felt, how good she felt.

Exhilarated. That was it. She felt exhilarated.

"I'm counting on it," Jack assured her, winking at her before turning his attention back to the kayak.

She glanced toward where he'd repositioned her kayak on the bank and tingles of awareness hit as she took in his baggy wet shorts, life jacket that covered a sleeveless T-shirt that had to be plastered to his chest, and a backward-facing baseball cap on top of his head to semi-contain his hair that curled and snaked to just past his shoulders. A scruffy shadow beard shadowed his face.

His arm muscles bulged as he gave the kayak one last tug forward.

When he turned toward her, Taylor didn't attempt to

hide her thoughts. She doubted she was that good an actress anyway.

The blue of his eyes darkened as he stared into hers. So much emotion in those depths. So much everything, she thought.

His brow lifted in question.

She'd already been caught and wasn't sure she cared that she had been. Lowering her gaze, she slowly took in all of him. From the width of his shoulders to the scrumptious chest hidden beneath his life jacket, to his narrow waist, hairy legs, and water-shoe-clad feet.

Sexiest river rat she'd ever seen.

A small smile twisted her lips as she met his eyes again.

"Whatever you're thinking, hold that thought forever," he ordered, his dimples dug deep into his cheeks.

Forever?

She hoped not.

But for the next month before he left for new adventures, yeah, she just might.

"Where are you staying while you're in Warrenville?" Taylor asked as they finished packing up their kayaks on the small trailer he pulled behind Jessica.

Jack made sure the straps holding the kayaks in place were properly tightened, then glanced up. "I've rented a farmhouse a few miles from the hospital. It's too big for one person but was furnished and available for a few months while the deceased estate is settled so it works. Plus, I like the wide open space."

"Oh?"

"Nothing around but rolling hills, farmland, and cows with a few barns, silos, and far-off neighbors. Once the estate is settled, the house and personal property will be auctioned off. At least, that's the plan of the former owner's children who inherited the place. I don't think they'll have any problems. It's several acres and has a nicely stocked pond for fishing."

"Fishing?"

He arched a brow. "Something else you've not done?"

"I wasn't hinting for you to take me," she said, looking cute in her braids and wet clothes.

Cute? Not exactly the right adjective to describe a woman as naturally beautiful as the one who'd barely been able to contain her enthusiasm during their ride down the river.

"I didn't mean to imply that you were, but I'd gladly take you fishing, Taylor. Just say when."

"Soon," she replied, glancing around to make sure they had everything packed and nothing remained on the gravelly ground.

"I look forward to it," he assured her, walking around the trailer to where she stood. "I had a great time today."

She grinned up at him. "Even though I lost my paddle and you had to tow me until we caught up with it?"

Jack's fingers itched to brush the tiny stray hairs back away from her face, to bend down to kiss her pert pink lips.

He cleared his throat, then said, "I'm just grateful that tree branch was low enough to snag it or I'd have been towing you the whole way."

Not that either of them had had to do a lot of paddling as the current had been good on most of the river with only a few areas where they could idly float.

"Yeah, so was I until you teased me to watch out for snakes on low-lying branches."

He chuckled. "Hungry?"

"Starved."

He'd packed snacks for them on their river ride, but breakfast had been a long time ago and they'd burned off the energy from their snacks hours ago.

"Want to see the farmhouse? I have steaks in the fridge I could grill for us."

Surprise lit her face. "Seriously?"

Not sure why she'd question his invitation, he asked, "Something wrong with steaks? I know you eat meat because I've seen you."

"No, not that. I just meant us going to your place for you to cook for me. It seems..." she shrugged "...such a normal thing to do."

He laughed. "Normal? Are you implying we don't usually do normal?"

"Nothing about what I do with you is normal, Jack."

"I'll take that as a compliment."

"It's meant as one and, yes, steaks sound delicious. I like mine medium to medium-well done. Please and thank you."

Jake's rented farmhouse was like something straight out of a picture book. An old but well-maintained white siding house with a navy roof, shutters, and trim work rested down a gravel road that was fenced on both sides. Cows dotted the pasture on both sides and to the left was the pond Jack must have been referring to.

The family must still have the land farmed because corn grew off in the distance as did some other crop. Taylor wasn't sure what it was. Soybeans, perhaps.

"Like it?" he asked as he pulled to a stop in front of a porch that sprawled all the way across the front of the house. A half-dozen rocking chairs were painted to match the house's navy roof and welcomed any visitor who wanted to spend time rocking away their cares.

Taylor loved it all. Warm, inviting, functional, like it had belonged here a hundred years and would be here another hundred.

"What's not to like?"

"If I ever settled down, I'd want it to be somewhere like here," Jack mused, glancing around the place with obvious admiration.

Taylor's gaze cut toward him.

"Mountains less than an hour away for climbing and hiking," he continued a bit wistfully. "Lots of lakes for skiing and swimming. Rivers and streams everywhere you look. Caves for exploring. Green in the spring and summer and amazing colors covering the hills in the fall. Snow in the winter for sledding and skiing in the mountains."

"I take it you like Tennessee."

He grinned. "Between all the big music festivals in Nashville, Memphis, Chattanooga, Knoxville, and the one in Warrenville, I end up spending most of my summers here, especially now that my mom is in Tennessee permanently."

Such a strange life he led. "Where is home, Jack?"

He shrugged. "Some music festival far, far away."

"An actual place?"

He shook his head. "Not really. Just a metaphorical locale that represents all the different places that made up my childhood."

"You never lived in one place that feels like going home when you visit?"

"Only time I ever lived in one place more than a few months was the year I stayed with my grandparents." He didn't look pleased about the experience.

"You lived with your grandparents?"

"A torturous half-year until everyone realized how miserable I was, being stuck in the same four walls all the time."

She couldn't imagine four walls containing Jack.

"At first, they put it down to me needing to adjust to the change, but I inherited their need to be on the move. Eventually, they realized their mistake and had me back on the road with them."

Whereas her parents lived in the same house they'd moved into when they'd got married and would likely live there until they died. She wasn't sure they'd ever left her hometown other than to attend her graduation from college. Even then, they'd not stuck around but had driven back home that very night, rather than sightseeing or spending time with her.

They were happy, content with their lives, so she didn't begrudge them what worked for them.

It just wasn't the life for her.

As the thought entered her head, Taylor smiled that she'd moved away from everything she'd known other than Amy, that she'd sought a new adventure, that she was living a different life.

Her life.

Mostly she was grateful for Jack because he was the greatest adventure she'd ever encountered.

"Come on," he said, climbing out of the Jeep. "Let's get the grill fired up."

Taylor's clothes had mostly dried on the ride to Jack's

farmhouse. But she felt grungy and when he refused to let her help, saying he wanted to do this for her as repayment for the night she'd cooked for him, she asked to take a quick shower.

"You naked in my tub?" he asked, then, grinning, asked, "You think I'm going to say no?"

Rolling her eyes, she asked him to point her in the right direction.

"Better yet, I'll show you."

Having already placed his steak away from the flame, Jack turned skewered vegetables on the grill next to Taylor's steak.

When she came to the backyard to find him, he glanced up.

She'd left her hair in her double braids and had changed into a different pair of shorts and tank top from the ones she'd kayaked in earlier. Her skin glowed a rosy pink, hopefully from her shower and not from too much sun. Her eyes sparkled, and her expression was soft, relaxed.

Relaxed looked good on Taylor.

Like it belonged, and she should wear it more often.

The back of the house had a patio and grill and if he cooked, it was usually there. Other than a few friends from work and Duffy a few days prior to Rockin' Tyme, he'd never had company at the farmhouse.

"Something smells good," she said, coming close to peek at the food on the grill.

"Yes, you do," he offered.

"Ha, I probably smell like you because I used your bath wash."

Lucky bath wash.

"Positive I've never smelled as good as you. This is almost done."

"Yay. Something about being around you makes me hungry."

"I know the feeling."

Her gaze lifted to his and she smiled. "Oh?"

He nodded. "Being around you increases my appetite, too."

"Um…guess we're both just hungry people around each other, huh?"

"Apparently." Jack cut into one of the steaks, making sure it was cooked somewhere between medium and medium–well done. "Perfect."

"Unlike your raw one there." She crinkled her nose.

Placing her steak on a plate, Jack laughed. "It's called rare, not raw."

She gestured to his steak. "Same difference, apparently."

He put his sirloin on a plate then put a vegetable skewer apiece on the plates. "Dinner is served."

CHAPTER THIRTEEN

"I ATE TOO MUCH," Taylor said, rubbing her belly. They'd cleared their dishes and had gone back outside to sit on the front porch.

She was sure Jack would have gone back outside, but she'd wanted to sit on the front porch. It had been so inviting. She wanted to rock.

So she rocked.

Jack was in the chair beside her but seemed more interested in watching her than in rocking his chair.

"Everything was really good, though," she continued, not content to sit in silence. Surprising because she felt sure she could while away many hours on this porch and feel at peace, but at the moment silence toyed with her sanity.

When he still didn't say anything, she frowned. "Jack, talk to me."

"I'm listening."

"Not the same thing as talking. It takes two to have a conversation."

"What do you want to talk about?"

Ugh. Why did he have to ask her that? And what was she supposed to say?

"Who's Courtney?" She wasn't sure where the question had come from, but somewhere in the recesses of her brain, the name Duffy had thrown at Jack had been agitating her, refusing to go away.

If she'd thought the silence had been thick before, it was nothing compared to the current heaviness of quiet.

"Jack?"

"My girlfriend when I was seventeen."

Okay. Not necessarily what she'd been expecting him to give as his answer. Why would Duffy have brought up a girlfriend from more than a decade ago?

"She had long black hair, the bluest eyes you've ever seen, and I was convinced gravity itself couldn't hold her down she was such a free soul."

Ugh. She did not want to feel jealous of his teenage girlfriend yet listening to Jack describe her, hearing the admiration in his voice, green filled her veins.

"She sounds beautiful." And Taylor's voice sounded envious.

"She was."

Was. Heaviness fell on Taylor's chest. Was. Did that mean…?

"I fell in love with her before I even knew her name." Jack sounded far away. "When she told me her name was Courtney, I knew she had to be lying because I'd have guessed Star or Rain or Cloud or Petal or something equally earthy, you know?"

She didn't, of course, but he wouldn't have heard her answer either way because he wasn't with her. Memories of a woman he'd loved had hold of him, and he was far away.

"When I finally found my voice I told her as much. She laughed and told me I could call her anything I wanted. I told her my name, and with that carefree laugh she had she said, 'Okay, Jack.' I was sixteen at the time and she was eighteen. Age didn't matter. Just being with her."

His eyes closed and he paused a moment, seeming lost in his memories.

"She'd run away from home years before and had been working music festivals for cash ever since. Sometimes parking cars during the daytime, sometimes working food booths, sometimes doing Lord only knows what to make ends meet." A short spurt of air came from his pursed lips. "I grew up around drugs and free-living, and was no saint, but Courtney got mixed up with some things better left alone. She hid it from me at first, but soon enough I saw the highs, the lows when she needed a fix. I hated it but was so in love with her I'd have done anything for her."

Taylor wasn't sure she wanted to hear more yet waited with bated breath for him to continue.

"We had been at a music fest in California for a couple of days and had another night to go. I was seventeen, almost eighteen by then. She was living hard. I don't know where she got the drugs, how she afforded them or what she did to get them. Like I said, I didn't want to know," he admitted. "One minute we were dancing and living what I thought was the greatest life ever and the next she fell at my feet and never woke up again."

"Oh, Jack. I'm sorry." She was. Sorry for the pain she heard in his voice.

"We had argued about how much she was using on occasion, but she wouldn't quit. Don't get me wrong, I was using stuff better left alone myself, but even so I could see the dangerous tightrope she was walking. I should have made her get help. Instead, I was as addicted to her as she was to her next high, so I turned a blind eye. In the long run, it cost me her." With tortured eyes, his gaze met hers. "I should have saved her, but I didn't."

"You know as well as I do that a person has to want to get help, Jack. You can't make someone overcome an addiction."

"Logically, I know that. But my seventeen-year-old heart has never believed it."

"I know you, Jack. If you could have helped her, you would have."

"It's where I met Duffy, you know."

She hadn't but waited for him to continue.

"I figured she'd just partied too hard and would sleep it off. But something inside me told me more was going on. I picked her up and carried her to the medical tent, praying she had just passed out and wasn't in any real danger, that she wouldn't kill me for telling the medics she'd possibly overdosed and wasn't picky about how she got her high. She crashed within a minute of me getting her to the medical tent. They tried to save her. Duffy and another man, a doctor, but she…was gone."

Taylor's heart hurt. She reached across the space between their chairs and took his hand. "Oh, Jack."

He sucked in a breath. "It was the first I'd met him, but Duffy spent a lot of time with me that night. I think he thought I was going to hurt myself and was afraid no one else would keep a constant eye on me. He never let me out of his sight. Not even when I went to the john."

He gave a humorless snort.

"I don't think I would have done anything, but I wasn't in my head that night. I was coming down off my own high and the light that lit my world had just gone out."

He swallowed hard.

"I didn't know who her family was, just her name. Duffy helped track them down, but no one came for her body. No one seemed to care that she was gone. Maybe that's why she'd left to begin with." He sighed. "Somehow, Duffy arranged for her to be cremated or maybe it was the State of California who did that. I don't know, just that Duffy was there and helped get her ashes for me. He saved me."

Fighting tears, Taylor squeezed his hand. "I'm glad he was there."

"Me, too." Jack swiped at his eyes, swallowed hard, then exhaled. "I'm not sure what would have happened to me had he not been working that night and taken a kid under his wing."

"You'd have found your way."

"Maybe, but I could have just as easily have slipped off that slippery slope that had claimed Courtney. Like I said, I was using myself."

"Instead," she reminded him, "you became a doctor."

"Because I became a doctor," he clarified. "I watched Duffy and that doctor work on Courtney, trying to save her life, and I knew that's what I had to do. I wanted to save lives, to make a difference to someone someday, the way they'd tried to make a difference for her and did make a difference for me."

Taylor's heart swelled at what Jack had gone through, at how something so devastating had not pulled him down but had lifted him up to become the man before her.

"You're a good person, Jack."

He snorted. "I've done some things that weren't so good during my life."

"Most people have."

* * *

Jack wondered if Taylor ever had. She was a good, decent person. He couldn't imagine her ever having done anything truly bad.

"I'm glad you stayed in touch with Duffy."

"Stayed in touch?" Jack scoffed. "He wouldn't leave me alone. He made me his pet project or the son he never had or whatever he likes to call it. Regardless, he has been there at every major life event since. University graduation, and then med school. And—" she'd think him crazy "—a few years ago he went with me to scatter Courtney's ashes."

He could tell by her face that she wondered what he'd done with them. It had taken him years to let them go, years to figure out where.

"We flew to Hawaii, hired a guide, went to the top of a volcano, and tossed her in."

Taylor's eyes widened. "What?"

It probably did seem crazy, but he had no regrets. Not for that.

"For years I tried to figure out where she'd want to be scattered. Almost threw her over a ledge into the Grand Canyon once, but it didn't feel right." He shrugged, then half smiled. "Being thrown into a volcano, that she would not only have approved of but she'd have loved it."

At Taylor's look of uncertainty, he took a deep breath then tried to explain.

"When a volcano blows, bits of ash are scattered through the atmosphere, even thousands of miles away. She'd be everywhere." A peace came over him. "Free, floating above the earth, seeing everything and slowly drifting down to become a part of everything." His voice lowered as he said, "She'd be everywhere. The volcano blew a year or so ago. *She is everywhere.*"

When she spoke, Taylor would probably demand he take her home. He wouldn't blame her. No way could she have anticipated his elaborate answer when she'd asked who Courtney was.

He didn't talk about Courtney.

Never with anyone other than Duffy on the rare occasion. That he so freely spilled out the horrid details to Taylor shook him. Why had he? He could have stopped with his girlfriend from when he'd been seventeen and left it at that. Taylor probably thought him crazy.

He was.

But she hadn't pulled away or demanded he drive her home. Not yet. Instead, Taylor's hand was warm, held his tight. But neither of them spoke for the longest time. He'd already said too much.

"That's a very beautiful tribute, Jack," she finally said. "She must have been a very special person for you to have loved her so much."

"I've never known anyone like her."

"I'm sorry you lost her."

"Me, too." Although, he wondered whether, if Courtney had lived, they'd have lasted or if he'd have tired of her abusing her body with drugs and whatever it took to get them. As much as he'd loved her, the man he was today wouldn't have stayed to watch such self-destructive behavior.

He was all about being a free spirit, but believed life was about a higher purpose, serving others. He liked to think that even had he never met Duffy he'd have found his calling, his purpose.

Knowing Taylor had to be tired of their depressing conversation, he stood from the rocker. "Let's go for a walk."

"In the dark?"

"You afraid?" he challenged, reaching his hand out
to pull her up from her chair.

"Should I be?"

"I promised you I'd never let anything hurt you," he
reminded her, and meant it. With everything in him he'd
do his best to keep Taylor from being hurt.

Taking his hand, she stood from her chair, laced her
fingers with his, and said, "Let's walk."

Taylor had lingered out in the cow pasture for as long
as she could.

Jack would take her home when they got back to the
house.

She didn't want to go back to the apartment.

She wanted to stay here, with Jack. Crazy, but she
didn't want to leave him. At the moment she didn't even
want to strip him naked and have her way with him—
although that was just beneath the surface.

What she wanted was to hold him.

Because Jack needed to be held. When they got back
to the house he turned to her. "Is your bag from when
you showered still in the house?"

She nodded.

"You want me to get it and us head toward your place?"

No, that wasn't what she wanted.

"I can get it." She could. "But if you want to grab it
for me, that would be great. I left it in the living room."

"Be back in just a few."

Taylor watched him go inside, then took off after him,

berating herself with each step. She was making a habit of following this man in hopes of ending up in his bed.

Only this time sex wasn't her sole motivating factor.

Hearing Taylor enter the house behind him, Jack turned toward her. He'd just spotted her bag on the living room sofa and was about to pick it up.

"I'm not leaving." She stared him straight in the eyes.

He arched his brow. "You're not?"

She shook her head. "I'm staying with you tonight. Here." Her chin lifted as if she thought he might defy her. "I want to sleep next to you and hold you and wake up with you."

Jack swallowed to moisten his dry throat. "Is that all?"

"For the moment."

Jack wasn't sure he was a strong enough man to sleep next to Taylor with her holding him and that was all. He felt as if he'd wanted her forever. As if it had been forever since he'd touched her, kissed her, shared his air mattress with her for a few magical hours.

"Okay."

His agreeing with her seemed to knock some of the wind out of her sails, because uncertainty flashed into her eyes. Whatever, she quickly masked it and smiled.

"Good answer."

"It wasn't as if I was going to refuse you saying you want to spend the night in my bed."

"Perfect." She smiled, then gave him a little *come hither* look. "I'm going to get ready for bed."

Jack glanced at his fitness band. "It is getting late, isn't it?"

Taylor yawned and he laughed.

She didn't have a clue how beautiful she was.

"You have a twinkle in your eyes, Taylor Hall."

Her lips twitched. "A twinkle?"

"Like the prettiest star in the night sky."

Eyes sparkling, she gave him a dubious look. "That's a big claim because you and I just saw some amazing stars."

"Not nearly as amazing as looking into your eyes."

She laughed, and it was a sound of pure merriment. "On that full-of-it note, get me a big, comfy T-shirt to sleep in, please."

Taylor followed him into his room. Opening a chest of drawers, he pulled out the top T-shirt, not surprised when it was a music festival one. He kept his wardrobe simple. "This work?"

Taking it, she ran her fingers over the soft cotton material. "I think so. Thanks. Okay if I use the bathroom first and borrow your toothbrush?"

He nodded. He'd just jump in the shower across the hallway while she got ready for bed. He probably smelled like a cross between grill smoke, river water, and cow pasture. Not the scent he wanted to wear to bed with Taylor.

Taylor had meant to hurry in the bath, but she'd heard the hot water heater kick on and knew Jack was showering somewhere in the house.

Staring into his bathroom mirror, she studied her reflection. What was she doing?

Staying with Jack.

Because Jack made her happy, was a good person, and she wanted to comfort him, to soothe away his sorrows, and give him happiness.

What makes you think you can make him happy? a nagging voice mocked.

She glared at her image, as if the voice had come directly from her reflection.

"Just watch me and find out," she whispered, then stripped out of her clothes, all her clothes, and stood naked in Jack's bathroom.

She took a cloth and washed herself, then helped herself to some unscented body lotion. She brushed her teeth and slipped on his T-shirt. It fell to just beneath her hips, covering her bottom, but just barely.

Perfect.

Reaching up, she touched a braid. If she left them in, her hair wouldn't be nearly so everywhere in the morning.

But she wanted her hair loose, not confined, and began the painstaking task of undoing her braids.

When she'd finished, she fingered-combed out her wavy hair. Wild. Crazy. Free.

Perfect.

Because tonight she was going to be wild, crazy, and free.

With Jack.

"You okay in there?"

Cheeks flushing at her thoughts and that she'd taken so long he'd felt the need to check on her, she called, "Fine."

Opening the bathroom door, she almost bumped into him as he stood just on the other side.

"Oh!"

He caught her shoulders, steadying her.

In her bare feet, he seemed so much taller and she looked up at him, smiled. "Thanks."

"You're welcome." He brushed his palms down her arms. "Since you were woken up so bright and early, I suppose you want to hit the sack immediately."

She glanced behind him at the big wooden bed with its antique-appearing quilt on top. "Hope that's okay."

"Anything you want." But he didn't move toward the bed, or at all.

"Kiss me," she ordered, staring up at him to watch the emotions play across his handsome face.

"Taylor—" he began.

"Kiss me, Jack. You said anything I want. I want you to kiss me."

Heaven help him, Jack thought. Or just heaven. Because pressing his lips to Taylor's, tasting her sweetness, was heaven.

"What else do you want?" he asked, lifting his mouth millimeters from hers.

She placed her hands on each side of his face. "You, Jack. I want you. I want you to kiss me, to touch me, to hold me and caress me and make love to me in that big old bed over there, and then I want to sleep in your arms. Is that okay?"

He shook his head, causing concern to fill her pretty brown eyes.

"It would be a travesty to label all that as just okay, Taylor. Okay means mediocre. Nothing about you in my bed would be mediocre."

Her lips curved into a smile, then she stood on tiptoe and kissed him.

Jack could no longer keep his hands still. He traced them over her arms, down her spine, her waist, cupped her bottom.

That's when he realized.

Pulling back, he stared into her eyes. "You're not wearing underwear."

She gave him a devilishly seductive look. "Is that a problem?"

Slowly, he shook his head, then slipped his hands beneath the T-shirt hem to palm her bare bottom. Yeah, it would be easy to just strip off his clothes and push her down on the bed and take her as quickly as she'd let him inside. But that urgency was what had happened last time. This time he wanted to see her, touch her, taste her—all of her.

That's what he set about doing.

Jack's mouth was driving Taylor insane. Absolutely mental.

She dug her fingers into his long hair, loving the luscious slightly damp locks between her fingers, around her hands. She arched against him. "Jack."

"Hmm?" He glanced up at her.

"Just Jack."

Her entire body hummed for him, every cell trying to draw nearer, to be the part touching him, being touched by him.

Over and over he brought her to the brink, letting her climax, float partially down, then lifting her back up, higher and higher each time.

Digging her heels into the bed, she tugged on his shoulders. "Now, Jack. Now," she demanded. "I need you now."

Within seconds he was above her, donning a condom, then inside her, stretching her in the sweetest way.

With the first movement of his body her insides trembled, then went full-blown earthquake.

She clung to him, hanging on because she was sure she was falling from some other world as he continued to move, continued to take her places she'd only dreamed of.

Momentum built, and she felt his waning willpower to hold back. Needing to feel his loss of control, to feel him give in to the magic between their bodies, she met him stroke for stroke, deeper and deeper.

"Jack!" she cried, realizing she was going to be the one to go tumbling over into orgasmic release yet again.

She reached the pinnacle, the highest place she'd ever been, and plummeted over to the other side, her entire body imploding into a colorful meltdown.

Which undid Jack and he followed suit, driving deep into her body before collapsing onto her.

CHAPTER FOURTEEN

TAYLOR DIDN'T RECALL a month having ever gone by so quickly. Not ever.

The past one had flown and, with it, Jack's days in Warrenville.

Eight days. Then he'd be gone.

"You've still not talked to him, have you?"

Sitting in their living room, Taylor glanced over at Amy, started to pretend she didn't know what her roommate meant, but decided against it. Why bother? Amy knew what was in her heart.

She shook her head.

"You need to tell him you don't want him to go," Amy advised, moving to the sofa to sit next to Taylor. "Tonight, before any more time gets away, before he gets away."

It wasn't that Taylor didn't want to tell Jack that she didn't want him to leave. She didn't want him to leave and wanted to tell him.

But she couldn't ask him to stay.

Every time she thought about doing so memories of how he'd described living at his grandparents' echoed through her head. Jack was a free spirit, not meant to be confined to one place. So, instead of defending why she hadn't, and wouldn't, ask Jack to stay, she went on the offensive.

"How about you? Have you talked to Greg about how this long-distance thing is wearing thin? Have you asked him about opening a practice in Warrenville?"

"I know what you're doing, and it isn't going to work," Amy warned.

"Neither would asking Jack to stay."

"You don't know that."

Amy was right. She didn't know that. She saw how he looked at her, felt how he touched her. He might say yes. But asking Jack to stay would be like asking a bird to give up flying to live in a cage.

How did one ask that of someone they cared for?

She did care for Jack. Way too much. How could she not when he made her laugh, made her feel things she hadn't known possible, made her step beyond the ordinary lines of her life?

A knock sounded at the door.

"Speaking of the lucky devil," Amy said, motioning to the door. "I should get that and tell him myself."

Jumping off the sofa, Taylor's eyes widened. "Don't."

Amy took on a pouty look. "You know I wouldn't really, but I think you should."

"Trust me, I shouldn't."

Sighing, Amy shrugged. "If you say so. You'd better let him in."

Taylor nodded. "He's taking me frog-gigging."

"He's what?" Amy looked disgusted. "I take it back. Let him go."

But her friend was teasing and they both knew it.

After they spotted the first frog, Taylor was done. No way did she want to participate in spearing a frog. Just the thought of Jack killing the frog had her turning to wade back out of the water. Loudly, and with as much splashing noise as she could make.

Hop away, froggy. Hop away.

"I'm all for learning new things," she told Jack, hoping her sloshing feet scared the frog away. She hoped it did, and that it sent all the neighboring frogs into hiding. "But you're on your own with this one. I want no part of murdering frogs."

Following her rather than going after the frog, Jack laughed and asked, "Not your thing?"

She shook her head. "If you want to feed me frog legs, I can't have seen those legs still attached to a body with eyes that looked at me," she warned.

He chuckled. "Fair enough. I brought fishing poles so if we didn't find any frogs we wouldn't get bored."

Fishing didn't bother her. Jack mostly was a catch and release fisherman, only keeping what he planned to eat.

"Fishing in the dark?"

He'd taken her fishing, several times in fact, but never at night. Just the weekend before they'd gone out with friends, including Greg and Amy, on a nearby lake and whiled the day away with water-skiing, tubing, fishing, and soaking up sunshine. That evening they'd had a fish-fry at Jack's and had all sat around eating, laughing. It had been a perfect day.

Every day with Jack was a perfect day.

"Some of my best fishing has been at night."

In the moonlight, she looked at him a little in awe. "Is there anything you can't do, Jack?"

He got quiet, then shrugged. "Lots, but I'll try most things once."

Such as living in one place. He'd tried that once. He'd

been miserable. He'd said so himself. Who was she to try to force that on him again?

"I know what you're thinking, Taylor."

He did? Her eyes were probably bigger than the full moon shining down on them.

"I keep thinking about it, too."

She blinked. He was?

"Eight days isn't long enough."

Taylor's breath caught. Was he going to stay longer? And what if he did? She kept thinking about him, about how he was a free spirit, but what about her? She'd had no plans to wrap her life around a man, to get so wrapped up in a man that, rather than focusing on learning who she was, she focused on him. Her plans were to build a career, to get to know herself, her likes and dislikes, to do the things that made her happy. Not to add a man to the equation who she felt she had to cater to.

Jack gave a heartfelt sigh. "But it will have to be."

She wanted him to stay, yet maybe, for her own sake, his leaving was best all the way around.

They ended up not doing much fishing but made love on a blanket spread near his pond. The moonlight created the perfect hue. Taylor didn't ask him to stay, not with her mouth. That she kept quiet. Her brain said he needed to go for, oh, so many reasons.

Her body, however, had a mind of its own and begged him to be hers forever.

Tracing a pattern across Jack's chest, Taylor snuggled closer against him.

She'd given up any pretense of going home this last week. Going home was a waste of precious time she could have spent with Jack.

"I can't believe tomorrow is your last day at the hospital," she told him, hoping her voice didn't convey how utterly bereft the thought made her feel. The music festival in Daytona started the following Thursday so she imagined he'd want to arrive on Wednesday to check things out. That left four days.

Four days to make a lifetime of memories.

"You going to miss me?"

"A little," she answered with false bravado.

He laughed. "Good to know where I stand."

She glanced up at him. "You know I'm going to miss you, Jack Morgan. Way more than a little."

Bending his neck toward her, he kissed her forehead.

"I mean, who is going to take me fishing? Or boating? Or hiking? Or skinny-dipping in the pond?"

"We never went skinny-dipping in the pond."

"No?" She feigned innocence. "We still have four days."

His body tensed beneath her and she knew whatever he was going to say wasn't good.

"About that…"

Her stomach tightened.

"Duffy called today. We've worked Daytona together for as long as I can remember. Last year, we went down a few days early and scuba-dived at an old shipwreck site. He wants to go out again."

Her heart pounded. "Before the festival?"

Jack nodded.

Taylor scooted back from where she'd been pressed against him and sat up. "How long before the festival?"

"I need to head out the day after tomorrow. He's booked us."

"Why would he book you without checking to make

sure it was okay? That you didn't already have plans?" Her voice had a panicked edge. He was leaving. Early.

"Because it's what we've always done, and it's never been a problem. There's never been a reason for me to stay anywhere once a job finished. He knows that."

His words shot arrows into her heart. She'd wondered if he'd told Duffy anything about her, if the older man even knew she was in Warrenville with him, that they'd been together this past month.

That this time Jack had a reason to stay a few days more.

He didn't meet her eyes. "I won't leave Duffy hanging, Taylor."

No, he wouldn't. Part of her understood and didn't want him to. Duffy had been a good part of his life for so long. The kind of friend one rarely found. Jack had to go.

But the selfish part of her wanted every last second with him.

"I know that's not when I'd originally thought I would be leaving."

She didn't say anything, couldn't say anything.

"I'm sorry, Taylor."

"It's okay."

Nope. Not even mediocre.

Jack leaving earlier than planned sucked. She'd thought she had four more days to say goodbye, that they'd work their shift tomorrow, then have tomorrow night and three days of just them.

Instead, she had a little over twenty-four hours, twelve plus of which would be spent at the hospital.

"I started to tell you earlier, but didn't want that hanging over our evening."

"I appreciate that." She almost wished she didn't know

now, that he'd just waited until the last minute, said goodbye and left. That way she wouldn't have had to count down those last minutes.

"I hear the hurt in your voice." He touched her face, lifting her chin. "Look at me."

She met his gaze. Barely.

"This past month has been amazing. You've been amazing."

She nodded. *Don't cry. You are not going to cry. No tears, Taylor. No tears.*

"I've never known anyone like you, Taylor Hall."

"Ditto, Jack Morgan." She faked a smile and reminded herself that she'd known this moment would come from the beginning, that he wasn't doing her wrong and that she shouldn't feel hurt. She should be happy for the experiences she'd had with Jack and ready to move on to the next phase of her life.

With the life she'd planned when she'd moved to Warrenville.

Just look at how she'd let a man flub up her plans yet again. She should be glad he was leaving so she could get on with her life.

She should be.

He leaned forward, kissed her forehead. "Thank you, Taylor. For everything."

The emergency department was slammed. A stomach virus had broken out at a nearby nursing-home facility and was running rampant among residents and staff. Due to their already fragile health, several residents had needed to be transported by ambulance for emergency room work-up to see who would be okay with administration of intravenous fluids to rehydrate them then sent back to the facility, and who needed actual admission for closer observation.

Other than with regard to patients, Jack barely got to speak with Taylor.

Which was okay.

They had tonight to say their goodbyes.

He'd never had trouble leaving anywhere, but he'd stayed in Warrenville long enough that he would miss the small Tennessee town.

Would miss Taylor.

One last night to make love to her, to hold her in his arms while she slept, to wake beside her and make love to her all over again.

Only apparently not.

"Taylor is sick in the ladies' room," Amy announced matter-of-factly. "I think she's caught whatever this bug is."

"Is she all right?"

"Other than the fact she lost all her stomach contents in less than three seconds?"

Jack winced. "I'm going to check on her."

Amy's eyes widened. "In the ladies' room?"

"What are they going to do? Fire me?"

"Yeah, I guess they wouldn't bother, with it being your last day and all."

He doubted they would fire him for checking on an ill nurse regardless, but he didn't care. Taylor was sick, and he needed to check on her.

"Make sure there's no one else in there," he ordered Amy. "I'm not worried about being fired, but I wouldn't want to walk in on someone unexpectedly either."

Amy looked skeptical. "Taylor isn't going to like you seeing her this way."

"Then she shouldn't have gotten sick with me being the doctor on duty."

"He's insisting he come in here, Tay."

Struggling to find the energy to lift her head from where it rested on her knees, heavy and throbbing, Taylor squinted at her friend.

Still fighting the nausea racking her body, she grimaced. "Please, no." Her entire body ached, felt wretched. "He leaves tomorrow. This…" she gestured to herself sitting on the bathroom floor "…is not how I want him to remember me."

"He looked intent on checking on you. I'm not sure I can stop him."

"Try."

"Too late."

The last came from Jack.

Rather than look toward him, Taylor lowered her forehead back to her knees. She wanted to curl into a ball and disappear.

"You were supposed to wait until I gave you the all clear," Amy scolded.

"You were in here long enough I knew Taylor was alone." His voice was growing closer. "Go keep an eye on things out there. If I'm needed, get me."

Nothing, then footsteps, the sound of the door opening and closing.

Amy had abandoned her. She didn't even have the strength to protest.

Jack bent, placed his hand on her back. "Are you hurting?"

Did the excruciating ache in her chest count? Or just the horrific cramps gripping her stomach?

His hand went to her forehead. "You're burning up with fever. How long have you been fighting this?"

Since a few hours after the first nursing-home patient had come in. She'd thought she'd be okay, writing her symptoms off to stress over Jack leaving even as they'd continued to mount throughout her shift. Fifteen minutes ago denial had become impossible.

She rarely got sick. Why today?

"You shouldn't be in here," she said, hearing the whine in her voice and beyond caring. "I don't want to make you sick, too."

"You won't."

"You're not impervious to germs, Jack."

He sighed. "I can't leave you on the bathroom floor. Let me carry you to one of the bays. I'll give you something to calm your stomach down."

The thought of him picking her up, jostling her around, did not appeal.

"I don't want to move."

He wasn't having it. "You can't stay here indefinitely."

"I don't plan on being sick indefinitely." Her stomach churned, threatening to miraculously produce something more. Impossible. No way could there be anything left. "Please, Jack. Send a shot with Amy, if you must, but let me stay here until it kicks in."

"Won't you look at me?"

"No. I hate you seeing me like this."

"I'm a doctor, Taylor. This is what I do."

"This is not what we do." She hugged her knees even tighter, mentally willing her stomach not to turn inside out in front of him. She felt Jack's tension, his indecision.

He wanted to force her to go to the bay, force her to do as he wanted, because he thought it was the right thing. Stubbornly, that made her that more determined to stay. *She* decided what happened to her, not him or any man. Right? Besides, she really didn't want to move.

"If you want me to send Amy back, that's what I'll do."

Stunned he'd agreed, that he hadn't scooped her up and carried her out of the bathroom whether she wanted to go or not, Taylor moved her head in an up-and-down motion or as close as she could get without raising her forehead from her knees.

He didn't sound happy about it when he said, "I'll get Amy."

Jack insisted on helping Taylor to Amy's car. He'd wanted to drive her home, but several of the staff were throwing a going-away party for him in the break room. It wouldn't last long, but he was anxious to leave the entire time he was shaking hands and hugging co-workers he'd genuinely grown to care about.

The main co-worker he cared about had gone home over an hour ago and he wanted to check on her before getting a few hours' sleep, then driving to Daytona to meet up with Duffy.

He didn't call, wouldn't risk being told not to come, just drove to the apartment and knocked on the door.

Amy opened it and shushed him. "She's finally asleep. Don't you wake her up."

His heart fell. "Can I see her?"

Amy looked torn. "I don't think she'd want me to let you."

"But you're going to." Hope glimmered inside and grew as Amy's expression softened.

Amy eyed him, then sighed. "Only because I like you and she's not the only one who's going to miss you."

He'd swear she'd just sniffled.

Jack hugged her. "You'll see me again next summer at Rockin' Tyme. Same time, same place. You know the drill."

She nodded. "Maybe sooner if I can convince Greg to move here."

Jack smiled, hoping things worked out for his friends. "Maybe so."

With care to be as quiet as possible, he pushed Taylor's bedroom door open and made his way to stand beside her bed.

She looked pale, fragile. But he knew better. Knew she was strong and would be okay. Better than okay. Nothing about her was mediocre. Taylor was a butterfly emerging from a lifelong cocoon and was only just beginning to use her wings. He was humbled he'd gotten to be a small part of her learning to take flight, to soar.

"Bye, Taylor. It's been fun," he whispered, so low he doubted it was even audible.

Unable to resist, he stroked his fingers over her hair.

Her eyes opened.

He should feel bad he'd woken her up. She was sick. But he couldn't leave without saying goodbye to her and knew he'd hoped she'd awaken at his touch.

"Shh," he warned. "If Amy finds out I've woken you, she'll skin me alive."

Although obviously still ill, Taylor gave a small semblance of a smile.

"Feeling any better?"

"A little." She glanced toward the night table where Amy had put a cup of ginger ale with a straw. "Please."

Jack held the cup out to her, positioning it so she could sip while he held the cup. She didn't take in much, but at least it was something.

Seeing her so weak, so unlike her normal vibrant self, threatened to undo him. How could he leave until she was back on her feet?

"I'll stay if you need me to. I'll call Duffy and tell him you're sick. He'll understand."

Face pale, she shook her head. "You shouldn't be anywhere near me. I'm contagious."

He took her hand in his, marveling at how fragile she felt. "You're not the first contagious patient I've been around, Taylor."

She nodded almost imperceptibly.

"Is there anything I can get you?"

She shook her head. "I just feel tired. I want to go to sleep." Which he'd woken her from.

"I didn't picture our goodbye quite this way." He hesitated, studying her hand within his. "If you ever need me, Taylor, for anything, a new adventure, whatever, you know how to get in touch with me. Always."

But he wasn't sure she heard him, because her eyes had closed, and her breathing evened out in sleep.

"Goodbye," he whispered, marveling at just how much he wanted to stay but knowing he'd stayed in Warrenville longer than he should have already.

It was past time for him to move on to *his* next adventure. So why was it so hard?

Taylor refused to just go through the motions of life. She'd been there, done that with Neil, and during the aftermath of their marriage and subsequent divorce. Had gone through those motions during her childhood with the parents she'd never been able to please, so she'd faded into the background instead. She'd existed without really living. She wouldn't go back.

Not now that she'd gotten a glimpse of what life truly could be.

What she was determined it would be.

She went out dancing. She went to the lake with friends. She found an art class, got access to a kiln, and started a piece, but had started over several times because she'd known it wasn't right, that what she was uncovering wasn't what was really hidden in the clay. She'd even white-water rafted with a group from work. She lived, took chances, was the first to volunteer to try something new. Some she enjoyed, some not so much. Either way, she was discovering what she liked and disliked. It was a good life.

She missed Jack and found herself wishing he was there to share her adventures, to share everything. Oh, how she missed his easy smile and twinkly eyes. Earlier that day, restless, she'd driven out to the farm Jack had rented. A "SOLD" sign had been placed at the end of the drive. Her heart broke a little at the knowledge she'd never sit on the front porch again, or fish in the pond, or make love to Jack in the big antique bed with its hand-stitched quilt.

But life went on without Jack Morgan.

Perhaps not as brightly or as sweet an adventure, but life was good.

If she'd learned nothing else, she'd learned she had control over her attitude and the direction of her life. She refused to let it be bad.

The piece of clay she'd been working on again earlier, however, was a different story. That was bad. In the corner of her bedroom, the box into which she'd packed her supplies called to her as surely as if someone were locked inside and pleaded for her to rescue them.

Unable to resist the siren call any longer, she flipped on the lamp and began carrying her supplies into the living/dining room combo. Within minutes she had a protective plastic cover spread over the small dining-room table and her fingers were covered in clay. Immediately, the wet earth soothed something deep in her soul and she began to pinch away bits of clay, molding and shaping, using her fingers, using picks and wooden sticks to free whatever, whoever was trapped inside the clay.

Herself, she thought. Jack had been right when he'd interpreted the piece she'd given to Amy. It was always her that emerged from the clay.

When she'd originally realized that was what kept happening, Taylor had wondered if her art was much like putting together puzzle pieces of herself, slowly letting who she was come into view, slowly getting back to a whole.

As her hands worked, a smile lifted her cheeks.

She truly felt whole.

Was that why she'd been so hesitant to let Jack in? Because she worried that, much like what she was doing with her clay, he'd slowly pinch away the pieces she'd worked so carefully to put back together? Did she worry he'd bend her and mold her into something different than the woman she was destined to be?

Being with him had felt so good, so liberating, it was difficult for her to imagine him stifling her the way Neil had done. But she'd been blind to Neil's true nature until after they'd married, until she'd experienced his cruelty in bed and life first-hand.

Her hand slipped, and she took off a bigger piece of clay than she'd intended.

Letting out a frustrated huff, she painstakingly added the clay back and worked until it was impossible to tell that anything had ever been missing.

Minutes became an hour. An hour became hours. Night became morning.

She sat. She stood. She moved around the table, leaned forward, stepped back, working on different angles as she slowly chipped away at the clay. Her neck ached and was stiff from how long she'd been working, but she wasn't tired. Her creativity energized her, pushing her forward, refusing to let her leave the table as she worked on intricate details that were taking shape.

When she was finished, she stepped back and eyed the piece.

She wasn't very good, doubted she ever would be even if a new instructor had told her she was a gifted, natural-born sculptor, but what she saw awed her more than a little.

And revealed a lot about where her head was.

Or more specifically her heart.

"Wow, Tay."

At Amy's exclamation, Taylor prised her eyes open, realizing she'd crashed on the living-room sofa, and peered up at where her friend was glancing back and forth between the table and where Taylor lay.

"That," her friend continued, "is amazing and you look like death on a cracker."

Stretching her stiff body, she wiggled into a sitting

position. "It's a piece of clay and, thanks, you look great this morning, too."

"Right and the *Mona Lisa* is just a painting."

"Did you just compare my work to the *Mona Lisa*? Wow." Taylor glanced toward what she'd spent most of the night working on. It needed to be bisqued, painted, and glazed still, but pride swelled in her chest as she stared at the piece. She smiled at her best friend. "It's not nearly that spectacular, but it's the best I've ever done by far, so thank you."

"It's amazing." Amy plopped down on the sofa next to her and stared at the piece. "If I could make something like that, you'd better believe I'd give it to Greg."

She didn't bother pretending that she didn't know what her friend meant. She knew. Just as Amy knew. As always, she'd made a piece of herself—but for the first time a part of someone else had emerged from her clay.

She walked over to the table, stared at the piece. It was abstract, but there was no denying the heart overflowing from the hands that held it.

Jack's hands.

Her heart.

Because Jack held her heart.

"Jack is a traveling man with all his worldly belongings fitting in a Jeep. I don't think he'd want to lug this thing around in Jessica."

She thought back to the day she'd gotten sick, the day he'd left, to his words as he'd stood by her bed. She'd pretended to be asleep because she hadn't trusted herself to say another word. She'd needed him to leave before she forgot how he had a wandering soul and how hard she'd worked for her independence and begged him to stay.

Not just until her illness passed, but for forever.

He'd cared for her. She knew he cared. Had she asked him, he might have stayed. But how could she bind him that way when the very essence of him was freedom?

"He's in Chattanooga, you know."

No, she hadn't known. She'd not heard from Jack since he'd left her room that night. Neither had she reached out to him. There had been nothing else to say. She was living the life she wanted, the life she'd worked hard for, and so was he.

Her fingers itched to run over the hands holding her heart. Jack's hands.

Things were as they should be.

Are they? Are they really?

"Just for two days," Amy continued. "He's working a tough-guy competition. Greg is driving down to see him tomorrow and take in some of the action. You should call."

Jack was in Tennessee. An hour from her. Oh, Jack. Just knowing he was near made the air in her chest feel thick, making breathing difficult.

"He knows where I am if he wants to see me."

Her comment to Amy echoed through her head, causing similar words to replay. Words she'd replayed hundreds of times over the past two months.

If she ever needed him, she knew how to get in touch with him.

What if she'd needed him before he'd left? Still needed him? What if she always needed him? What then?

Nothing had changed. Jack was a free spirit. She wouldn't be the one to attempt to shackle him.

She was a woman who had fought hard to win her independence, to find her voice, to find herself, and she wasn't willing to give it up.

"What about you?" Amy asked. "You know where he is. Do you want to see him? Does he know you want to see him?"

She wanted Jack to be happy, not trapped in a white picket fence world with her.

Who says you have to live in a white picket fence world? Or that you even want to?

She'd been raised to think that was what she wanted, needed, but hadn't she learned to think for herself long ago? Hadn't she put aside others' expectations to discover what her *own* expectations from life were?

Her gaze cut to Amy's. "Who says I even want to live in a white picket fence world? To live a normal nine-to-five life?"

"Huh?" Amy clearly hadn't followed her thought process.

Excitement building within her, she leaned over and kissed her roommate's cheek. "I love you, Amy, but you may be roommate-less again soon."

Amy's eyes widened. "What?"

Taylor hugged Amy, then pointed at the piece of art. "I need to tell him about that. I need him to know what I know."

Amy grinned. "You're headed to Chattanooga, aren't you? Wait for me! I'm going with you."

Eyeing the man sitting across from him, Jack took a sip of beer, then leaned back in his chair. He and Duffy had gone to a bar and grill along the riverfront within walking distance of the medical tent they were working the next couple of days.

The men and women competing were typically in tip-

JANICE LYNN187

top shape, but in the process of pursuing their best times often dehydrated and injured themselves.

One of Jack's main jobs was to make sure someone was safe to go back out after an injury or collapse. These people had been training for months, years, and most would work through an injury, even if dangerous, if allowed to.

They finished off their drinks and headed back toward where competition "headquarters" had been set up.

As they were walking, a woman caught his eye, making him think of Taylor. Not that she was ever far from his mind, but these days any platinum blonde had her popping into his head.

Only this one had his pulse pounding.

If he didn't know better, he'd swear the woman was Taylor.

Then he noticed the familiar woman with her.

Taylor was in Chattanooga and Amy was with her.

"Hey, isn't that…?" Duffy asked, sounding surprised, but not quite as authentically as he should have. Duffy must have known they were in town.

"Looks like it." He braced himself for however Taylor responded to seeing him. Had she known there was a possibility she'd bump into him here? Greg knew he was here and would have mentioned the competition to Amy. Maybe they'd all decided to drive down to check out the event. Or was Amy playing matchmaker again? Had she messaged Duffy to find them and was throwing him and Taylor together?

Taylor spotted him, looked uncertain for the briefest of seconds, then flashed a big smile on her pretty face.

A big, genuine smile. A smile that lit up his world

and had every nerve cell straining to get near her. She stopped walking, her mouth dropping open.

"You cut your hair!" she pointed out unnecessarily.

He reached up, ran his palm over his bare neck. "Why are you here?"

Probably not the best intro to seeing her after two months had passed, but it's what popped out of his mouth.

"Good to see you, too," she replied, turning to Duffy and giving him a smile of his own. "Duffy, how are you?"

Duffy hugged Taylor, then Amy. Taylor gave Amy a look and, taking her cue, Amy locked her arm with Duffy's. "Let's go for a walk, my friend. We need to catch up since I missed out on seeing you at Rockin' Tyme."

Duffy didn't hesitate, just abandoned Jack with Taylor. Yeah, his friend had known Amy and Taylor were there.

"You didn't answer my question," Taylor reminded Jack once they were alone.

No, he hadn't. He glanced around them, wanting to be somewhere other than where they were. They could walk to the bridge, go to the park, but with the competition there would likely still be too many people around.

"Let's walk down to the riverbank," he suggested. There might possibly still be people around, but it would be less crowded at least.

Glancing toward the Tennessee River, Taylor nodded. "Okay, if that's what you want."

Taylor had rehearsed what she'd say to Jack a thousand times in her head on the drive to Chattanooga. Now that she was with him, had set eyes on him, she could barely string two words together.

Maybe his haircut and being clean-shaven had thrown

her. She'd never seen him without his hair being long. He looked amazing, but she missed his tousled, *I don't care* look.

He wore his khaki shorts and a T-shirt—one of his Rockin' Tyme shirts, which made her smile. The shirt seemed fitting for her arrival and what she wanted to tell him. She'd acknowledged that she'd torn free of her chrysalis and emerged a different woman after her divorce. But she hadn't found her wings until Rockin' Tyme.

Until Jack.

He'd encouraged her to spread those wings and take flight, teaching her to trust in herself and soar. His voice hadn't overridden hers but had instead encouraged her, lifted her. No matter what happened, no matter what he said, she would be fine, would continue to fly.

She'd just fly higher with him beside her.

"You here for the tough-guy competition tomorrow?"

She laughed at the absolute absurdity of her competing in the event. "I'm not near tough enough for that. You?"

He grinned. "Working medical."

"What's next for you, Jack?"

He hesitated to answer and she wondered if he'd tell her to mind her own business, that he didn't want her to know his schedule or showing up where he was.

"I've a little time off coming up, then I'm headed to Las Vegas for a few weeks."

"I've never been to Las Vegas." Yeah, that had been wistfulness in her voice.

His brow arched.

"I've not been to a lot of places," she continued. "But I plan to change that."

He stared at her and she didn't blame him. She wasn't making a lot of sense.

"I'm quitting my job, Jack." Which probably didn't make sense to him either. He didn't know that she'd saved every spare dime over the past year, had quite a nice little nest egg, and if she lived tight, could get by for quite some time.

Concern twisted his face. "What? What happened?"

"You happened."

His brows drew together as he visibly tried to make sense of what she was saying.

"Warrenville will always be special," she continued. "But I want to see the world, to travel and not define myself by where I live or work."

Had she not been watching him so closely she might have missed the flash of disappointment that appeared on his face before he said, "I'm happy for you, Taylor."

That flash of disappointment nearly did her in. She didn't understand why he'd be disappointed, but she pressed onward. This was too important to lose her voice, her nerve now.

"What I want is for you to be happy for *us*, Jack."

"Us?"

Here went everything.

"You told me if I ever needed you, that I knew where to find you. Well, I've found you, Jack, so it's time for you to tell me exactly what you meant by your comment."

They'd stopped walking along the riverfront and had gone halfway down the bank between the walkway and the water.

In the moonlight and glow from the riverfront buildings Jack studied Taylor's face, how her eyes sparkled, how her chin lifted in defiance of anyone who stood in her way.

She was beautiful.

And not saying things he was prepared to hear.

"If you need me, I'll be there. You know that."

"That's what I thought you meant. What I hoped you meant," she corrected, then met his gaze head on. "I need you, Jack."

When words failed him, she continued. "I want to travel with you, Jack. To see the world with you."

Was that what she'd meant?

Jack took a deep breath. "That may be a problem."

Taylor's face fell. "I… What kind of problem?"

A wry grin tugged at his lips. "I've recently made changes to my schedule and won't be traveling nearly as much in the future."

Uncertainty darkened her face. "What?"

"You once asked me if I ever thought of some place as home." He smiled at the memory, at his recent realization. "I never had, but now, when Warrenville comes into my head, I get nostalgic." He shrugged one shoulder. "You might say homesick."

Her mouth opened. "Oh."

Studying her, he said words he'd once not ever expected to say. "I'm coming home, Taylor."

Eyes big, full of emotion, she asked, "When?"

"As soon as this competition is over."

"You'll be in Warrenville until you leave for Las Vegas?"

"Yes." Telling her he was coming back to her felt good, felt liberating. "And I'll be back as soon as Las Vegas is over."

She swallowed. "You're moving back to Warrenville? But…"

"Is my moving back a problem for you?"

"No, but…"

He might feel good, but Taylor looked torn as she said, "But, Jack, you'll be miserable."

Taken aback at her comment, he asked, "Why on earth would I be miserable if I moved to Warrenville?"

Then it hit him, threatened to knock the wind from his chest and buckle his knees. "You're not going to be there, are you?" He could smack himself in the head. "All this to be with you and you're going to be gone."

Her lips parted, her expression brightened. "You're moving to Warrenville to be with me?"

He nodded. "It's not the town that made me homesick, Taylor. It's not being with you." He looked her straight in the eyes and told her what was in his heart. "You are what makes Warrenville home. You are home."

Taylor could stand it no longer and closed the short distance between her and Jack, practically throwing herself into his arms.

"I've missed you so much."

She wasn't sure if she said the words or if he did, just that he lifted her off her feet and hugged her to him.

"I don't want you to get heavy feet, Jack," she told him, placing her palms on his cheeks and staring up into his eyes. "And, I sure don't want to be what weighs you down. Not ever. That's why I'm leaving Warrenville. I want to be with you, wherever you are."

"Then I guess you're going to be spending a lot of time in Warrenville."

"We don't have to stay there. I'll go with you. Really."

"That's not going to work. I've a farm to take care of."

"What?" Then it clicked, and her jaw dropped. "It was you who bought the farm, wasn't it?"

He lifted one shoulder. "I live a simple life. The farm was a good investment. Besides, I have a lot of good memories at that place."

"But…why would you buy it?" She couldn't even begin to imagine what the farm had cost him.

"Because I have to have somewhere for us to live."

"You want me to live there?"

Snorting, he ran his fingers through what was left of his hair. "I thought I had a few more days to plan this, to come up with something grand to convince you to say yes."

Taylor's heart missed a beat.

He took her hands into his. "I want you to live at the farm with me, Taylor. Or wherever it is you want to live. Wherever you are, that's where I want to be."

"Jack," she whispered, fighting back moisture that was prickling her eyes.

"Say yes, Taylor. Tell me you'll live at the farm with me."

His words about his grandparents blasted through her head and the thought of the farm becoming a gilded cage that locked away his free spirit tore at her.

"No, Jack. I won't."

Jack's ears roared. He'd thought…no matter what he'd thought. Obviously, he'd misunderstood.

He let go of her hands but she grabbed hold of his.

"I came here to find you, Jack, to tell you that wherever you are is where I want to be." Her eyes searched his. "We don't have to live at the farm or even have four walls of our own. So long as I'm with you, that's what matters."

He'd botched this. Then again, he really had thought he had longer to figure out what to say to her, to figure out what he was going to do next.

"I love you, Taylor."

Like that. He hadn't planned to just spit those words out. Had he had time to plan, he'd have come up with some elaborate way to have told her, some special way that a woman like Taylor deserved.

Her eyes widened, then softened as a smile lit up her face. "That's why I'm here, Jack." She placed both palms on his cheeks, cupping his face. "Because I love you, too."

"You do?" His ears had to have heard wrong. He'd known she cared, known they were good together, but he hadn't let himself dream that she might love him.

"Don't act as if you aren't fully aware of how I feel about you, Jack Morgan, because you know I love you."

Had he? He'd not outright thought it, but maybe she was right. Part of why he'd bought that farm was because Taylor loved him and only a fool would let that love go to waste.

Especially when that love was reciprocated a hundredfold.

"I'm not just the rebound sex guy?" he teased, running his fingers into her hair to caress her.

"Oh, you're the rebound sex guy," she assured him. "But you're also my forever sex guy." She studied him. "My forever everything guy. If you want to be."

Jack brought her hand to his lips and pressed a kiss there. "For the record, I've never wanted anything more."

"There you go making me wonder if you're for real again," she accused as she stood on tiptoe and kissed him. Kissed him for now and forever after.

EPILOGUE

TAYLOR WASN'T SURPRISED to see the group of guitar-picking men in front of her tent at the Rockin' Tyme music festival.

At the end of their shift in the medical tent, she and Amy had gone to wait in the shower line then wash away the day's grime.

Duffy nodded in acknowledgement of their return but kept singing about mommas and cowboys.

Taylor leaned over to kiss the top of Jack's head, brushing back a stray shoulder-length hair that had escaped his man-bun as she did so, then sat in the chair next to him to watch them play. With the songs she recognized, she sang along. Loud and carefree and full of enjoying herself. When Jack finished singing a number, she let loose with applause.

Duffy shook his head and gave a pretend disgruntled sigh. "Same groupie two years in a row."

"Same groupie rest of my life," Jack corrected, causing the rest of the gang to launch into good-natured ribbing.

Taylor smiled. The past year had been amazing. She and Jack had moved into the farmhouse. They'd both taken PRN positions at the hospital. She went with Jack on most of his events, working at the ones she could get hired on with, and just attending the ones that hadn't needed another nurse. Her favorite so far had been car racing. She'd loved that boisterous crowd.

They'd found a happy balance of white picket fence and adventure.

Jack nurtured her need to dig, to carve away years of toxic layers to uncover who she was inside. Nurtured and, much as she did with her clay, helped her discover who she was and to embrace that woman.

Who she was loved him with all her heart.

Lost in thought, she'd missed that Jack had set his guitar aside until his getting down on one knee caught her eye.

"Jack?" Heart racing, she asked, "What are you doing?"

"What's long past due," he said, taking her hand in his and giving it a reassuring squeeze.

Her blood pounded through her veins.

"Will you marry me, Taylor?"

"Jack?" She could barely breathe and his name came out as little more than a hoarse whisper.

"Because you are the greatest adventure of my life," he continued, his eyes warm, reassuring, happy. "And I can't imagine my world without you at my side."

That he'd so perfectly echoed what she'd just been thinking, what was in her heart, Taylor couldn't hold back the moisture stinging her eyes.

"Yes!" She nodded. "Oh, yes."

"'Bout time," Duffy piped up from behind Jack.

Amy nodded her agreement. Everyone around them clapped and gave their approval as Jack stood, pulled Taylor to her feet.

"I love you," he said, kissing her.

"I'm glad," she whispered back when their lips parted. "So very glad, because you're my greatest adventure, too."

* * * * *

COMING SOON!

We really hope you enjoyed reading this book. If you're looking for more romance, be sure to head to the shops when new books are available on

Thursday 25th July

To see which titles are coming soon, please visit
millsandboon.co.uk/nextmonth

MILLS & BOON

Coming next month

DR RIGHT FOR THE SINGLE MUM
Alison Roberts

'I learned then that you just had to get on with it,' Laura said, her voice soft enough to make Tom lift his gaze to catch hers. 'You get to choose some of the cards you play with in the game of life but others just get dealt out, don't they? There's nothing you can do about that except to play the absolute best game you can. And you have to fight for the people you love. For yourself, too.'

It was impossible to look away from those warm, brown eyes. She totally believed in what she was saying. Laura McKenzie was quite prepared to fight to the death for someone she loved. There was real passion there, mixed with that courage and determination. He was seeing a whole new side to the person he was so comfortable to work with and it was more than a little disconcerting because it was making him curious. Apart from being an amazing nurse and clearly a ferociously protective single mother, just who was Laura McKenzie? No... It was none of his business, was it?

The half-smile that tugged at one corner of her mouth made it seem as if she could read his thoughts and sympathised with his small dilemma.

But she was just finishing off her surprisingly passionate little speech. 'I guess that's the same thing, isn't it? If you're fighting for yourself that means you can't do anything other than to fight for the people you love.'

Okay… That did it. Tom had to back off fast before he got sucked into a space he had vowed never to enter again. He didn't want to think about what it was like to live in a space where you could love other people so much they became more important than anything else in life. That space that was too dangerous because, when you lost those people, you were left with what felt like no life at all…

He had to break that eye contact. And he had to move. Making a noise that was somewhere between a sound of agreement and clearing his throat, Tom slid off the corner of his desk.

'I'd better get back to the department.' He opened the door and there was an instant sense of relief. Escape was within touching distance. 'As I said, we'll work around whatever you need. Send me a copy of the chemotherapy calendar and I'll make sure Admin's on board for when you're rostered.'

Laura nodded as she got out of her chair. 'Thank you very much.'

Her formality was just what Tom needed to make things seem a little more normal. 'It's the least I can do,' he said. 'The least we can do. You're a valued member of this department, Laura. We'll all do everything we can to support you.'

Continue reading
DR RIGHT FOR THE SINGLE MUM
Alison Roberts

Available next month
www.millsandboon.co.uk

LET'S TALK
Romance

For exclusive extracts, competitions and special offers, find us online:

f facebook.com/millsandboon

🐦 @MillsandBoon

📷 @MillsandBoonUK

Get in touch on 01413 063232

For all the latest titles coming soon, visit
millsandboon.co.uk/nextmonth